P9-BZN-483

RIDER AT THE GATE

ALSO BY C.J. CHERRYH

*CYTEEN:**
The Betrayal
The Rebirth
The Vindication

RIMRUNNERS

HEAVY TIME

HELLBURNER

TRIPOINT

Published by Warner Books

*Winner of the Hugo Award for Best Novel

C.J. CHERRYH

RIDER AT THE GATE

A Time Warner Company

Warner Books, Inc., 1271 Avenue of the Americas, New York, NY 10020
A Time Warner Company

Aspect is a trademark of Warner Books, Inc.

Printed in the United States of America

ISBN 0-446-51781-X

FOR JANE
SINE QUA NON
Especially the beginning—

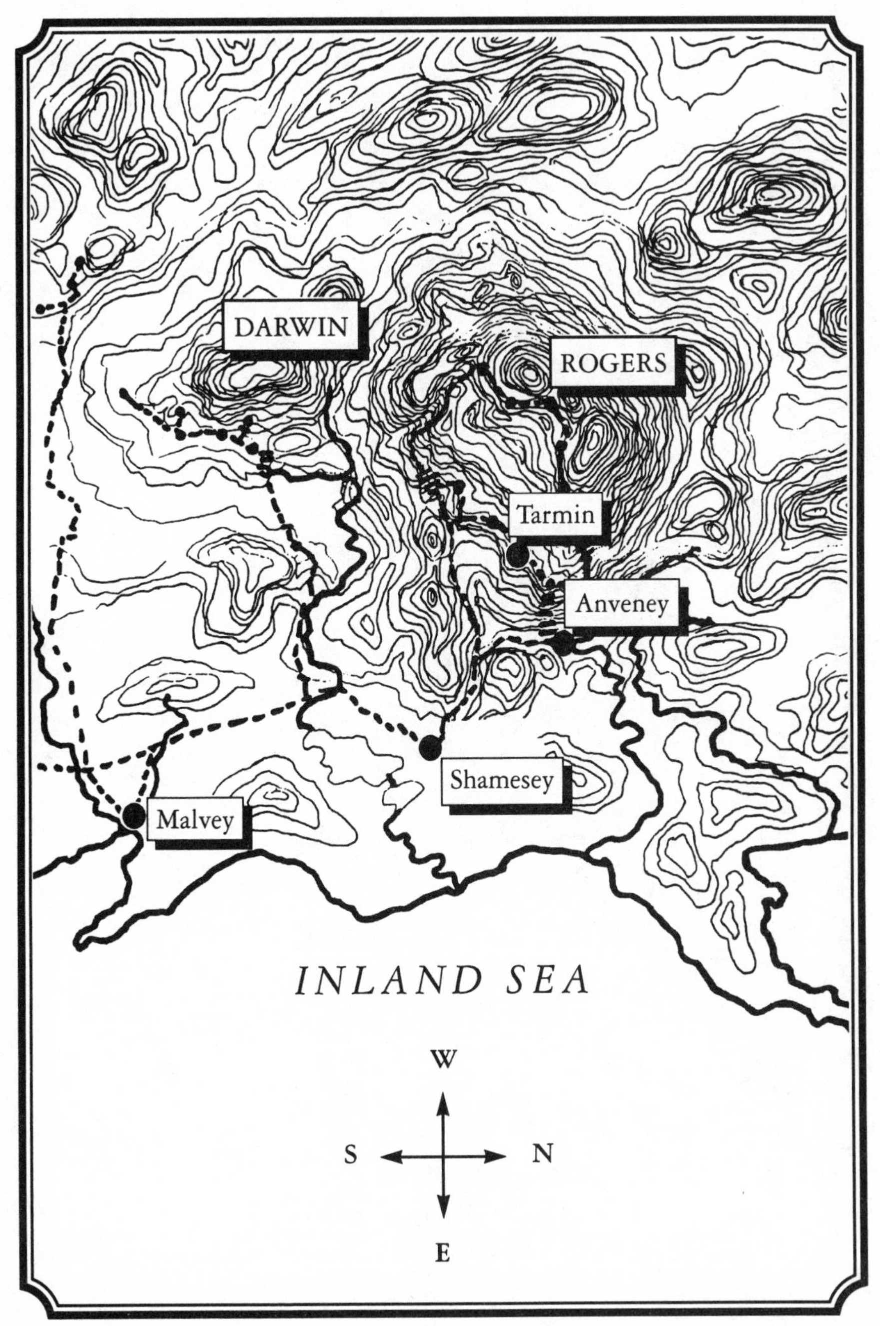
DARWIN
ROGERS
Tarmin
Anveney
Shamesey
Malvey
INLAND SEA
W
S
N
E

RIDER AT THE GATE

Chapter

— i —

THE FIRST OF THE TRUCK CONVOY HAD SCARCELY TOPPED THE RISE that would lead them down to Shamesey town when three riders broke free of its line and raced up on a gust of autumn wind, past the bell-arch of Shamesey camp and through the open gates behind which over a thousand riders and nighthorses were encamped.

These three, strangers all to Shamesey, swept into the camp commons without any more warning than that, borderers by their dress and manner, atop nighthorses out of the High Wild. Two of them stopped just inside the gate while the third rode down the main street of the camp, searching.

They were a grayness to nighthorse minds, these three from the convoy, two out of range, the third a shifting flutter of images passed to nearby horses and from them to the Shamesey riders' minds, an uneasy sending that masked that pair's intent from the nighthorses, who held no secrets one from the other.

But it required no nighthorse sense to know that these three wanted something; more specifically, they wanted some*one.*

A scattered few Shamesey riders, camp-boss Lyle Wesson among them, hearing the disturbance among the horses, deserted their tables in the Gate Tavern and gathered on the encircling porch. Lyle Wesson walked alone down the wooden steps and stood in the dusty tavern yard to meet that third rider, this guide and guard (he perceived so on the whisper of information coming to him from the horses) to a line of trucks now rolling unescorted toward Shamesey.

Unwise to leave a convoy unattended even within sight of Shamesey, largest and most secure of all the Finisterre towns; if they had done that, it was a breach of procedures for which these three might pay dearly in subsequent hires.

But as the rider from the convoy drew up near them in the tavern yard, Lyle Wesson and all the nearby riders saw—imaged in their own minds through the stranger's horse—the blond young man the convoy's guide had come looking for.

More, the Shamesey riders felt a terror closely held under the stranger's façade of calm: terror and a gnawing insanity under which these three riders had labored for days.

"Stuart is the name you want," the camp-boss said aloud, more than uneasy at the prospect of that unsettled sending set loose through his camp. "He's somewhere about. Get down. We'll stand you and your mates a drink. Someone will find him."

The stranger shook his head. "Not here," he said, scantly controlled, and leaned heavily on his horse's withers. "Tell him. Outside." The nighthorse under him threw its head, shook out its black, cloudy mane, and with no more decision of the rider (those around him were in a position to know) it spun and fled back toward the two riders who waited at the gate. Those two turned beforehand and dashed beneath the bell-arch and out onto the road.

The third followed them at no less speed.

The riders and the camp-boss, who had most immediately felt the fear unraveling the peace, breathed a collective sigh of relief at having that much space between Shamesey and the madness those stranger-riders carried with them.

"Find Guil Stuart," the word went out: the boss spoke aloud to the riders he sent on that job, a message without nighthorse image: it was a human attempt to contain that madness.

But a solitary nighthorse, in the hostile, curious way of its kind, had come near enough to skim the image-rich surface of human thoughts, and gone off, unknown to the camp-boss, to carry what it learned to its den-mates.

So the contagion spread, inevitably, through the encampment.

It took a man a considerable walk to accomplish the circuit of Shamesey camp, that protective circle of riders and horses who lived between the double palisade walls of Shamesey town's perimeter, riders who slept in hostels near the horse dens, met in taverns similar to the Gate Tavern, and lived in their separate settlements within that ring. But that image had made the rounds of the bell-gate section of the rider camp and was traveling down the ringroad to the next station before the camp-boss had even climbed the steps to the Gate Tavern.

The image had reached the fourth tavern and cluster of hostels long before the bell rang that signaled the arrival of the convoy at Shamesey town gates. It was a smallish, blond man the stranger wanted, a young man, a borderer, the rider of the horse that imaged himself as fire, pain and dark: those who knew Stuart called the creature Burn.

The image mutated and acquired opinion as it sped further: a solitary young man, a sullen, prankish horse, both prone to fights; a pair that roused dislike in some quarters of the camp, respect in others—disdain among the Shamesey riders, which image held more of Shamesey opinion of borderers in general than of Stuart in particular.

As a result of those acquired opinions, it might have been four and five different men the message sought before the image was halfway through the fifth cluster of brown plank buildings. Nighthorse sendings were like that when they flew through a camp: they were images and emotions, no words. Sometimes a rider or a horse mistook the individual in the message and shaped the image to something more like someone he did know—an image that also passed on, confounding the search: sometimes it found no names in human minds, and sometimes it acquired other, mistaken names as it met the leading edge of the spoken rumor.

But the main thread, camp-boss Lyle Wesson's order, running by human word of mouth at various distances behind the nighthorse sendings, held no doubt at all: Guil Stuart and the nighthorse Burn were the rider and the horse the strangers wanted at the bell-gate. They were present in camp; there was danger in the high hills; and, arriving with a truck convoy, some business had come to the gate that strangers who knew Stuart had feared to bring inside the walls—only prudent hesitation, where so many nighthorses were gathered.

Bad business. Bad news. A contagion that no one in his right mind would want to receive.

In the better part of Shamesey town, the very core of Shamesey—where wealthy wooden houses were bright with painted flowers and red and blue eaves, where gaslights glowed wanton waste on the street corners even at early twilight—no one even noticed the event, except that the bell had rung which signaled a convoy coming in.

Merchants left their dinner tables and headed out for the marketplace, as late as it was, to spy out what goods had come in and with what prices. Well-dressed children ran out to see the trucks and annoy the drivers. Others in the town center turned out for curiosity, if nothing else.

The better part of Shamesey town would never feel the fear and the distress that ran the circuit of the rider camp, but that was, after all, why the rich built their houses so far from the palisade walls, so that the riders and the world over the hills would never intrude into their peaceful lives. That insulation was the privilege of their wealth, which they gathered from their labor and their trade, and which they planned to enjoy forever, nothing changing, preferring to build atop each other rather than crowd closer to the camp.

But in Shamesey slums, the insulating ring of human squalor lying between Shamesey town and Shamesey camp—where the bell meant little but rich merchants getting richer—the residents sensed that nighthorse rumor like a presentiment of storm. It was a sensation so convincing that some stopped their business on the streets and others flung up their windows to search the skies in the west, the ordinary direction of bad weather.

But when the western heavens showed clear in the final glow of sunset, the slum-folk directed their anxiousness instead down their streets of ramshackle, unpainted board buildings toward the encircling walls of the rider camp; and, with the helplessness of the poor who had to live nearest the camp and the images that seeped through those wooden walls, they cursed and spat for fear of nightmares.

The Fisher household felt that storm-feeling in their drafty third-floor flat, a flat which lately had new stoppage for those drafts and smelled of fresh paint and plaster. The Fishers paused in their supper and looked toward the window—as Danny Fisher's fork hit the plate and flung beans in an arc across the table.

"Hell!" Danny cried, which one didn't ever say under his parents' roof. He wasn't thinking clearly as he began to get up. He only realized his intention as he cleared his chair and it scraped on the floor.

"Where do you think you're going?" his father demanded.

His mother said, "Danny, sit down, finish your supper. The bell's none of your concern."

But he couldn't sit down. The feeling was dreadful, as if his mind were going every direction at once, and he had to wonder, didn't his family feel *anything*?

His youngest brother, Denis, shook at his arm, saying, "Danny, Danny, sit down, what's the matter with you?"

His mother was upset now, and his father was angry, ordering him to take his seat with the rest of the family and act like a sane human being.

But he had to get to the camp. He had to find Cloud. He headed for the door.

His father shoved his chair back, too, yelling at him to come back and do as he was told. His father crossed the room in two strides and grabbed his arm hard enough to bruise it. Then his mother was on her feet, and grabbed his father's arm.

"Let him alone!" his mother yelled.

"The boy can act like he's sane! The boy can sit down and finish his supper!"

"We have neighbors!"

"Fine, we have neighbors! They all know our son's crazy! It's no news to them!"

"Don't you yell at me! Sit down! Everybody sit down and eat your dinner! I'll throw it out if nobody's going to eat it!"

Danny didn't feel anything but that dissociation, that terrible coming-apart. He jerked at his father's arm. "Let me go, dammit, I've got to go!"

His father's hand cracked across his face. His father started yelling at him, something about God and religion, devils and hell.

But devils and hell weren't here. Something else was, something as frightening and far more imminent.

Danny freed himself, not because his father couldn't have held him, even lately, but because his father had let go in seeming shock—while his mother pounded on his father's arm with her fist, screaming about 'that creature' and how it would come into town and they'd all die if he didn't let Danny go to it. Denis was bawling, screaming at them to stop fighting. His older brother, Sam, stared at all of them from the table—Sam didn't argue with their father, Sam wanted the machine shop when their father was gone, nothing more, nothing less, so Sam just shoveled down another spoonful of beans.

Danny grabbed his coat, his scarf, his hat from the pegs beside the door.

"You don't have to come back, you!" his father yelled. "You're damned to hell, dealing with that beast, you know that? You're going straight to hell!"

"Shut up!" his mother yelled. "You don't mean that! —Danny, he doesn't mean that!"

"Yes, I mean it!" his father shouted, and the fight was in full cry when Danny shot the bolt back, banged the door open and raced down the rickety stairs.

He was halfway to the bottom, two steps at a time, before Denis overtook him. Denis got a grip on his coat, screaming at him to stop, he didn't want him to go, papa didn't mean it, he couldn't go out there, the devil would get him and drag him and that horse down to hell if he went back there.

Danny wasn't even aware of shaking Denis off. "You just go!" he heard Denis screaming after him. "You just go ahead! God's going to send you to hell! Papa says God's going to send you to hell and I don't care!"

It was meaningless noise to him. He ran the stairs, rushed out the door and down the street, breathless.

People everywhere were stopped, gathered along the walks, looking toward the wooden walls of the camp. He'd never felt anything the like: it was bad, it promised the town worse dreams, and people shied away from him in the streets, seeing not a kid who'd grown up in their neighborhood, but a rider's fringed leather, a rider's clear purpose in the midst of the stifling storm-feeling.

Trucks jammed Gate Street, which led down to the bell-arch, trucks crowding one another, engines growling in their uphill climb toward the market and the warehouses buried deep beneath the town center: protection for the material wealth—and the vital food supplies that were life to everyone, merchant and slum dweller alike.

Only the riders could survive without. Riders could survive without the town; the town could never survive without the riders.

Tanker trucks lumbered in the midst of the canvas-covered cargo trucks, huge, long rigs the drivers ordinarily chose to park outside the walls. Tonight they were in the line, seeking shelter from the coming dark.

Danny wove past the gawkers at the corner. It was a big convoy, maybe the last before the winter closed the passes.

"Don't listen!" a street preacher was shouting. "Heed not the beasts! Death and damnation to the followers of the beasts! Pray! Shut your hearts against the creatures of this world and pray to God for deliverance!"

The feeling on Gate Street was overwhelming. Maybe part of it was the exhaust from the trucks: fumes welled up in the narrow street, under a dilapidated overhang of buildings so old and so close that at the gentle imprecisions of the uphill road the tankers ran their tires up over the low curbs and threatened the eaves and people on the sidewalks.

Danny wanted to run. He felt as if he couldn't get enough breath. Diesel stung his eyes and his throat as he walked double-time.

Terrible thump. Some driver rear-ended the truck in front. Second collision, then, as somebody else stopped too short. Panic was contagious. The truckers felt it.

"Pray for your children, that they follow not the beasts!"

He was strangling in it.

Fear raced through the camp, provoking a general surveillance over the main street from the doors of rider hostels and nighthorse dens alike. The camp-boss and the several riders who had first come out to meet the arrivals had set up their own watch over the situation from the vantage of the Gate Tavern porch. Nighthorses who had drifted into their vicinity had shied off into the twilight, spreading the message that the camp-boss was not pleased.

The tide of disturbance had rolled all the way through the camp and back again. Consistently now it imaged a thin, smallish man with fair hair, recognizable to some, not to others; it imaged strangers at the gate, and horror in their company.

That image stirred hate in some quarters, and that hate roused other angers waiting to explode, tempers set off by nothing more than the darkness of the feeling. Fights broke out that had nothing remotely to do with Guil Stuart.

But it was hate for Guil Stuart that had sent Ancel Harper in particular searching after his cousins; and anger and fear flowed through their meeting at Hami's Tavern, a bar mostly claimed by the riders of Hallanslake district. Nighthorses wandered through the open portico of the tavern, and the feeling in that precinct was not good.

Hallanslakers, Harper included, knew Stuart.

And unlike most of the riders in Shamesey camp, Ancel Harper recognized the threat lurking about the edges of the message. He, unlike most riders, had felt it before and never wanted to feel it again.

He knew, and controlled that knowledge: a man who dealt with nighthorses learned to keep his past from infecting the present. Nighthorses didn't think easily in terms of past or future: a careless rider's own imagination could all too easily become real for his horse, and come from the horse back to him.

Stuart hadn't caused what had happened—not directly—as Stuart hadn't caused this newest disaster—directly. But that hardly mattered: Guil Stuart was the kind of man trouble always happened next to, and there wasn't a friend Stuart had in this Hallanslaker tavern . . . not now and not before some poor sod out there had died with the horror this death had about it.

Because that was what lurked at the core and around the edges of the stranger's message: death come singing to as many as wanted to listen. Harper and his associates knocked back two rounds of drinks in quick succession, not the only patrons trying to drown the feeling that pulled at old feuds and seethed up through old matters long settled, even among themselves.

"Damned *fool*," Harper said, as the horse-borne image made yet one more round of the camp, but what he imaged in his own mind was, in particular, a young fool, quick to offense, too quick to pull a knife—

Drunk at the time, as Harper himself had been, night camp on the road, hard decisions to be made; and Stuart in no good mood. But neither had Harper or his brother been in a charitable mind toward a sullen outsider.

Gerry had died years later, of something Stuart hadn't had a thing to do with, just the breaks as they happened in the High Wild. Gerry was dead and Stuart was alive . . . nothing to do with each other, those sets of facts, those events that left one man alive, one dead; but it wasn't damned *fair*, in Harper's thinking, and Harper didn't want to see the face that kept intruding into his mind in constant image, preoccupying his attention like an unwelcome, waking dream.

Most of all, he didn't want to feel what he was feeling in the air. He didn't want that sending that was rubbing in the fact of Stuart's presence in the camp like salt into a wound: Stuart, Stuart, *Stuart.*

Damn his trouble-prone, arrogant, son-of-a-bitch ways that plowed ahead into a situation when smarter men said stop, don't go. Men and horses had breaking points, and the High Wild, when a man or a horse grew careless, always won. Minds snapped. Illusions became fact. A man wandered right into his death, blithe and believing, until madness sucked his companions down into that delusionary hell with him.

So somebody else had died. On Stuart's side, this time. One of Stuart's friends, most likely.

Good riddance.

Harper carried a scar across his ribs. Stuart had one to match. So had Gerry. Draw, it had been, then—thanks to a trucker's interference. Hallanslakers had said no go, and maintained a convoy wasn't safe on the mountain. Hallanslakers had had damned good reasons for saying so, including the higher fees they ought to have gotten for doing it; but Stuart, the only outside rider the convoy had hired on, *he'd* pushed, claimed of course they could make it, and *he'd* bring them through—for no extra charge, as if money didn't matter.

And Stuart, of course, had gotten his way, his way being far more palatable to the trucker boss, so it was go on up the road at the same fee despite the risk or lose their reputation and look like cowards to the clients.

Two Hallanslakers had died on that haul, swept away down the mountain, thanks to a snapped cable and toppling truck that had nearly taken Gerry out as well. Knocked cold, he'd been, by that free-flying cable that had taken Gerry's partner down.

Stuart in the number of the dead? The man whose stupid-stubborn fault it was they were there with that faulty cable? that unstable truck?

No such luck.

And Gerry hadn't fought Stuart again. Gerry hadn't fought much of anything after that trip, not even after his cracked head healed. Gerry was never the same after that. Gerry had taken hires he shouldn't have taken, loned it across the mountains in a season he shouldn't have. Gerry's sense was gone, thanks to that cable, and Gerry's heart had gone, swept down the mountainside with his partner, and that was that.

A brother couldn't hold him. A brother couldn't stop the change in him. Gerry'd been on his own when he died. He'd chosen that, as others who lost partners chose to die. He'd ridden out to his death. His horse . . . they'd had to shoot it when it came to camp without him. They'd had no choice. They'd been lucky: for a moment, it had been sane.

The feeling in the camp grew darker, and more angry: nighthorse politics, sexual politics, that shivered on the autumn wind.

Death. Sex and death and a rider Stuart knew and slept with.

Harper had his knife with him. He *knew* where Stuart was now, disquieting feeling. He knew that the ripple of query had just gotten to Stuart.

Stuart knew and the ripple came racing back again, through nighthorse minds and human, a feeling like the pause between the lightning and the thunder.

The camp-boss watched from the Gate Tavern porch as Guil Stuart came walking toward the camp gate, following that reverse tide of rumor. Slight, smallish, dressed in brown fringed leathers: the reality behind the image. Stuart's long blond hair was loose, a borderer's vanity—and he carried knives, one in the boot and one on the hip.

That was a manner, as the saying had it. A definite manner which gave not a damn about the rules of no-conflict that prevailed in a camp this size . . . a manner that flatly challenged the camp-boss to call him on it.

But say that Stuart wasn't the only one, and that Stuart carried at least two of his in the open: a clear warning. Say that the camp couldn't enforce the rule: there *were* riders—especially borderers like Stuart—who had specific reason to guard their backs, generally against other borderers.

Borderers, the rider-guides born to the High Wild, were the ones who knew the routes at the extreme points of settled land. They were a necessary fact of rider society—they stayed in Shamesey camp only during the winters, when the routes were closed to trucks and riders alike; and Shamesey locals, the guards over cattle and town edges, hadn't the knowledge the borderers had of each other. No one local knew who was right and who was wrong in their quarrels, out in the far land where civilized law didn't apply and where those knives settled grievances.

So Lyle Wesson, sipping a slow, speculative pint on the porch of the Gate Tavern, kept entirely out of it, not seeing anything in his venue in question.

Borderer business. Borderers looking for each other, carrying bad news, was what Wesson picked up. He couldn't identify some of the other feelings he was getting on the backwash out of the farther camp—he didn't like much of what he could identify, so he kept a purely human ear to the matter, awaiting human specifics.

More than an ear: Dart, old himself, limping a little (it was arthritis in the hindquarters, an affliction they shared, with the winter nip in the air) left the comfort of the nighthorse den nearest the tavern to stand watch over the commons, too.

And as Stuart approached, on foot, Dart imaged <dark,> —and something so unquiet it shivered along the nerves.

"Man's walking," Ndele said, moving out of the doorway to stand at Wesson's elbow.

"He's being followed."

"A man can't help that," Ndele said.

Truth. That Stuart chose to walk and not ride gave Wesson, who disliked and distrusted borderers in general, a better opinion of him: Stuart, for his part, had meant to keep it a human matter.

But a living darkness trailed Stuart as he passed them without a word, headed for the three strangers waiting for him just outside the gate. It trailed Stuart through the gathering dusk, regardless of Stuart's intentions, a head-down, angry darkness with which no rider would be willing to argue.

Stuart's horse. Defensive. Outraged.

Dart flung out a feeling of ill and warning, protecting the porch from that outrage, and trotted across the street, positioning himself between his rider and the source of that dark anger.

Opinion all along the street solidified around that pair as they passed through the gates and the strangers' message reached its target.

No question now: rogue was the word on the wind. That was how humans called it. What nighthorses imaged was something roiling and dark, and that was what Wesson perceived in Dart's image.

Rogue horse at least: that impression came through the horses, and maybe—far worse news—rogue rider, somewhere out in the bush.

He didn't know where, now, that image was coming from. It had no direction, but it was spreading like wildfire, and even the image was deadly dangerous. It was more than imagination nighthorses shared with human interlopers. Insanity came quite, quite naturally in this season of mating and rivalry. So did death.

There began now to be another presence in the uneasy flux of images: a young red-haired woman, a borderer, on a nighthorse that imaged itself as, no qualifier, just the bright and largest Moon.

"Aby Dale," Ndele whispered, and Dart's presence carried a gut-deep certainty of the woman's death, and a landscape so real, so particular in detail, that Wesson would swear he'd been there. "She's dead," Ndele said. "A fall. On the rocks. She was with the convoy. She died."

More riders gathered, soft movement on the boards of the porch. Images proliferated, rocks running with blood.

On that instant young Danny Fisher came skiting in, shied off from the man at the gate, and darted, distracted, along the palisade wall, looking for his horse, Wesson could guess, among the nighthorses that maintained an uneasy vigil at the den near the gate. Wesson caught and held his breath until the fool kid was clear of the situation.

Town kid. Shamesey kid. If the boy had fallen afoul of Stuart, it would have been his business. And Wesson was, personally, very glad it wasn't.

Chapter
— ii —

DANNY FISHER CAUGHT THE RUMORS IN FULL FORCE AS HE CAME through the gate, in a flood of images both true and half-true.

And, stopping along the gate wall in a shiver of shock, he discovered the general focus of the trouble was the man who had just walked past him.

In that time-stretched moment he realized he *knew* Stuart—knew him for a fair man, a borderer, true, but never the bullying sort: far from it, Stuart had sat on a rainy spring evening on Gate Tavern's porch, sharing three drinks with a kid who, at that time, could only pay for one, and telling a towner brat who'd dared—*dared* come to a borderer to ask, how he could ever hope get the long-distance convoy jobs he dreamed of.

Trips the like of which Stuart was clearly born to—born *on*, Danny had caught that in the way you knew some things even when the nighthorses weren't near, things that just echoed to you—a muddle-headed junior had trouble distinguishing the sources of what he'd gathered out of that moment. Maybe he'd heard them from Stuart himself; maybe he'd recalled small details from casual remarks Stuart had made earlier at the bar—he didn't know, now.

But Stuart hadn't grudged information to him. He'd come to Stuart half expecting ridicule—or worse, an indecent proposition, borderers having no good repute among lowland riders. He'd been mortally scared, and desperate, walking up to that table, offering to buy Stuart a drink in return for his question, and Stuart must have picked up on that fear. Stuart had laughed, given him an amused and immediate Calm down, he was spoken for.

And because Stuart's Burn and his own Cloud had both been nearby, he'd caught the image of the rider who'd laid personal claim to Guil Stuart . . . beautiful, beautiful rider, beautiful seat, maybe glossed by Stuart's memory, he didn't know that either, but he'd been instantly set off his balance and mortified with embarrassment, because, of course, he'd realized Stuart had read his suspicions of him through and through.

But now, watching the man walk out the gate alone to face some kind of bad news—news that Danny suddenly, illogically, felt centered on that woman so important to Stuart—he shivered in the unmistakable darkness and skittishness in the horses' minds, and wished he could do something. He felt outraged when someone muttered, 'borderer' in that tone that implied Stuart and trouble deserved each other.

It wasn't *fair.* He almost blurted out something to that effect, junior that he was, but talking out of turn could start what he by no means could finish: it was a group of Shamesey men, six of them, years senior to him, and you didn't contradict the seniors.

Then he first heard, aloud, from the same group, the word *rogue horse*, and almost lost his supper, because it at once echoed off everything that had brought him running out of town. *Rogue* was that going-apart. He'd heard a rider tell about it, a man who didn't need to say he'd talked to somebody who'd personally seen it, because the images had carried a detail and a feeling that haunted a junior's sleep for nights after.

But rogue couldn't have anything to do with Stuart, or Burn, or Stuart's beautiful border woman. It couldn't. That awful word didn't happen down in Shamesey lowlands. It was campfire stories, it was ghost tales around the hostel fires in deep winter: other riders had objected just to the telling of the story with the horses at hand. They'd said it was irresponsible to pass that image at night, when things were spookier, a word that belonged up in the highlands, in the extremes of dangers riders and horses faced up there and you always hoped they exaggerated—some creature, a horse or a bear usually, got brain-injured and started doing things a sane one just wouldn't do, sending at a range a sane one couldn't, coming right into encampments to kill, playing canny games with trackers while *it* hunted its hunters. It didn't for God's sake come down to Shamesey gates and civilized territory to trouble a town of Shamesey's size.

It didn't touch someone he knew in real life, or disturb his family at their own dinner table.

The tail-end of the convoy had just filed by the open camp gate, on its way into the city gates, headlights shining in the twilight, and behind that last truck, he could see Stuart cross the road to meet with the riders waiting there, all mounted, all waiting.

He had the most terrible feeling then, like chill, like forewarning . . . he suddenly realized he was picking up expectations out of the ambient. Every horse around them was disturbed by what they picked up from human minds, like a buzz of gossip, everyone anticipating/dreading/wanting calamity to the man they were watching. The feeling around the gate grew stiflingly close, charged and irrational.

Rogue, rogue, rogue, kept circling through his mind and maybe others', that dark, nasty *feeling* that clicked into place with a clear impression of a twilight mountainside, a memory so specific he could have recognized that place if he'd ever been there; different than he'd felt with the man who'd told a story and given impressions into the ambient secondhand, right now he felt something . . . so powerful, so horrible . . . so *present* with them . . .

<Body on the rocks, limbs broken, blood everywhere.>

"Dead," he kept hearing, words, as humans talked. Dead, dead, dead . . . while Stuart stood on the other side of the road and out of earshot, arms folded, head down, mostly, so one couldn't read his face as he talked with the mounted riders.

Then a sudden crisis hit the ambient. Danny held his breath as Stuart abruptly strode away from the meeting and turned upslope on the grassy hill, heading away from the camp.

The three riders who had spoken with Stuart held their horses still, and Danny felt a terrible, smothering fear, so vivid it became his own, and made his heart race.

<Autumn leaves. Rocks. Blood.>

He put out a hand to find something solid. His fingers met rough bark . . . his eyes told him it was a tree trunk on the mountainside, along that perilous road; but his brain knew it was only the palisade wall.

<Blue eyes, pale face, a thread of blood down from the nostril. Autumn hair on sunset stone.>

Sight dimmed, senses drowning. Some other rider jostled him, likewise on the retreat. Everyone was clearing the area.

Then a wild squeal erupted out of the dark behind the gates, a heart-stopping squalling.

"Let him *go*!" someone shouted aloud . . . *shouted*, in the camp. The sound shocked the air as a nighthorse broke through the thin screen of bystanders, not bolting uncontrolled into the dusk, but treading catfooted, shaking his mane and throwing off such a cold feeling of ill that senior riders crowded each other to get out of its path.

<Burn,> it imaged itself, in a violence that raced over raw nerves and ran red. It whipped its tail then, crossed the road and spooked the messengers' horses as it launched itself uphill toward Stuart, running full out.

He scarcely saw Stuart catch its mane as it cut across his path on the hill. Stuart swung up and astride, a solid piece with the darkness that raced along the shadowy grass of the hillside . . . they ran and ran, until Danny couldn't see them any longer with his eyes. Only the feeling of <loss> and <harm> remained, shivering down his arms and disturbing his heart.

Meanwhile the three riders who'd met with Stuart crossed the road, coming quietly toward the camp gates—a darkness themselves, mind and body, they and their horses. The men nearest the gates began to push them shut as if they could wall that menace out.

For an instant the feeling in the air was horrid, full of death. The gate-closers gave back, mission not accomplished, and the riders came through.

Danny shrank back against the wall, breath dammed up, his head swimming with visions of blood and rocks as those riders passed, and his nerves feeling, far worse, the *separation*, the taking-apart that he hadn't recognized when he'd first felt it in the town. The anguish and the anger of a rider's death rippled and echoed through the area around Shamesey gates like a stone tossed into a quiet pond.

Something warm breathed on his neck then, a presence that had slipped up on him quiet as a breeze, a frightened, spooky mind that didn't like what it smelled/saw/felt from the strangers and meant to safeguard his rider from them.

He didn't need to ask, and he tried not to image . . . which did no good at all: he turned and reached for the refuge of Cloud's midnight neck, tangled his fist in Cloud's mane, stood there in the shelter of Cloud's warmth, only then beginning to shiver.

<Dead horse,> Cloud was imaging. <Blood everywhere. Dead rider.> It was the same image he had seen, the same image the strangers had brought with them through Shamesey camp gates, and the face of the dead rider was, he was increasingly sure, Stuart's border woman.

Stuart's grief came shivering through him then, as if it were washing off the hills. The iron bell that tolled for inbound and outbound convoys began to ring again, distraction to horse and rider senses. They would drink, tonight. They would dance, make love, anything to numb the night. That, in Danny's young experience, was a proper rider funeral.

But there was no joy, no celebration of life. Violence boded everywhere about. Murder raced out into the hills and echoed off the slopes, into the streets of the camp. He'd only heard the faint stirrings of that anger, that bitter, killing rage, let loose in the town—disturbing the streets, maybe reaching his family, maybe prompting the anger at the table. But here it rang through his bones and stirred the pain of his jaw where his father had hit him. Here it prompted him to rage next to tears. The violence, the confusion that had broken forth in the camp, now, in force, threatened all of them. He felt it tugging at his reason.

He saw it in the eyes of the small boy who wove his way past the leather-fringed elbows of the rider crowd. He recognized that thin, white face as someone familiar to him and didn't even realize for a heartbeat that he was looking at his own brother Denis. In that moment he saw Denis as he'd never seen his brother before, a thin, scraggy, amount-to-nothing kid. He saw how fear and hard work were setting a mark on Denis that was on their father, on their mother, on Sam. It was death happening, it was the damned, doomed mark of the masses who huddled in walled towns, the sons and daughters of starfarers, as the preachers constantly reminded them, afraid of the world they lived in.

Denis came running and grabbed him around the middle, terrified, wanting him. Danny shoved back as Cloud's fright hit his nerves. He struck out instinctively just to get Denis away from Cloud, screaming: "Get out of here! Get *out* of here! Go home, you brainless little fool!"

In the next instant he felt the sting in his hand and saw Denis sitting on the ground with a hand pressed to his cheek, all shock and hurt, tears in his eyes.

The shock he felt was what stopped Cloud. That was *all* that stopped Cloud until he turned and shoved desperately at Cloud's muscular shoulder, trying to image to Cloud that this wasn't an enemy, this was a part of him . . . he *ordered* Cloud to go away, and Cloud surged against his push in a fit of jealous anger.

"No!" he said, shoving back, and imaged <Danny hugging Cloud. Danny wanting Cloud. Danny wanting the boy. Quiet water. Pebbles under quiet water.>

<Dark,> Cloud sent back. <Lightning. Thunder. Cold rain.>

"Behave yourself!" Nighthorses understood some words, more than a few words, when they wanted to; Danny was mad, now, and Cloud was mad, but he was madder, and scared: it was his brother's life at stake.

<Lightning.>

"Denis." <Boy at table in house. Boy following him through Shamesey streets, past trucks, crying, upset. Angry people in the house.> —That did no good. Cloud was angry at the people, angry at the boy, and Cloud didn't want to know who Denis was: the complexities of human family relations were beyond Cloud's imagining. Danny shoved hard at Cloud's shoulder. "Go away if you can't behave. Cloud, go away. Now!"

Cloud shook his neck, an obscuring flurry and flutter of mane, then backed a step and whirled with a stinging lash of his tail. But he sulked a little distance away from them, temperous and snapping at an equally surly horse in his immediate path.

Danny turned toward Denis then, not wanting to deal with the boy, still trembling as he was with Cloud's fighting anger.

But Denis wasn't there. He'd not felt him go. Cloud hadn't told him. It wasn't important to Cloud.

Dammit!

There would be murders by morning. When the camp shook to nighthorse dreams, the slum of Shamesey caught the fever. Old feuds, old angers, old resentments, would boil up in the taverns and the houses tonight. The rich sat safely insulated in town center. But no one in or near the camp palisade could be immune from the madness that had broken loose—when all the camp swarmed with images, when all the riders had the same dread of their own dark imaginings.

Clearly a Shamesey kid who'd left the common path had no place in his own home tonight. He couldn't face his father or his mother or his brothers—especially not Denis . . . a realization which settled and occupied a numb, vaguely angry spot in his heart.

He thought he ought to feel overwhelming remorse, loss, something. He knew in his head why his father had hit him. He even forgave his father in his heart, the way the preachers said he had to do. He knew the desperation his father felt in the face of his middle son's sure damnation, and his middle son's tempting Sam and Denis and their mother to go down that same hellbound road.

But that road was *his* breath of life. What he held dearest and most vital violated everything his father held rational or sacred. He couldn't possibly explain to his brothers what he felt when he touched Cloud—his father called it proselytizing for the Devil, leading his brothers into temptation.

So he'd personally rejected God. He hadn't meant to. But once he'd begun to hear the beasts, he'd begun to hear the whole world as it spieled down to winter and licentious riot. He'd felt in it the urgency of all life . . . even of townsmen and the placid cattle that had come down from the stars with them: delicious feelings, forbidden feelings his parents didn't talk about and he could only hint at with his friends because they weren't, he'd understood, the feelings his friends had. They were constant, they were preoccupying: pictures in his mind and feelings that charged those pictures with sensations that ran over his skin and roused desires he had to seek privacy to deal with. He'd prayed, and the pictures came into his prayers. He'd worked until he sweated, and he felt his own skin alive to the air.

He lived now in the flux of beast-sent images that invaded his mind moment by moment. He shivered in the feelings of lust and anger that alternately took his body, the outpourings of disturbed minds, when he should be repenting for hitting Denis and defying his father.

Except no matter what his father believed, riders did have feelings the preachers would call good. Even the horses had them—a thing no rider could explain to the preacher-men, a thing riders couldn't even tell each other, it just was. When you got a number of horses together and enough riders to pin their thoughts obsessively on a set of images, they said you *could* hear beyond the stone's-toss that was a horse's ordinary range. Shamesey regularly proved it. And the pain people felt tonight was because riders couldn't ignore each other.

He couldn't ignore the rider alone out there. He couldn't forget the pain that had rung through Shamesey camp, that still rang, in the iron tolling of the bell. The images tumbled one over the other in his skull, the woman, the rocks, the blood. He didn't easily distinguish (they said a rider's ability to judge such things got better, over time) what was his memory of what he'd just seen imaged and what he might be hearing from riders in the camp, or at this very moment, even from Stuart, at a range no nighthorse was supposed to attain. Horses in pain reached inexplicable distances, did things they weren't supposed to know how to do—junior riders said so, around their own fires. He'd never heard a senior rider say it.

But that horse's pain, which he thought he'd felt when he'd had his hand directly on Cloud, had gone straight to his nerves in a transferred disturbance of a nature and subtlety he'd never felt before—if that was the source of it. The pain and the anger running the hills out there could be why he'd hit Denis—recoiling from Denis' emotional outburst as he ran to him. Cloud could only see that wild emotion as an attack on his rider—and Denis didn't know: Denis couldn't *feel* the air around him. A boy who understood only Shamesey slum couldn't begin to believe that things in the outside world didn't feel or react the way he did. And Denis was his own world, being twelve-going-on-thirteen, and in that world of all things he believed as so, Denis could only know his older brother had gone crazy with his horse and slapped him to the ground. So much for Danny, Denis would think, go on and go to hell, Denis didn't need him, anyway—he could hear it as if Denis had yelled it at him, without Cloud's help.

So, —that was well enough, he couldn't make Denis see it, and Denis had some major adjustments to the world-as-it-was yet to make, some edges yet to be worn off his hellbent sense of right and proper. Denis had it in him. Denis could learn. Denis wasn't Sam.

But, God, he *didn't* need to have hit the kid that hard, no matter that Denis was being an ass.

The way his father, equally scared, equally angry, seeing him in danger, had hit him.

The camp gates shut, the bar dropped. Cloud, venturing close to him again, spooked off with an angry whuff of breath, the wildness Cloud had before storms, deserting him as the other nighthorses, gathering here and there among the riders, shifted and snorted in the gathering dark. A group of them spooked off the same way Cloud had, a muted thunder down the street toward the farther reaches of the camp.

The riders around him turned up their collars against the night wind, thrust their hands into their pockets and, shying from their own horses, went back into the commons, onto the street, to go back to their own precincts, or into the tavern to drink and to numb the feeling.

To kill the anger, as all strong feelings had to die, quickly, in the huge, unstable assemblage of Shamesey camp. It was the rule.

Danny joined the general drift down to the commons, trying to subdue his own bit of that prickling storm-sense, trying to forget the set-to with Denis, trying to forget his father shouting at him and telling him go to hell. Everyone was on edge—his father had, he was increasingly convinced, been feeling the rogue-sending when he'd hit him. His own nerves had certainly been at the snapping-point when he'd hit Denis; and Denis had been on the raw edge, to run at him in fear, risking Cloud's vicinity, when ordinarily Cloud scared Denis out of reach.

He'd never seen mind-to-mind panic in action—although the boss-man, Lyle Wesson, had had the universal Talk with him, when first he and Cloud had come into the camp, novices, confused and hostile and scared of everyone and everything. The camp-boss had told him in plain words that, being young, he was bound to be stupid with his feelings at least several times, and that he had better get control of his emotions, fast, or find himself out on solitary cattle watch for the next three moon-chases.

He remembered that brush of Stuart's presence at the gates, now, when his own insides had been in turmoil and his brain hadn't been thinking, just . . . he'd wanted, ached for company, the way Stuart ached for company in these precarious autumn days . . . and Stuart's border woman was for some reason the image that kept coming at him as if it were his own loss, the unattainable substance of his wishes, a beautiful, fringe-jacketed rider in the High Wild . . . copper-haired woman with the red leaves on all the hills, the object of more than one of his furtive midnight fantasies.

He was disgusted with himself, finding his own juvenile privations echoing off Stuart's earnest grief. It wasn't remotely even forgivable, God! The rider Stuart loved was a mangled corpse in the images running horribly under the surface of the minds around him, Stuart's private pain was echoing at him out of the night and *he* had thoughts like that. No wonder even Cloud wouldn't stay by him, in the confusion of mating urges he was feeling in his blood—it was too painful and drove Cloud too crazy, when there was enough craziness natural in the edge-of-winter ambient.

He didn't know why he should ache after a woman he'd never even met, a borderer who wouldn't have given a junior a passing glance on his best day.

But Stuart had passed that close to him, with horses nearby—and a human mind, he suspected by now, was a flittery, fragile thing, very much unsure what belonged to it by experience and what came to it from elsewhere.

Or—shuddery thought—if it was Stuart he was still hearing, if it was Stuart's thought coming at them from the hills across the road—by all he knew, by all he'd heard, also at a winter fireside, only rogues could send like that. But Stuart wasn't. His horse wasn't. He wouldn't believe it. Chains of such misfortune were legendary, one rogue triggering the next—but it was stupid ghost stories, that was all. Horses and sometimes bears and cats did legitimately go rogue, that part was real—horses got kicked in the head in some mating-fight, or got a high fever that damaged the brain, and a rogue horse—probably a wild one: there were wild herds on Rogers Peak—had spooked that convoy up in the mountains and sent a rider and her horse off the edge of the road. All that was true.

But now, and for no sane reason, all of a sudden *rogue rider* was echoing around the ambient, fear spreading out to attack Aby Dale's partner—as if *Stuart* had just gone unstable, just like the ghost stories, only because he'd run from the camp and gone out alone. But wasn't that what you were *supposed* to do if you couldn't hold something in: get away from the horses, get calm, get quiet? Stuart wasn't crazy. Stuart wasn't any rogue. It wasn't fair or reasonable for people to think so.

Was it?

<Cloud?> he questioned the dark, but Cloud didn't answer him. Either Cloud had gotten out of range, or Cloud was refusing all dealing with him until he'd gotten himself in hand.

<Quiet water,> he thought, trying to calm his rattled nerves. He very much wanted Cloud's comfort right now. He wanted Cloud to

be near him—<soft, beautiful nose, inquisitive black nose, ears up, Cloud walking with Danny.>

But nothing came back but <rocks, and blood.> Constant, now, came the erotic urges of horses heading into winter rut: sex and rivalry and anger. So much anger, no focus, and so much fear of instability . . .

He couldn't even image <still water,> as disturbed as he was. He looked at the ground as he walked, at the dust, gaslit from the poles in the tavern yard, determined to notice detail. That was the last mindless defense against an invading image. He strove to see individual grains of dust, in the half-colored texture the gaslights and the lantern light gave to the ground. He noticed how the footprints in that dust were different, the town-made boots, and the ones more individual, borderers, the sharp, tri-partite hoofprints of the horses under and over them.

In that preoccupation he came up among the tables where the commons gave way to Gate Tavern territory, under the gaslights, where old Mastraian had his hands full. Mastraian's town help were bringing out ale by the pitcher-full: nervous kids, slum kids glad to have any job, even one the preachers said risked their souls, and, working along with them, rider kids, as yet horseless, and a few riders so new or so young they welcomed a tavern job to keep themselves and their horses fed—forage being no viable choice in Shamesey's civilized lowland, where even open pasture had owners.

He was a second-year junior. He was far richer than that. He had his winter account with the camp-boss, money for camp store, the hostel he stayed in, and another account with Mastraian, beyond what he'd given his family in Shamesey—he even carried a little cash in his belt-purse; and the tavern would thank a customer for cash tonight, he was sure, from anyone who carried it—there were just too many customers, over half the camp having followed the disturbance to the gates, for the harried staff to keep tabs.

So he laid down a five on the porchside counter, in exchange for which the counter help handed him an empty mug. He found himself an empty place at a table, shoulder to shoulder at the end of a long bench with other juniors and a couple who didn't look at all to be juniors, man and woman, maybe even borderers, he wasn't sure.

A mug and five meant you could sit at a table, pour from the pitchers the servers set out, and drink yourself gradually stupid, which he was determined to, tonight, for the first time in his life. His father would be furious if he knew, and quote the preachers about ale and riot. His mother would be disgusted, and say he was a stupid kid in bad company, squandering money. Of course. Squandering was his mother's word. It didn't matter if it was your money. If you spent money or time on something she didn't like, you were squandering it.

He was never so conscious of the wall dividing the camp from the town, and him from his family. He'd never had a hangover. He wondered was it as bad as seniors said. He'd spent more money plastering his family's walls than he'd ever squandered in the Gate Tavern. He'd bought clothes and gear he had to have, nothing extravagant. He'd bought sweets for Cloud . . . who didn't at least cry over how wonderful the money was and call him a sinner damned to hell in the same evening.

The high, reedy sound of a flute had started up, another joined in oscillating discord, and then the drummers started a wild and noisy rhythm.

Nobody could be planning sleep in the surrounding hostels tonight. A flood of riders left their tables and started dancing in the commons, some with drinks in hand, men and women in a mingled line.

His table mostly cleared in that first wave, and he refilled his mug and joined what was getting to be a rowdy first-dance line. A handful of borderers had started a contest of sorts, the show-outs holding forth inside the meandering lines—lowland riders didn't do the borderers' steps, didn't do the single-dances like that: he wouldn't dare go out with them, but he watched, asking himself if he could keep his balance, if he could do those steps, and trying a couple of them in the line-dance.

He found a couple of juniors, both male and girl-less, when the line broke up into sets. They danced through one mug and a refill—he didn't know one of them except as Lane, a kid from the far side of Shamesey slum himself. He didn't like Lane much, but that was no requisite for sets. They danced themselves breathless and drank half the refill down.

Then a couple of borderers, already way too many ales down, were spinning past each other with knives flashing, coat-fringes flying. The sets line bowed out for fear of mishaps, while the drummers went crazy, and the hired-help dodged down the line, filling outheld mugs and spilling astonishingly little.

(Follow not the beasts, the preachers said. Avoid ale and riot. Dance is the Devil's enticement.)

He had his mug refilled without asking—without noticing it was about to happen; and, out of breath, tried a few of the steps he'd seen. . . .

Arms hooked his of a sudden, and he found himself snatched and spun into another set, arms snagged by two sweating men he didn't know, both drunker than he was, and as suddenly found himself spun out onto a dance circle, where two borderers beckoned him in, wanting him, he feared, to play the female third—

"No knives!" he panted, and the two, holding each other up, roared with laughter, grabbed his free arm, and snatched him into a dizzy circle-dance. Then he just concentrated on footwork to the drum, round and round and round, with gulps from the mug in between, matching their consumption the way he matched their steps.

Sweat was pouring down his face, despite the chill. He'd picked up the step, and thought he was doing damned well at it. The beat became the whole night, the whole universe, so long as his balance lasted.

But after two rounds he'd no breath for anything but to take the good-natured, hard slaps of high country riders on his shoulders and to weave away, thank God, still able to find his way to a table and sit down before he made a public staggering fool of himself.

A server filled his mug. He'd lost count of how many he'd had out there. Assured of a stable bench under his backside, he sipped the ale, not because he wanted the alcohol, but to ease a throat raw and dry from panting.

Most of the dancers were still going, but the two borderers, after deriding the junior for flagging, had fallen down at other tables.

The sounds he heard now were all of drums and flutes, the sights all whirling bodies, recollections of gaslights spinning past.

Human images, human company . . . humans couldn't image to each other without the horses close, and with the horses absent, human minds could grow quiet, exhausted, blind, deaf, and voiceless. The rogue-presence was gone, its burden lifted. Funerals ought to be loud and raucous, and one could hope the dead woman could somehow know they'd thrown a good one—borderer that she was, the camp she'd been intending for her winter-over at least knew she was gone, and, in that, acknowledged they all were mortal. They wished the dead rider a good hereafter, if there was one, or at least wished themselves drink and dance and noise enough to make the dead hear the party.

It might ease Stuart's mind if he heard the drums out there in the dark. He hoped Stuart did know he and the red-haired woman had friends in camp. He hoped Stuart might come in and have a drink and sit and mourn in sanity, giving the lie to the fools who, in their stupid, idle speculation, put the rogue business on the man who'd only loved that rider—because he'd made them *feel* it; he'd shoved it at them hard, and their nerves were jangled.

God, he wanted his family to be safe tonight. He wanted to know Denis had made it home to bed before the craziness started in the town, as he very much feared it could. It would be better in town once the dancing had started and angers fell in camp. It would be better for the town if, in the Shamesey taverns, there could be dancing, too, or prayers in the churches, or whatever calmed hearts and tempers—since the preachers said dancing was the Devil's way.

No question that the slum could hear the drums: many the nights of his life he'd heard the like from that third-floor flat, lying in his bed, scared of devils. His family would hear the drums and flutes tonight and know there was dancing going on. His mother would be angry and his father would be praying to God to forgive their wayward Danny for dancing and for drinking and for being with low minds, that was what his father called it, words he'd surely gotten from the preachers.

Low minds, consorters with the beasts.

He'd not asked to be a rider. But nobody, not even the boss-man (and he had asked that among the first agonized questions he'd ever dared ask the boss) *nobody* knew why horses picked somebody, or why, as the boss said, they'd sometimes travel unaccountably long distances in search of someone, the way Cloud had done for him.

Cloud had just, in the autumn of his second year, wandered down to Shamesey looking for someone of a description that somehow he guessed he happened to fit.

Maybe Cloud had found no prospects in the high villages. Maybe he'd been so persnickety he'd decided to search a really big town, because there were just more to choose from. Cloud had been persistent about it once he'd arrived. Cloud had hung around Shamesey hills, coming down to the town gate at night, scaring hell out of the gate-guards. The whole town had heard that the night-watch had been shooting at a horse, which so far they'd been lucky enough to miss, and the town council had been recipient of an angry ultimatum from the riders, who took strong exception to the firing.

At the time, he'd been solidly on the gate-guards' side, frightened for his town, believing absolutely in his father's hell, and night after night suffering strange dreams nobody else—he'd tried to figure if he was the only current case—admitted to.

He'd been steadily losing sleep and having nightmares about the gates and the gunfire ever since what the kids called the devil-horse had shown up. His dreams had finally grown so vivid and his mind so sleep-cheated and frantic that, after a day of agonizing over the prospect of another night of such dreams, he'd marched down to the camp to protest to any rider he could find that he was a good God-fearing kid, to state that riders were clearly responsible for protecting townfolk, and to ask that rider how to stop hearing it.

The rider he'd asked at the safe limit of the gate had taken him, in his extreme reluctance, right inside the camp where he'd never been and straight to the camp-boss, whereupon the boss had looked him up and down for the scrawny, unlikely kid that he was, and drawled, as if there was certainly no accounting for tastes, "The horse wants you, that's all."

Then the boss-man had asked him his name, and said he'd be

living in the camp, soon—told him plainly that he really didn't have any choice about it, that when a wild horse was sending like that and you started feeling it as that personal, then pretty soon you were going to start hearing everything that came along, every little burrower at meadow's-edge, every bird that perched on the roof-trees . . . the world would never be quiet to you, ever after.

The boss-man had said that if you got a Call and lost that horse, you'd never, ever sleep again, and probably you'd go crazy . . . so he might as well take a hike into the hills and let the horse find him.

The boss-man had lied to him, he'd found out. He'd actually had a choice. But in the conviction that he hadn't, he'd walked out of the Gate Tavern and lost his breakfast, right at the camp gate, he'd been so scared of hellfire.

Then he'd heard the horse in broad daylight. He'd seen it waiting for him in the hills across the road, hills he couldn't even see with his eyes from inside the gate: he'd been getting images that strongly, from that far away. He'd never realized it.

Clouds across the stars, that was the way Cloud called himself. Clouds scudding fast, before a storm wind. You couldn't say all of it aloud, with the rain smell and the shivery chill and all, and he'd been completely, helplessly swallowed up in it—he'd seen nothing but that starry sky when he'd begun to climb that same grassy slope that Stuart had run, and met, past that hilltop and another one, a horse that decided, finally, it had found a fool who satisfied its juvenile itches.

Found a fool that knew where to scratch, of course. Cloud was a glutton for human fingers.

Found a town-bred fool who'd fall off and near break his neck half a dozen times before he quit insisting he was going one way when Cloud knew very well he was going another.

It hadn't been easy for a young fool in any sense. Bruised and skinned on various parts of his body, he'd been, when he'd written down a message to his family and sent it by a town kid.

He'd thought a lot about hell in the two days he'd waited for an answer from his family.

He'd said, in that message: I can make more money being a rider, —because his father and his mother understood money.

He'd said, —We can get the apartment fixed. We can buy a new drill, one of those electrics—we can bring in a line. He knew his father lusted after that, most of all.

His mother had written back—he still kept the letter, folded up, in the lining of his coat: Your father hasn't accepted it yet. But he says you can come in. He doesn't want to hear about the horse. Come to supper Sunday. We won't talk about the camp.

That had been the agreement, the condition under which he was acceptable at his family's dinner table. That and the money he brought. His evident prosperity. As things were now . . .

A lump started gathering in his throat, and he washed it down with forbidden ale. Now it might be a while before mama could talk papa into Sunday dinners again. Maybe papa's anger would stretch into winter—there wasn't much time left in the year.

You couldn't get hire in winter, to speak of, but there was spring when all the goods had to move at once, and if he could somehow come back next spring with a lot of money, papa would be happier.

And they might have worried about him, a little, if they didn't hear from him. He could sit in camp all winter and not write. Just let them worry. Let them wonder if *he* was mad at them. Or if he was all right.

Papa just didn't like to think about the drums and the drinking and the fornication, that was what papa called it. He hadn't ever had any chance to fornicate, himself, but it wasn't something you could argue with papa. In papa's mind fornication and wickedness was what went on in the camp, all the time, and after the work of summer and fall, winter was one long misbehavior, that was what papa called it when papa was being delicate in front of Denis.

When papa was mad, however, he found that papa had other words, some of which he hadn't heard even from his friends in Shamesey streets, words that made him mad, and made him ask what you learned in church when you got to be his father's age—*he'd* never had that in his lessons.

But if he'd outraged his father and embarrassed him in front of the church by showing up in rider style, he'd profoundly embarrassed his mother, who had to face the neighbors and her customers, and them of course all asking questions—like where the money came from to paint the apartment, and what went on in the camp, and she wouldn't know, she wasn't interested in hearing it from him—but nobody was going to believe she didn't. That was the position he'd put his family in.

The preachers said once you started hearing the beasts of the world, you couldn't ever stop, you couldn't come back . . . because once you heard one, then you started hearing all the beasts, even the little ones. So you slipped deeper and deeper into damnation and became like a beast yourself.

That was one thing the preachers said that had turned out to be true, but not quite the way they'd said: it wasn't like hearing words. Sometimes you'd just see things, when you were riding out and about the hills. You'd see yourself and your horse going down the road, and you'd know you were picking something up from some little creature somewhere, under the bushes or up the hill.

And it just wasn't that bad. They were gentle images, most times, a little spooky toward dark, but you learned very quickly to tell what was sending it—and mostly the feelings they brought with them were anxiousness, or curiosity: very few wild creatures wanted to come near a nighthorse.

As for the sex his parents imagined . . . God, that was a joke. If you were a townbred junior, you just lay in the dark when the images came past you from somebody else, as they did, and you tried to imagine you'd found some rider girl who didn't think you were pond scum, but there weren't many girls among the juniors. Shamesey girls didn't come out to the horses. They were too scared of hellfire, or no horse had ever wanted one. And there were rider girls, but they all had boys they'd grown up with. So that left a Shamesey rider on his own at night.

But, oh, there were women who came into camp, full of mysteries a sixteen-year-old couldn't possibly deal with, women in fringed leather and carrying knives, sun-tanned and wonderful, women who bunked down mostly with senior riders they personally knew . . . a lot richer than he was, and not needing a junior to tell them his sweaty-palmed aspirations.

The horses eavesdropped, at the same time, and sometimes

spread feelings all through the den, until, if you were in the vicinity, God help you. . . .

Cloud was a pushy horse, and devious, and Cloud flirted with all the mares. Cloud drove him crazy sometimes.

Like now.

He finally knew exactly where Cloud was: in the dark of the den by the gate, not that far out of Cloud's range when Cloud was excited. And Cloud was sniffing after a mare who was more than interested.

He couldn't stop it. It wasn't even his right to stop it, the boss-man had told him that, and the boss-man could as well have left it off the list of particulars: Cloud would have made him know his rights and dues beyond any doubt at all.

The dancing was still going on, a little slower, as everybody ran out of wind, but craziness was running the camp, with the autumn cold in the air. So, of course, when he was so buzzed he staggered, Cloud, with the images of blood and dead females in his head, had to think, tonight, of sex. God, Cloud *had* no sense of moderation.

Nor did the mare.

Damnation, the preachers said. A nighthorse had no kindness. Animals had no souls.

Cloud had no shame, that was sure, and he didn't know how to be near human beings when Cloud was doing what Cloud was doing at the moment. He'd danced enough and drunk enough; he decided he'd better stagger off to bed, which, wobbly as he was, was just too far, in a cheaper hostel clear around the circuit of the camp. He only needed a place for an hour or so where nobody would bother him, where he could suffer Cloud's mate-courting in private, and sober up enough to walk home, and he didn't want . . .

Oh, God.

He had to get up fast, dazed as he was. He couldn't stay in the tavern yard. He stood a moment, while images came and went, to be sure of his feet.

Then he wandered through the area of the dance, walked his unsteady way down the street toward the nighthorse den next the gate, which, sense told him, was where Cloud was doing his courting.

Chapter
— iii —

DANNY DIDN'T WANT TO GO INSIDE THE DEN. HE WENT ONLY AS far as its wooden wall, next the end where the earthworks were piled up to make its sod wall and roof. There he sat down on a pile of moldering canvas, overwhelmed by the night and the images, shoved his arms between his knees and tried to subdue an arousal so intense it didn't let him think. He just stared blankly back at the tavern yard down the street, an island of light, like one of those other worlds the teachers talked about, men and women drinking at the tables, men and women dancing with each other under the gaslights.

He saw couples pairing up—one pair very drunk, completely distracted or as far from their own beds as he was. They didn't wait. They just did it in the far side of the hostel, in the alley where they probably thought nobody was watching. He tried not to look, but he did, and worse . . . much worse . . . he grew angry along with watching them. He wanted to kill somebody at the same time, and that *feeling* was going through the camp, back again—when it had left them alone for the last hour or so.

Stuart . . . was aware. He suddenly realized that Stuart was watching the camp. Stuart wanted . . . he wasn't sure what. The angry feeling was coming through the wooden walls, it was coming through the ground, and his eyes were suddenly full of tears he didn't know he had. He kept wiping them, and they kept coming, while, somewhere nearby, Stuart wanted . . .

Death. Sex. The red-haired woman.

He *felt* Cloud courting the mare, felt the union, the mare's sensations as well as Cloud's, and he couldn't stand it. He got up from his place by the den wall and paced the street.

The urgency and the anger grew less when he was walking. It slowly became endurable. He walked back and forth in front of the den, but the nighthorses were all disturbed, now, arousal was epidemic, and he found himself walking back down the street toward the tavern, toward company he didn't really want, but there were human minds there, and the feeling near the walls and near the den had been dangerous and full of complex urges he didn't understand. If it was Stuart, it was gone now. Or farther away. But he didn't want to stay that near the horses if it started up again.

The dancing had gotten down to drunken singles, monofocussed on the intricacy of the steps, while the single remaining drumbeat had grown erratic.

He wove back through the tables, at which some slept, some sat talking in small, sober knots, saner than he was, wiser than he was. He kept getting images, maybe his own memory, he didn't even know any longer, the feelings of a dark body, an intense misery of hurt.

Overwhelming awareness as a man brushed past him with a contact like electric shock. That man grabbed his arm, faced him about in a fit of temper. He felt the anger, he instinctively flinched from the blow—

But he felt something else flowing through the painful fingers, burning straight into his gut, and he couldn't breathe.

"Damn *kid*," the rider said, as if that meant dirt.

He jerked his arm free. The sexual feelings didn't stop. The anger didn't stop. The rider grabbed him a second time, hard, by the wrist.

No. Not Stuart. It was the riders who'd talked to Stuart outside.

They'd brought the rogue-image inside with them. They'd felt it up on Tarmin Height. *They* were the source of the fear—and the image. Not Stuart. The riders at the gate had been right to try to shut them out.

But you didn't start a fight with anyone with the horses involved, not if you could help it, not for anything. Not for your life, if you had the least chance of saving it yourself. The men at the gate had let those three riders in, and the whole camp was in rut and anger and fear.

"Easy," the man said. The grip on his wrist hurt, and he was scared, but Cloud wasn't there to rescue him right now, Cloud was deep in the sensations of a den gone mad with mating.

"Kid! *Dammit!*"

He tried to get free, tried to draw a breath. The rider wasn't the dark body he felt. He tried to see where he was, ignoring Cloud's presence, ignoring what Cloud was doing.

"Friend of Stuart's," the man said. "Friend of his. Get a breath, kid. Get two." The stranger popped him across the face, backhanded, enough to sting. A bench came up against the back of his knees and he fell down onto it. "Dammit, kid, come *down*. You're sending it, d' you feel it, do you taste it, are you deaf?"

The stranger had his attention, now, holding his wrist, trying to pull him out of the fog, but nothing human or sane got through the ambient. There was sex, there was anger, there was grief . . . they were both caught up in it. A vast, shapeless anger rolled out of the town streets toward the gates. He felt its frustration and its fear; he heard the sounds of voices, heard that sound of human beings in a mass, disturbed and angry, outside the camp walls.

A shot went off—from the gates, from the town, from inside the camp, he couldn't tell—the report rang off walls and echoed off the hills.

The rider let him go, turned to shout at people at the tables, yelling to get the boss, to get somebody to stop it.

He didn't know Stop what? except for that anger rolling past the camp, toward the road.

<Rogue-feeling. Trucks racing on a road too steep. The lead truck going over, the whole convoy going too fast, the truck missing the turn, falling and falling . . . like the copper-haired rider . . . falling down and down among the rocks . . . >

He didn't want any more. He didn't want to hear it gone over and over, and see that woman die and die again. It was Stuart's message. It was Stuart's dead. He wanted Cloud. He *wanted* <Cloud,> calling in a night gone mad.

Second burst of gunfire.

The night exploded. He lurched to his feet, he cried out to his horse, "Run!" and he was <sliding down off Burn's back,> he saw <dry grass blurring under them in the dark. . . .>

<Horse running,> he thought. <Horse running, running, running in the dark.>

He heard Cloud answer, somewhere near, he heard <someone shouting. . . .

<*"Open the gates!"*>

<Gunshot.>

Close, quivering echo. Pain hit his right leg and it folded. He fell on one knee, and a mass of riders broke around him, followed the man who'd grabbed him, all running toward the shut gates. Bullets were still flying outside, a ringing, erratic volley of shots. The echoes came back off the hills—he'd heard hunters' rifles echo in that strange, hollow way. All his life he'd heard it. He'd heard it the nights they'd shot at Cloud.

"Hold it!" the call went out from somewhere down the street. "Hold those gates! —Dammit, *stop where you are*!"

The order went out not only from the camp-boss, it went out from Dart, too, who was never far from the boss-man, and it shot straight to the nerves.

<Gates open. Riders mixing with angry townsmen, men with rifles, nighthorses sending anger, anger, *anger*—>

<Still water. Instant *ice.*>

The old man who walked past him and down to the gates was crippled. A stick supported him. The nighthorse that came up near him was one-eyed and scarred, but Dart was one *loud* horse, a force, with Lyle Wesson to back it, that made nerves twitch and ears prick up. Danny stood still. Movement had stopped, stopped in the image, stopped in reality, out beyond the gate.

But the horse out there on the hill went running, running, and the rider staggered up, pain shooting through his leg. Danny sat down on the bench and shivered in the dying mental echoes of the gunfire.

<Rider ahorse,> was the image that came to him, to everyone, he believed, up and down the street. <Horse running into the dark.>

Stuart had grabbed that mane and was away. The mob that had poured out of the town—an irrational, hating thing, as crazed as the rogue-sending—couldn't take Stuart now.

His leg still ached, telling him that Stuart hadn't escaped unscathed. He didn't know why he shared it, but he felt the pain acutely as he got up, and limped, alone in his area of the street, toward the gates.

<Danny.> He saw himself, his hand clasped to the hurt on the side of his thigh. He felt the condemnation he was due, anger at a junior who had, he realized it now, been dangerously sending out into the ambient.

"I'm sorry," he whispered when he got to where Lyle Wesson stood, hands clenched on his walking-stick.

"Damned fool," the boss said. "Did I tell you, or not?"

He tried to image Stuart's helping him. The image went askew. It was just Stuart, the way he'd been that day on the porch, a stiff, rain-smelling breeze stirring his hair and the fringes of his jacket. A downpour grayed the commons. He'd thought even then that it was no bad thing to be a borderer, free of towns and free of family . . .

. . . free of a father who, however he excused it, hit him and consigned him to hell.

He didn't want the whole camp to know that, but, humiliated, he feared they'd all heard. He thought of <wind in the grass, wind bending the stalks>: that was the earliest image the boss had taught him to send, to be invisible.

But he wasn't the only area of disturbance. He heard shouting out in the dark beyond the gates, he heard voices raised in demands. The town wanted the riders to do something. To hunt the rider down. The town came to the camp with its fears for its safety, its peaceful sleep—the rich feared for their right to go on as they always did, oblivious to the Wild beyond their walls, and they *demanded*—

The town could go to hell, he thought, with a lump in his throat. The town didn't know. The town didn't remotely know what he was, or what he saw, every day. He lived in a wider, more vivid, more connected world than he could make his father or his mother or even Denis understand.

Danny Fisher damned sure didn't belong in this town any longer; he'd felt it, in the echoes of the gunfire that still echoed in his brain.

The lump in his throat grew larger. The leg ached. He wasn't aware of Cloud, now, but that was the way it ought to be—the camp was settling, minds were growing quieter, the pain in his leg was diminishing . . .

He was terribly scared when he thought about what had happened, how the whole camp, the whole *town* had been on the edge of crazy. Everybody was scared now. Even the camp-boss was scared of the craziness that had almost driven them to do things and feel things in one mind.

Mass-hallucinations happened, the borderers reported, in snowed-in winter camps. They *didn't* happen in the biggest city in the world, in a gathering so large, so precarious in its size the riders themselves argued whether they ought to put limits on their numbers and draw lots for who stayed.

"Break it up!" the boss yelled out across the commons, and rounded on sobered, scared riders. "Quiet, dammit!"

Himself, in Wesson's near vicinity, in Dart's, able to feel the brunt of Wesson's anger, he wished he were far, far elsewhere.

"Damn you all!" the boss said. "Do you know what you did, yet? Have you come to your senses? Quieten down! All of you, *quiet*!"

He tried, obediently, not to think at all, and the feeling around him grew measurably less raw, less miserable. The ambient tumbled around him with images of <still water> and <quiet sky> and <gently waving grass.>

But he'd seen Shamesey tonight in a way he'd never seen it. Everything he hated about town and everything he feared about the sheer power of so many minds pushing and pulling at him had crystallized tonight.

Maybe it was Stuart's feeling he still had: it could be. He didn't know, but walls had come down tonight—walls between people, walls between townsmen and their precious self-deceptions about safety. His family was so glad of the fresh plaster, so glad of reliable food on the table.

But know a thing else about him? They didn't even want to wonder. They didn't want to understand their hellbound son.

The preachers said they'd come in ships down from the heavens, the preachers said they'd begun as glorious beings with a God-given mission to subdue the land and make the fields safe for humankind and their cattle . . . which meant to go out and make towns and fields and roads as many and as fast as they could.

But, doing that, you had to deal with the world as it was, and you had to have the riders, and somebody had to deal with the creatures of the sinful world, which the preachers said were a temptation and evil.

So how did you work it out, that God arranged it so some people had to sin so the rest could go to Heaven?

Because if not for the riders, no town would stand, and human beings wouldn't ever have survived their first winter against the predators and the nighthorses that loved human minds, *loved* human senses, and lusted after their company.

And how did you work it out that the whole wide world was out there full of food, and his mother and his father worked so hard to buy what they could take for free if they just went outside the walls.

He wasn't sure. Just . . . there had to be riders.

Hear not the beasts, the street preachers said.

And, while the boss-man called the riders fools, and while others said they couldn't just let Stuart go off as crazy as he was acting, and they had to do something to stop him before he killed somebody, his own heart was still aching from what he'd learned and his leg still throbbed with a gunshot that hadn't come near him.

Wages of sin, the preachers would say.

Chapter — iv —

No shot had touched Burn, the two of them running and running on Burn's strong legs. Burn flung off such a dire warning it became total, mind-absorbing thought for both of them. . . .

But came a mortal, moral weariness, finally, on the grassy brow of a hill well and away and above Shamesey town.

Burn's sides and gut were aching. Burn's legs shook with exhaustion as he slowed and wandered at a slower pace on the dark and dangerous slopes.

Burn stopped, then, with a shake of his neck and a snort of disgust.

Guil Stuart looked down from the height on the cluster of Shamesey lights, lonesome island in the dark of the Wild . . . and wished it no good, not Shamesey and not the other coward towns. Burn would run farther if Burn could. Burn's anger and Burn's desire for blood was no less because he was exhausted. Neither was his.

But Burn was a self-saving creature, sane for both of them. Burn would never destroy himself in some mad desire to escape what a human brain, in its own weighing of priorities, had begun to realize was no immediate threat to them.

Exhaustion was the enemy. Cold was, in this edge of lowland autumn. He began to realize Burn's aching lungs and wobbling legs as a distress separate from his own crazed pain, and he slid down from Burn's bare back to give Burn relief from his weight. He managed, gingerly, leaning on Burn's sweating side, to take his weight on the wounded leg, which proved to him that at least the bone wasn't broken.

A bullet-trace, he decided, feeling it over with his fingers; leather breeches had split on a nasty raw gouge across the side of his leg, above the knee. He walked a little distance across the steep, grassy slope of the hill. It was to test the leg, that was what he said to himself.

But he couldn't rest yet. He couldn't stop moving. He wasn't tired enough to sit down and try to absorb the shock in plain sight of those smug, safe, lights. He'd start thinking if the pain stopped, and he wasn't ready to think. He couldn't realize anything yet but bits and pieces.

<Aby dead. Lying on the horse. In the rocks.>

Jonas . . . Luke . . . Hawley . . . they'd carried on and gotten the convoy through. Aby'd ridden point at Tarmin High Loop, coming down Tarmin Climb.

<High, steep, winding road. Lead truck following Aby, rolling down to the fatal turn, where the woods came near the road. Rogue horse—coming from somewhere on the mountain—crazed, sick from injury—spooking the truckers—trucks going faster and faster—>

Images came at him. He wanted not, not, not, to see. He walked harder and faster, until the pain was affecting his balance, blurring the city lights and the stars and his recollections alike.

He slipped on the grass. <Guil falling down,> he saw in his head. And did, sideways, hard, on one hip.

He grabbed a fistful of grass and ripped it up. Flung the resultant clod at Burn, wanting no images, no thinking.

But the images assailed him anyway, out of his own brain, out of Burn's, he wasn't sure.

<Tarmin Climb. Sunlight. Omen and death in every rustling leaf. The riders going in a group, behind the trucks, not suspecting. Aby alone in front.>

He thrust himself up to his feet, wide-legged, staggered further, wanting the pain, cold wind on tracks on his face . . .

<Road in the sunlight. Trucks winding down the mountain, slow, heavy-loaded with rough-cut lumber, with bales of furs, with broken machinery, craftworks, and such, out of the villages of Rogers Peak, with the mid-sized tankers supplying the convoy as well as the villages.

<Jonas preoccupied with the tankers, that pushed the limit of length that could get up and down that eroded roadway, bringing them up last, so if there was bad road and trouble they'd not take out the road in front of most of the trucks, and not stall the whole convoy on the steep downhill grade . . . now the long straightaway before the turn—>

That was the instant, the very instant—

He *didn't* want to see it.

<The road—no idea and no warning that there was a danger ahead of them. Horse on the mountain—rogue-sending—>

Jonas, he had no doubt, would have been up there riding point with Aby if he'd known any danger in the area. But Jonas and Hawley and Luke had been riding tail-guard, all of them worrying about the trucks, some of the driver-apprentices riding on the running-boards to watch the treacherous edge, to call out warning where the tires were—he'd *seen* that road himself, in Aby's mind, at night, when they lay close and safe and warm—

"The horse went with her?" he'd asked Jonas, when he'd talked with Jonas and his partners outside the camp gates, because he'd known, he'd known all of it he could possibly face in Jonas' first thought, and believed in that first heartbeat that Aby had died in a slide, not uncommon on the road.

"It wasn't a slide," Jonas had said, then, grimly, arms folded, eyes downcast to the withers of his horse, and he saw <Aby lying next dead horse. Blood. Aby's red hair.>

And immediately—maybe not Jonas' intention—he'd gotten all that the nighthorses had seen, all that the riders knew. He'd felt for himself the disintegrated horror of the sending that riders and truckers and horses had picked up at the edge of that woods on Tarmin Height.

<Something in the woods. Something deadly, at the forest edge, something disjointed, dissolute . . . distant, then. Calling for them. Wanting them. Wanting them all.>

Riders never used loud voices. Sometimes you got almost out of the habit of speaking aloud or parceling out thoughts in human words. Sometimes you forgot you had a voice, or what to do with it.

He'd have screamed at Jonas to shut up, let him alone. He'd forgotten how to make such sounds at need. Or, rider-born, never learned how at all.

"Stuart?" Jonas Westman had said, maybe wanting to tell him more than he had already said, but he couldn't bear it. And Jonas had known, and thought <Snow. Cold, white, trackless snow,> as Jonas would, when things went wrong. "Guil. We'll hunt it. We'll get it. . . . "

But he'd already started to run—run and run to clear the vicinity, run until his lungs hurt, until pain and lack of wind had wiped his mind clear.

Run until Burn had caught him, and carried him away up the steep hill.

He'd had no idea even where he rode, after that. And he'd thought . . . his first sane thought . . . that he had, for numerous reasons, to go up to Tarmin before the snows closed the passes. That had made sudden, necessary sense to him. Kill the rogue that had killed Aby and haunted the convoy down the mountain. Jonas didn't want to go back. Jonas had enough bad dreams.

And he'd known, when he'd thought that far, in the carefully guarded, piece-by-piece way he dared let conclusions form in his mind now, that he needed his rifle, that he'd left in his hostel room. All he owned was there.

<Gates in the darkness. Bell-arch of Shamesey camp.>

<Main gates opening, to Shamesey town itself. The night-guard with their long rifles . . . >

The gun and the gear he needed was all he'd asked, his own belongings, when he'd gone toward the gates. He thought, at least now, that he'd only wanted that, and that he'd never harbored any darker intentions against the camp.

But the town had come out to resist him—for no reason.

<Death. Hate. Dissolution and open space, rider and horse swept away in front of tons of metal, at the turn. The truck going off the edge in dreadful slowness, the driver trying to clear the truck, door open, as it slides off the edge . . . but the rider and the horse go quickly and together.>

<Dead. Dissolved. Blood on the rocks. But the riders can't go down to her, can't reach her, where she'd fallen, without risking lives. Boss trucker is angry. The riders, spooked and uncertain, leave her for the slinking carrion-eaters. Damn them. Damn the lot of them.>

The night-watch had shot at him out of fear. The riders of Shamesey camp had kept within their gates—for fear of him.

That should tell him something of what sane people felt in his anger and his intentions, and maybe the townsmen had been right. He didn't trust himself to try another approach to the town, least of all to talk to Jonas, whose decisions had been coldly, professionally correct. Save the convoy. Get it safe. The dead could wait for the scavengers. Even Aby.

The hazard of autumn was in the wind and the grass, in the cold which seeped from the air into the bones, like solitude, like chill, like foreknowledge of luck turning brutal and foul. And his anger was too profound, too broad, too unreasoning to be only his anger. Other resentments had gotten loose in Shamesey camp. Other reasons had risen up and taken on life in the town. It was no place for an angry man to stay.

He wiped at his face. The ache in his leg so long as he walked absorbed all his logical thinking, a cherished, protective pain. He wasn't thinking at all clearly in such weather. Nighthorse instincts were in the way, coloring everything, making everything raw emotion . . . even before the rifle shot had resounded off the walls, even before the blinding red and the pain had washed across his mind.

Just . . . he couldn't think clearly now what to do. He was thinking Burn's thoughts, and they were all anger; all selfish . . . bitter . . . anger . . . at the town that wasn't at fault for wanting lumber and comforts for the winter.

He wanted someone to die, he wanted to see it, he wanted to do it with his own hands . . .

He wanted Shamesey town to know a woman had died so that they could have light and heat and repair for their walls, and they could go to hell for it.

But she was only a rider, only a damned-to-hell rider, it didn't matter to them, they didn't need to care. Shoot the horse if a rider went like that. Make sure it was dead. That was all they'd want to know.

He could take to the hills, go south, not north, and he and Burn could forget what they couldn't mend—they didn't need to avenge Aby's death. It just was. What had killed Aby and Moon had no relation to anything, no grudge, no personal reason. It just was. And if in winter snows it came down the mountain, if it haunted the road next season, if it killed villagers or townsmen, what did he care?

If Shamesey went without lumber or tin next year, what should he care?

That more riders could die by the thing that killed Aby, all right, he did care, little that it deserved. He didn't owe any of them, didn't get any damn help from them, not even from Jonas. He didn't know why he shouldn't let someone else hunt the thing. He could live elsewhere. He could find other hire. No place and no person mattered to him with Aby gone. *She* had brought him into towns. She'd always been the go-between for him with people.

But his dreams wouldn't change until the rogue was dead. And he would dream about it. He'd wonder every night whether it was still out there, still surviving, still sending out the images that lied to horse and rider about what was friend and foe, or where the edge of the road was. . . .

Walk and walk, and walk, and he found himself walking north

across the slope. He found Burn trailing him, aching-tired himself, waiting for a foolish rider to fall down again.

<Guil sitting down. Legs ache.>

<Town lights,> he imaged in his own turn, not consciously thinking. Town was just too close, too dangerous, too loud, too evocative of anger.

<Hills and grass in the moonlight,> Burn answered him. <Hills and grass. Hills and grass.> Burn shook himself, and snorted. An image of blood and raw meat. <Kill cattle.>

Burn didn't forgive. Burn might lose his train of thought and forget. But Burn didn't know how to forgive.

It was why he kept walking.

"Hunt him down," was Ancel Harper's word in hastily convoked Meeting, in the tavern yard under the gaslights, in the small hours of the morning. "He's Shamesey's problem."

No, Danny Fisher wanted to say, and half-choked on the impulse to rise and protest.

But other, senior, riders stood up from the benches without hesitation and said no, there was no call for such drastic measures.

"He wanted what's his," one of that number said. "His belongings are all in camp. He has a right to ask for them."

"He has no right, after what he's caused," somebody else shouted, and a dozen riders from Hallanslake got up and added their voices.

"We come down here to the lowlands for a quiet, safe camp," the Hallanslake leader said. "I know what I'm talking about. A man running up in the hills is one thing. Coming down to town is another. Stuart's gotten riders killed. He's a spook. He's always been a loner and that horse of his is another. He's got a grudge and he's not going to let it go. I tell you, you stop it now! You hunt Stuart out of the district, or you shoot him *and* his horse!"

"No," the general murmur rose in rebuttal; Danny said so, too, under cover of the others, but the Hallanslake rider didn't give an inch.

"That's what you do, that's what you have to have the guts to do. That's a borderer up there hovering over this town. He knows what he's asking for, staying around here, spooking the town into riot. You got fifty, seventy thousand people in town here, a lot of them not liking each other. You want to think, boss-man, about what could happen in the streets the other side of that wall if he panics this town? Stuart's as crazy as what killed that woman up in the hills—that's how they go, one to the next—the sickness spreads. You got to shoot both of them, fast, so they don't know one's dead! It spreads, boss-man! I've been there! I know!"

No! Danny Fisher thought, and before thoughts could get far:

"No," the camp-boss growled, and hammered the table with his fist. Crippled in a fall, and survivor of one horse already, Lyle Wesson might ride when he had to go any distance and he might use a stick when he had to cross between two tables in the tavern, but the strength in the man and the force of mind in old Dart made the skittery, jittery feelings in the air subside instantly, and let a scared junior sink gladly back into his seat with his objection unmade, at the same time the Hallanslakers sat down, sullen-minded and angry and not giving in.

A junior *hadn't* any right to speak ahead of the seniors, except he was Shamesey-born, and they were Shamesey townsfolk who'd shot Guil Stuart tonight, calling Stuart a threat, which wasn't at all the truth, the way Stuart's horse wasn't a rogue. He *knew* it wasn't, but more surely, Cloud knew, the rest of the horses knew, and the boss-man knew, so the whole camp had to know. They were here to talk about the rogue that had spooked a convoy off the road on Rogers Peak, and here were Harper and his friends talking as if Stuart was the real threat, right here in Shamesey. The whole camp had lost their minds. Or it was the spooked riders, the ones that had come in with the news. *They* were here, and maybe the source of what Harper thought he felt. Fear of a rogue had gotten loose in the camp, and after that, it came from everywhere. But a junior couldn't stand up and say his seniors were all being fooled.

Fact was, half the riders in the meeting weren't wholly sober, some were surly—a couple were unconscious, face down on the tables, though a whole lot had sobered when the gunfire went off, and more when the boss-man had said there was Meeting, now, fast.

He was one who had sobered mightily, even before Wesson's call—and he'd tried, well knowing that he wasn't at his sharpest, and far from experienced in a situation like this, to do exactly what the boss had said, namely to keep his mind quiet, because even with the whole Gate Tavern yard and the open commons for the Meeting, even with all the horses except Dart requested out of the gate area so that humans had to say things aloud to each other and not image at all, he wasn't sure things didn't leak out and get back and forth to horses and humans anyway, the way they'd certainly done a couple of hours ago, when the horses had all caught the same image at once.

Ancel Harper said he'd seen a rogue once. He said he'd seen a dozen riders go with it. He said it was like what they'd just felt, only a hundred times worse . . . he said a rogue could send over an entire valley, and trick you into seeing things where they weren't, and make you want it bad until it killed you, because that was what it would do when you got close to it.

Harper said there was one cure, an ounce of lead.

Harper and the Hallanslakers—Danny had never met anybody like them in camp, riders who just didn't listen to what people said, who, when they got an image and a horse was near, turned it inside out, to what they wanted. In his mind, *they* were crazy as the rogue, but he tried not to think that: they also carried knives, and he didn't think they were an empty threat.

But by the time he'd figured out what Harper and his lot stood for, there were more moderate voices, older riders, to stand up one by one and severally and demand that the camp-boss should deal with Shamesey town and negotiate Stuart's right to come back when he was indisputably sane, as riders could clearly judge better than townsmen.

"Now wait," another rider stood up to say, now, Yeats, a senior Shamesey rider. "Now, I don't agree with the Hallanslakers, that we need go shooting at shadows—but I don't hold we should take Stuart's side against the town, either. It sets a bad precedent, a *bad* precedent, backing a rider who breaks the major rules."

"Now, wait a minute," a woman said.

"Rules," Yeats said, raising his voice, "as seem clear enough to us. Stuart stayed on in the area, Stuart came near the walls. The watch hadn't a right to shoot, but they were skittish, they had a crowd out there—"

"Damn right, they haven't a right!" came from the back.

"It was Stuart's doing that a crowd gathered," Yeats shouted, "and it was Stuart's fault! If Stuart had a sane thought left, he should have got the hell all the way out of Shamesey fields when he knew he was losing his hold. But he doesn't want out of Shamesey district, does he? That's why he's stayed out there!"

"God's sake, Yeats!" A borderer stood up, wobbly on his feet. "You got his gear and you got his gun—he come back after his gear, you damn fool!"

"I got the floor! I'm saying we got excitable townsmen all over, we got horses upset, we got riders upset—it shows clear enough what we've been saying for three years, now: boss-man, you got to thin the camp down—"

Riders hooted, from all over the assembly.

"Yeah, you go first, Yeats!" somebody yelled from back in the crowd, then the drunk borderer was yelling something, not sitting down, and Wesson banged on the porch with his cane. Dart started imaging <Still water. Still grass,> until at last Yeats and the borderer sat down, and the silence was thick enough you could breathe it.

Yeats was off on a different issue: the number of riders gathered at Shamesey—and Shamesey riders had argued before against letting the camp get as large, and consequently as unstable, as it was—but the riders that came from outside said it was just Shamesey riders wanting exclusivity on the best jobs and the comforts of the biggest town there was.

"Jim," Wesson said, "keep to the Stuart business."

"It *is* the Stuart business," Yeats said. "This is what we're going to get more of if we don't thin down the winter-camp and put some restrictions on how many out-of-district riders we're going to camp here! Shamesey valley's big enough—build a camp down at the end of the valley! Build it up on the foothills! There's no way the snows are going to cut off valley roads!"

"Yeah, on whose land?" somebody yelled. "The town council isn't going to give up a foot of pasture!"

Yeats was right, in Danny's estimation.

Unfortunately so was the rider right when he yelled out about the council not giving up any land: rich people decided everything, and the rich people in Shamesey didn't feel the dreams that came through the camp walls on an uneasy, stormy night, didn't lose sleep the night through with the autumn urges—only people like his family did, old and young alike, and girls got pregnant and godly folk prayed and sweated and prayed to send the devils away. It was the lowtown folk who'd come out with guns. People like his family. It was people like his father and his mother and his brothers who'd gone stark crazy and shot at Stuart.

People of the same town-bound, mind-blind sort that he'd used to be, before Cloud called him in his dreams.

He hoped Denis hadn't gotten swept up in the crowd that was shooting; he desperately wanted to know where his family was and that they were safe. But he couldn't go into town tonight. Maybe not for a lot of nights. Couldn't—a lump formed in his throat—so much as offer his help to his father to keep him safe, when he could do as much for any trucker in the outback.

"All that's beside the point," a borderer stood up to say. "What Shamesey is, Shamesey chose to be. It can't ever go back to being a small town. We get your trucks through and we got our right to camp here. And the whole damn valley had better get off Stuart's back. This town had better hope Stuart goes up to Tarmin and finds what's up there before winter falls, or you're losing Anveney *province*, Shamesey boss. That thing that got Aby Dale won't stay away from the villages up there. And maybe if it gets a village or two, it might come down to Shamesey to hunt around spring melt. When a horse goes bad, it *wants* human company, and there's nothing but a bullet through the brain can stop it. So you better quit arguing about how many riders we have in this camp and Stuart and your piddlin' rules—and start worrying about that rogue horse up there!"

"That's saying Stuart's going to do a damn thing he ought!"

Ancel Harper stood up to say. "He's not going to stay away from Shamesey. He'll be back."

"That's tomorrow's trouble!" a borderer shouted, and stood up. "And it isn't proved, Hallanslaker! There's never been a rogue come into this district!"

"You'll see it proved when you've seen a man and a horse go bad—and I have, Reney, I've seen it, don't you tell me what's not proved! I've felt it, don't you tell me what's like and not like! You want to *feel* it, Reney? Come outside camp and I'll show you!"

"That's no call to go after Stuart!"

"I'm telling you he's a danger. He's already spooked the town—and he's not going to let go and go away. You got people out with guns in the town streets, Wesson. You're going to have people killed over there if you don't get Stuart shut down—"

"Hold it, hold it, hold it!" Lyle Wesson yelled, pounding the table. But people had started shouting at one another, and got to their feet, and started yelling at each other about hazards to the camp, about outsiders, which Stuart was, and which the Hallanslakers also were, but the Hallanslakers seemed to have forgotten that point, or Harper had. Harper started yelling at Lyle Wesson that they had to hunt Stuart and his horse, and Lyle Wesson banged his stick down on the table.

"Shut the hell up!" Wesson shouted. "And let's talk about the trouble in Tarmin Height. Let's talk about clearing that road of a hazard, and keeping the thing away from the villages up there on the Loop this winter. That's our business, if you'd shut the hell up and quit stirring things up, Harper!"

Tarmin was where Stuart was going, Danny Fisher thought, certain as sure. The skin on his arms stood up in gooseflesh. His legs just moved—and he was standing, and the boss was looking at him. Everyone was.

"Stuart's going up there," he said, too quietly, he thought, but a leaf-fall would have made a sound in that silence. He sat down again, hugged his arms about him and wanted not to make another sound.

Lyle Wesson said, "Going up where, Danny Fisher?"

"To find what killed her and that truck driver. He's going up to Tarmin to stop it, just like you said."

"He's shown no sign of leaving, yet," a Hallanslaker shouted. "What's the kid got? A phone line to God? Stuart's a danger to the whole camp! Shoot him *and* the horse before he comes back! The town may not have a second chance!"

"No!"

It was a voice he'd heard before this night—one of the strangers, the one who'd accosted him, the one who'd called him seriously to task for giving way to his panic. "The kid's right. He's going up there. Absolutely that's where he's going."

"So you say!" the Hallanslaker shouted. "We got this town at risk! You're not going to get any help out of Stuart!"

And another of his lot: "The Shamesey riders already say the camp's too large, the town's too large—you let a rider run amok around Shamesey fields, what do you look to have? Murders in the streets? Bodies stacking up like cordwood? You don't trust Stuart'll do any damn thing he ought to. Hell with him handling the Tarmin rogue—he spooked the whole damn town! Shoot him, I say! Then *we'll* handle the Tarmin problem!"

The ambient was miserable. The rider next to Danny got up and left.

He stayed. He said, standing up again and forcing the words through a throat that seemed too small, "He's wrong."

"Who's he?" a Hallanslaker asked. "Who is this kid, some kin of Stuart's?"

His voice stalled. He cleared his throat with an effort and prayed it wouldn't crack. "I'm not any kin of his. But he's already left. He's not crazy. He's done what you say and left the town the way he's supposed to. He just wants quiet for a while."

"*How* do you know?" one of the Shamesey riders asked him, and he retorted,

"I heard him go."

"Heard him go. Sit down, junior, till you know what you hear and don't hear."

He was standing alone against a senior, mad, uncertain of his facts, his face gone hot.

But another man stood up, Stuart's friend. "Kid's right."

"Then that's you and the kid," Harper yelled, on his feet again, "against all of us!"

"Four of us," one of the other strangers said, on his feet, and the other man stood up. People started yelling again, and more and more people were getting up, Hallanslakers and other borderers in a shouting match.

"All right, all right," Wesson shouted, banging his stick on the boards. "So shut up! If he goes to Tarmin and deals with it, our problem's solved, if everybody just calms down. Just shut up and let a man breathe."

"Somebody better go," a Shamesey woman said, "somebody better track him to be sure he clears the area."

"Somebody better be sure what's up on Tarmin gets dead," a Shamesey senior said. "Somebody should have taken care of it when the thing showed. Convoy or not, you had your best chance—"

"We had three of us left!" the foremost stranger said. "Aby Dale was our convoy boss! We were short-handed as was. We had trucks to get down off that road! You ever been outside a pasture, Shamesey man?"

<*Ice,*> hit the ambient. A winter's day. And the crack of Wesson's cane. "Shut it down!" Wesson said. "Enough damn should-haves! They didn't have that option so long as they had the convoy in their charge!"

"So?"

Debate started again. Riders swore, and more of them got up and stayed on their feet.

Wesson banged his stick on the porch rail. "Stuart's Dale's partner. He has a right—*first* natural right to deal with that thing on Tarmin Ridge. But so have the villagers on Rogers Peak a right to their safety. And so have townsmen down here in the plains a right, and us in their camp, we've got rights! If Stuart has gone up there, well and good. But if he can't do it . . . "

"It's not our responsibility!" the Shamesey rider yelled. "I'm not risking my neck up there!"

"Yeah, go guard cattle! Nobody asked you!"

Shouting started again. Danny sat down and sat still, trying not to shiver, trying not to think. Horses had strayed near enough, called by the disturbance of their riders. They made the very air electric with disturbance. But Dart was nearest of all of them, and Dart was damned angry.

"Shut *up*!" Wesson yelled. Danny's fingers were clenched so tight on his seat they ached, and for a moment he couldn't breathe.

But the lead stranger, unlike others, hadn't sat down. "Bossman." He held the center of attention, his arms folded, face grim and downcast. "*Friends* should go after him. If he goes over the edge . . . friends should make sure of him and do what has to be done. Or help him get that thing. We're ready to go up there."

"You naming yourselves?" Wesson asked.

"Three of us," the man said. "Jonas and Luke Westman, Hawley Antrim, all out of the MacFarlane. We'll take his belongings to him, we'll catch up with him and we'll bring him back sane. We'll have that thing out of the heights. Aby Dale was a close cousin of Hawley's."

"Settled, then," Lyle Wesson said.

Discontent prickled through the air, a quiet muttering, no one satisfied . . . or someone utterly dissatisfied.

"Beds and quiet," Lyle Wesson said, levered himself up with his cane, and abandoned the porch for the inside of the tavern, where the powers in the camp repaired to talk about things juniors didn't need to know—Danny knew that much about the politics of Shamesey camp.

And he supposed it would happen now the way the boss said. He hoped it would. He looked askance at various individuals of the retreating crowd, hoping he hadn't made a permanent and grievous mistake by speaking out like that and setting himself up to argue with his seniors. He didn't know why he'd done it, except his father always said he never could keep his mouth shut.

He walked away across the yard, onto the commons and the street, wanting Cloud, wanting the steadiness and the quiet Cloud could give him. He intended to take Cloud back to the den far around at the hostel where he stayed.

But he felt a restraining hand on his arm—and looked around in panic. He'd not heard the rider who, soft-footed and shadowless in the dark, had overtaken him.

"Why'd you speak up for him?" It was the leader of the strangers. The one who'd spoken most.

"I don't know. Stupid, maybe."

"You know him."

"He helped me once. We talked. He didn't have to. He gave me good advice."

"The leg hurt?"

He didn't know how the man knew. He wasn't limping. He started away into the shadows of the street without another word, but he didn't see the den, he saw <rider on the hill.> He heard <gunfire echoing off town walls,> and flinched from the shot so badly he almost fell.

The rider wanted his attention. And got it, with that transmitted memory.

"Jonas is my name," the stranger said. "Jonas Westman. You heard him louder than we did. Why?"

"I don't know!"

"Kids do sometimes. Kids don't know to stop. Don't know to wall things out. Don't know when they're hearing and when they're making it up."

"I didn't make it up. It hurt."

"You could be a help to us. You could be a real help. Stuart knows you. You can hear Stuart. You want the high country. We can take you there."

He didn't know how the man knew what he wanted—or whether Cloud, who longed for the High Wild, had betrayed him . . . because when the man offered, he suddenly wasn't thinking only about helping Stuart, he was thinking about why he'd gone to Stuart with his question in the first place, he was remembering that longing he had that wasn't logic, just a condition—like dreaming about the unattainable stars. And Cloud wanted to go. Cloud wanted to take him up to the High Wild where Cloud had come from—Cloud hated Shamesey, hated the cattle, hated the town and hated the smell and the crowding; and that town was all his very junior, townbred rider could give him.

He wasn't sure Cloud wasn't listening now. He felt that all-over tingle of longing that wiped out every clear consideration to the contrary.

"You have a partner in camp?" Jonas Westman asked. "You got leave to take? Anybody to go with you?"

Rider conversations ran like that, when the horses were too close, mediating half of it. He didn't know he'd agreed. It played hob with negotiations. And Jonas Westman knew his answer: he caught the echo back from Westman, a kind of confused imaging, <the house, Denis . . . in the streets, with the gunfire going off.> The kid would have been scared.

No. He'd have run to see, the stupid kid.

"No kin in camp," he said, reasoning that Denis was beyond his reach. Or his harm. "In town, yeah, family, —but I could drop dead. I'm nothing to them."

The borderer had to know the ambivalence in the anger. The hurt. The offended pride. He'd not made friends in camp. The juniors from Shamesey district, even the rider kids, were all too touchy, too protective. Everything in juniors felt raw, exposed, feelings left open to every passing opinion—and he was, right now, scared of this Jonas Westman in the same way he'd been scared going to Stuart with his questions.

And as careful as he'd been, Stuart had had to slap him down, and remind him to mind his own edges, just the same as this man was telling him—this man who'd learned everything about the aching ambition of his young, debt-plagued life in two short seconds, while he still knew nothing whatsoever about Jonas Westman except that he called Guil Stuart a friend and was, if things went wrong up there, willing to shoot Stuart and Stuart's horse both. But this wasn't a bad man. He didn't think so. They'd been spooked. But they'd *tried* to keep the terror bottled up and not to let it loose: they'd certainly helped settle things down at the meeting.

"You going?" Jonas asked.

"Yessir," he said, feeling he'd just stepped off a cliff. Pride didn't let him go back on that, not even when the agreement was just a second out of his mouth. "Depending on my horse."

"Always depending," the senior rider said. "That's a given. Come on. Let's talk."

It was harder and harder to back out, when he found himself trekking along with the stranger through the edge of the gaslight, knowing he'd talked himself into something Cloud wouldn't let him back out of. He was sure now that Cloud knew and wasn't saying no, not to the proposition nor to the company he was in.

<Mountains. Snow,> he kept seeing, and <gray, scudding clouds around the peaks.>

Cloud's name, in its endless variations.

Cloud's freedom from Shamesey smokes and the minds of cattle.

How could Cloud's rider say no to that?

Chapter

— V —

THE SUN WAS COMING. THAT WAS THE SURE PROOF THAT THE world had rolled on without much giving a damn. Something died, something became something else's supper, something brand new saw the dawn, and the world was still here.

Guil Stuart became aware of that fact, sitting, blanketed in grass, against Burn's warm and breathing side, and watching the stars go out above the plains that began at Shamesey town—watching what, in the mountains, you couldn't see: the edge of the world, where the illusory daylight began, unraveling the night along a long seam of light.

Almost cloudless morning.

Nice day.

His leg hurt. Damn stupid, walking on it. It didn't want to bend now. He supposed it would, once he warmed up: his legs were numb and his backside was feeling the chill seeping up through the grass mat from the ground beneath. His hands were icy cold . . . he'd come away with no hat, no scarf, no gloves, and he'd waked with a pale rime of frost on the ground, on the leaves of knifegrass he'd cut for a lap-robe, and on the toes of his boots. If he moved, he might lose the grass he'd so meticulously arranged, which would expose his arm and shoulder to the icy cold, while the other arm, the one against Burn's body, was comfortably warm, so he chose not to move, and not to disturb Burn's sleep.

It seemed not but an hour or so ago that they'd settled to rest, unable to go on, Burn aching from the effort and unwilling to take another step. Burn had settled on the ground to sleep, not Burn's habit when the ground was this cold, but Burn's legs were tired.

So, having been so bright as to have left his pocket matches and his glass with his guns and his trail gear (God, it was slovenly camp habits he'd fallen into lately, having no glass and no matches on him; but, hell, he hadn't expected to be on his own in the Wild in what he stood in, either) he'd done the best he could. He'd cut the tall plains grass for a mat to keep Burn's belly warm and for a cover for himself. He'd been too tired to weave strip-and-tie mats—the cold hadn't been that bad, and his eyes had kept shutting while he worked.

But he'd worked up a sweat doing it. And hurt the leg, like a fool. But it was numb with the morning cold, not too bad. The side of him next to Burn was downright warm.

If he didn't move, Burn wouldn't.

Aby died, and the morning after, the uncaring sun came up, and the man who, alone in the world, ought to be broken-hearted, was busy preserving his own warm spot in the frosty dawn, moving his toes in his boots to be sure they would move . . . first small venture of his mind out of its deliberate search for pain and distraction, and it wasn't so bad, the world wasn't, the cold wasn't, the sun wasn't. It was incredible it all went on, but it did, and he found *he* did, miraculously sitting on the other side of a black pit he just couldn't look into yet.

He wasn't interested to look. Aby was gone and there wasn't anything profitable in that dark, crazed night past, the night he could remember only because some fool townsmen had tried to blow his leg off.

Fool rider, far more to the point. He'd risked Burn, going down there in the mood he was in, and he was bitterly angry with himself for that. He'd lost all his gear but the knives he carried, but, hell, he deserved to lose it for what he'd done, and Shamesey could keep it for good, before he'd go whimpering back to Shamesey camp gates, saying he was all right now and could he have his guns back? He knew why the gate-guards had fired at him—it wasn't a justified fear: he hadn't been beyond controlling himself until they'd shot at him, but that didn't matter in townsman accounts. They just wanted what they wanted, thought what they wanted to think, and they could go to hell and keep what they wanted.

His frame of mind didn't matter much to the camp-boss either, who just wanted peace in his camp, and no troubles. Wesson might even agree to take him back into camp, but there'd be somebody tagging him the entire winter, and there'd be quarrels lurking. He'd been surprised to find Harper and his cronies in camp when he'd gotten there. He hadn't liked it, and he wasn't limping back there to try to restrain his temper in Harper's case, not this season. Figure that Harper would push until he got something. There was too much between them.

Death happened. Riders died. Mostly they died young and by surprise, a nasty quick accident in storm or slide or some hole in a river-bottom. Moon had gone along with Aby, which was the best way, rider and horse at once, nothing untidy, a minimum of pain . . . Aby couldn't leave Moon. That pair couldn't be split.

He could take to the road and go on down toward the coast, to Malvey town. He knew riders who might winter there, and he liked them better than he knew or liked folk in huge Shamesey camp.

Ava Cassey might be at Malvey, freckled Ava, who . . .

. . . who wasn't Aby, dammit, who was far short of Aby's measure, and who, good-natured as she was, didn't deserve to put up with a man constantly moping about that fact. The horses didn't leave you much illusion. No polite lies. No self-deceit, for that matter.

A lump gathered in his throat. The stinging in his eyes wasn't the cold. The rime-ice showed white crystals on the grass as the sun slowly widened its eye—showed white on his boot-seams, on his toes, but Burn was a warm lump against him, and under Burn's mane he had a warm place for his fingers.

He sat there watching the sun come up, watching the sky become pinkly opaque, and the autumn grass go to golds and pale browns, with here and there the dark brown seed-spikes of what was, in summer, gold and red-flowering fireweed.

The frosts came steadily now. Most mornings like this one showed rime. Green and gold-green died. The browns and the reds came into their own season, on the foothills first, then on the rolling plains.

So very few times anybody could count on seeing that change. You thought you'd see it forever. You thought you were immortal. But what had Aby gotten? Twenty-six times the seasons turned, twenty-six autumns, twenty-six times to see the fireweed die and the snows fall, and three and four and five of those times being a clingy brat kid who didn't pay attention.

You got only so many nights to see the stars. You got only so many sunrises. Shouldn't a man go out from under roofs and look at them?

Maybe that was the poison in towns like Shamesey, or grim, gray Malvey, where factories smoked the pristine sky.

Only so many times to make love. Only so many frosty mornings.

A man should wake up and know he couldn't buy one, not for all the townsmen's money. The days came to you and you didn't know how many you'd get.

He couldn't know, for instance, if he'd ever see the seeds of those brown spikes grow up gold again, or the flowers flaming red. He should have looked more carefully at the summer fields.

He should pay attention to the frost this morning. He should look at the wispy pink of the clouds and know he was using up his ration of them.

<Bacon frying.>

That was the happiest thing Burn knew. By which he knew that Burn was awake and pigs were in danger.

<Fat bacon. Smoky taste. Warm on a winter morning.>

"Haven't got any bacon," Guil muttered, and moved a hand to

scratch beneath Burn's abundant mane. "Wish I had." He could taste it. He began to ask himself was it fair to Burn to go up to the privations of the highlands for the winter, and not to go back to Shamesey town, to comfort he could, at cost to his pride, bargain for.

<Snow falling,> Burn imaged. <Deep and thick and clean. Blizzard in the High Wild. Us in a snug warm cabin. Bacon frying.>

Burn had such faith in him. He didn't know where to procure the death of pigs.

Except . . . there was a place on the way to the upland, the high passes. There was a factor Aby'd taken hire with; and there was, in the way of towns, a bank in Anveney.

They said if you put funds in at Shamesey you could get them out at Anveney; or down in Malvey; or clear to Darwin.

He'd never tested that idea before. He'd always carried all he owned, until he got to camp, put funds in with the camp he'd winter in—and had this year; but there was an account he and Aby held, Aby's idea; and he'd put his carrying-cash in it, the way Aby had said. He'd been relatively sure he could get *that* out again at Shamesey, if he walked into that Shamesey office and said hand it over . . . now. The Shamesey camp-boss had said it was as good as having it on account with him, and as safe.

He'd doubted it. But he'd done it, the way Aby asked him to.

He was less sure about Anveney, and this business of getting money out where he hadn't put money in. But maybe what Aby believed was true. Shamesey had phone lines up to Anveney. Wherever the phones worked—and they worked, intermittently, at least, in the lowlands, until the first ice-storm of the winter—the money was supposed to be available. Merchants certainly seemed to do it . . . although townsmen looked out for each other and cheated riders when they could.

Well, he could see. He could try. There was that man in Anveney whose shipping business Aby had worked for on a regular basis—it had been Cassivey goods in that inbound convoy, he'd seen the flags.

And knowing that was the job Aby had taken, he wanted to ask Cassivey some questions, too, like what in hell had been so last-rush important a convoy had to go up there, risking the weather, risking the movement of creatures who always became more active and more dangerous when winter was threatening and the urge to mate and feed up fat took prey and predators alike.

But that led to darker thoughts he didn't want to think, and to anger he didn't want to entertain.

Burn just thought of bacon and wheat-cakes frying, in abundant grease.

Danny didn't own a rifle. He had a pistol, fifty years old, a good one, though the ammunition was of a large caliber that was hard to come by. He'd paid for it what you'd pay for a good rifle, but a high country rider didn't encumber himself with much else, and he'd thought it would be a good idea to have the firepower, for his sake and Cloud's. He'd bought that before he'd promised anything on the replastering and the paint for his family.

In the same way he'd gotten a good flat-brimmed hat to keep himself from sunburn, and a good, heavy coat, with a lining gone to rags and the elbows patched, and with a new patch and some stain on the side, of which the second-hander didn't know the cause . . . but it was far better than the new ones he could have afforded. It was beautiful, buttery-beige cowhide and had fringes as long as his hand. He'd bought new, bullhide boots to fend off the brush, boots made for his feet, and fit for walking, when Cloud decided that he'd had enough of carrying a healthy young man.

He owned, besides that, one truly good knife; and, of course, his trail kit, with fold-up pans for eating and cooking.

Plus a couple of second-hand blankets, with frayed edges, but he'd hemmed those up, which had given him a lot of practice with his stitches . . . you could see a considerable difference between where he'd started and where he'd finished.

And he couldn't, especially on this cold dawn, forget the wherefrom of all of it, because Guil Stuart had given him a list, once upon that rainy afternoon, of the gear he most urgently had to have, and told him besides how to get the best quality and who to deal with, and when to take second-hand and when not.

Because, Stuart had said, that's a high country horse you've got, and if you really want to go, he'll take you there someday. Likely he'll take you there even if you don't want it. Count on it, if you take my advice.

Count on it just as surely, too, as he'd discovered his very first long convoy trip, that Cloud wasn't any pack-animal. He'd stowed his stuff, except his pistol and a single reload of ammo, in the supply truck, and kept on good terms with the drivers, because Cloud wasn't the one of the two of them that was going to carry any packs, thank you: Cloud didn't like anything but his rider on his back, and Cloud didn't tolerate loads of gear on his rider.

His gear right now was adding up to a fair weight, when he included in the makings for biscuits and a slab of cured bacon and the jerky. He'd gone to the suppliers first thing as their doors opened, and asked outright for what a traveler would most need in the High Wild. Jerky was lightweight. A couple of slabs of bacon of course solved the oil problem for the biscuits, so he didn't have to have a container of that, but there were six kilos of flour and soda to carry for a long stay in the high country, as would be, if the roads became impassable.

Cloud would hunt, when weather and time permitted; but what Cloud caught, he might not want, so he took fishhooks, line and cord. The extra rounds for the pistol, which he couldn't count on getting in the high country, weighed like sin, but that could provide meat he'd otherwise have to carry up there. He began to ask himself what the balance was between weight he could carry himself and how willing he was to go a little hungrier. Flour weighed more than jerky, value for value. But jerky cost more.

You traded with your traveling companions. But you didn't ever, Stuart had warned him, want to get down to needing to trade. You never came out ahead.

Spare blade. Razor, for more than shaving, and a good oilstone.

Clean rolled bandages, sewing kit that was for your clothes or you if you needed it; awl and a piece of leather to wrap it in that could become ties if you needed them. Burning glass. Waxed matches. Spare shirt, spare socks, and heavy underwear. You could literally die of a soaking rain and a strong wind up in the hills. He'd heard too many stories about freezing to death after a slip in a mountain stream, or going hypothermic in a rainstorm that wasn't even cold enough to make snow, because the wind always blew up there, strong and cold, especially when the sun was going down.

He'd heard every horror story in camp, and a lot of it encompassed good advice, he was sure. But he didn't want to look, either, like the novice that he was, and he'd tried to get his load down to as small and as light a set of packs as he could possibly make, counting he'd maybe been extravagant in food. He didn't own a proper pack-kit for it, but he'd had enough of canvas sacks that got soaked, last time he'd gone out, and he'd stitched together a real oiled-leather kit—with a great deal of swearing, his fingers repeatedly bloodied by the awl and the needle-butt; no fancy seams, either—oiled twine and thongs instead of proper leatherworking and buckles to connect the bags together. He'd thought he'd save money. But it didn't, when he loaded it, hang quite the way he'd planned. Worst of all—it was new, raw leather that hadn't even been rained on.

The Westmans and their cousin Hawley, who'd blazed through the supplier's before him with definite knowledge of what they needed, had gathered at the den exit, at the main camp gate. They were lean and tanned, they *and* their gear were weathered alike to a general impression of browns and blacks and tans against the solid black of their horses. They were the sort of experienced-looking riders that convoy bosses probably never even dared ask how many times they'd been to any destination.

But, unexpected and unwelcome witnesses, a cluster of idle younger riders had gathered in the vicinity of the gates, standing with backs against the hostel wall, and Danny found himself far more public than he had ever planned to be as he walked toward the rendezvous by the gates. His private obligation had gotten him a reputation-making hire, he suddenly realized, and he was the center of his age-mates' attention and gossip—maybe even the object of their envy. He tried not to think that: the horses might betray anything he thought, though he got none of the expected catcalls and heckling from the junior bystanders. He was only aware of the senior riders' impatience in waiting for him.

"Ready?" Jonas asked and, not waiting for his answer, Jonas

vaulted up onto his horse's back—a flashy move, a show-out move, one Danny hadn't perfected and Cloud didn't much like.

Cloud wasn't even out of the den yet. He wanted Cloud to hurry up. Please. <Riders leaving.>

And true to habit Cloud came sauntering leisurely and calmly out of the log-and-earth den and into the morning sun. Cloud shook himself all over as he reached the daylight, making a haze of dust, Cloud having (depend on it) rolled in it; and for a moment as horse met horse the ambient was full of images, all uneasy.

Cloud moved into the vicinity, refusing to take any orders from Jonas' horse, flatly, no. Every horse in the trail party was male and older, autumn was nippish in the air, and the Westmans might be a working partnership in which a new horse and rider weren't necessarily welcome—but that didn't daunt Cloud in the least—Cloud was <young, strong male horse.>

Teeth clacked, *snap*, just short of a nighthorse rump, as Cloud passed Jonas' horse to the rear. A foot cocked and slyly kicked back, again a miss, all calculated, all narrowly short of mayhem—just a trial of personalities.

Jonas swatted his own horse across the withers, and the meeting last night flashed across Danny's mind, <himself, from Jonas' view,> skinnier and plainer and more junior than he thought he was. He'd learned their names last night, when he'd agreed to come with them: Jonas and Luke Westman and Hawley Antrim, who was somehow a cousin of theirs and related to Aby Dale. Their horses . . . they imaged themselves, and no rider could totally figure a strange horse's name on meeting: but in their riders' word-names, they were Shadow and Froth and Ice respectively, a chilly set of impressions in the ambient.

<Cloud by calm water. Quiet, pebbles under the surface.> He laid a hand on Cloud's neck. <Danny riding.> Shadow had annoyed Cloud, and Danny really, desperately hoped that Cloud wasn't going to make him start out the trip walking, in the company of senior riders, with all the juniors lined up at the gate to watch.

He made a solid try at getting up on Cloud's back, determined to do it on the first attempt, and determined that Cloud not move away from under him.

To his relief he landed square on, and immediately Cloud took a snap at Froth's rump, moving closer, momentary jolt.

But Jonas had started riding toward the gates, and the others followed, the horse called Froth not without a snap back at Cloud in retaliation.

<Still water,> Danny kept thinking, as he followed the three out the gates of Shamesey camp. Nobody got thrown, nobody bit anybody: he let the three senior riders go well ahead as they rode in leisurely fashion past the gates of Shamesey town.

He thought then—he was suddenly sure that he *should* have sent a note to town, telling his parents where he was and what he was doing. For one thing, it would make his parents worry about him for a satisfactory several months.

—Off hunting a rogue horse. Don't worry. Back before summer. Love, Your Son.

He really, truly wished he'd done that. They deserved it. His father deserved it.

And, thinking that, he lagged farther and farther back, away from the casual images the three seniors let flow back and forth, because he didn't want to think about his family in their range, or eavesdrop on their business, either, feeling himself on scant enough tolerance.

He'd be on trial with them for the first while, he was sure: they thought he was useful because he could hear Guil Stuart farther than he was supposed to. They said it was because he was a snot-nosed junior who couldn't control what he thought, and in spite of the fact that that was his use, he didn't intend to broadcast everything in his head all the way to catching Stuart, or annoy them with his junior-rider insecurities spilling over at them.

So, first to keep from thinking of home, and then to keep from thinking about the trip ahead and the chances of trouble, he looked at the grass moving in the breeze. He noted the footprints of a timid scavenger that had crossed the road last night. Field-rats, he thought. Somebody had been careless with the garbage. Probably the garbage-wagons had spilled over when they went out yesterday to the dump. Out there—the province of truly junior riders—you got vermin so thick the ground moved.

Cloud's skin twitched. Garbage-guard was a job he'd never done but a week. He'd have starved first. Cloud didn't want to think about it, and switched his tail energetically, thinking instead of <mountains. Evergreens. Looking down on the plains> until his head was crowded with those thoughts.

He'd meant to look back at least once while they were near enough, but he'd decided not: the juniors might be watching from the gate. He did only when they rode past the shoulder of the hill, when the road wound around it and he knew it was his last chance before it cut off sight of Shamesey town.

But all he could see from there was the wooden wall, the pastures, the fences out across the valley.

He saw the cattle-keepers taking the cattle out for their daily pasturage, far in the distance. The junior cattle-guards were the little moving dots of darkness far in the lead. The herds of cattle and sheep and pigs went out like that every day, rain or shine, until the snow fell.

He might be doing that all winter, instead, earning a few coins, or, at best, riding winter watch on the phone lines that ran along the road to Anveney and down the coast to Malvey, watching for breaks and guarding the crews that kept them working.

The lines ran beside them as they traveled, following the road. They were all that let you believe that human civilization stretched out into the Wild. The shadows of them went on and on across the land, a convenient perch for birds that preyed on vermin in the grass. He saw them, dots along the wire, as the sun grew higher. He heard their buzzing cries. He sometimes had that strange out-of-body notion that he was watching himself ride along with three other riders; but that wasn't a bird sending that impression: that was some creature a little closer to the earth and with a bigger brain than any bird had. It was watching them from the rocks that cropped out of the grass on the west side of the road. The cattle-guards might need to look sharp, later in the day.

The riders ahead of him didn't speak. He had other, less spooky images, sometimes: Cloud's, of the High Wild, he was sure that was what he was seeing, <sun shafting down through tall trees.>

<Pastures ringed by those same trees, and rocks covered with

snow.> Cloud switched his tail as he walked, quite certain where he was going now, quite content with the direction, but not—not communicative or sociable with the horses ahead of them.

Cloud was uneasy, Danny thought, and saw the twitch of Cloud's ears, the backward slant of them that accompanied a thought of <clouds gathering gray and dark. Clouds flashing with lightnings.>

<Cloud in the den last night, Cloud with images of high hills.>

<Lightnings flashing. Wind blowing.>

Danny shivered. He slapped Cloud with his hand to distract him. "Don't be like that. They're older, is all, you silly sheep. Don't pick a fight. There's three of them."

<Rain falling on the riders ahead. Soaking rain.>

Cloud wasn't happy with the riders or their horses. He wasn't sure Cloud understood what they were after, coming out here, except the chance to go into the highlands—which Cloud did approve.

Cloud, he thought on the instant, didn't see any real reason to be following the tails of three other horses. Cloud could take him where he wanted to go. Cloud didn't need a guide.

And in that thought, also, he suffered a clear, cold realization where he was, on the dusty road far from Shamesey town and Shamesey camp, headed north into territory he knew was dangerous for the weather alone—to be stuck there probably for the whole winter, in company with three strangers he'd only just met, of a class of people reputed for wildness and strange manner, and whose only recommendation was being friends of a man, also a borderer, whom he only remotely knew.

<Rider dead in the rocks.>

"No," he muttered, disquieted. He toed Cloud in the ribs. Cloud tossed his head, threw a cow-kick to jolt his rider.

He couldn't ask why Cloud thought that way. He couldn't find an image to argue with, nothing but the same dead-rider image that Cloud threw him. <Burn going out the gate,> he tried to inform Cloud. <Stuart on the porch. Bacon and gear. Lots of bacon. Biscuits. Stuart in the High Wild, on Burn.>

Cloud threw his head and sulked. <Rain. Rain. Rain and thunder.>

So Cloud was just generally disappointed in their company, disapproving of anything but <quitting the group and going off by themselves.>

<Sunlight through clouds.>

"We can't," Danny said. "We promised. And maybe Stuart can't get this thing by himself. This thing's bad, it's real bad, Cloud." He didn't want to think about it, but he wondered if Cloud had any real idea what they were chasing up into the hills, or how it connected to the dead rider. And the wondering alone connected it.

<Dark woods,> Cloud imaged, so vividly, so threateningly for a moment he couldn't see the riders ahead of him or the hills or anything. <Spooky feelings. Shivery.>

"Somebody's got to get rid of it." <Dead horse. Gray clouds breaking to sunlight. Us, in a green meadow. Mountains.>

Cloud's ears came up. <Mountains. Danny and Cloud in mountains. Valleys below us.> With a kick and a toss of his head, Cloud dived uphill off the road, jolted slantwise across the hill as Danny grabbed a double fistful of mane.

"Stop it!" Danny yelled.

But Cloud didn't stop it. Cloud had the mountains in his mind, and that was all he wanted to see.

"Dammit!" Danny yelled. <Danny falling off. Danny hurt.> "Cut it out, Cloud! Stop!"

Cloud didn't stop.

<Mad,> Danny imaged, and began to figure where he and Cloud could part company without his breaking an ankle. He slid to one side, displaced their center of weight, and hung on to Cloud's mane, put his feet down a couple of times, sliding on the grass, before Cloud sulked to a slower pace.

<Cloud and Danny on the road.>

<Rain. Thunder. Soaked road.>

Danny planted his feet hard, on the grass, and skidded, holding on to Cloud's mane, his packs swinging around him as he jolted over a series of uneven spots on the hill.

Cloud just kept plowing ahead, dragging him with him, imaging <mountains,> while he returned raw anger, that was most of it, and, <road,> when he wasn't fighting for footing. He was determined to win the fight, determined he wasn't going to give in with the seniors watching from below, not if he had to walk for the next three days.

But Cloud was mad, too. Cloud took out on a particularly steep uphill and Danny braced his feet the harder—until his feet hit a rock. His grip on Cloud's mane jerked Cloud's forequarters around, threatening to bring them both down.

At once he gave up his grip on the mane, which put the downhill under him—he fell through empty space, curled to protect his head, landed with his baggage under his back and skidded downhill over the slick, dusty grass.

He fetched up finally on a small grassy hump, momentarily out of slope to slide on, with the laughter of the strangers ringing out from below the hill. His feet were pointed upslope—between which he saw Cloud standing staring down at him.

He rolled over, struggled against the downhill slant to get his feet under him, and got up, with the thong-tied packets banging about his arms, without the weight of the pistol in its holster. He saw it downslope, beyond him, and he slouched down the hill in a fit of temper, recovered it to its holster and sulked on down to the road, walking aslant on the hill, because the Westmans and Hawley, having had their laugh, were going on, leaving him to sort it out, and he had to overtake them, afoot or ahorse, they clearly didn't care.

He was mortified. He didn't look back to find out where Cloud was. He limped on down toward the road, intending to intercept them, still finding bits of dry grass to pick out of leather seams and brush out of his hair.

Cloud couldn't resist making him look the fool. It was one thing when he dumped him in front of the juniors. It was another, when he was working, when matters were serious and he was out on the road. He was furious with Cloud. The seniors were clearly disgusted with him. Their riding on meant they were testing him, whether he could get himself together and catch up.

And then he either misjudged where he should intercept the

others, or misjudged how fast he had to follow, because by the time he reached sight of the road, having crossed over the shoulder of the hill—they were nowhere in sight.

He went downslope, not believing that they would have left the road and turned off cross-country, but not sure of that until he saw their tracks in the dirt of the roadway.

So he followed them, having no suppositions whatsoever that Cloud was going to leave him. Cloud was up there in the hills, not far, probably watching him, but he wasn't going to acknowledge that fact.

So Cloud wouldn't carry him. Then Cloud could trail him along the heights of the hills, playing his little games while he fell farther and farther behind the Westmans, and while the Westmans laughed at Cloud's foolish junior rider, that was all Cloud had gained.

Meanwhile he was hurt. He'd bruised his backside, his shoulders, and all but knocked the wind out of himself. He had itchy grass down his collar that he couldn't reach. He'd hurt his ankle when he hit the rock that caused his fall, and it was probably swelling. He might be lame for life. He hoped Cloud was satisfied, making him look like a fool, which Cloud had to do every damned time it was really important to convince somebody that he knew what he was doing, and he hoped Cloud really enjoyed his temper tantrum. Cloud's rider was humiliated, and bruised, and ready to guard cattle for the rest of their lives.

Which would probably happen to them. He'd fall so far behind the other riders he'd never catch up. He and Cloud would have to limp back to Shamesey camp alone, their reputation would be ruined, all the high country riders would know he wasn't to be relied upon, the juniors would laugh at them, and they'd never, ever, ever make it to the mountains.

He wasn't sure Cloud heard him that far up the hill. He was too mad to care. The other riders were out so far ahead now he no longer tried to overtake them. He could only hope they stayed on the road, and didn't put him to tracking them across open country, at which he wasn't as good as he needed to be.

He could lose them if they got off the road and he'd be out in the dark alone with the goblin cats and the willy-wisps.

He was *damned* mad.

<Rain> came to his mind.

Maybe that was his thought.

Fine, he said to himself, and sulked along, limping with his sore ankle on the rutted road, a mere track the trucks maintained, dragging chain on the undercarriages to keep the weeds down. It was a fine road for trucks. It was perfectly fine for nighthorses.

It was a damned sorry mess for human feet.

It was a damned long walk, measured in telephone poles and sore joints, and in the tracks of the riders in front of him, riders doubtless laughing at him. And he was more and more sure that Cloud was up there on the heights, as steep as the hills had risen above this section of road.

Maybe the other riders could stop for noon break, but he didn't dare stop, for fear of not overtaking them before dark. He kept thinking, irritably, <Rain falling.> Cloud understood that. <Rain falling on hills. Rain falling on rocks and grass. Rain falling on Cloud.>

And eventually, when his steps were growing shorter and shorter, and his tailbone decidedly hurt with every step, he saw a dim image of <boy with a silly lot of baggage swinging about him, far, far below the hilltop.>

<Rain,> he sent. He'd learned stubbornness from Cloud.

<Danny getting down from Cloud. Danny falling down the hill.>

<*Danny going off over Cloud's shoulder,*> he sent back, the maddest he'd ever been at Cloud.

<Danny getting down.>

The argument kept up, until he changed tactics, thought about pain and sore feet and bruises, thought <snow,> and <still water.>

Then he was aware of Cloud's presence closer than had been. Cloud met him as the road took a bend and a climb, Cloud standing on the hillside, and then walking along, head down and ears flat. Danny threw him only the most casual of glances, and limped, badly, thinking about <woods and rocks and the dead rider.>

Dirty trick.

He heard Cloud behind him, then. He didn't have to look. He could see himself, ahead of Cloud, limping along with the stupid baggage.

He heard Cloud closer, a whispering in the grass, a soft breathing.

<Rain,> Cloud imaged.

<Raindrops on still water,> he thought, and Cloud shoved him between the shoulders.

<Cattle,> Cloud thought.

<Water still, reflecting Danny and Cloud.>

Unfair, of course. Humans couldn't image on their own, but humans were tricky and inventive when they got the knack of it.

Cloud peevishly dashed raindrops onto their still reflection. Cloud understood his tactic.

But Cloud couldn't drown the reflection. Cloud wasn't as mad as the human in question was determined—and the human in question wasn't stopping or getting into details. Danny just kept limping ahead, in the tracks of horses nice enough to carry their riders.

<Cattle,> Cloud thought. <Cattle. Cattle. Cattle in Shamesey camp. Cattle dropping manure in the street.>

Cloud *could* combine images when two thoughts crossed in his head.

And they clearly had.

Cloud came up beside him and slumped along pace for pace. They walked along maybe half an hour before Danny thought <Danny riding,> and Cloud stopped and waited for him to climb up.

He didn't do so well getting up this time. He hadn't the strength for a swing on Cloud's mane, he just planted his arms across Cloud's back, jumped up and landed belly-down, tangled in the strings of his baggage, to work his way across Cloud's back in a maneuver he would be humiliated to do in front of the strangers he was trying to overtake, while, annoyed by a knee in his kidneys, Cloud began to amble on his way, giving him no grace whatsoever.

But Danny didn't argue. Cloud was going his direction.

<Mountains in the winter,> he thought, to please Cloud. <Snowy rocks.>

<Three snobbish nighthorses from the rear,> Cloud imaged, <with cattle tails.>

"Cloud. Behave. Dammit." He'd not had so much trouble out of Cloud on the regular hire they'd taken. He'd worked with other riders. He didn't know why Cloud should take so profound a dislike to horses that were going to guide them to the High Wild, that would be their protection by their experience and their riders' guns once they reached an area they might not be able to cross safely on their own . . . granted anything went amiss.

<Cattle,> Cloud persisted sullenly.

Then Cloud threw his head and looked back, just the red-edged corner of a nighthorse eye, cast along their backtrail.

Nostrils widened.

<Horses,> Cloud imaged, and stopped joking.

Did we miss them? was Danny's first thought—stupid thought. There were multiple nighthorse tracks under Cloud's feet at the moment.

They were *following* three horses. But Cloud was looking behind them.

He thought of the horse who'd gone out the gate, following Stuart: <Burn.>

<Horses,> Cloud persisted. Cloud didn't think it was one horse he was hearing back there.

Line riders, Danny thought. Inspecting the phone lines.

But it wasn't the day they usually went out, when he thought of it—unless they had a break in the line that shut down the phones, which would bring somebody much faster.

So who among the riders would go? Danny asked himself and Cloud, trying to see if Cloud could recognize the horses.

But Cloud didn't answer his perplexity, except with this same dark image of more than one horse, on ambiguous ground, except that there was Cloud's wind-image in it, the sweeping of the images, coming and going, distorting to many and back to a conservative two or three.

<Trucks?> Danny asked.

Cloud shifted footing, snorted to clear his nostrils of stray scents and sniffed again.

<Horses,> was all Cloud could give him, but this time they had riders, less certain an image—just the illusion of shadows atop shadows.

Not wild horses, then. Not likely, unless Cloud was getting not the scent but the desire of the horses for humans.

A wild lot wasn't something to meet in the autumn. And they did go on the move in this season.

<Cloud running,> Danny suggested. But Cloud didn't, Cloud only started uphill and off the road, where Danny didn't want to go.

Danny swatted Cloud's shoulder, wanting <going on road. Us in bushes with bad horses.>

<Dark horses streaming along the road,> was Cloud's thought.

And Cloud picked up the pace.

<Water,> Danny thought, not the still-water of silence, but <Cloud wading. Cloud-wavery-scent image running away in water.>

Cloud didn't think so. And maybe it was true: they were so close the scent-image came to them on the wind from their backs, and strange riders were almost certainly back there—it was too persistent to be anything Cloud just remembered. But the wind came to them treacherously as it did in the foothills, reversing its ordinary direction in places, coming almost east to west, when nearly the opposite was the rule on the road—and they could only trust the wind would shift again.

A human knew that. He wasn't sure Cloud did. What ruled Cloud's decision was likely the surety that he didn't smell humans in the direction he took and he did smell them at their backs.

Trouble was what they had to reckon it. Towns were the safe zones. You didn't trust what you ran into in the Wild—not solitary riders or groups of riders. That was the law Danny Fisher knew. Maybe it was a townsman way of thinking, but Cloud lit out at that fast-traveling pace Cloud could hold for long, long runs—Cloud had learned that humans didn't put their noses down and smell tracks, but they saw them and they understood them by processes that had never occurred to Cloud.

<Tracks in dust. Wavery riders on solid horses on road.>

That was what Cloud reasoned—maybe as far as the fact that nighthorses without humans didn't use roads.

And Cloud wasn't staying around to meet them.

Chapter
— vi —

GUIL STUART SWEATED LIGHTLY IN THE NOON SUN, WATCHED THE brown grass pass under his dangling feet and Burn's three-toed hooves, and avoided the thoughts bobbing to the surface of a distracted, several times jolted mind. He rode northerly still, not using the road, but overland, up over the rolling, grassy hills, on the same course which he had begun to choose in their first panic flight.

Burn had other ideas, making a slow, quiet intrusion into his vision.

<Domerlane road,> Burn imaged for him, the characteristic two stones with the old rider signs, that exact view of the mountains, so for a moment Guil didn't find himself on this road at all, but well south of Shamesey town, high in the hills where the Domerlane left the MacFarlane High Trace, the mountain ridge towering on the right.

<Winter snows,> Burn sent, and, falling enthusiastically under

the spell of his own imaging: <Domerlane camp and female horses.>

<Mountains,> Guil thought, then, slipping into a moment of weakness, <mountains clean with snow in the winter, game running on the slopes. Mountains above the MacFarlane. Kantung Peak.>

Then, abruptly: <Aby lying dead on the rocks. Aby and Moon together,> because that ugly image leapt into his mind whenever it found the chance.

He stopped it. He thought of water. He thought of bubbles on the surface.

<Aby giving sweets,> Burn recalled pleasantly. <Aby smiling. Wind blowing red hair, blowing red leaves in the woods. Aby standing on the hillside. Warm thinking. Moon wanting sweets from Aby's pockets.>

Guil resisted the imaging at first. But he did recall that day with pleasure. He remembered Aby laughing, playing keepaway with Moon and Burn.

<Dodging on the moonlit hillside. Moon darting this way and that for pockets.>

A lump arrived in his throat.

<Guil and Aby,> Burn imaged, <holding hands. Taste of honey, smell of dew and grass and Moon and Aby and Guil. Moon and Burn mating. Guil and Aby mating, sweet smells, good feelings everywhere.>

The whole moonlit moment rebuilt itself, lived vividly and faded into the present sun and chill breeze, as if it were the same day.

Wind and grass, sun on autumn colors. On the left hand the mountains loomed up, the Firgeberg, the backbone of the continent. The wind came down from the foothills with a chill that shivered through the grass, cold and clean enough to wipe away the stink and madness of Shamesey camp.

<Hunting,> Burn sent him. <Heart beating quick, quick feet moving ahead of us, chasing willy-wisps through the brush. Delicious.>

Burn had no long memory for distress. Troubles came and they went. Horses died. Horses were born. As long as it wasn't Burn, Burn didn't stay concerned.

<Guil cooking nice meat, fat crackling in the flames, warmth in the dark.>

One more sunrise. One more sunny afternoon on the hills. A rationed number of them.

But Burn also had no memory for money. Money ran counter to Burn's sense of the world, and Burn forgot where bacon came from. Burn's rider was supposed to have it, that was all.

<Guil laying down shiny coins on counter. Man taking coins, giving bacon. Anveney streets.>

<Cattle.>

<Pigs,> Guil sent.

<Bacon,> Burn thought, much more cheerfully. Burn imaged the slow rolling of hills northward.

And they argued for a while about the connections of Anveney town, banks (a concept Burn refused to deal with, as a repository for things worth bacon: naturally one would immediately get what was worth something, and not leave it anywhere) and humans (not high in Burn's thinking right now, since humans had lately had rifles shooting at them). Burn was vastly put out by humans and would be put out so long as Guil's leg hurt, because it made Burn's leg hurt. Almost. Well, close enough.

When they rode alone Guil could sink into trains of almost-thought and exist in Burn's realm of sun-on-back, humans-at-distance, food-the-day's-necessity and sex-on-opportunity. Sometimes in the high hills you ran into a partnership like that, one where you couldn't talk to the man except through the horse; and Guil supposed in the long run they were happy enough—never work, never come into a town, they'd barter sometimes, food and skins for clothes or a knife. Usually when you met them, the human half wanted to trade, the horse was skittish—and the rest of the time you just got a spooky feeling in the brush, the intimation of something that might have been there for a moment, might have looked you over in a slightly predatory or slightly fearful way . . . wild things did that sometimes, before they ran.

He was glad enough to sink into that kind of nowhere at least for the day. The leg ached when he didn't. The stomach complained it was empty when he didn't, and he didn't care he was hungry, really—he hadn't energy left to care.

But somewhere toward evening Burn found the stream that crossed the road well north of Shamesey, a smallish stream—Guil was relatively sure it was the same one—cold in this season; and Burn wanted to cool his legs and drink and—definitely—find something to eat.

So Guil sat down there and tended the wound he had gotten, the ugly rip that by now was somewhat scabbed and not wholly clean. He took off the breeches and sat on the bank, dipping up water to wash the wound and numb the pain, which was so miserable once he'd worked the pants off that Burn took himself from the vicinity, went a distance down the stream and slammed his three-toed foot down on something that wriggled.

Burn ate it then, alternately washing it in the stream. It was not particularly nice; it was not the sort of thing Burn saved for cooking, and Burn had the grace to keep his tidbit out of range of a queasy stomach to eat it.

"I don't suppose you could catch a fish," Guil said aloud, and thought <fish.>

Burn snorted, and wandered off along the stream, nosing into this and that, sampling the water. Burn came back to him with, <mudcrawler, mossy big shell.>

He wasn't that desperate.

<Plate-fungus.>

No.

<Scraggy pucker-berries.>

He was disgusted. <Guil riding,> he imaged, and got up to put his pants on. Burn came back to him, took him up again, uncommonly patient still with this carrying business.

<Valley,> Burn imaged, having settled on that goal, imaging a good winter and enough to eat. <Mountain meadows. Meandering stream.>

He dreamed in that still sunlit but nippish ride, of the valley where he had been a boy, in the first spring he remembered. He wondered where it was, and whether it was what he remembered. He thought of it, in bad times.

And perhaps he did gloss it a bit, being light-headed with pain and hunger, with the meadows spangled with starflowers and the delirious yellow spikes of mollyfingers, in green lush grass; but that was the way he liked to remember it—which was probably, he'd long said to himself, why he'd never found it.

Burn took up his dream readily enough, embellished it with the restless longings of his own kind: a valley, a far, far different place from the safe, smoky dens of Shamesey hostels, where riders and horses lived in such muddy, smelly, close quarters.

A clean winter, a wide winter, with all the white valley to hunt. Tarmin. Then this place.

"Promise," Guil said. "I promise."

Burn twitched his ears back and forth.

"Don't know 'promise,' do you? Probably it's good you don't."

<"You don't,"> echoed back to him. Burn could image sounds he didn't know, so far as his horsey brain could remember them. Or cared to remember them. Then a visual image. <Mollyfingers and green grass.>

Mollyfingers didn't grow in the lowlands. They wouldn't grow where factories sent up smoke, or in places like Anveney, where men ripped copper and lead out of the earth and made beautiful, poisoned pools, bright blue and milky white.

<Cattle,> Burn thought, sulking, and then again, quite cheerfully, the sunlight in his thoughts belying the evening—<mollyfingers and clean new grass.>

Twilight was getting scarily deep scarily fast in the folds of the hills, with the sun already over the mountain rim.

Maybe the riders Cloud had smelled behind them had stopped for camp by now. Danny hoped that the Westmans had.

They'd come back to the road finally. He'd found their tracks where the dust was thick, and where a horse's toe had scored the occasional rock. He could track at least that well: from an old rider on his one long trip he'd picked up enough of the art at least to read whether a horse or a man was running or walking, how loaded his quarry was, and—if a human was involved—how tall that human was and maybe what the gender was.

But he knew precisely the riders he was tracking; and he was scared, to tell the truth, not alone now of the riders they'd feared behind them, but of a night alone out where he'd never been alone before if they didn't catch up before they ran out of daylight. He caught little strange vignettes of himself and Cloud seen from low to the earth or high on the hill or out of the brush, so he knew that small hunter eyes were watching them, nothing big, nothing that would bother a horse—yet. He had his pistol by him and he decided, considering having fallen on the hill and having had it slide free, that a tie-down would be a very good idea, but he wasn't going to tie it in the holster now, thank you, he wanted to be able to draw it very quickly, and not shoot himself or Cloud, if an emergency happened. He was afraid his hands would shake if he had to aim. He was afraid of shooting in panic and hitting the men he was tracking. A townbred junior rider had no business alone out here, he was increasingly convinced—he'd never been alone in the dark in the Wild before, and he *didn't* know what was watching them from the brush.

The Westmans might have slowed down just a little, he said to himself. They might have helped, damn them, when he'd fallen, instead of laughing and riding on.

They'd asked him to come with them out here. Jonas had said he'd improve their chances of finding what they were looking for—so why had they let Cloud dump him? Damned funny joke, maybe. But he didn't think so.

Neither did Cloud. Cloud sent an uncomfortable hostility, daring the Westmans or their horses to stop anything Cloud wanted.

"You embarrassed me," Danny muttered to the darkness under him, blacker than that gathering around them. He couldn't make Cloud understand ideas like that, he didn't think so, at least. Senior riders said that horses did come to understand, eventually, about human thinking—but a young horse was full of horse notions, and it wasn't until they were ten or fifteen or so that they began to take up on fine points like embarrassment.

Or the politics of humans with each other.

Well, so maybe young humans didn't pick up on things like human politics too well either, the way he didn't understand why older and wiser riders would have left him. Why boys his own age would have done it, he could figure just fine: plain stupidity. But he didn't think that was the case with the Westmans, who were borderers like Stuart, who understood what the dangers were.

So borderers played rough jokes on each other, and expected juniors to take more than they dared hand back, the way every other senior did . . . but they were friends of Stuart, and Stuart hadn't laughed at him.

He tried to think it was some sign of trust that they did leave him, and figured he'd catch up, and figured he'd take care of himself. Maybe it was a sign of respect, or an expectation of him—or something.

<Cattle,> Cloud thought. <Jonas Westman hitting Shadow, at the gate.> Cloud hadn't missed that. Cloud didn't like it in the least. Cloud didn't like Jonas Westman *or* his horse. <Shadow-horse pitching Westman in road. Cattle tail on Shadow.>

Cloud vehemently didn't like the Westmans. Cloud certainly hadn't indicated anything about that when Cloud had nudged him into going. Maybe it had always been Cloud's notion that they could kite up to the High Wild and desert the Westmans to their business with Stuart, but that wasn't the way Danny Fisher understood an agreement, thank you. Humans made promises and humans had to do what they said they'd do, and that was that. Maybe he hadn't made Cloud understand that point, or maybe Cloud didn't want to understand.

Or maybe, with somebody following them, it was time for Cloud to use his nose and his horse-sense and get them out of danger.

Whoever was following them could be somebody who didn't like the Westmans. It could also be somebody who didn't like Stuart, like that bunch in the meeting . . . and they'd cut your throat soon as look at you: Danny had that feeling, and Cloud didn't disagree.

Whatever went on among riders, there was usually—and always before in his experience—a convoy and a lot of riders, or at least a boss of some kind, to buffer the feud, and if nothing else, to give one rider or a group of riders excuse to ride apart from one another and keep out of each others' thoughts. But here there wasn't any convoy boss to provide a young rider fearful of being put upon by his seniors the least small contact with town law.

He was off with people where there just wasn't law at all . . . where seniors ran off and left you at a pace faster than any convoy was ever going to travel. He'd thought of helping somebody, their friend, no less, and this was the pay he got. The preachers said, Do unto others. And it wasn't working that way.

It was darker and darker. There were singers in the grass he couldn't identify, there were images that could come from a goblin cat pretending to be something small and harmless for all he knew. . . .

Cloud snorted suddenly, and <horse> flashed into mind.

Danny took a fistful of mane and a deathgrip on his pistol butt. Cloud was imaging the smell, that kind of fluttery darkness a horse made on the landscape ahead of them, which was growing more frequently wooded than he liked, and generally uphill for a long while now. <Nighthorse,>the image was, in Cloud's better nightsight: a shape against the brush.

But Cloud didn't act disturbed, just disgusted, and jolted forward into a trot.

<Cloud stopping!> Danny sent, or thought he was sending: he was holding on with his grip on Cloud's mane and his knees tight on Cloud's sides, so nervously tight that Cloud shook his mane and snorted the scent out of his nose.

<Cattle,> was Cloud's comment. <Rear end of cattle.>

Then they went jolting right off the road and through brush that made Danny have to duck his head and hold onto his hat with the hand that was supposed to be holding the pistol in its holster.

<Smell of smoke,> Cloud sent then, even Danny could smell it; and he could see the nighthorse as a blackness going quickly through the stand of trees in front of them. Danny had a terrified thought that it might be the rogue come downland . . .

But smoke led to fire and the gleam of fire through the brush to the stray nighthorse who had clearly come out to look them over as they approached; and the nighthorse—he was sure now it was Froth—led to three riders seated at a campfire and cooking supper.

"Well," Jonas said, hardly looking up. "Made it, did you?"

<Cattle,> was his own quick thought, no more pleasant than Cloud's. But you didn't do that with a senior, you said, meekly getting down,

"My horse and I worked it out." He wasn't sure he wanted now to say anything about people following them. He wasn't sure he wholly trusted present company to be friends of his, any more than the people behind them, but the thought that he might say something was enough, with the horses all about.

"What riders?" Jonas asked, with no levity whatsoever.

"I don't know," Danny said. "I didn't stay to ask. We were downwind as we caught scent of them . . ."

"But you don't know whether they got wind of you."

"Possible they did, sir. I don't know." They thought he was stupid. He wouldn't exaggerate what he *did* know: it was too serious a matter. "We kept the wind with us and got out of there, cross-country. Cloud thinks there were more than two, less than ten, that's all we could tell."

Hawley was stirring the coals with a stick. He flung it into the fire. There was silence, and a confused group image of the meeting, of the principal rider who kept arguing to shoot Stuart.

"Harper," Jonas said. "Damn him."

It was undeniably the right image. Danny recognized the face. He didn't know what more than the business at the meeting lay behind Jonas' knowledge of this Harper, but he got a confused image of a fight, blades flashing, fringes flying—imprecise target in a knife fight, that was what the fringes were good for, he'd heard that. Borderers.

And he wondered if they were going to put out the fire at the news and run for it, maybe higher into the hills, and off the trail. It was what he might do if he were Jonas and he thought Harper and several of his friends were behind him with hostile intent.

"Sit down," Jonas muttered. "We're not budging."

"Yes, sir," he said, and sat down and shed his baggage on the ground beside him. It was dirtier and more scuffed than it had been in the morning. Maybe it looked a little less like a novice's gear. By some miracle he still had the gun in its holster and it made sitting uncomfortable. He took it off, and decided, in the smell of bacon and sausage starting to cook, and the sight of tea on to boil, that he was very glad they weren't going to budge.

But he thought he should figure out what the rules were.

"Do I put in, or cook my own, or what, sir?"

"What're you carrying's the question."

"Bacon and biscuit-makings mostly."

"You can put in tomorrow. We made enough. You got jam?"

"Yessir," he said, thinking then that he'd been too judgmental, and they'd figured all along that he'd make it. "Got jerky, too. Fair deal of it."

"Save it. You mix up the breakfast dough, leave it set the night. There's clean water. You wash up."

"Yes, sir." That was Luke Westman who gave him that order, and it was fair. "So what about this Harper, sir?"

"There's time," Hawley said. "There's plenty of time to settle with that one."

How? he wanted to ask. Did they mean have a fight, or wait in ambush and shoot them, or what?

"Scared?" Jonas asked.

He hadn't planned to shoot anybody. Jonas had talked about it in meeting as something they'd do if there wasn't a choice . . . but it hadn't seemed what they had any intention of doing.

And now there was this Harper following them, who might, Danny thought with a lump in his throat, shoot *them* as easy as thinking about it. Harper had been all too eager to go shooting at people *and* horses right up near Shamesey walls, which was unthinkable and dangerous as hell to the camp and the whole town. It didn't encourage him to think that Harper was any more reasonable out of reach of those walls.

No camp-boss out here and nobody to tell town law what had happened between a group of stray borderers with feud on their minds.

There was a real chance he might not get home next spring. Things could happen out here, very final things, he began to take that into truly serious account—things nobody would ever know about except the ones that pulled the triggers.

He just didn't know right now why these men had ever needed a junior in their midst, or what good he really was to anybody. He wished he hadn't come. He wished he'd asked somebody like Lyle Wesson what his mature judgment was of his going off like this, somebody who might have said Don't do it, kid, you don't count for anything out there.

He got a dark, chilly feeling then. There was one of the horses he couldn't pin down—Froth was easy to identify, agitated most of the time and full of temper; and Ice just didn't communicate much.

And that left the horse named Shadow, just the faintest thought, just the skitteriest images, a hostility you couldn't get hold of.

Shadow didn't like him and didn't like Cloud, that much he picked up, and Shadow was always there, behind the other two, lurking behind Froth's jittery everywhere images and Ice's unfriendly quiet . . . Shadow didn't swear like Cloud did, Shadow just sent hostility slipping out around the edges of what was going on, so maybe it was easier to feel unwanted, and easier to feel danger in the night.

<Cattle tails. Kick and bite. Lightning flash and rain.>

That last was surely Cloud, and Shadow didn't like it.

"Keep it down," Jonas Westman said, while their supper cooked. "We've no need for that, boy. Calm that horse of yours."

"Yes, sir," he said, asking himself what about the situation deserved calm, and how, the same as at home, everything got down to being his fault.

They didn't have any preachers here to say so. But it seemed a reliable commodity, guilt. You could get it here cheap, handed out like come-ons to a sale.

"Not my damn fault," Danny muttered. "Cloud and I can go by ourselves if you don't need us."

"Did I say that?" Jonas asked. And Hawley Antrim, Ice's rider:

"Nobody said that. Just calm down. Horsefights feed off quarrels. And we don't need that kind of trouble."

"Yes, sir," he said. Everybody was sir, being senior. And they weren't telling him in any sense what they were doing waiting here, or whether they'd found any sign of Guil Stuart. He knew he hadn't come across any tracks but the ones he'd been following. But he'd been up in the hills a good deal of the time.

"Gone overland," Luke Westman said. "Same's we could, but we know where he's going."

"We don't need to hurry." Jonas said, put another stick on the fire, and adjusted the frying pan. "Stuart won't appreciate interference. He's an independent type. We let him handle the business up-country, if he can."

It seemed dangerous to him, and not too helpful to Stuart. He wanted not to have an opinion, but they kept coming up. He kept his eyes on the fire and tried to keep his mouth shut.

"Don't trust us?" Hawley asked.

Nosy question. It scared him just thinking about it. There were a lot of ways a junior could get into trouble with men like this, as rough as this. He didn't want trouble. They had Stuart's gear in those extra packs they shared out, everything he owned. Hawley carried Stuart's rifle, having none of his own. At least he thought they meant to deliver it all to Stuart.

"Easy on the kid," Jonas said. "He's noisy enough. Quiet mind, kid. Quiet. Think about supper. You'll be fine."

You could get fiber from knifegrass. You stripped off both the edges with your fingernails and you braided the strands you got. You could braid as many strands together as you had the skill for, and Guil just round-braided it as he rode, with a little wrap of nighthorse hair when a piece quit and the end wouldn't quite stay tucked on the splice.

The result was a tough cord. You wouldn't break it by pulling on it—it'd cut right through the skin of your hands.

It was also fine-gauge enough that it made a fair fishing line; a notched large thorn, carefully scored about for the cord to tie on, made a decent small hook, a dry twig tied into the line a convenient float, while he was sitting on the bank of a fair-sized stream. He dropped a rock into a shallow to trap a handful of minnows, baited his hook, cast near a low branch that touched the water, and waited.

<Burn eating fish,> Burn thought.

"Pest! You had yours. This is my fish."

<Delicious fish frying in fragrant bacon grease.>

"Do you see bacon? Do you see a frying pan?" <Rider hostel in Shamesey. Guil's gear in corner of room.>

Burn sulked.

Effectively enough Burn got the next fish. Guil filleted it while he was waiting for another to bite. Burn couldn't manage the bones, but he so loved the taste, almost as much as Burn loved sugar-cured bacon.

Fish wasn't bad, raw. He drew the line at other things. He hadn't the makings for fire, hadn't the energy for fire-making, even given that he did, now, have the cord for a bow-drill; raw fish was good enough.

And he found a number of spotty-neck shellfish along a rocky edge, which were also fine eaten raw. Burn got a couple of them, which pleased Burn mightily—a knife left them in ever so much nicer condition than cracking them open under nighthorse feet, and Burn liked for his to be washed in water before eating—in beer, if it was available.

It wasn't. Burn sucked down his dessert and resumed his proper watchful duty, protecting the two of them from goblin cats, feral nighthorse pairs in autumn lust, and other potential hazards, while idly nipping the tops off tasslegrass, eating only the seed-bearing part, the extravagance of autumn.

Meanwhile Guil limped about, cutting soft-needled branches along the wooded streambank. He heaped up a fragrant pile of them in a sheltered spot, and when he had a large enough pile, Burn helpfully sat down in the middle, rolling out a nesting spot.

"Get up, dammit! *My* bed, Burn."

<Sweet smell. Warm nighthorse belly. Guil in sunlight.>

"Oh, hell," Guil muttered, and went on cutting branches, to make their bed wider.

Danny lay down to sleep tucked in blankets, near the coals. There never yet had been a whisper from the riders he was sure were following him, and now he asked himself whether the Westmans believed him that such riders had ever been there.

But of course they had to. Riders couldn't lie to each other.

At least, juniors couldn't lie very well. To anyone.

He hadn't picked up on everything that was going on, that was sure.

He wasn't wholly surprised when Cloud came over and settled down on the ground next to him, sharing the fire warmth, sharing his own warmth, sharing his muddled, half-asleep nighthorse thoughts with him, that ran mostly along the general content of the ambient.

A ghosty was in the brush watching them, not a specific thing, just one of three very different creatures that townsmen gave the same name to, and he didn't know much better. Cloud knew what it was, Cloud wasn't spooked by it, and no cattle-guard needed be, except sometimes the little creatures would spook the cattle just to have them away from their territory.

The ghosty wanted them to go away, too, probably. But it was scared of Cloud.

Danny just wished other things were. And he was glad that Cloud spent the night close to him. They were clearly on the uphill now, headed into the foothills of the Firgeberg. They were committed to the mountains. To all else it meant.

He really, really wished to keep his mind quiet and let the senior riders rest. Hawley was on watch, he was aware of that. So was Ice, and he didn't think much would get past that horse.

He didn't think the senior riders believed that Harper, if that was who it was, intended to do them harm. Harm to Stuart was another matter. But as long as they stayed their pace, the common thought he picked up was <them staying in one group, ahead,> and <Harper's party in the other, behind, neither meeting.>

It wouldn't help for him and Cloud to have another argument. He wanted Cloud to know that. He wanted Cloud to agree to stay with him.

He wasn't sure what Cloud's answer was. He shut his eyes, but that made pictures behind them, of the hillside and the dark, fluttery smell-shapes following them. He stared into the dying coals and that was better.

At least the shapes the burning edges made were all random and without motive.

Chapter
— vii —

SLEET BEGAN TO COME DOWN IN EARNEST, WHITE DUST RATTLING against the evergreens—not an unusual occurrence if it were midsummer on Tarmin Height: the Firgeberg spawned occasional sleet year-round.

But when a flurry came on an autumn morning after quakesilver leaf-fall, a rider, however well prepared, looked anxiously to the sky above the woods and the mountain for a hint of what might be rolling in.

<Cold, frosty breaths, feet crunching snow.> That was Flicker's thought, but Flicker's rider thought snow would not come yet.

<Melting drops on green needles, sun shining,> Tara Chang sent back, riding along the wooded road. <Road free and clear, white lines of sleet blowing across the dirt, sticking in the autumn leaves.>

Flicker tossed her shaggy head, shook her mane and still thought differently, sending unease out into the air. They'd intended hunting if they had the chance: they'd escorted the road crew out to their camp yesterday, they'd turned them over to Barry and Llew, who were stuck out there shooting dice for penny stakes, their horses equally bored, making sure nothing ate the road crew, who were all Tarmin folk, and who'd generally, but not universally among the riders, be missed.

If the sleet spooked them, the crew they'd just delivered safely would be insisting that Barry and Llew take them right back home, and the whole crew would be chasing her heels all the way back to Tarmin, after yesterday's trek getting foot-dragging fools in an ox-cart out there. . . .

But she didn't blame them: one didn't take chances once the weather began to turn, and the road crews had one of the nastier jobs, crawling out and around slide zones, shoring up the road with timbers they had to drag by ox-power out of the woods—they managed with oxen, because they couldn't waste fuel for trucks up here, where it didn't come by nature—or at all cheaply. The village tanks, since the last convoy out of Anveney, were full-up, and they'd stay that way until they needed the emergency heaters in the village common hall for days when the ice closed in and the wood ran low. Tarmin year-round burned wood for its stoves, and by autumn had barns full of hay that kept the goats alive and the oxen strong for such winter-hauling as the weather demanded.

And they never waited until the last minute to see to those stores. Tarmin always remembered the story of Parman Springs, which they'd been telling as long as Tara had heard stories: a rider coming into Parman Springs one winter had turned up with every last building taken down and burned but one—and the wall breached. Not a living human being was ever found, just a little scatter of bones.

That had been back in the boom days, when every lowland fool with a notion of instant riches had flooded up into the mountains, and the disasters had come yearly, when new-made camps either set themselves with no regard to the avalanche traces on the slopes, or never asked themselves why several big boulders sat on the flat they'd chosen; when stubborn lowland-bred miners had used transmitters for non-emergencies and thought that rifles could deal with the consequences.

The survivors had stayed to log and do the little winter mining that paid off, winter being the heaviest mining time because the temperature in the shafts was constant and bearable in months when logging, which sometimes paid better, was all but impossible. Verden, the other side of Verden Ridge, on the High Loop, was all underground, the whole settlement having discovered what its digging was really good for. They piped fresh air in and vented smoke out—precariously, to her mind—up a complex arrangement of flimsy tin pipes.

Spooky place, and dirty. It depressed even miners, from what she heard in Tarmin. Riders didn't like it and wouldn't go inside. She had, once, out of curiosity, and come out again anxious for sun-warmed air, having no desire to do it twice.

She wanted the sky over her head. Truth be known, she liked the snow, she liked the quiet months of isolation that the weather enforced in the High Wild, when there was precious little work for riders but hunting and trading off the take to the town butchers and the tannery for the nasty end of it. She'd no steady partner, but she'd two lovers and no shortage of intelligent company, and a couple of junior female partners who weren't permanent, but who might become so. The juniors were partnered with each other, were in more than autumn lust with the boys—the boys, as they called the senior riders—and whatever they called them, 'the boys' damn sure beat their competition over on Darwin.

So she'd shared-in and found herself as happy as she'd been in her life, settling in with a group of riders, all of whom, senior or junior, she could count on in any pinch. She'd gone hungry and she'd slept alone in her junior years, completely on her own since her mother died—and after five years of hell, first as a junior and then as a senior riding Darwin Ridge, she'd ridden into a camp on Rogers Peak too easy to live in and too hard to leave. She'd become pinned down. Tied. Permanent, in a way she'd once, in her footloose youth, sworn she'd never be.

<Steak cooking.> Flicker was definitely interested in camp and food and nighthorse company, out of the skitter and scatter of her thoughts. <Tarmin camp, fires and ham roast.> Flicker was also glad enough to know where such things always resided—glad, too,

to be going back to civilization all in one long push today, and not minding the long walk. Flicker never liked road guard and Tara had had her own fill of it this fall. It was boring, and this late in the year it meant standing around in windy places in the sleet where there was nothing to eat, and nothing to do but shift from one cold foot to the other and try to keep the wind from blowing up at your underside.

Until even a rider might hope, after a few weeks on duty, for a goblin cat or some such to make a meal of the crew, so she could go home.

But a rider didn't make such jokes around nervous villagers. A rider just sat and watched the ambient with nighthorse senses, trying to keep a restive horse from equally bored and very vivid amusement.

So, having served their time in purgatory on the last trip to Verden, and Llew and Barry having gotten the short end of the draw, she and Flicker were homeward bound through the spitting sleet.

Flicker was putting on her winter coat early this year—had been at it for a month, and the sleet stuck to the longer hairs of her body, and to her ears and mane. Flicker had voluntarily picked up the pace since that fleeting thought of pork roast: she was enthusiastically bound for Tarmin, and way-stopping at one of the two lonely storm shelters on their way, then having the next day to turn around and ride out through the snow to restock it (there being no rest for a Tarmin rider when a shelter wanted stocking) was not in Tara's plans, either.

If they traveled late, they could make it on in with no real need of a way-stop. It was the first winter squall of the season lurking up there about the peak, but not a serious one, she had the skill to bet knowledgeably on that outcome—and the skill to cover that bet and save them both if things went wrong. No mere storm was going to stop them for more than a nasty cold night in the open if they misjudged, and they'd winter-camped many a night out in her starving junior years over on Darwin, where the weather was, if only in her memory, very much worse.

But there'd been a spooky feeling on Tarmin Climb—the worse with the wind howling about the rocks. The road crew there had found an accident, a wrecked truck, logs strewn all to hell and gone up and down the rocks at that hairpin that started the only 20 percent grade on the Climb, a notorious turn, and not the first truck that had ever lost it all on the curve. That section was old road, hard to improve because of where it was located, and often as crews from Tarmin and the higher Ridge villages shored the slip zone up with timbers and fill, it eroded. It was a battle with the weather and the wear of the trucks' brakes on a grade the road crews couldn't improve without blasting a whole lot of mountain down and maybe, by what she'd heard, making matters much worse.

So it was one more load of timber and rock to go up there to stabilize that roadbed before winter snows and spring melt made little runnels into major slips. The crew was running a race with the winter and it looked like they might lose this one, though they damn sure could get cut timbers in plenty from the wreck down there.

Dead truckers, for sure—that there had been fatalities was evident both from the condition of the truck and the fact of scavengers numerous about the vicinity. It was possibly as much as a month old, or maybe more recent, part of the last convoy Tarmin had handled, which had joined its High Loop segment coming off that downhill and turned on down to the lowlands, outrunning the winter. Of the driver and his backup they'd not even find the bones intact by now. Unless somehow they'd jumped clear or been rescued the day it had happened, they were gone. The scavengers that night would have made quick work even of personal effects, and the convoy boss doubtless knew the names and next of kin of the dead truckers, so there was no point risking necks. The road crew had hallooed and banged on pans when they'd discovered the wreck, making absolutely sure that there wasn't some survivor holed up in the truck cab—occasionally such miracles happened; but you didn't really expect them.

There hadn't been any response, and she heartily agreed with Barry and Llew: it was just too dangerous, for no real hope of survivors after so long a time, and considering that silence, for a rider to go climbing down that slide where no horse could defend him against what else might be interested in the wreck. Death drew predators as well as scavengers, or one became the other very quickly when they found themselves a nice soft-skinned prey that didn't image back. Next spring when the weather was better and all of nature was calmer, they'd salvage it for metal.

Flicker imaged slinky little shadows. Flicker didn't like the roadwork or the carrion-eaters. <Bite and kick,> was Flicker's thought. <Trample.> Flicker *hated* little things that ran out under her feet on narrow trails.

Then Flicker stopped cold in her tracks, so suddenly Tara jolted a little forward and caught herself with her hands against Flicker's suddenly rigid neck, wondering what in the world Flicker had heard besides the sleet rattling among the evergreens. Immediately the ambient had gone unpleasant. That was Flicker's opinion: she felt that tingling along her nerves, but there might be something more specific she couldn't sort out of Flicker's nervousness.

"Damn," she muttered—she didn't like things she couldn't figure from Flicker. She thought, urgently, with authority, <us going on now. Staying on road.>

Flicker wasn't budging. Tara kicked her gently in the ribs, but Flicker just stood.

Second kick. Harder. Something was in the area. Something was sending in a way she couldn't quite pick up, maybe just a ghosty, doing its I'm-not-here. Maybe Flicker was just spooky with the weather.

"Come on." Third kick. Flicker came unstuck from her momentary paralysis and started on her way, step and step, one, two, three, four, her hoof-toed feet scuffing the leaves louder than the sound of the sleet in the branches. Flicker was imaging something that just whited out.

Tara didn't understand. She'd never known Flicker to do that before. Not her usual soft flutter of light, but a glaring <white-white-white,> as Flicker traveled with that about-to-move floating feeling that advised a rider to keep alert for a sudden jump or a shift of direction.

If it was a beast sending that unease she'd felt for a moment, it was one she didn't know. And she'd thought she knew everything in the woods of Darwin and Rogers both.

<Going faster,> she imaged. But she couldn't get through that <white-white-white> sending. Flicker kept her steady pace. Tara kicked her lightly, once, twice; and Flicker moved up to that traveling shuffle nighthorses could keep for hours.

That got them out of the area faster, at least, assuming it was something that laired nearby, not tracking them. Tara slipped the tie-down off her pistol and thumbed the safety off, riding with a fistful of Flicker's mane in the uneasy, constant feeling that Flicker might dive right out from under her.

It was a long while later the feeling slowly localized, as some danger—she was reasonlessly, absolutely certain—lying behind them, which meant they had finally gotten far enough ahead they had achieved that separation; but Flicker forged ahead for a time longer as if she was nose into some heavy wind.

Then the feeling just lifted. Flicker shook herself as she walked, snorted, kept going at a slightly slower pace.

<Goblin cat,> Tara suggested. She loved the High Wild and the woods. She enjoyed riding alone . . . but now and again came one of those small, cold moments when the woods seemed foreign and lonely, when the sounds all seemed right, but muffled and faint, and when before and after seemed to change places.

Flicker didn't agree with her image. She couldn't tell what Flicker thought.

<Ghosty in the bushes,> she thought then, shakily, telling herself it was only some particularly clever small creature—a spook, a fast-moving one, maybe not a kind she was used to.

But she couldn't convince herself of that. Maybe she'd gotten scared at something and scared Flicker with her own human imagination.

That could happen up here, especially in the woods, especially with the snow flying and whiting out the details of things. Humans had to have edges. Humans had to know the connections of things, and human minds made them up if they didn't get them. There were stories about riders who'd spooked themselves and their horses into serious trouble, losing track of the land and where the drop-offs were; but she wasn't a scatterbrain, she wasn't inexperienced, and neither was Flicker.

She just didn't like what she'd felt back there, she still didn't get a clear image out of Flicker—and she'd never in her life felt Flicker do what she'd done.

It was a cold, cold morning, overcast about the mountain ridge above them, as the road wound in slow, gentle ascent toward the rising wall of Rogers Peak.

It was a mountain Danny had grown up seeing from his third-story window, a peak drifting disconnected from the earth in misty distance above Shamesey walls—a place a town kid had regarded as remote as the stars the preachers talked about. He'd never imagined himself in those days as a rider—certainly never thought he'd be traveling to that mountain, hunting rogue horses, or rescuing villagers. But the closer they'd traveled, the more solid the mountain became, not a daydream now but an environment of stone and gravel and grass, under a high dark wall of evergreen.

The more solid the mountain became, the more the business they'd come to do seemed both too close and too unreal to him. He heard nothing wrong. He felt nothing besides themselves and the occasional spook, the impression of being watched that was just the Wild, that was all. It went on all the time, nothing threatening—even reassuring, a sign that large predators weren't in the area.

It was definitely colder, a knife-edged wind where the road wound into the open, the sort that made one's ears ache, and Danny, like the others, rode with a lap of his scarf over his head and his hat on tight.

He looked back now and again as the road offered a downward view of the land, wondering anxiously if he might see any trace of the riders Cloud had heard lower down—which didn't at all seem to worry Cloud now. Cloud was feeling energetic, snorting, flaring his nostrils and watching every flutter of leaves and wind-wave across the grass—grass which was giving way to an advance guard of scattered evergreen, not just occasional stands of trees, but the edge of real forest, at which Danny had looked all his life, seeing it only as a darkness on the mountains. Cloud moved here and there on the track, generally annoying the three other horses, while Jonas and the others pointedly ignored his presence. The other horses were trying to be peaceful, Danny thought: they seemed to realize that Cloud was excited about the mountains and were forgiving of his behavior.

He wanted no more trouble. He'd had a go at the land alone, it was damned spooky out there even without the remotest hint of whatever might be on their backtrail, and he hoped Cloud would be content finally, now that they were headed upland.

He'd at least calmed himself enough he could be sure he wasn't sending out a constant broadcast of his concerns, and he was sure that made Cloud calmer.

But he couldn't but look over his shoulder from time to time.

"They're not going to be that careless," Jonas said finally.

"Yes, sir," he said meekly. Yes, sir, after being left on his own in the wild seemed the best answer to anything and everything Jonas or any of the others said to him. He was not going to get into trouble again. He was *not* going to afford these men an excuse to look down on him.

Cloud had to try to bite Shadow just then. Had to, though Cloud deliberately pulled the nip short of Shadow's flank—deliberate provocation, status-battle, and nighthorse tempers flared for a jolting moment.

"Boy," Jonas said.

"Yes, sir," he said, embarrassed, taking Cloud's rebellion for his fault, which only made Cloud madder.

"You have a problem, boy. Do you think you can fix it, or do you want to ride home now?"

<Juniors laughing,> was his immediate and mortified thought. "He's just never worked with a group. I'll pull back some."

"You going to spend your life pulling back some, or what, boy?"

"My name's Dan, sir." It had to be Cloud's influence. His face was burning. His heart was beating hard. He might pull back from making a direct and personal challenge of Jonas' authority—that was farthest from his mind; but he wasn't going to tuck down and take it from all of them for the rest of the trip, either, and that was one boy too many for Karl Fisher's son. "You asked me to come along to help find Stuart, and I take that for a promise. But I don't pick up anything right now. So I'll ride back behind till I do, thanks."

"Got you," Hawley said dryly. "Kid's got you, Jonas. It was your idea to bring him. I told you."

Jonas wasn't happy. Or didn't look it. Danny started to signal behind Cloud's ribs with his heels. Cloud fell back on his own, sullenly imaging <fight.>

But <fight> wasn't what came from Jonas or from Shadow. Some impression slid past him, something nebulous and fast and without edges, a piece of something he didn't understand, and Jonas dropped back, too, in clear intention to speak with him, as Cloud and Shadow went unwillingly side by side.

"Kid," Jonas said. It was an improvement on 'boy.' And Danny caught an impression, now, of a meeting among the three men after he'd left them last night—that and talk on the trail, yesterday evening. "I didn't figure the complications, a kid getting into this. Maybe you'd *better* go back."

"I don't want to, sir." The juniors would know—he broadcast the fear of that humiliation without in the least wanting to. He tried to image himself on convoy, instead, riding guard with senior riders. He'd done that: it was the truth. "I can pull my own weight, I've no question."

"I have. You can't stay on your horse. That's bad news up there."

"Now, ease off, Jonas." Luke Westman had dropped alongside, on Jonas' other side. "I can recall the day."

Jonas sent him a surly look. But everybody got the image, Jonas taking a tumble right over Shadow's neck. And Hawley had to laugh.

Danny ducked his head and thought urgently, desperately, devout as a prayer in church, that Jonas looked important and professional and—his traitor mind added—rakish, experienced, absolutely unflappable at disasters, the way he'd like to look.

That brought a silence from Jonas, further guffaws from Hawley and Luke, and he'd rather have died, right then, fallen right off Cloud's back and died right on the road at their feet.

"His horse is a damn problem," Jonas said—and just once Danny got something of an image: <convoy, somewhere,> he didn't know the road. <Lot of trucks. Trouble.> "Danger to the kid, is what that horse is. Same as the kid is a danger to him."

Threaten Cloud, disparage Cloud? Not to his face. He wasn't going to put up with it. <*Cattle,*> he thought, to that idea.

"Ouch," Hawley said, and Jonas and Luke were frowning, while Hawley shook his head and imaged <Quiet grass. Quiet water.>

"Damn strong, is what he is," Luke said. "Noisy horse. Must have learned from that old sod Wesson. —But bullying your way through doesn't serve you well out here, kid. Take a strong dose of quiet. You aren't in town now, and strong sending like that can bring all sorts of attention. —*Don't* go surly with us. That's *good* advice."

"You want me to leave?" He was mad, he'd been insulted all he was willing to bear, he'd embarrassed himself. He couldn't stand it.

"Go backtrail in that kid-fit, boy," Jonas said, "and you'll find trouble that won't give a damn about your sweet feelings. Throw some water on that temper of yours, first off. Your horse doesn't need that kind of trouble. You're no help to him. *You* keep him agitated. You twitch, all the time. Knees. Feet. Elbows. Let the horse for-God's-sake *alone* ten minutes in an hour."

Damned outsider didn't know what Cloud needed and didn't need. He did.

"I said, throw some water on it. You're a fool. If you want to fight about it, you and I can get off right here and settle who's taking orders and who's giving them."

"I never said—"

"You don't have to say anything, town-kid. You shout it. You didn't grow up with the horses, you never have got it through your head that full-throttle isn't the way to take a steep, and you haven't had anybody give a damn enough to tell you how damn noisy you are, have you?"

<Stuart,> flashed to mind, and mad as he was, he was embarrassed, sure the man was reading it all out of his mind, somehow.

Which was stupid: the horses couldn't figure human experience. The horses wouldn't know how his father dealt with him. Horses didn't clearly know what a father was, scarcely recognized a mother . . .

God.

Cloud jostled under him, angry at his distress, he realized, and he tried to calm Cloud with his hands. He couldn't organize his thoughts. They were scattering every which way . . . <beads hitting a floor. Mama's necklace. Mama and papa yelling at each other.>

<Mama and Denis and Sam and a roof over his head most of his life, and the drafts coming through until there was plaster—>

"Kid. Get down. Get off."

"I don't want to fight you." <Knives. Fringes flying. Blood hitting the dirt.> He was scared of Jonas. He'd die in a knife-fight, he had no question. He didn't know how to fight except with his fists. And Cloud didn't want him to fight—Cloud shied off on the road toward the edge, ears flat.

"I didn't say fight, I said get the hell off. I want to talk to you, fool kid."

He wasn't sure. It might be a trick. Probably to humiliate him. Cloud wasn't pleased. Cloud thought <Bite and kick,> and argued with him to get in range of Jonas. But the other riders were trying to calm the ambient and keep the horses apart.

Then Jonas was sliding down. So he did, floppy baggage and all, ready to <fight.>

"Just walk with me," Jonas Westman said, and waved his arm in the direction they were generally going.

He still thought it still might be Jonas' intent to drop him. But they could shoot him if they meant him real harm and not just to deal out the knocks juniors took. He tried, shakily, to calm Cloud down.

"Kid," Jonas said. "No trick. Talk. Come on."

He wasn't sure what Jonas had to say to him was going to be better than hitting him. It was probably going to be direct and rude and it was probably going to make him mad, and he didn't know if he could stop Cloud now that he wasn't on Cloud's back.

"Easy." Jonas put his hand on Danny's near shoulder as he came close enough, Jonas let it rest there while they walked, the two of them, while Shadow and Cloud trailed after. Danny threw a look back to be sure Cloud was all right, but Hawley Antrim had his horse between.

Jonas squeezed his shoulder. Hard. "Kid. Easy. You're not the only kid in the damn world, you've just got to damp it down a little. It's not hard. Be not-here. Be quiet as you can, take a breath or two. Quit moving. Keep your elbows and knees and feet for God's sake quiet, anybody ever tell you?"

"I don't want to go back. I *owe* Stuart."

"Yeah, yeah, yeah. That's fine. Nobody ever showed you the finer points, did they?"

"He did." <Rainy day. Stuart telling him about the outfitters, who to trust.>

"Yeah, well, that's well and good, too. But there's more than that. If I send you back to town now, and I ought to, I never bargained for Harper and his night-crawlers, but you'll be mad as hell, you'll get in with that bunch, and you don't want to understand, Danny-boy, just how bad it can get in bad company. They're not good men." Something slid like a ghosty right over his mind. He couldn't grab it. He wasn't even sure it wasn't a ghosty, and he was scared, feeling the silence that Jonas Westman could muster, and knowing . . . knowing that this was the man who'd upended all of Shamesey camp and half the town when he'd come in looking for Stuart. This was the man with the horse that imaged itself constantly changing, shifting—you didn't know what you had. You didn't know what Jonas thought, not really, not ever.

"Easy," Jonas said, and that hand was still there, pressing hard, almost to the point of pain. "Easy. What you've got to learn to do, kid, is quiet down, don't give people so much help hearing you. You can do it. Easier for you. You're older than that horse. What is he, three, four?"

He didn't want to talk about Cloud. The man had insulted Cloud. Had insulted him.

"My name's Dan . . . —Dan."

"That's fine. When we know each other I'll use it. Shut up, shut down, stop being scared."

"I'm not—"

"Hell you aren't. Scared of us. That's foolish. You ought to be scared of who's on our tail. You ought to be scared of the job where we're going. —You ought to be scared as hell of Stuart, if he doesn't get himself quieted down, are you hearing me, kid? You get a damper on it or you flame out of control all the time. If you do that, you won't have many friends, no mates . . . that's Stuart. That's Stuart, boy. That's why he's where he is. That's why he's got enemies. That's why he's got damn few friends, tell the truth."

"He's all right." <Stuart on the porch. Rain coming down. Telling him who to trust.> "He never did me any harm."

"How long have you and that horse been together?"

"Couple of years." One and a half was a couple, wasn't it? "I'm not stupid."

"Yeah. Fine. Easy to say, harder to prove. I've got a temper. We've all got tempers. But a horsefight doesn't serve anybody, least of all the horse, trust me on that."

He didn't want Cloud hurt. He was scared he'd gotten Cloud into—

"Calm down." The grip on his shoulder did hurt. "Boy."

"My name's Dan."

"That's fine. We've all got names. Don't be so definite. Be smoke. Be fog. I can teach you, if you're not like Guil. If you'll listen. Otherwise you'd better ride back and stay safe."

<Riding up to the high country alone. Taking Cloud home.>

"Damned fool," Jonas said. "Not a choice."

"I told him I would," he muttered. "Cloud wants to go. It's where he's from. Even Wesson says. You can't send me back. If I leave you got no say where I go."

Second painful squeeze. "Town-brat. You don't know what you're up against. You can't imagine the high country in winter."

"I know about it. I know it's hard up there."

"You also know there's a rogue up there that's killed a rider ten years in the business. You know you're damn bait, kid, that's all you've got sense to be, the way you shout into the dark. *That's* why I brought you. Wise up."

"So I can do one thing real well. My name's Dan."

"Danny. All right. A little less pride, a little more clear thinking. Do you have to go up there being bait? Or do you think you can do better than that?"

"Maybe." If Jonas had something to teach him about slipping

around things, he could learn it. If Jonas was just being nasty, he didn't care. Staying with Jonas got him up there to Tarmin Ridge, up in the honest-to-God high country. Any mountain would have done. That was what he most wanted.

"You just calm down. Calm—down. Hear?"

"Yes, sir."

"Damn lot to learn, Danny Fisher," Jonas said then, and dropped his hand from his shoulder, the two of them walking along in front of the horses.

"I'd rather Dan," Danny muttered.

"It's Danny. It's *kid* when you foul up. You *earn* Dan."

Still made him mad. But he quieted it down. He imaged <peaceful clouds> and <clouds over mountains.> "All right," he said. "I can do that. When I want to."

"Good," Jonas said, and didn't seem to dismiss him. Danny didn't know what to do with himself then—whether to go back to Cloud, fall back and leave the man alone . . . or what.

"Name's Jonas," Jonas said. "I earned it. —You tried talking, kid?"

"Yes, sir." His father had pounded 'sir' into him. It got you off without being hit.

"Jonas," Jonas said. "That's Luke, that's Hawley. Try not to shout, damn you."

"I'm sorry, sir. I—"

"Jonas. Try it."

"Yes, sir." That wasn't it, either, but it just fell out. His tongue tied up. He wanted Jonas to let him go, he wanted . . .

Cloud moved up on them. So did Shadow. So did Ice and Froth with their riders. <Calm water,> Danny imaged. <Still water. Danny walking quietly with this man. Danny upset—>

He *couldn't* keep the negatives out of his thinking. <Still water,> was the best he could do consistently. <Clouds over mountains, sunset.> He felt like a fool. And knew everyone heard him. <Danny unhappy.>

<Cattle,> Cloud sent.

"Kid," Jonas said.

<*Quiet* water. Cloud standing in quiet water.> Best he could do.

<Danny giving Cloud sugar-lumps. In camp,> he had to amend that, because his pockets were empty of sugar-lumps. <Danny sitting with men.>

<Cattle,> Cloud still imaged. <Cattle rear ends.>

"Cut it out," Danny muttered, not looking at Cloud, but Cloud knew that tone and knew the thoughts in his head with a very clear understanding when he was getting on his rider's nerves.

<Cattle everywhere.>

"Sorry," Danny said to the men around him, and went back and patted Cloud on the shoulder, walked with his arm under Cloud's neck, patting him under his mane. Cloud kept sulking, but that was because Cloud was getting his way. "You behave," Danny muttered. When things got bad, he used words, mystery words, things Cloud didn't know, and Cloud got frustrated, because Cloud knew something was going on Cloud couldn't have, couldn't see.

Cloud hated the town. Cloud hated his family. Cloud hated townsmen. Cloud hated people around them. Cloud wanted just him. Alone.

That was scary. That was real scary, when he realized that small truth.

The sleet came down thickly now, whiting over the dark shapes of evergreens, sticking on Flicker's black coat, dusting Flicker's mane and up-pricked ears. Pace, pace, pace down the trail at a steady clip; the images from Flicker were still all spooky, distracted, wavery—like smell-images, but stranger than that, and Tara Chang told herself she wasn't going to stop at the storm-shelters. They'd make it, no matter how heavy the storm grew. She wasn't bedding down tonight alone in a log shack out in the middle of the woods. She was determined about that matter long in advance of getting there.

But it was a serious decision. It might be a spooked, unwise decision, with the sleet having turned to honest snow by the time they passed the shelter on the trail.

The shelter sat unoccupied, Tara knew that in the same way she knew the ambient and saw no smoke from the chimney. She had no doubt it was stocked and ready for winter—Chad and Vadim had escorted the teams out with the winter supplies the first leaf-turn:

clean blankets, grain, preserved meat in strong, pilfer-proof tins, medicines, cordage, anything a storm-trapped rider might need.

She might be foolish. The way ahead of them was turning as white as Flicker's frantic imaging, and there was safety in those thick log walls and those heavy shutters, if one could keep the doors barred. The shelter would hold her and Flicker both, no question.

But no shelter could help if a rider, in the grip of predator-sent illusions, chose to unbar a door or open a shutter. If you got yourself besieged indoors by a persistent predator, illusions came through walls, through shutters, through barred doors, illusions to confuse a horse and beguile a fool human into lifting a latch.

Flicker snorted and shook herself, never slacking pace as they moved on down the road. Tara agreed by doing nothing and they both committed themselves to the try for at least the next shelter, if not for home. It was a very uneasy feeling in Tara's several looks back, as the shelter lay farther and farther behind them, as woods closed between and the storm showed signs not of abating, but of getting worse.

It might well have been a mistake, Tara thought. Not necessarily a fatal one, but a rider didn't get too many such mistakes for free, not in a long life. Staying the night there might have been a mistake, too. She didn't know. She had no way to judge now, either the weather or the uneasiness about the Wild that still crawled up and down her nerves.

As bad as the weather was looking now, the road crew she'd just taken out to their work might indeed be coming back, all of them, scared by the same storm—so if she'd stayed at the shelter, she might not have been alone for more than the night. If the road crew did decide to winterize the equipment and break camp, Barry and Llew would push through the night if necessary, at whatever pace they could with the ox-teams. They'd offload everything, cache even the supplies, if they didn't like the look of the weather; and the stolid-seeming oxen could move fast, if they moved unladed, not as fast as nighthorses, but they might be headed for that shelter, all the same.

If *she* were in charge instead of Barry, the way it was looking now, no question they'd chuck it and leave that exposed mountain flank before the drifts built up.

Barry, though, was a get-the-job-done man. Village-bred, not a born rider. Villagers liked to deal with him. He made sense to village-siders, and Barry had agreed with this jaunt out to flirt with the weather and been willing to sit out there freezing his fingers and toes off. Not to mention other useful parts.

A cold gust blew up the skirts of her coat, found its way into her bones, and she buttoned the weather-bands tightly around her glove cuffs, then took her hat off to get a closer fit on the scarf that protected her ears from frostbite. She slid the chin-cord tight when she put it on again, and turned her collar up. She had a knitted hood in her inside pocket. It made her face itch and she hated it.

Most of all it restricted her side vision, and she wanted to know what was around her, on the edges of her vision, even if it was misty white and the misted shapes of trees.

But, <white,> Flicker imaged, whiting out the world except the trail in front of them, as if they were nowhere in the universe but this small patch that was real; and Flicker kept up a steady pacing gait, creating the world constantly ahead of her.

Spooked, she said to herself. Too much thinking on disaster in this perilous season. She imaged <scavengers in the rocks, wrecked truck> until she realized she was doing it.

She imaged <winter storm on the mountain> and <frozen bodies> without running it past her thinking brain, and Flicker couldn't tell the difference. Panic her own horse into a heart-attack, she could—like some fool first-year rider—come in with her tail tucked and the willies lurking in every tree. She knew better, and she told Flicker <calming down, slowing down.>

But that shelter was a long ways behind them now, and the next chance lay a good distance ahead.

<Death on the rocks. Hidden ledges.> Dammit! She couldn't stop thinking about it.

They knew the trail. Despite the whiteout, she was sure they hadn't left the road. She could see the markers on the trees arriving out of oblivion and passing by in Flicker's constant, even strides.

Possible that some new creature had moved into the woods. Humans weren't native to these mountains—not even native to the world they lived in, the seniors said so: now and again something did show up that nobody'd seen, pushed by the storm winds, driven by fiercer predators or by some unguessable notion of prey to be had this side of the mountain divide, she didn't know. Sometimes a wild horse would show up with an image you didn't want to know about. Nobody claimed to have met everything there was to meet in the woods; Flicker was all the opinion she trusted now, Flicker felt something she didn't like . . . void and the smell of death, that was what began to come through the ambient, something that crawled with scavengers and came out of the storm, neither dark nor light. It was everything. It was nothing at all.

But it was prickling at the edges of her attention.

Flicker jolted forward into a sudden, neck-snapping run. <Rocks and logs,> Tara imaged in alarm. She had a fistful of mane, and took a second one, closer to Flicker's head, jerking on it. But in the next instant her own panic overwhelmed her. She believed something was behind them—she threw a look over her shoulder, as Flicker hadn't, and saw nothing but white light and the ghostly trees jolting and blurring past with Flicker's reckless strides. <Run!> she thought in fright, looked back, looked to the sides and forward, and again she looked back, and then she thought, an instant's amazed chagrin—and absolute conviction: it's not there. It's not there now.

Flicker slowed, breathing through her mouth in great, cold gasps—and kept making a little forward progress, just a little, a walk on a wider-open stretch of road. There was still one more shelter ahead, the last between them and the village, but Flicker's reaction to that image, too, was a spooky, wordless no, Flicker wouldn't stay there. Flicker kept walking, picked up speed on the downhills and trudged up the climbs, an ox-road and as level as the roadbuilders could make it. The place felt safer now, and if Flicker wanted to rest, Tara was for it.

But she didn't get off, because if that sending came down again, she didn't rely on Flicker staying sane or remembering that she was leaving her rider stranded. There was a limit, even to their long partnership, and a goblin-cat confused even a nighthorse, if that was what it was.

Hours on, well into afternoon, they came to that second shelter. Flicker's legs and chest were spattered with ice now. Flicker's breath huffed in great heavy pulses. <Rest,> Tara wanted, afraid Flicker would run herself into a heart attack. <Dark behind us.>

Flicker imaged only <cold> and <white> and retook her beat, pace, pace, pace, pace, steady and scared.

The falling snow slowly took on a kind of dim gold haze that passed to a hint of blue, heralding night, one of those snowy, moon-up nights that might have no boundary from the day. The second shelter was no-return now. It was farther back than it was on to Tarmin, and the night was blued and pale.

<Camp walls,> Tara imaged, and swore that if they just made it to Tarmin camp there'd be warm blankets and whatever Flicker wanted. Ham. Eggs. A rub-down as long as Flicker wanted.

Flicker wasn't taking bribes. Flicker wasn't listening at all. Flicker just kept going, in a fear that wasn't at all panic, a fear that just didn't let go, didn't allow rest.

Until between one stride and the next . . . the fear dropped away from them, different than its prior comings and goings—it just all of a sudden didn't exist, might never have existed, leaving a nighthorse running and forgetting why and a rider who never *had* clearly known the cause.

Flicker slowed to a shuddery walk, snorting and blowing and slavering onto a chest spattered with ice—walked, with wobbly steps, and Tara slid down, her fears of phantoms in the dark replaced by a real and present fear of Flicker collapsing under her rider's weight.

<Warmth,> she imaged. <Camp and light and warm air, Flicker walking, Flicker just walking, safe now, safe . . . >

Flicker wasn't sure. Flicker was confused where she was, but in that confusion she kept listening to her rider, and Tara kept walking, holding a fistful of Flicker's mane to be sure they stayed together. She cast through the haze of snow and blued night, picking out what the markers told her was the trail, despite the trackless blanketing of snow.

She smelled the smoke of cookfires, then. She imaged <camp walls,> and <rest,> and shoved at Flicker's shoulder, terrified of the ordinary dark for the first time in her adult life. She imaged it without intending to, and that got Flicker moving, a last shaky effort uphill and onto the flat road outside the gates.

<Gates opening,> she imaged, before she reached the bell. But it was a snowy, sleepy night, and she had to grasp the rope with a numb, gloved hand, rouse the sleeping horses inside, and ring fit to wake the whole town, telling them there was a rider in from a dark that seemed deeper and more threatening at their backs now that they had the gate in front of them than it had a moment ago out in the midst of the storm.

"Come on," she muttered to the insensate wood, and hammered on it with her fist. <Tara and Flicker, freezing, snow on both of us. Vadim. Chad. Sleepy, lazy riders. Gate opening. *Gate opening. Danger in the woods.*>

The spyhole opened. They were being careful tonight. An eye regarded her before someone lifted the bar.

"Need help," she said. It was Vadim who had answered the gatebell, and Vadim who shut the gate behind her as she led Flicker in, heading for the nighthorse den where warm bodies kept the air a constant temperature—where other horses, other minds, were solid, friendly, ordinary.

Images flashed back and forth as she met that warmth, Flicker's <white-white-white>, the other horses' queasy, unsettling fright at the dark outside.

She couldn't stop it—she couldn't get Flicker to stop—couldn't come out—couldn't escape—couldn't stop the light—

"God," Vadim said quietly, coming into that flood of panic.

She was lost in it, trying to shut it down. She felt smothered when Vadim put his arms around her, hugged her against him—<fright and love and warmth.> Vadim was sending <danger> and <horse> but it was remote from her, lost as she was in cold, lost as she was in her desperation to get air, to breathe, to move. She writhed free without meaning rejection. She felt Vadim's consternation at that fleeting contact, felt it in the ambient, the horses all waked to fear and malady . . . they didn't know, at first, what had come among them: <Cold,> Flicker sent. And <white.> no ordinary calm-sending. Flicker was lost, too. White was a veil of snow and light behind which they'd both taken refuge, and now in its shifting substance, Flicker couldn't find the exit.

"Tara!" Vadim shook her till her head snapped back. Till she *could* see the dark around them. He hugged her till her joints cracked, kissed her, breathed warmth on her.

"Get help." She'd been too cold to shiver. In the still warmth of the den, in Vadim's attempts to warm her, his sending that she couldn't take in—she found the ability. "Water. Cold water. Need more hands."

When you were this cold you started with cold water compresses, and you kept increasing the heat in the water little by little. If she and Flicker were alone she'd do it herself, but there was help. Chad and Luisa and Mina were in the barracks, and with a <Tara sitting, Tara waiting in the den> Vadim went running out into the snow, *running*, scared for her, when nothing she'd ever met could scare Vadim.

Vadim hadn't been where the danger was. He hadn't felt it stalking behind him. He only had the echoes. And by that shapeless, dark fear of his, she knew how desperate it had been—still was, in her mind.

"We're all right," she said to Flicker, pressing close against Flicker's shoulder, thinking <den, camp, riders and horses, all around us. . . . >

In not very long at all, her partners came running, Mina and young Luisa, all appalled, saying there was a rogue, they'd had a phone call clear from Shamesey, they'd wanted to come after her, but Vadim and Chad had held out against their going outside the walls—<wanting> (young fools that they were) <coming out into the woods to find her; town gates were all guarded; they were both angry—>

<Safety,> Tara kept saying, half-aware of them, shuddering at the thought of them going out into the woods unprotected. But it was constantly Flicker uppermost in her thoughts, it was Flicker

she desperately tried to make aware of the camp, the den—the horses Flicker knew as her den-mates, as close to her as her human partners were to her rider.

Flicker just kept imaging <white,> only <white,> as if, even in safety, she still couldn't come back from that place.

Chapter viii

MAN'S A DAMN GHOST," HAWLEY SAID, AT THEIR WIND-BLOWN campfire that night, high on the road, in a clump of evergreens that gave them a little shelter. There was no sign of passage but the ruts the trucks had made in the road. The prints of horses on the dust were old, hardened mud; the tracks of game were newer. They hadn't turned up tracks or sight or scent of Guil Stuart or, for that matter, any sight at all of whoever they'd sensed following them.

Maybe we imagined it, Danny thought against his day-long inclination. He was, by now, willing to doubt his perceptions and Cloud's.

Maybe I misled everybody.

"It's sure a steep climb if he's gone straight up the ridge," Luke said, meaning <Stuart.> "Question is, how bad was he hit? He could have gone to ground somewhere, if he was bleeding heavy."

The question turned unexpectedly to Danny then, when his mind was half-elsewhere; but Jonas was next to him, looking at him, so that a crawling-feeling went up and down Danny's skin.

Jonas wanted, Jonas was impatient, that came through, and Danny's wits went scattered. <Gawky kid sitting on ground,> also came through to him, along with a feeling of irritation.

"Boy," Jonas said. "You'd tell us if you had a thought of Stuart's whereabouts. That so?"

"Yeah, but I don't. Sorry."

Jonas kept pushing at him. Friendly in the morning. Jonas' back to him all afternoon. Everybody talking. Except him. <Cloud increasingly unhappy—>

He rolled to his knees, intending to leave the fireside and go over to Cloud's vicinity, where he was comfortable and welcome.

"Kid," Luke said, not half so harshly. Luke was the friendlier, youngest one, the one he didn't want a fight with—Luke maybe knew it. He couldn't tell what got through to other people. "Sit down. Sit down, all right? Just a question."

It wasn't just a question, he thought, with upset still roiling in his stomach. The question he was asking himself was about his own competency, a question so wide and general through his life he didn't want to consider it except piece at a time, and most of all he didn't want to consider it with them.

But he didn't want a fight with Luke, so he sat back down, arm around one knee, and found a dead seedpod to break up into dry pieces.

"Ought to have stayed with mama," Jonas muttered.

"Yeah, fine," he said back. "You want an answer, Jonas, sir? I don't know where he is. I'm not hiding him."

<Cattle.> He was unhappy, Cloud was unhappy.

"You're being loud, kid," Jonas said.

"Yeah, well, get off me. Doing the best I can." He didn't look at Jonas or the rest of them. The seedpod was far more interesting. It had four inside chambers, with hard, round seeds, brown in the firelight. Crunch. Four, six, a handful. He tossed them at the fire, one, two, three, trying to land one where it would burn visibly. Two hit, off, the third landed under the glowing archway of branches at the edge. Achievement.

"Kid." That was Hawley. He didn't dislike Hawley. He really, really wasn't sure about Jonas.

"Kid's adjusting," Jonas said. "And he *doesn't* know."

Truth. Jonas always talked nicer *about* him than Jonas talked *to* him. He didn't know why Jonas couldn't do a little adjusting himself.

Didn't know why Jonas had wanted him if nobody was going to believe him, except that remark Jonas had made about him being bait, and he didn't take that altogether as fluffery. They might have intentions like that, using him that way, to draw Stuart in; and no reason they shouldn't tell him so.

They probably thought he was lying about people following him, trying to make himself important, trying to cover his trailing in late the way he had, as if there was some big, awful danger out there and he'd escaped it on his own.

Serve them right if somebody did come up on them. And he'd warn them, of course, but they wouldn't listen. They were seniors, and knew everything.

"Kid," Jonas said. "Calm *down* for two minutes, have you got it? We can send the horses off a ways so you and I can have a discussion, if you want."

"No, sir," he muttered. Nobody was sending Cloud anywhere he didn't want Cloud to go. But it wasn't smart to quarrel with men who carried knives for more than fire-making. It didn't even take a junior's intelligence to figure that out.

"Guns are quicker," Jonas remarked dryly.

He was sending, again. Dammit.

"The kid's just upset," Luke said. "Lay off, Jonas. You're pushing him too hard."

"Damn right I'm pushing him. We leave *him* at Tarmin village first chance we get. The rogue'd have him for breakfast. Go right for him, it would. I don't plan to get him killed."

Madder and madder. Insult and concern. He couldn't read Jonas' signals and he couldn't say whether Jonas was right or wrong. He wanted to go to Cloud the way he'd started to and not have to listen to them. He'd no need of lectures. But he'd been told to sit down, by the only one of them who was civil to him, and if Luke got mad at him the trip was going to be hell.

Cloud ambled up into the firelight, snuffing at the ground, insinuated his big head over Danny's shoulder and rested it there, imaging <grass in the sunlight. Sweet-smelling.>

Danny patted Cloud's cheek, and Cloud's soft nose investigated his pockets, wanting <sugar-lumps> he was sure his rider ought to have.

Cloud didn't do things totally unselfishly.

"What I still can't figure," Hawley said, "is what he's doing."

He meant Stuart.

"Maybe he thinks the camp's sent out hunters," Luke said.

"They have, of course," Jonas said, and it took Danny a second and more to realize Jonas meant themselves, that *that* was what they were. It didn't even count whoever was following them. He told himself what he'd perceived was real, no matter what Jonas thought. It was a damned stupid mess, over a rider who hadn't done anything—*anything* but go to the gate trying to get his belongings back.

Which they had brought with them. Supposedly to give Stuart's belongings back to him when they found him.

But he wasn't so sure what Jonas' personal motives were.

He was probably sending again, but Jonas ignored it, just kicked the cook pan into the fire for the fire to clean. There wasn't much grease. It made a flare, and the flare died quickly. He'd have to wipe it down in the morning, with a twist of grass, nasty job. But the youngest rider always got those jobs, it was a law of the universe.

"Suppose he did get hit worse than we thought?" Luke asked.

"I don't think so," Danny muttered without even thinking about it, and wished he hadn't opened his mouth on any of their business, but Luke asking was different from Jonas asking, in his estimation, and by that comment, he'd committed himself. He found his hand resting on his leg above the knee, remembered the pain of the gunshot across the skin, the shock to the knee bones and tendons, vivid memory—he'd played it out a dozen times in his head and he did it for them, the whole image, to answer Luke's question.

"Didn't go through," Hawley judged with a grimace. "Went past. Burned him good, knocked him down, is all."

"Good," Jonas said, not meaning about knocking Stuart down,

meaning *him*: he suddenly figured he'd just done exactly what Jonas had been trying to get out of him, exactly the way that Jonas expected, and he *hated* Jonas for the satisfied look Jonas cast in his direction. But he held onto Cloud's forelock long enough to distract Cloud when Cloud jerked his head up. Cloud's hair burned through his hand. And Jonas won. Jonas was used to winning.

"Kid's damned good when he wants to be," Hawley said, which doubly confused him, about whether Hawley was serious or sarcastic, as Hawley, immediately off on another tangent, imaged <steep mountains, rider on dangerous slope.> It looked like Guil.

"Maybe not," Luke said, not about him being good when he wanted to be: it was the rider-image Luke shook apart, in favor of <level trail>; a definite place, it seemed to be, but it could be any place. *They* knew what they were imaging. He didn't. He sat there with places he'd never seen flying back and forth through his vision and no knowledge what the question was.

From out of nowhere Jonas put his hand on Danny's knee—scared hell out of him, that too personal, powerful touch—shook him right out of his thoughts. "Gone across to Anveney?" Jonas asked without paying further attention to him, and the image of town and smokestacks Danny had never seen in person was certainly Anveney the way he'd seen it before, in his head. It was a place, he'd learned, that riders didn't like, except Anveney paid well . . . and it was the only place of all the places in the world besides Shamesey he could have identified without their help.

Jonas hit his knee, meaning Shut up, Danny thought; stop thinking into the ambient.

"Man's got no supplies," Luke said.

"Question is if he's got money," Jonas said.

"I wouldn't leave *my* stash under any hostel mattress," Hawley said. "Not in Shamesey town."

Insult his town, while he was at it. There were limits.

Another pat of Jonas' unwelcome hand, and Jonas wasn't even talking to him. Jonas was thinking about a building somewhere else, a place with bars on the windows, a jail, Danny thought at first, and then thought not, it was a business. "Has he," Jonas asked, "got a draw on Aby's account?"

The question surprised Hawley, angered Hawley. Danny didn't know why. Then it seemed to perplex Hawley, who scratched his stubbled chin. "Hell. She never said."

Jonas asked: "How much was in there?"

"Healthy amount," Hawley said sullenly. "It's not his."

What did they do? Danny wondered. It sounded like an account at a bank, and money the dead rider had had there—that they thought Stuart might have gone to get.

There was an uneasiness in the air, Hawley's Ice, Cloud, Jonas' Shadow all suddenly on edge. Jonas wasn't at all happy.

Hawley wasn't.

Hawley had gotten the money the dead rider owned, out of a bank, somewhere not in Shamesey—which was maybe Anveney. Danny didn't know about banks or how you got money out of them. He'd never been inside one. Papa kept his money on him, or in the hiding-place under the floor, which he didn't want to think about with these men seeing it. . . .

"Kid," Jonas said sharply, and laid a hard hand on his knee. Shook at him.

"Sorry." He knew he'd slipped this time, and dangerous men were close to anger with each other all around him, a long lonely way from anywhere.

"No," Jonas said. "We're not angry, boy. Hawley has a right to the money. He's her kin. He evidently proved it to the bank." <Jonas and Hawley at a counter, or something like, a woman talking to them.> "Just, it's a damn complication." <Stuart with his back turned, Stuart walking somewhere in town streets. Stuart with this same bank employee woman.>

<Aby Dale,> another sending imaged. <Red-haired little girl, big black horse.> But the sending stopped in anger.

"Everybody calm down," Luke said. "Just calm down."

"The damn kid's a distraction," Hawley muttered.

"You went in there," Jonas said, "you took that money out."

"I had a right!"

"You could have by-damn said, Hawley!"

"I'm *on* that account. Look, I'm her cousin."

"Dammit, Hawley!"

"If you had a word you could have said it, Jonas. You knew I was going to the bank. What did you think I was going to do? I got the card. She give me the card."

"Calm down," Luke said. "Hawley, it's all right. You did all right."

"Yeah, all right," Jonas said. "If he goes there, if he knows about the money—"

"I had a right!" Hawley said.

"You had a right," Luke said. "There's no question you had a right. —Danny, you want to get up and move the horses back? Do us a favor?"

"Yes, sir," Danny said, and got up—the horses were crowding in, snappish and pushy with the argument. He gave a shove at Cloud. <Cloud in the dark, away from the fire. Danny, too.> That was easy, another, harder push on Cloud's shoulder, Cloud's understanding that they were both to leave the fireside, but dealing with the other horses was a scary matter. The seniors' horses didn't want any town kid pushing them around, didn't want to take orders from him—

He walked in among them and suddenly a queasy darkness flittered through his mind, shapes and shadows and a violence that sent him a step back, disoriented. <Bite. Kick> was in the ambient, from two sides. "Cloud!" he said, and made a futile grab at Cloud's mane as horses squealed and heads darted past him, teeth bared, big bodies swinging about perilously close to him as shoulder hit shoulder.

Another spin. Cloud and Shadow. Heels flew past him and he jumped back barely in time.

"Shadow!" Jonas shouted.

It just stopped, horses jogged past each other in abortive attack. Shadow's teeth snapped on empty air. Cloud's heels kicked up and managed to miss.

He was shaking. <Cloud and Danny walking,> he insisted, furiously, and <quiet horses grazing,> but he couldn't call their true names in his head, not with the knowledge their riders had; and meanwhile their riders were having an argument at the fireside. They wanted *him* out of the way because he was loud—and the horses were on edge, with each other and with Cloud on general principle. He tried to calm tempers all around, imaging <quiet grass,> but he couldn't call the silent names, not the way their riders could.

He'd seen Shadow's name when the fight started, that fluttering succession of treacherous shadow-shapes. It was a dreadful name—he truly didn't mean to think in that hostile way of Jonas' horse, but it wasn't a name that slid easily past the nerves. He'd mistrusted that horse from the first moment he'd dealt with it, and he didn't turn his back on it—he was scared of that horse in a way he'd never had to be scared of a horse.

And in the aftermath of the encounter he'd just had, when he recalled Shadow's heels flying past his head, he was twice afraid. He didn't want to think of what could have happened to him if he'd not moved fast enough or if the fight had gotten serious with him in the midst of the horses.

Which wasn't the way to deal with horses at all. He fought his townbred nerves. He tried to separate them out, put Cloud to one side and keep the other three from snapping at each other or him, and they kept getting around him to make another sniping attack.

"Here." Luke Westman came to help him, clapped him on the shoulder, which did nothing to help his knees, and shoved Shadow out of a not-entirely-inquisitive approach with the back of his fist—swatted Shadow hard on the rump when he didn't retreat. <Danny swatting Shadow,> came into Danny's head—*he* for God's sake hadn't thought it, he was scared even to think of hitting that horse—Luke had launched that threat into the ambient on his behalf, Behave or the kid will hit you.

He didn't think it a help. But Luke waved Froth away from him and came close up on Cloud.

"What's his name?" Luke asked, meaning the inside name, the real name Cloud called himself—but he wasn't sure that Cloud wanted Luke to know that name. Cloud was laying his ears back and wrinkling his nose as was, and he didn't answer Luke. He just shoved at Cloud's chest and wanted him apart from the seniors and their horses.

"Be careful of him," Danny said. "Cloud, behave. Don't bite."

"He won't bite," Luke said, taking something from his pocket.

He held it out. Froth muscled in and got the treat. Candy. Cloud wanted it. But Ice sneaked his head in and got the next one Luke magicked out of his pocket.

<Cattle,> Cloud sulked, and then Shadow intruded, slipped up behind Froth and Ice so slyly and so smoothly Danny didn't see him until Shadow's neck snaked out and Shadow nipped the third candy Luke's pocket produced. Cloud was outraged.

But immediately Luke's other hand was out, offering one to Cloud . . . <sweet, delicious sweet> was the image in the ambient, from Luke and the horses, Danny realized, and felt Cloud wanting it, inching toward it. Sugar-candy was what he'd promised Cloud for good behavior, when he hadn't had one, and there it was, not from his hand, but from Luke's.

Cloud's mouth was watering, <Cloud sneaking it right off that hand, hating that cattle horse licking the man's other fingers, ugly shifty horse . . . >

Cloud was going to—

"Fingers!" Danny said, earliest manners-lesson Cloud had had to learn, where treats stopped and a rider's fingers began.

But Luke had curled his hand around to hide the treat for a second, then showed it again, just halfway, teasing, did it twice, blink of an eye, had something else out of his other pocket, in his other hand, that Shadow got before Shadow created a fuss.

Cloud's head darted out, Luke's hand wasn't there, and Cloud jerked . . . except there was the candy again, quick as a blink, right there, <sugar-smelling, fruit-smelling, sweet—>

Cloud nabbed it, jerked away, and backed off, jaws working on his prize. Hostile. Enjoying the sweet. Thinking he'd gotten away with it.

"He's fine," Luke said. "You ought to let that horse of yours around people more. It's good for him."

<Mad.> Danny didn't know what he felt: he was glad Luke hadn't lost a finger, glad it hadn't sparked a horse-fight—<mad> that Cloud had fallen for it . . .

"Kid," Luke said. "What *is* your grief?"

"Nothing." He couldn't own to what he felt. He didn't know

why he was mad, except Luke knew he'd promised Cloud that candy and Luke had no right.

"Nothing," Luke echoed him, and <mad> was in the ambient now, horses milling about, Luke growing irritated with him, Danny felt it. "Kid, —*why'd* you take up for Stuart?"

That came from out of nowhere, when he was ready for an accusation. "I don't know."

"Man did you a petty little favor. You're traipsing clear to hell paying him. Why? What's it to you?"

<High country. Papa hitting him. Mama yelling. Snow and trees in Cloud's mind. Stuart on the tavern porch talking to him as if he was really somebody.>

"Who hit you? A relative?"

"None of your damn business."

"Yeah, none of our business. Till you screw up and need somebody to come after you, none of our business."

<Stuart. Surly and mad. Him, Danny Fisher, same expression, exactly the same stance.>

"Like Stuart?" Danny retorted. "Me? I don't even know him, all right? I don't see where he screwed up. He was doing fine till you came along with your lousy news." <Stuart talking to him. —Luke, standing there in the dark blaming him for being mad. Giving candy to Cloud.> A lump came into his throat. So he found one man who'd talk to him like a human being, one man in the whole universe who helped him who didn't have to. He'd thought a couple of nights ago he'd found another in Jonas. He'd thought he'd found somebody else who stood by his friends. Which was a joke. <Stuart running up the hill, away from the three of them.>

That didn't sound like friends to him. And he'd had friends, one or two, no matter what Jonas said—well, at least the boys he'd hung around with in town, until he'd gone and taken up with Cloud.

They'd even tried to get past that, his town friends had. At least they'd tried. Gone on seeing him and hanging about with him, when he came back into town, maybe to shock their other friends, but, hell, it was more than he could say for Jonas and the rest of them, sitting smug on their horses, watching Stuart lose his grip on sanity in the upset they'd brought him.

<Stuart running up the hill. Them sitting watching. Rogue-feeling spreading like poison in the camp.>

Suddenly it was a resolve and a certainty to him: he couldn't stand any more of their company. He stalked back to the fireside, grabbed up his gear and started hanging thongs from his shoulder and stuffing gloves in his pocket as he walked back to Cloud—<us leaving this place.>

"Can't take it?" Jonas sniped at him, from the fireside. "This the way you honor contracts? Is this what you do to drivers you're hired to?"

It was an attack the same way his mother attacked him. He was used to it. He jammed his hat on, reached for Cloud's mane, the lump in his throat grown to painful size.

"Kid!" Different voice, Hawley's. It made him flinch out of the flashy swing up he intended, but it wasn't going to stop him: he chose the steadier, belly-down mount he knew he wouldn't fail.

So he wasn't good. So he got up like a kid. He was on Cloud's back, and Cloud turned away from the fire.

"Kid. Use your damn head. Where are you going?"

"What do you care?" <Us downhill,> he thought, and Luke came and tried to get into his path. <Luke riding to stop him,> was in the ambient; but Jonas said,

"We don't need him. If he wants to tag us he can follow. That's all."

He'd expected more interference. He'd frankly expected more concern. He sat there on Cloud's back staring down at Jonas, mad, damned mad, and Jonas stared back at him.

"You're a magnet for that thing, kid," Jonas said. "You know that? You and that horse—making all that noise. You care about that horse? No?"

"Go to hell," he said. He wished he hadn't. But he'd said it. Now he couldn't slink back to the fire. He stared down at all of them from Cloud's back, then wanted <downhill,> and <empty road,> not <going back to Shamesey.> Just <empty road.>

"Doesn't solve your problem, kid," Jonas' voice pursued him into the dark.

But Cloud took him onto the road and upped the pace to a trot, downhill into the dark of a clouded night, with a wind cold and keen as a knife.

He already wanted to go back to the fire. He knew he wasn't fool enough to ride straight uphill to Tarmin Height, first and alone, taking Cloud into what an experienced rider like Aby Dale hadn't been wary enough to survive.

But he couldn't find a way to go back and duck his head and take it anymore—he couldn't see getting Cloud hurt in a horse-fight, either, and he saw it coming if he didn't give in: Jonas was pushing for it, because Jonas intended to run him the way he bossed Luke and Hawley, and once you started taking Jonas' orders, he had the strong suspicion, it got harder and harder to break away from what Jonas wanted. A small group riding together wasn't at all like Shamesey camp, where there was a whole thought-deaf town to escape to when you felt thoughts crowding in on you; and when the town got too bad to tolerate, which usually took a few hours, there was Cloud to come back to.

And if everybody in the world pushed them too far they could go out to the hills and hunt for three and four days and not need anybody. He'd managed to stay out of trouble. He'd never gotten Cloud into a fight. He wasn't about to. Not three on one. Jonas knew it. Jonas kept pushing.

Bad decision maybe, that had made Jonas drag him along; so Jonas had thought better of it, and maybe Jonas had found out he wasn't going to knuckle under easily—but was Jonas going to say he was wrong and manage the situation as civilly as possible until they went their separate ways? Hell if he was. Jonas couldn't take somebody who didn't think Jonas had done right by Stuart. Maybe that was Jonas' conscience talking to him. Maybe it was just that Jonas was born a son of a bitch. It didn't matter.

He had to wonder how Stuart's partner had gotten along with the man. Why Aby Dale was lying dead up there on the ridge and they'd gotten away safe.

Then they'd gone over to Anveney to draw Aby Dale's money

out of the bank before they broke the news to Stuart at Shamesey. That was two, three days to make that detour, with some trucks that had to go that direction, he was sure—riders had to take their charges where they were hired to go, and that had to be the case. Hawley hadn't told Jonas about taking the money. That was a point in Jonas' favor. But hell, it hadn't been exactly a straight line they blazed with their bad news, had it? And there were telephones. If they were running a race with the weather getting up there, they could have phoned. They could have told Stuart without the rogue-image in the ambient with him at the time. Maybe he thought of that because he was a town-kid. But they knew there were telephones. Now Stuart's *friends* had his money the way they had his gear, to give to him, of course. And Stuart was out there with nothing, and going all the way up to Anveney, to the bank, he supposed, to find it out.

His throat ached. His chest hurt. Cloud slowed to a walk, mad, too, thinking <kick men, bite horses> until Danny reached down and patted his neck.

<Men by quiet water, three men at the table, with mama and papa and Denis and Sam . . . >

Sometimes the images that came up were outright stupid. He didn't know why he put those three men in the apartment with his family. They didn't belong there.

He was mad at them and mad at his family. Luke asked who'd hit him, which was none of Luke's business.

So what if he was mad that papa had hit him: he knew why papa had hit him, which Luke didn't understand: papa hit him when papa couldn't talk, the same reason he'd hit Denis—it was just something men in his family did, and it never meant you didn't love somebody, it just meant you'd gotten to that point your throat wouldn't work and the words weren't there, which was when you loved somebody a whole lot and they did things you didn't understand.

Sometimes thoughts came up that didn't make sense, as if they'd always lived in different spots in his brain and suddenly, because some nosy fool went asking into things he'd no right to ask, these separate things got together in scary combination, notifying you things didn't match up right, they couldn't make sense, and maybe the only safe way to deal with thoughts like that was to send them apart from each other before they messed up something in your life you couldn't put back the way it was.

Same way he'd found he was at odds with what the preachers said, once there was Cloud. And he was going to hell, but he still thought about God.

Same way he loved his family, and got madder at them than he ever could at Luke and Jonas, and Luke and Jonas made him mad at his family all over again. Luke and Jonas were messing with what he thought, messing with what he *was*, that was what they were doing—trying to bend his mind around to directions he couldn't figure. Luke thought he was like Stuart. Luke didn't think Stuart was a good thing to be. Neither did Jonas. Probably Hawley didn't.

He was Aby Dale's cousin, which he guessed explained why Aby Dale had been with them this trip and not with her partner, Stuart. But it didn't explain the other things. Hawley hadn't said about the money. He'd kept that even from Jonas. It wasn't easy to keep secrets with the horses around. *He* couldn't do it. But some senior riders had that reputation—he'd run into them, and you didn't know that they were different from other people, you just wouldn't know, that was the problem—but word got around about some, that they lied really well. He just wished it had gotten around about Jonas and Hawley before he'd been so gullible.

And hell if he or Cloud would come and eat out of Luke's hand. He was mad that he'd almost liked Luke. He wouldn't give in to Luke's tricks.

Cloud hadn't either, not really. Cloud had just gotten his candy and backed off, still mad, still free of debts. Cloud just always knew things. Cloud was smarter than people sometimes. Cloud wanted to kick the men to the moon, was all, end of problem.

<Kicking men,> Cloud thought, pleased with the thought, going along quite energetically—but he wanted Cloud to slow down on the road. They'd gone far enough they wouldn't hear him, no matter how loud he was.

Not far enough down the road to run into trouble, either, if there was anybody back there.

Jonas, damn him, knew he'd be following them tomorrow—Jonas had flatly said so. There was just one way up from here, he was on it, and they thought they could have him back any time they wanted to slow down and let him overtake them.

The hell with that, he thought. Jonas could get used to not getting what he wanted.

Cloud was quite happy with <going away from Jonas> and <looking for place to stop and be warm.> But when, on his thought of <daylight,> Cloud began thinking <going uphill in daylight, us alone, up through evergreens,> then Cloud formed a queasy sort of area <ahead of them, on high mountain, something bad, something shapeless.> Cloud switched his tail and laid back his ears at that, rethinking in Cloud's way, what to do about that <danger on the mountain.>

Cloud had gotten the rogue-image the same as all the riders and horses had, and, Danny well knew, gotten it from time to time from Jonas' bunch, but Cloud wasn't necessarily going to understand it the way a human would—a horse had to know all the sides of something before it didn't at any random moment surprise him; and the notion of the rogue they might have to deal with—now that Cloud had remembered that danger—still was going spooky-strange on Cloud. They said horses didn't think in future-time, but Cloud did. The rogue was just kind of a dark blurry spot in the future, dead center in that funny edge-of-vision blind spot horses had right in the middle and top of what humans saw, out of which most scary things came, because of the way a horse's eyes were set. There was a bad horse in that danger-spot—Cloud didn't like <shooting horses> but Cloud didn't like that shivery spot, either.

Cloud also knew (thanks to the dogged tracking of human thoughts, far less skittery than horses' thinking) about the three men they'd ridden out with being a problem and about men they'd smelled behind them who might become a problem. That was another hazy spot in Cloud's geography.

In his own way, Cloud even seemed to know about Stuart—a human mind could keep Cloud thinking on a subject and going over and over it and not forgetting any of the pieces of it: that was what Cloud got from human thoughts, the sheer dogged stubbornness to hold on and put pieces together. And Stuart had been a lot in various human thoughts on this trip.

So Cloud had begun, in the mostly-now way Cloud thought, to decide tonight was more complicated than yesterday—and Cloud wasn't, consequently, acting up on him. Cloud was being disturbingly sensible and doing exactly what he asked, in spite of the fact Cloud had a jittery feel to his slow gait.

<Looking for a sheltered spot. Looking for a place in the trees.>

<Finding Stuart up on the mountain. Riding with Stuart under evergreens.>

That ambition had danced at the edge of his mind for the last couple of days—he'd not dared think it when Jonas was belittling him all the time, but now that he was alone with Cloud he could haul things out of the dark spots of his probably immoral mind and at least look at them and try to sort out the stupid notions from the really stupid ones, and the embarrassing things and all the rest he'd die before he dragged out in front of Jonas.

That <Danny and Stuart> picture was just too stupid, too impossible, too indecent a wish, counting Stuart was grieving over a woman who was, in Stuart's mind, at least as much a wife to him as his mother was to his father.

More, he hadn't even thought about partnering yet—hadn't planned to find anybody until he was older. The juniors he could partner up with were all desperately busy looking out for themselves and handling the horse problem, which didn't seem to come easily even for kids born to the camp. It was just a hell of a lot of cheek for a junior even to think about Stuart taking him on under any circumstances.

But that day on the porch, with the rain flinging a gray sheet across all the world else, Stuart had trampled right over the defenses of a scared junior's inmost thoughts and learned more about him in five minutes than his parents or his brothers had figured out about him in a lifetime. Stuart had looked straight into him in one terrifying moment, calmed him down and maintained that calm contact through what remained at once the most devastating and the most exhilarating exchange of his life—Stuart had told him, one after the other, the answers to questions he didn't remotely know how to ask, questions he didn't even know he *should* ask, and in parting, Stuart had wished him luck, honestly wished him luck in his life and even given him a lead on the first real convoy job he'd ever had.

He hadn't had that feeling figured out when he'd started off with Jonas—that night, with the drink and the craziness running through the camp, he'd been so in awe of Jonas he'd believed he was dealing with Stuart again—but he'd gotten smarter fast on this trip. He'd felt somebody else trying to do with him unwilling what Stuart had done to him in that one shocked moment—the way Stuart had just blazed right on through his normal tongue-tied stammering, faced him at a level of need nobody in his whole life had ever gotten into—and not criticized, not carped at him, not lectured him, just seemed to take him as he was, in spite of his spilling the deepest, most embarrassing secrets of his life into Stuart's view.

Stuart had thrown advice back at him that had echoed right off his longings and drawn more and more of his secret hopes into the ambient. It gave him to this very moment a sense of disbelief when he reconstructed that hour or so—so vivid it was like meeting God, that was what it had felt like. So vivid it had scared him out of sleep for a week. So accepting of a kid's stupid ideas and stupid questions he couldn't believe it had ever really happened, and in a certain sense he'd been scared to death to go near Stuart again, because he didn't want to find out it wasn't real—or wasn't the way he remembered it. He hadn't gone back to him. He'd wanted to come back wiser and be able to *talk* to Stuart with some sense in his head.

Then Stuart had disappeared from camp—gone off wherever Stuart normally worked, the summer long.

But all Stuart's advice had been true. And he'd not even known the man was back in camp this fall until Stuart had brushed by him at the gate.

So, God, yes, he was going up that road. He didn't need Jonas for a preacher to tell him where right and wrong was. His father, never mind his faults, had taught him what was fair—<papa working late in the shop, papa fixing Koz's wheezing old sewing ma-

chine and not charging his time, because that machine was Koz's whole living, and they knew the old man couldn't afford it; papa saying, yeah, well, and not answering Sam's question about the bill.>

But mama knew. Damn right. Mama who kept the accounts, mama knew. <Mama saying, Shut up, Sam.>

Sam never *had* figured it out.

There were moments he was damned proud of his parents. They might all fight, except Sam. Papa might be sure he was going to hell, and they might be cheating, dishonest townsmen to rider eyes, but that was the riders' mistake, to lump everybody together. His father didn't ever cheat; and he didn't need moral lessons from a man who let his friend go off alone and hurt into the dark.

And he didn't need Luke's tricking Cloud into taking any damn candy, either, not at the price Luke wanted to sell it for. If he wanted to give Cloud candy, he *gave* it with no conditions, and he didn't want more than Cloud was willing to give him back.

He picked his spot among the trees at roadside—he rode in among the trees, the branches brushing him with the gentle force of Cloud's moving. He slid down as Cloud stopped, rubbed Cloud's nose with gloved fingers, then flung down his packs and set about cutting evergreen boughs to go under their blankets.

He didn't need Jonas to survive in the Wild, either. He was determined now to show them. He hadn't *had* to have their help. He'd turn up not when Jonas decided to collect a terrified kid but whenever *he* decided to, whenever they really, really needed to know what he could tell them, yes, he might be there, and he might tell them what they asked—if they minded their manners and dealt with him like a human being.

Or he'd find Stuart himself and ask Stuart whether he wanted to be found.

Then to hell with Stuart's not-quite-best friends in the entire universe. A winter in the high country, him and a senior rider, and (even if Stuart wasn't interested in another partner) he could learn from Stuart God-knew how many things. He had his gear, he had a clear notion where Stuart had gone, given they'd named Anveney and a reason Stuart would go there, and he had an absolutely clear idea where Stuart would ultimately go. The main road he and Cloud were on led near Tarmin to another ascent, up to a loop all around to the villages of Rogers Peak—he knew that for certain.

That was where Aby Dale had died, up on that high road, as the convoy was coming down. He even knew the names of most of the villages on the mountain; and he knew that there was another old road to Tarmin up directly from Anveney—an old, tight-turned road almost unused these days except by line-riders.

They'd passed the Anveney lowland turn-off when they'd gone only half a day from Shamesey gates, about the place where Cloud had thrown him and he'd hiked over the shoulder of the hill. But if Stuart had gone down that other way, and over to Anveney the way they thought, then there was no reason for Stuart to ride all the way back to pick up the road they were on—Stuart would get up to Tarmin the old way. Trucks might not use it now, but a horse could.

So he didn't need to wonder where Stuart was or where he'd come in and pick up the road to the accident—the Anveney-Tarmin road would join theirs before it went on up to the other villages on the High Loop of the Tarmin road. Stuart would go past Tarmin and up to that same road where the wreck was.

So he knew where he had to go.

And in his wildest dream, counting Hawley had made off with Stuart's money, Stuart could be real glad to see a kid with a gun and ammunition and winter supplies.

Favor paid. He'd like that. He really would. Stuart's respect of him—God, what wouldn't he do to feel he'd won that?

That occupied his thoughts as he made their bed of evergreen fronds, and as he settled down to rest in his wind-shadowed nook and Cloud settled down by him, providing him his body heat.

In Cloud's mind everything was right again, after all this <mad> and <not mad> at the men, and most of all the money-thing, which Cloud never had gotten straight, whether it was a kind of food or guns or whatever.

<Cattle,> was Cloud's assessment of Jonas and his crew, utter disgust.

But Danny didn't think of cattle—he thought instead of slinking predators. Shadow-horse still gave him the shivers.

And when, momentarily, he recalled Shadow's self-image, Cloud's skin twitched under his back as if something were crawling on it.

Fire warmed the den from the old fireplace they only used for the horses in the bitterest cold. Water was heating, and cloths went into it.

<White, white, white,> was the ambient, <white> so Tara couldn't see the den except through a veil, <white> so she burned her hands on the kettle and the hot rags, and bit her lip and kept at sponging Flicker down. "Rest," Vadim begged her. "Lie down at least, Tara, you've done enough. Let us take care of her."

But she wouldn't. She hardly heard until Chad seized her arm with painful force and made her face him. "You're contributing to it. Tara. *You're* falling into it, same as she is. Pull out."

Chad hit her across the ear hard enough to make her eyes water. Flicker threw her head and kicked out, lost her balance and all but had her feet go out from under her . . . Flicker was exhausted, hardly able to stand, and wouldn't lie down, wouldn't rest. Tara knew that. She was in the same condition, no different, legs shaking.

Rogue horse, they'd said: the marshal had had that warning in a phone call up from Shamesey—while she was on the trail.

"It's *you*," Chad said, and shook her and slammed her back into a post. "Sit *down*, Tara, *sit*! *You hear me?* You're upsetting her!"

She jerked away. "Her lungs will fill," she said, imaging a death she'd seen, long ago, on Darwin. She wasn't a horse-doctor, she didn't know how to get Flicker out of this and neither did Vadim or Chad or Mina, or, God save them, young Luisa. She just kept working, kept agitating, for fear that Flicker would give up. She warmed Flicker's legs and flanks and chest. She brought oil-fragrant smoke and made Flicker breathe as much as she could in the drafty den.

And Vadim and the rest, her own sometime partners Mina and Luisa no mean force in the attempt, kept visiting their own horses, imaging good things, imaging treats and food and the warm den, fearing contagion, but not letting that to the front of their minds.

They curried and rubbed and bathed and combed—with Vadim's and Chad's steady good sense, they dragged any thoughts of the snow back to the warm, safe dark. They dragged any reckoning of the howling wind back to the crackle of fire in the fireplace. They kept fighting for their sanity and their lives, not entertaining for two seconds running the fear and the anger that wailed and roiled out there in the storm, and not bolstering, either, the defense Flicker still raised . . . they wouldn't echo it, wouldn't stand for it, wouldn't give way to it.

Tara knew that they were keeping her sane as well, keeping out the storm, keeping away the white that threatened their collective reason. They were her friends, her refuge, her safety. She tried to tell Flicker that. She imaged their faces for Flicker. She imaged light and warmth and a den and horses Flicker knew. She began to fight for warmth against the white, to image <ice melting, fire on the ice, snowflakes melting on nighthorse back, sun coming up, bright, bright sun.>

It was all that they could do: outlast the storm and look for the sun to rise. The night and the howling white were all about them, a thunderous snow that echoed off the mountains and shook the nerves.

And the white remained a veil, and the dark was too ready to seep into the image, as if the sun would never, ever rise.

Chapter — ix —

SOMETHING *WANTED*, THAT WAS THE FEELING. SOMETHING CALLED and called, lonely and desperate, and it wasn't scary at all, just so terribly sad that Brionne ached for it in her heart. In her dream she stood in the middle of the woods where the snow had just fallen, the soft kind of snow that made soft sparkles under a golden sun, the kind that sat thick on the evergreen branches and fell in wet spattery clumps when the least breeze disturbed them. Otherwise the ground was all smooth rolling lumps and tiny hills, a beautiful, shining surface that no track had yet disturbed, since only she had come there.

In her dream she stood looking toward the dawn, where gold and rose sifted through the evergreens. She stood knowing that she was the only person in the wide world, herself, Brionne, the blacksmiths' daughter, who could see this sight and hear the singing presence that made all the forest magical.

In her dream a nighthorse came out of the woods and across that smooth, gold-glistening snow, a black horse with a midnight mane that all but floated on the dawn winds, a tail that drifted like a cloud of blackest smoke. The horse made the only other tracks in the world. Its neck arched as it regarded her with a wary eye, its mane and its night-black coat glistening with the golden light.

It called to her aloud with that soft, strange sound a nighthorse could make when it chose. It called to her in the silence with unbearable longing, with all the power of a nighthorse mind.

She *wasn't* just the blacksmiths' daughter. She knew that. She instinctively hated the smoke and the soot that lived about her parents' shop and her parents' house and about her brothers. She *knew* that someday somebody magical would come and lift her out of the ordinary and workaday. She had an artist's hands, too fine ever to wield a hammer, her father said. She had fair skin, and a face that—her mother said it—would break hearts, and she should never scar it with the sparks from the anvil, or let the soot get into her skin.

Papa called her their own angel, pretty and fragile, but gifted, everyone said so. Mama said her face, if she took care of it, could be her fortune, and theirs, and she'd go down to the valley to marry and live with a rich merchant, in a fine carpeted house with linen closets and a fine brass-grilled furnace, the sort of house Tarmin village only heard about.

But most of all she knew . . . she *knew* in her heart she wasn't like the rest of Tarmin village. She was never meant for the soot and smoke of her family's trade that was irrevocably to her the preachers' very hellfire.

Sometimes she'd dreamed that the ships from the stars would come back, that they'd look over all Tarmin village, and take just her, because she was special, and the star-folk would see it.

She talked to the little, harmless creatures that came at forest edge, a small wickedness, by what the preachers said, but she'd learned she could hear them. *She* could hear them, and her two older brothers couldn't—it was her special gift, and she kept it secret. She tamed them to her hand. She had names for them all and fed them with scraps, and they fought with the cat, dreadful squalling at night, but the cat always won.

And sometimes she went to the rider camp and talked to the riders, who admitted to her how, for reasons no one knew, sometimes horses came for people who weren't born riders.

So maybe the ships wouldn't come—she was older and wiser now, all of thirteen. The ships hadn't come, not just in her thirteen years, but in hundreds of years, and the preachers said they never would, that the wickedness of humanity had surely destroyed the star-folk. But if that was so, there were the horses.

The riders' horses whispered secrets to her. The wild things ate from her hand. She clung to that gift of hers as something of promise, that if there weren't to be ships (which she began to decide now was, after all, unlikely) still—*something* had to account for the feeling of difference she had, *something* had to come of her special gifts. *Something* had to offer her an escape from the humdrum of Tarmin village. And escape that meant going down to some strange town in the valley was no good, if she couldn't have her mother and her father and the neighbors *see* her fine things.

So in her dream of dreams the escape should come to *her*, the very way the wild things came. It was a sign, she decided, the sort that the preachers talked about, and it wasn't wicked, her talking to wild things, it was never the wicked wild creatures she talked to, it was only the pure little nibblers at grain and the little teases that skipped about at forest edge: they weren't what the preachers called creatures of lust and blood. They didn't think such thoughts.

Most of all, the nighthorses ate from her hands, and she could image to them in her mind, and hear them, too: she imaged to them that they should tell all the wild nighthorses they saw, and particularly the stallion of the herds, that there was a very deserving rider to find in Tarmin village.

Because that was her dream. Some wild one would come searching for her, a wild horse, maybe the king horse, more beautiful than any horse had ever been, and that wild horse would know immediately that she had qualities no one in town, no one even among the riders remotely imagined she had. Neither of her brothers, and no Tarmin rider, not her mother or her father, no one in all the world knew what she imagined and what she imaged, otherwise—because she told secrets to the horses in her mind, the way the riders did. She saw their images from farther away than her brothers, or anyone, and she didn't run away scared the way they did just of the shallow ideas they could pick up: she could *talk* to the riders' horses—she could talk even to strangers' horses that came with the truck convoys. Oh, the riders who didn't know her were always anxious about her walking about inside their gates, but she immediately made friends with the horses. She brought them sugar-treats and sat and talked for hours to them in the way horses liked humans to talk. They imaged her in their minds as <sun-hair> and <sugar> because they loved her.

And in this dream she had, that wild horse came, not an ordinary horse, like Flicker and the others that served the riders, but the most beautiful, the most special horse came treading softly over the snow, eyeing her sidelong from under its long forelock, and saying its secret name in her mind, which she could just almost hear. . . .

But she waked, for no reason, with that Name still just echoing at the edge of her sight.

It wasn't just a dream. It wasn't. She lay awake in her parents' house in which you could always smell the soot and the stench of hot iron, and even with her eyes open she could feel a strange, wild stirring in her mind. She lay still, afraid that the dream would escape her, and she wanted very much to hold the textures of it, the feeling of it in her heart.

The vividness of it stayed a long, long time. She could shut her eyes and have it back, that place, that moment, that vision.

She hugged the feeling to her, knowing now it was real, undoubtedly outside the walls, one of the wild ones. She heard it calling and calling to her.

The preacher man said if she said her prayers every night God wouldn't let the beasts talk to her, and she wouldn't have to worry about anything in the world if God was taking care of her. The preacher man said she could tell God if she was afraid and God would blast the beasts that wanted to talk to her.

But if she willfully talked to the beasts, they told her in church, if she did begin to seek them out, she'd surely go to hell.

But the smell of hell was in papa's forge, and the substance of her heart's desires were out there, with the snow, the beautiful clean snow.

Mama certainly wasn't going to be happy if she ran away to become a rider. Mama had much rather she marry a rich lowland merchant. Mama would be worried about her ruining her skin and her hands.

Papa would call her his pretty angel and ask the traveling preachers to pray for her soul and hope for the horse to run away—but she grew so willful she knew she'd pray against papa, because she wanted to be a rider, and papa couldn't stop her from anything she wanted, he never had. She'd do as she pleased, and mama would be mad and papa would be worried, but in the end she'd have her way, and they'd accept her—or if they stayed mad, she'd run away for good and not come back except occasionally, remote and grand in her fringed leathers, with the look of distant places about her.

And she'd talk to mama and papa if they were nice, but her brothers and their friends would stare daggers at her and she'd look right back and scare them with the images she could send. The neighbors would all be envious about the money she would make. And the Tarmin riders who said stay away from the horses, they'd respect her, they'd be sorry they'd ever scolded her, and *her* horse would be finer than theirs, the convoy bosses would pick *her* because she'd look better than all the rest, and she'd have a reputation far and wide over the mountains—go with Brionne, they'd say, Brionne's the best. She'd ride out the gates of Tarmin camp with the convoys and she'd wear a knife with a white shell handle like one she'd seen, with a beaded fringed jacket, black as her horse, and bright blue beads: she liked blue beads—and it was all *true*, it was all possible, because a wild one had come, exactly the way she'd known it would.

She couldn't get up yet. It was still dark between the shutters and mama would wake up instantly if she heard her moving about. So she lay abed savoring the feeling and the planning—she lay listening for a long time, longing for daylight to shine through the seam of the shutters, so she could go out and look for the horse she knew was waiting for her—oh, it *couldn't* go away with the dawn. It *had* to wait.

Mama and papa wouldn't just let her go. But mama and papa wouldn't of course hear the horse that was calling so loudly out there, and if they heard it they would never suspect it came for their daughter. Her brothers were a little cleverer, mostly because they spied on her all the time, and they'd surely tell, so she couldn't let on she was going anywhere special—most of all she couldn't let on she was excited, even if she could hardly contain it. She'd say she was going to the shop, that was all, and if she was clever and fast, they wouldn't know when she slipped away from them.

It was forever until that first faint light came.

Then, impatient, her breath hissing in the cold of her room, she slipped out from the covers, dressed quickly in warm ordinary clothes, struggled into two of everything, one too small and one a little too large, watching in the mirror so she didn't look as bundled up as she knew she needed to be to face the outside cold.

And, secretly dressed for blizzards, she sweltered through breakfast in the crowded, overheated kitchen, where mama had been baking biscuits: it was bacon and of course the biscuits, and she saved both pieces of bacon and stole a couple of whole biscuits for the horses—some of it, she thought then, hugging the thought to her . . . for *her* horse. She took two more, when nobody was looking, because she might be out all night.

"Brionne! Done your lessons?" mama asked when she snatched her new red coat and her scarf and hat to follow papa out the door.

She stopped in the clutter of boys and noisy footsteps. She was momentarily at a loss. Mama insisted *she* learn accounts and excused her brothers to be rowdy. And mama *couldn't* keep her in. Not today.

"I'll have it all this afternoon," she said, very quickly, and was fast enough to shut the door so that she didn't hear mama's scolding; and, not hearing, of course wasn't obliged to do what mama wanted.

But it was not to papa's forge she was bound, putting on her hat and her coat while she hurried in her brothers' wake through the new-fallen snow. She veered out of their track at the corner of the house, and, still buttoning buttons, went running a zigzag course down the tracked public walk, then across the street and along the front of the bakery.

She couldn't hear the horse calling now, but the wild ones came mostly at night. They gave a village bad dreams; but the people they favored to hear them clearly would begin to waste away with longing to go after them, that was what all the stories said. Even people who were afraid of them had to go out to them when the Calling came, and if they didn't find their horse soon, they might perish in the snow and the cold.

But she wasn't afraid. She'd waited for her Calling. She welcomed it with all her heart.

She turned the corner at the baker's, where the water tanks were, and ran from there to the Little Gate, which let riders come from the camp into the town, though on purpose it was too small to let the horses pass it.

The Little Gate had no lock, only a pull-latch, and she came and went there as she pleased, always a little careful that the watchman down at the big main gate didn't look this way and see her, because he'd surely take her straight to her parents.

But Tuck at the main gate would be having his breakfast, she was confident of that, besides that the Little Gate wasn't really Tuck's business at all, least of all one to make him come out in the morning cold. She slid the latch aside, slipped over to the rider camp, and pulled the gate silently to behind her.

Once when she was seven the other kids had dared her to slip through the Little Gate. She'd told them she was scared, and of course never let on to them the secret that she'd done it already a hundred times. She'd never once let on that she could talk to the horses, either, because if she did, then her brothers would have told their parents everything she did forever. Then they'd have had the preacher to pray over her, and they'd have watched her *ever* so much closer.

Now that she was older, her parents knew that she occasionally went to the camp and that occasionally she talked to the riders, especially when her father had some work to do and she delivered some message to or from, as she loved to do.

But her mother lectured her severely about rider men and immoral thoughts, which embarrassed her, and would have mortified her if the riders had ever, ever heard her mother talk like that. Riders weren't at all the way mama said. They never hurt her nor even said an indelicate word nor thought an indelicate thought in her presence. They treated her like their sister. They talked far nicer than her brothers, and the men especially would talk to her and tell her stories.

Which made the women, like Tara and Mina, mad. They were probably jealous, or at least they protected what they had, namely the men, from her influence. She didn't mind. She took it for a kind of compliment that they were so worried. And Vadim and Chad were the handsomest men she knew, just ever so nice to watch, and now—

Right now she most wanted to find Vadim. He was usually up and about early, and she knew Barry and Llew and Tara were away working on the road: she always knew what went on in the camp.

But she was equally sure that Vadim and Chad and Mina and Luisa were in camp, and with any reasonable luck, Vadim or Chad might be outside working, so she wouldn't have to deal with Mina.

She wanted to ask Vadim if they'd heard anything last night. She was bubbling over with excitement about her dream, and she *knew*, she just knew that he'd be happy for her and tell her if there were any secret things she should do or say to call the wild one in.

If just Vadim and Chad were there, she could ask their advice and know they'd listen and tell her what to do, whether her horse was waiting out beyond the walls and she should go to it, or whether her horse might have gone away by now. She might have to wait until night, and she might have to stay in the rider camp—they might hide her, so her parents couldn't keep her in.

Because now she belonged—and as she came toward the den, she tried to feel what the riders called the ambient: that meant the images that were going on. But she could only get an impression of snow, and of course snow was the weather—it was snow lying everywhere, snow thick on the roofs, a blanket of almost untracked white across the yard from the shelter to the horse den this morning, and the sun coming up in a golden glow above the palisade wall—so, so like her dream.

By the tracks she expected just Vadim, but, just by something odd in the ambient, perhaps by her newly quickened senses, she suspected something strange even before she slipped into the entry of the horse den—walking carefully, carefully between the shoulder-level entry walls, because they'd cautioned her about startling the horses.

She was astonished and dismayed to see Tara back, Tara, looking exhausted, with her arm over Flicker's back, and Chad and Luisa sleeping in a stall, on pallets on the wood-chip bedding the horses used.

Odd, she thought. It was very odd, them sleeping in the den. She was completely unprepared for Tara to glare at her out of the deep shadow and equally unprepared for a sudden wash from somewhere across her vision, like a veil of blinding white.

"What in hell are you doing here?" Tara snapped out of that whiteness.

Brionne was so shocked she stood stark still until Tara and dark flashed back on her.

"Get out, go home. Dammit, *get out of here*!"

Flicker had waked up, and again all Brionne saw for the instant was <snow.> She couldn't orient herself in the world. She couldn't find a backward step. She was trying to do what she was told, and felt behind her to see whether there was a post in the way. She only saw <dark> fighting with the <white> imaging, she saw Vadim through the <white,> and the other horses . . . then Chad and Luisa and gloomy, sullen Mina.

"Flicker's sick," Vadim said. The haze of white was thick and cold, very much like snowfall. But where Vadim stood was dark, and solid ground. "This isn't a good place for kids right now. Do what she says, go on home."

"I brought biscuits and some bacon." She decided to be generous. It was important to her to have the riders like her. Even Tara. "Would Flicker like it?"

"No," Flicker's rider said sharply. Tara was purely jealous, Brionne thought angrily; that was why Tara was mad. Tara was always stand-offish, and protective of Flicker—and of Vadim and Chad, too. She'd always had an inkling there was something going on between Tara and Vadim and his partner which her mother would call very immoral, and Vadim and Chad both hung about with Mina and Luisa, too—she suspected things she felt very uneasy about in the ways of the camp.

But Flicker did truly look not to be well, and the feeling in the air ran up and down Brionne's nerves—so maybe Tara was just mad and distracted and yelling at everybody. Brionne backed away, bumped a post and felt her way around it.

"Go home, Brionne," Chad said gently. "It's not a good time to be here."

She was hurt, all the same.

Angry. It was all Flicker in their attention. They were supposed to be so sensitive to the horses, and they didn't even know that she had special news, they didn't know why she'd come—

But then, maybe Flicker was occupying all their attention. They looked as if they'd not gotten much sleep last night. Even Vadim seemed cross with her. It was a dreadful disappointment.

So she retreated outside into the dawn and scuffed her way across the snow-carpeted yard, wondering what she was to do if she didn't have their help.

And what if, because Flicker happened to be sick and the riders were being surly and Tara was jealous of her, her horse got discouraged and heard Tara's nasty temper and didn't come back? It was Tara who was against her: she knew it was Tara's fault. Tara was always telling her get out and leave the horses alone, and she wouldn't even put it past Tara to pretend Flicker was sick just so she could get everybody's attention on *her*.

Clearly Tara was having things her way right now. The riders were all out there in the horse den or out on the road fixing washouts, and Tara had the center of attention right now in camp.

But just then, just when she was thinking that, she felt that strange prickly feeling the horses sometimes made on your skin when they were trying to get your attention.

Maybe, she thought, feeling that strangeness running up and down her arms, maybe it's still out there.

Maybe it didn't go away last night.

Maybe it's still waiting.

And nobody at all guarded the main rider gate, that, with a simple inside drop-latch, led to the outside and the snow.

* * *

<Horses with riders, daylight on the road.>

Danny woke with that vivid impression, different from a dream, as Cloud moved to gain his feet. He scrambled to his feet, too, struggling with the blanket and the springy mat of evergreens under them.

Cloud didn't recognize the horses—didn't know who he heard, but Danny felt direction as Cloud did, and looked toward the road beyond the screen of evergreens.

The Westmans were in the other direction, and the riders coming from the downhill of the road were near enough to have waked Cloud—nighthorses wouldn't miss them in the ambient if they got any closer at all: the group of horses was louder in the ambient than one horse was, but there was no way they could stay hidden as those riders went past, and they had a steep wooded hill at their backs, a sheer drop across the road . . .

<Memory of the riders at dusk, smell-shapes spooking them lower down the mountain. Men following us up the road.>

Cloud bet on <us running,> but <guns,> Danny thought then, and patted Cloud's shoulder, because Cloud was on the edge of spooking out into the open to argue with the intruders. <Guns!> Danny insisted, frantic with apprehension, and took a firm grip on Cloud's mane, a grip which unexpectedly he needed, because Cloud took that hold for him mounting up, and ducked into it and bolted for the road.

"Cloud!" Danny gasped, trying to stop him, but Cloud plowed ahead.

Danny's feet were sliding. He was about to lose Cloud. He took a bounce on the uneven, root-crossed ground and made it to Cloud's back in a single move, to his own astonishment, as Cloud burst through the buffeting screen of branches and onto the roadway, uphill.

He was leaving his blanket and all his baggage behind. He'd at least slept with his gun, scared of the isolation, but he couldn't stop; he clung desperately as Cloud headed uphill, with the sheer drop off the road on their right hand. He tried to get Cloud to go <off the road, into the woods,> thinking that he could take the steep, wooded way over the rise of the hill and come down again after the oncoming trouble had passed them.

Cloud was willing. Cloud bolted through a battering of evergreen branches, took the uncertain footing of laddered roots and rock, and wove among the trees, headed aslant up the rise.

A shot splintered bark off a trunk beside them: Cloud veered uphill, and he slewed entirely off Cloud's back on the downhill side, still hanging onto Cloud's mane, trying to get footing to swing up again.

"You!" somebody yelled, and he looked downslope as Cloud backed and tried to maneuver on the hill. A man came riding up on him, the horse imaging <gun firing.> Danny dragged his pistol out of its holster, maintaining his grip on a fistful of mane on a horse that didn't know which direction to face.

"Hold it, hold it!" the other rider said. "No need." But that rider had a pistol in hand, aimed generally toward him and Cloud. "Just come back here. Need a word with you."

He wasn't sure. Maybe the man had simply been trying to get his attention after he spooked—but shooting at people wasn't how he wanted a word with them. The man wasn't alone. Another rode up through the woods, weaving among the trees.

He was still on foot and downhill from Cloud, where he couldn't mount up without maneuvering. <Cloud standing,> Danny imaged desperately. Riders wouldn't ever shoot a horse except as an absolutely last resort, he believed that, but he'd believed in Jonas yesterday morning. Now he stood with a sweaty fistful of Cloud's mane, willing Cloud not to spook, his knees quaking under him.

That man came up with the first. He'd thought he might have detected a south-hills, Hallanslake accent, and he saw now for certain it was Ancel Harper. Harper was holding a pistol aimed at him while one more rider was closing in.

He was scared half to death. He'd never in his life dealt with a gun aimed at him. He saw very clearly now that it wasn't just a misunderstanding, and he didn't want to face these three men trembling like a fool kid, but he didn't know what to do about his situation, he didn't know what he should have done to escape it, and Cloud didn't know, either. Guns had shot at Cloud before, but

Cloud hadn't had a rider who fell off, the last time guns had fired at him, and nobody had wanted Cloud to come toward them under that circumstance, either, the way these men wanted him to do. Cloud was mad, and confused, and the ambient was thick with nighthorse threats, the Hallanslake horses' and Cloud's.

"So what do you want?" Danny asked, trying to sound madder and more confident than he was scared—but it didn't work at all. His voice wobbled.

"Sitting out here all alone," Harper said, and the gun in Harper's hand never wavered. "No place for a kid. Where are the Westmans?"

"I don't know. Tell the truth, I don't care. I'm tired of being bossed."

"Are you?" Harper said flatly.

"I'm tired of people acting crazy. What's the matter with everybody, anyway?" He managed high indignation, and told himself that Harper wasn't 'sir.' Nobody who pointed guns at him was ever voluntarily 'sir.' He made up his mind to that right then, as scared as he was.

"Friend of Stuart's, are you?"

"No." He managed to be surprised *and* mad. "I know the man, that's all. I never dealt with him."

"Not what I picked up in Meeting. Not what anybody in Shamesey camp picked up. What's your name, kid?"

"Dan—" He almost said Danny. "Dan Fisher. Yours is Harper."

"We know each other?"

"Same place as you know me." Thoroughly bad odds, Danny thought. He fell back on his bad-boy days, his town days, old friends and a habitual insolence to seniors—before papa had jerked him sideways. "I've got no personal stake in this. Jonas tried to hire me, but he didn't pay me and I got tired of being told when to breathe. I'm going home."

Harper slid his pistol back into the holster, threw a leg over and slipped easily down from his horse's back. "So he hired you, did he? For what?"

You didn't lie, near a horse. "I heard Stuart the night they were shooting. Jonas thought I could hear him loud enough on the trail to help out. I couldn't. So I left."

"Maybe you'd like to travel with us."

"You paying?"

"Yeah," Harper said. "Your neck, if you follow orders. And maybe a junior's share of the bounty, if ever happens they put one on the rogue. Not unlikely they will. So you could go back with pocket money."

What was smart to do? Say go to hell, to three borderers with guns? Danny shoved his hands in his belt. "I keep my gun, collect my gear back there . . . yeah, I'll go for a junior's share."

"Gun's not part of it," Harper said. "Kid like you, a cannon like that? You ever fired that thing?"

"I'm not going up there with no gun!"

"Kid, you haven't figured it yet. You're going up there stark naked if you want to argue with us, but you are going. No gun. You want a strip search while we're at it? Or you want to hand the gun over? You don't need it. Blow you right off your horse, the kick it's got. Guy like Watt, here, that's his size gun."

The man named Watt grinned. Big as a boulder and built like one. Horse as big as any Danny had ever seen.

And Cloud thought <fight.>

Danny snatched a handful of Cloud's mane, patted his shoulder, bodily pressing against him for a moment, imaging <gun in holster, man talking with Danny,> trying the forced calm-down from Jonas he'd resented yesterday. <Quiet water,> he insisted, sweating, trying to lower the force in the ambient. <Clouds reflecting in water.>

Cloud's ears were flat to his skull.

"Yeah," Danny said quietly, quickly, and started unbuckling the gun before Cloud got himself killed. "I've got my gear and supplies back there." He concentrated on the quiet. It kept his mind busy, kept his knees from shaking and wobbling. He imaged his camp downhill. Cloud nipped at his knee, caught a lipful of leather, still wanting <fight> and arguing about it.

But he let the gun and holster fall to the ground.

Harper motioned back the way they'd come. "Quig, get his stuff."

"Yeah," the other man said, and turned his horse about on the hill and went after the stuff while the big guy, Watt, got off and collected the gun he'd dropped.

In the deepest well of his thoughts he was sorry now he hadn't stuck tight to Jonas and said yes, sir, no matter what. Harper left no doubt who gave the orders with this bunch, and who was meaner, or smarter, or whatever it took to get that obedience out of men both bigger and stronger than Harper was.

"Get on your horse," Harper said, and Danny turned Cloud around on the hill to put his preferred side uphill.

Cloud moved as he was about to get up.

"Cloud!" he hissed, scared, because he wasn't all that steady in his knees, and wasn't sure his nerves weren't most of the reason for the upset he felt in Cloud. "Stand still, all right? Just stand still."

Cloud's ears were still flat. <Bite,> Cloud imaged, a shivery, angry sort of image, and Danny took a double fistful of mane, wanting him quiet, quiet, quiet. Please God. <Going to mountains. Harper and these men and us going to mountains up the road.>

He made it onto Cloud's back, and Harper and the others led the way to the site downhill, where the man called Quig was putting his blanket rolls together and gathering up his supplies.

They stopped there. Quig handed him up his packets and his blankets. He sat there between Watt and Harper until Quig had finished and gotten back on his horse.

Harper brushed close to him. "You ride alongside me, hear?"

Cloud didn't want be close to Harper or his horse, Cloud was consistently thinking <bite,> but Danny gave Cloud a mild kick to get him moving. <Quiet water,> he thought. The kick made Cloud mad. Everything did. But they went out into the morning sun and onto the road.

Following Jonas and company.

Not on Stuart's trail, he was relieved to think, Stuart having gone—

Shit! he thought, remembering the look of that town—heart sinking.

" . . . Anveney, is it?" Harper asked him.

"Yeah, well, that's what Jonas Westman thinks. That's all I know."

"Why does Westman think that?"

Try not to think of something. <Hawley patting his pocket, image of <money.>

He truly didn't know what more he could do to foul things up.

Chapter

— X —

In the busy days of summer, before harvest and after spring and open market, riders took hires as many as they could and went wherever along the roads their commissions took them, traveling with steady partners if they could, but if that wasn't possible, and a convoy had only so many berths, you took the job, that was all—because you always had a winter to get through, three dead-white months when nothing moved, when only the juniors made any money at all, and that was paltry change. If you were a high country rider, you made very good money during the summer itself, often the highest paying convoy right at the risky edge of autumn, when some last moment situation or late-realized shortage mandated that goods move somewhere fast.

The reliable riders got those offers—the shippers gave priority to the riders who gave *them* priority over other shippers, and if you had such a regular hire, depend on it—rather than risk losing a customer, you arranged a place to meet your partner for wintering-over, and you satisfied that special customer. Aby and he had end-season requests enough, usually separately, and they'd always arranged a place . . .

The MacFarlane, most times. He wished to God Aby had agreed to the MacFarlane with him this year, which would have put Aby far to the south instead of on that road.

But one of those last-moment commissions had come through, and as he guessed it, the high-pay end of it had been from Anveney *up* to Tarmin and the mining and logging towns.

Which meant Aby must have gotten a call from her Anveney shipper.

He still wanted to talk to that man, once he'd settled his own essential business on the mountain.

Anveney was a town riders avoided if they could. The spur over to Anveney was not so well-maintained since the townsman ambient had gotten tense between Shamesey and Anveney districts. Cargo still went, but the two districts quarreled about everything including responsibility for road maintenance, and the area where each claimed it was the other's responsibility held potholes big enough to take a truck tire.

Anveney was northernmost of the towns—and the branch road out of Anveney east could take you downland and east to Carlisle, on the Inland Sea, if you stayed with it long enough, a trek through tedious days of barren flat and sandy ground, fit to make you and your horse see mirages. And once he'd finished his business, the Anveney west road was a way up to Tarmin, at least for riders in a hurry—not the way Jonas had come down, he was sure: modern trucks couldn't take the steep grade.

What had come into Shamesey in that convoy with Jonas had been mostly lumber, logical enough for a cargo coming down from Tarmin district on the main road. Then the Anveney-based trucks and (the riders being short-handed) probably the whole convoy would have detoured over to Anveney (you *never*, for any reason, left trucks sitting unprotected in the Wild) before taking the Anveney spur road home to Shamesey: fuel was expensive, but it cost less than trucks.

Anveney copper sheet and Shamesey flour and beans and canned goods had undoubtedly been the upbound load, a before-winter shipment of supplies or equipment, on which Tarmin had elected to defray cost by shipping lumber down to Anveney and Shamesey. He knew the reasons and the directions things moved at the edge of winter. His job was to know; and he reckoned possibilities now in scatter-witted preoccupation, reconstructing without overmuch difficulty the reason Aby had been with Hawley and Jonas. The Westmans came north only rarely, but not so improbably: jobs had been slow in the south hills, a lot of rain this summer, as he well knew, and Aby was a good bet to be in this district come fall; they'd have come to ask her to get them hire. Which she could do: better to convoy with riders you knew than ones the truckers picked, and Aby was an experienced senior guide whose recommendation counted.

She wouldn't, he decided, have anticipated any danger yet in the weather: Aby was a good weather-doctor, rarely missed a prediction. She'd have held her favorite client up for a hefty fee, having a better knack than some for making a run sound risky (no lie, if your chief guide made mistakes with the weather) for making herself sound knowledgeable (she was) and for generally convincing the shipper that they'd lose the best rider in the region if they didn't keep Aby Dale satisfied with her situation. In part what they paid for was the expertise Aby had to say no if she didn't like the feel of it and the guts she had to go ahead if she knew she could make it.

You only needed to be wrong once. And nobody could have predicted what had happened.

But damn the discussion they'd had at mid-summer, a discussion that had drifted to the dancing and the music and the electric lights of Shamesey camp. *She* liked it. She'd gotten snowed in last winter and left him stranded in Shamesey. She'd wanted him to come back north two winters running to the damn town, which was smoky, overcrowded, with an ambient that never let you rest. She called it excitement. He called it enough to give you a headache. He'd been stuck there *last* lonely winter waiting for her while she was snowed in.

But she wanted it. Wanted—

His rebel mind suddenly, as it would, conjured corpses.

And worse, worse, the *feeling*, the going-apart, the lost, dreadful disintegration that occupied that place high on the road, where the evergreens came close to the unstable ground of that bad turn, and the outward view was empty air.

He shook. He pressed his hand against his eyes, blotting out the light around him. He remembered Aby living, Aby on Moon, blithe and beautiful, coming down the road in the safe lowlands.

Burn shivered under him, ripple of skin up his shoulders. Whuff of confusion. <Aby dead,> Burn imaged, vivid, brutal, *necessary* question.

He confused Burn, and Burn dragged him back to what was. Burn couldn't help it—and he couldn't. He'd dragged Burn into thinking Aby might be waiting there, when Burn knew Aby was dead, and what was Burn to think?

That was one difference between horse-mind and human: once Burn had realized death, regretted it, disposed of the matter, Burn wouldn't go raking it over and over at the turn of a breeze. And where did what-wasn't-real lead a horse or a rider, anyway?

He had to get the thing that had killed Aby. *Had* to get it. It didn't know any better than it did, its story was probably as sad as Aby's, but it had destroyed Aby's life and gotten a piece of his he couldn't get back from it until he settled the question. For hours at a time he'd be all right, and then for a few minutes confusion would close in on him so he couldn't breathe, and he'd lose his thoughts between past and present in a way Burn couldn't handle.

<Maybe death, maybe life> was one thing. <When winter comes> was one thing. <When Aby's alive> couldn't make sense at all.

<Dead,> he imaged now to Burn, hurt as it did, in order to straighten the matter out and assure Burn the truth he remembered was so.

And, equally confused, once in an hour he might think, To hell with it, ride south and forget it. You can't bring back the dead. Aby won most times; she didn't, once; she lost, is all. Fall of the dice. The riders up at Tarmin can handle their own trouble.

Then something would nag him saying, But all those people up there—riders not necessarily aware what's moved in, unless the thing's gotten noisier in the ambient. More deaths, after it got away with Aby's.

And the way he understood the affliction, rogues didn't *always* make a lot of noise. Some were very quiet. Very canny. A mountain village, unlike a lowland town, had only a few riders, and they'd have to divide themselves between hunting the horse and defending the village.

But: Damn stupid villagers, he'd think then, and hate them all; and ask himself who cared, or why he should care if they couldn't take care of themselves. If they couldn't take care of themselves they had no business living where they did and least of all crossing *his* path. He wasn't a town rider. He stayed generally to the High Wild, dealt with the convoys, got their precious lumber and fuel oil to them, and minded his own business otherwise. He'd had a bullet burn across his skin, thanks to townsmen.

And then, on a breath, the painful lump in his throat would come back, a stinging in his eyes, a desire, villagers or no villagers at stake, to blow that thing to bloody hell.

The average was anger, and hurt, which couldn't lead him to sit safe and secure down in Malvey, ignoring the situation, even if at moments he wanted to.

It didn't lead him straight up to Tarmin bare-handed, mad, and stupid, either. It led him steadily toward Anveney, because he needed a gun. If he could reach their money at the bank in Anveney, he couldn't think of a better use for what he and Aby had saved for the winter than to buy something to blow so many large-caliber holes in that thing daylight shone through.

Give it a chance at him, the best bait and somehow, in his mind, justice in the offering.

Give it the one chance that thing would have had at him if he'd been with Aby the time she most needed him—and give *him* the chance *he* would have had if he'd been there, kill or be killed. Jonas had been all prudence. Get the convoy down, leave the rider for the scavengers. No damn *way* he would have left Aby lying at the foot of that slide and not gone down after her, convoy or no convoy; and hell if he wouldn't have gone into the woods after that thing. Hawley he'd have thought would have had the loyalty to her to leave a safe, well-armed, downward-bound convoy, solo, to track Aby's killer down. He hadn't done it. He'd run. Aby had died with nobody near her with the guts to have gone after her killer.

Nighthorses caught the contagion of anger very readily, and believed human images very easily. Sometimes Burn likewise wanted to go <south> and forget it, too, in search of <females.> But more and more as the hours passed and they came steadily northward toward Anveney, Burn's images became <the mountains in the west, and the high forest gone dark and dangerous>—that was Burn's image for what Burn himself didn't like to shape in his thoughts.

<Gun,> Burn thought now, at least Burn's image of a gun: <flash of fire, smell of smoke.> Burn was very much in favor of guns when they were on Burn's side of an argument, Burn whose name was <fire> and <dark,> and whose temper climbed to the top of the ambient so, so quickly. If Burn's rider wanted to kill something, then Burn was ready. Burn would enjoy a hunt.

But <gun> was all that could settle a rogue, a good rifle best of all. And if one had to go shopping for death, Anveney was a fit place for it—any caliber, any proof, any strength, in Anveney of the poison pools and the poisoned earth.

And when they reached the cut-off where a horse-trail went west to the rider-stone that sat at the cross-country crossroads, Guil slid down and wished Burn gone to that stone, a route that wouldn't take him into Anveney itself.

<Guil walking. Burn going overland. Meeting on the road to the mountains. Big rider-stone. Marks like so.>

Burn heard his <stone> just fine—and imaged instead <bad-smelling smoke,> and <machines> and <dead cattle. Dead grass. Dead trees. Dead willy-wisps. Guil and Burn walking on road to mountains side by side.>

<Gun in Anveney,> Guil reminded him, and added: <bacon,> followed by <Burn going on the road alone, Burn waiting at the stone.>

Burn snorted and ambled off the road, nosing the grass without eating it. Burn left no doubt. Burn didn't think there were pigs in Anveney.

<Trucks in town,> Guil argued. <Bringing pigs. Bacon. Guns.

Sides and sides of bacon. Hams. Guil bringing packages to Burn at the stone.>

<Poison blue pools,> Burn remembered, not quite out of range. <Dead grass.> Burn had seen the zone around Anveney once, and that was enough.

<Us meeting at stone,> Guil insisted. "Go, Burn, dammit. Get moving. Don't give me trouble. I don't want you breathing the stuff."

Burn sulked off a distance, in no hurry. But Burn wouldn't at all like it once Burn had to smell the smoke.

Burn's rider, on the other hand, had to breathe the smell from the moment he walked over the rise and caught the wind.

Burn's rider had to look on a barren land, the smokestacks and the ruin they made, a dusty, barren land oppressive to any sane man's heart, but clearly some liked it that way.

And utterly silent—a silence that came of leaving not only Burn's range, but leaving the range of every living creature, because nothing flourished in this land of metal-laden air and dying grass. Walking down the last grassy hill was like walking down into a lake of silence, no easier to tolerate because he'd been here twice before. He experienced the same increasing desolation, the same little catch of breath when he'd had enough and wanted to go back.

No holding of breath would stop the stench or bring the world-sense back. No life. Nothing to hear—not the little creatures of the world that talked constantly to him and Burn; not the noise of a camp, the constant presence-sense that he was used to, in camp and outside one.

It didn't exist here.

Six huge smokestacks sat on the shoulder of a low hill and a huge town, rivalling Shamesey's size, sprawled off onto other hills—with little hillocks of tailings around the pits that surrounded Anveney, out across a barren landscape as far as the horizon.

Lakes of incredible poison hues. Smokestacks that lifted the worst and deadliest of the airborne ash above the town, so they said—but only humans, it seemed, could live near those tailings piles, or the run-off basins where the water collected in those pools:

white and brilliant blue and bright green, beautiful, if you didn't know you were looking at death.

Copper-mining, chemical-making . . . if it was poison and other towns wouldn't touch it, Anveney would. Let the smoke blow and the water run and seep into the river and run to the sea: Anveney didn't care.

Anveney supplied all the world with copper, tin, gold, silver, and lead—iron for trucks and guns came from over the Inland Sea, ported in at Carlisle, moved along Limitation River by barge. He'd never been that far east, himself, but he knew coal came inbound there. A handful of lowland riders shepherded those barges along the shorelines and guarded their contracts equally jealously, as *their* right—but they based themselves at Carlisle, and went only as far as the zone of die-off, so he'd heard. Coal likewise came from across the Inland Sea, smoky stuff to feed the furnaces of the big foundries and refineries and to supply the lights of Anveney, likewise freighted in by barge—while Malvey sat on natural gas and oil, a source of fuel on *this* side of the sea, a mere six days ride to the south of Shamesey.

But it wasn't distance that kept Malvey oil out of Anveney, or made them buy their fuel from middlemen in Shamesey. It was townsmen politics. Malvey's oil heated Shamesey as well as Malvey houses, as it did Tarmin villages, in winter emergency. It ran the generators that ran the electric lights, smoky stuff, too, but its smoke didn't seem to kill the ground.

Anveney smoke did. Anveney smoke ruined the ground in a wider and wider desolation made, as Shamesey claimed and any fool could see, by smoke and downfalling pollution out of Anveney, smoke that didn't always blow toward the vacant lands, Anveney's pious claims to the contrary.

Shamesey, lying southeast, had protested and demanded that Anveney shut down its furnaces on those days when the wind was blowing toward Shamesey and its farmlands—but Anveney consistently refused, first on the grounds that it wasn't possible, the furnaces couldn't shut down entirely on a given day; and then demanding that Shamesey pay exorbitantly in grain and fuel for any days the refineries were out of operation.

So the two regions quarreled and counterclaimed—it was news the rider camps cared about, since the fools held trade and rider pay and villages' winter supply hostage to their ongoing dispute. Anveney didn't need riders to guard their town at all, Anveney said, because their walls and their guards defended them, even out in the remote mining pits.

The stink and the poison defended Anveney, that was the truth all riders knew, and even townsmen in Shamesey had an inkling. The plain fact was that no creature in its right mind would come near Anveney, first for the stink that clung to everything, in that zone where the smoke spilled its most odoriferous content to earth—and second, for the more alarming effects: a stranger to Anveney felt he had contamination on his skin. He'd been here once, himself, and his skin had itched until he'd bathed in clean water, which argued to him and surely to any creature with a brain that it couldn't be good. It was why he wouldn't allow Burn close enough to eat the grass on the edge of this place.

But humans somehow survived here. Humans mined and refined the metals, and when Anveney shipped its ingots and sheet metal outside the envelope of its poison, it still needed riders to guard the shipments.

Anveney both needed what its poisoned soil wouldn't grow or graze, and held its own goods back if it didn't get the price it wanted. Other towns wanted copper to make the wires for the phone system, which never worked when you needed it—but at least it didn't draw predators like the radio did; townsmen wanted the phones enough to keep paying riders to fix the lines and guard the crews that put up poles that fell down in the ice storms all winter.

Lately Anveney and its little network of high-country mining camps with their copper and such had all made one union, and wouldn't sell except at their prices. This was the next escalation of the smoke wars.

So now Shamesey, latest he'd heard, was trying to arrange some kind of terms with Malvey, since Anveney was as desperate for food as Shamesey was for electrics and copper sheet for rich families' roofs. Shamesey reasoned that if Anveney got hungry enough it might shut down its smoke when the winds blew southerly. Shamesey had made alliance not only with Malvey and *its* union, but with other, smaller towns in the grain belt, which dealt with Shamesey markets, and began to hold back grain and to create stockpiles of copper against Anveney's price-fixing and smoke-dumping, saying that Shamesey could do without copper longer than Anveney could do without bread.

It was a damned stupid situation. Guil had heard both sides of the argument all his life, at varying degrees of immediacy, and didn't comment, as riders didn't generally voice opinions on town politics to their employers or to the truck drivers, whose trade was gossip as well as cargo. Talk like which side was right confused the horses and worried riders, when towns got to quarreling—nobody needed more ill feeling near the horses than they naturally had coming at them, but when the smoke wars heated up, things generally grew uncomfortable; and the smell of Anveney, both the stench and the town-wide atmosphere of fear and grievance, made it hard for a rider not to have opinions. Bad enough the refinery jobs at Malvey, including the chance of blowing sky-high in a truck accident.

But . . . Aby had argued, in her dealings with Anveney, the pay's good and I can camp out till they arrange the papers and get the trucks to the gate. I don't have to go into town but once a trip.

Well for her, he supposed, wondering once, in Aby's near company, how good in the blankets this Anveney shipper might be.

Gotten his ear boxed, he had—deserved it, he was sure; Aby'd been only half joking when she immediately after pushed him into the blankets and never did answer the question.

Come with me, she'd urged him again, last spring. Talk Burn into it. You've got to see the country up there.

I do see it, he'd said. She'd imaged him her route again and again.

And she'd said, pleading with him: With your own eyes, Guil. You've got to feel it. You've got to be there.

But he'd refused. He'd made his commitment to Malvey; he'd elected to run his risks with the fuel tankers up to Darwin. He had his hard-won customers down south that he didn't want to let into the hands of anybody else, for fear they might call on that somebody else next time.

And truth be told—he'd grown a little tired of her evasions.

So now he was walking to Anveney town alone, his eyes feeling the sting of the smoke when the wind gusted a fickle current down-valley.

Anveney's Garden, riders called the place, the area all around and northeast of Anveney, where the soil lay completely bare and prone to erosion, gullies leading to gullies leading to a wash that ran down to a river that ran through barren banks a long, long way before the inpouring of other streams began to put more life into Limitation River than death could take out. Even that far, neither riders or horses would eat the freshwater fish, which grew strange lumps on their bodies.

No riders wintered over in the district, that he knew of, either. During the summer if you looked over from the Tarmin main road, you could generally find a plume of smoke in the hills, a handful of riders resting up for a day or two, waiting for some convoy to organize; they'd wait in that still-green zone, always outside the dead fields.

Only a few weeks ago, Aby had been among them.

Chapter — xi —

Brionne's feet were cold, her fingers were cold. She tucked her hands in her pockets and kept walking, brushed by evergreens which dumped the burden of their boughs and spattered wet snow onto the melting crust.

It was a beautiful morning. It wasn't golden anymore. She'd walked through that angle of the sun. But it was a shining morning, still. Glistening white, the sun gleamed in snow-melt off tall branches. It was the kind of morning that would lead to glossy melt by afternoon, and a freezing icy crust again by night, in Brionne's young experience. The snow tomorrow morning would crunch underfoot and make hollow shells where footprints were—and you'd slip walking around the edges of the house where the run-off made thick ice. She knew. She loved the snow.

And when the kids of Tarmin village gained permission to go outside the walls it had always been with riders all about, but Tarmin wasn't afraid of goblin cats. Tarmin folk and riders both went out to skate on the mountain lake, and Tarmin children, when the riders were near, went out to build snow forts and sometimes, especially if you were lovey with boys, just to walk to the Rim and see the valley, with rider pairs to watch them.

It was scary being out on her own. But she wasn't truly afraid. Her horse surely knew she was looking for it, her horse was only testing her in making her walk so far from the walls, and if there should be a goblin cat, her horse would never let it come close to her. If there was a nest of willy-wisps, her horse would hear her call and come to her rescue, if she couldn't, as a rider could, drive them away simply by imaging as loudly as she could.

I'm here, she called to her horse, not with her voice, but the way the riders spoke, the pictures you made in your mind.

And there came . . . oh, so suddenly you'd never know it had happened . . . the view of a girl in a red coat, with a blue scarf—of course that was herself. Of course it was. And sometimes, the riders said, you could get that kind of image from willy-wisps, but it didn't feel scary like willy-wisps, it felt . . .

. . . so, so lonely.

She pushed aside a branch to pass between two trees, and suddenly was sure where she was going, so sure she half-ran the next wooded slope, arrived at a clear space in the woods, and in that clear space the sun fell, and in that sunlight . . . the most beautiful horse, its mane so thick and long it cascaded down its black shoulder, and all the clearing touched by sun that made its coat shine like silk.

Her horse regarded her with one forelock-obscured eye, dipped its head and pawed the snow anxiously before it took a tentative step forward, its three-hooved foot taking ever-so-light a step before Brionne dared commit herself.

"Are you mine?" she asked, and went on, breathlessly, feeling a little foolish to be talking with no human to hear. "My name's Brionne. I'm thirteen. I live in Tarmin village. I heard you last night. What's *your* name?"

Another step.

"I'm not afraid, you know. I talk with the riders all the time. I talk with their horses. There's Quickfoot and Flicker and . . ."

A third step. A fourth. Brionne forgot everything, every word.

The horse stretched out its neck and Brionne quickly pulled her glove off and held out her hand . . . felt the chill of the air on her bare skin, saw the horse wrinkle its black nose and bare its teeth. The center ones were large and square and yellowed—jarringly real—out of time with this white glisten of morning. The corner ones were longer and sharp; and for a moment staring at them she doubted her safety—but she stayed still when the horse's nose approached her outstretched hand.

The velvet black lip came down as it reached her fingers. She laughed shakily as she felt the hot, moist breath puff over her hand, she touched the delicately molded softness of the horse's nostrils as it breathed in her scent.

Another step, hers or the horse's, or maybe it was both, and she could touch with her fingertips its long forelock. Another step, and she could run her fingers through that incredible long mane and put her arm about the horse's neck and shoulder, and hug it tight. Its mane was like finest, softest, floatiest wool against her cheek, stirring with any wind. Its winter coat was warm and silky. She let go a shaky sigh, feeling shivery just feeling it.

She knew the horse should tell her its secret name then. "Brionne," she said, thinking about herself, the way her horse had, imaging <a red-coated Brionne, coming through the trees.>

Then she couldn't see the woods around her. She saw only <dark, and the bright and shining moon.>

Of a sudden Flicker's hindquarters buckled and she sat down hard and fast, knocked a post askew with her rump, and Tara dropped the pan she was carrying, hot water all down her leg, and ran to Flicker, flung herself onto her knees on the wet straw and put her arms about Flicker's neck.

There was no more <white.> There was <den,> and <tired horse.>

Tara shook, holding to her, pillowing her head against Flicker's back. Flicker shifted a little, matter-of-factly seeking a more comfortable position for her forelegs, and Vadim and Chad talked to each other in human words, quietly relieved, wondering if they should try to get Flicker up again.

truck—but none of them that he knew had ever asked. Anveney folk centered all their hopes on the mines, the metals, the mills; they depended like parasites from the moneyed monster Anveney was. It shook them off and they sank in the mud and died—all the while their faith so feared the intrusion of another, alien thought into their minds they'd die before they worked with a horse.

And by what he knew, they equally feared the uncertainties of a rider's life—meaning hunting for their supper. Anveney folk might *have* no supper. But they seemed reassured that they were *sure* they would have no supper.

They suffered no surprises. The poison above the town did make spectacular sunsets . . . that was all you could say for it; but Guil doubted they appreciated the colors above their gray, sooted walls. He'd touched enough Anveney minds for a lifetime, among those drivers who regularly came back to this town when they had other choices. He'd tried to penetrate their sullen, argumentative insistence on certainties. They afflicted him the same way dire illness did.

He'd felt an irrational fear ever since he'd passed the guarded town gates, first that the walls were closing in and then that the successive concentric rows of buildings were shifting and entrapping him. Even when the buildings became wider spaced that anxiety persisted, on the broadening way down which, if it were Shamesey, the convoys would come, assembled in the town square with excitement and honking of horns and cheers of passers-by.

In Anveney, depend on it as one depended there were rich townsmen at the heart of everything, there *was* a town square, but to his borrowed memory it was all official buildings and rich houses with sealed windows, while convoys assembled and onloaded and offloaded at warehouses outside the town wall, out by the tailings-heaps.

The buildings came in better repair as the road inclined uphill, the pavings mostly clear of muck. Here a shop stood open-doored, with moderate traffic of buyers, and there, the smell of bread from a bakery wafted out locally stronger than the general stink of the valley air. The bakery stood next a house with bright red doorposts and a red and blue door, a level porch with the rail intact and iron bars on the windows. Touches of color became riot further down the street; red beams with blue trim at the corners of neat yellow and white buildings, a carving of flowers on a wall inset—they all had a dusting of soot, and the flowers were black-edged. But the colors were cheerful.

The folk who walked here (more idle folk than in the lower town) wore townsmen's long brown coats and broad, flat hats, men and women with woolen trouser hems innocent of soot. Children waddled about like stuffed dolls in overcoats on this nippish day, children with round scrubbed faces, more color in their cheeks than in the poorer part of town—no few masked in gauze, leaving only the eyes exposed. They stood and gawked at the sight of a rider walking down the street. Their elders stared, too, and drew the children away.

He'd reached town center, where he was sure the bank must be, an open square with all too many silent minds and staring eyes for his liking, a marketplace not like friendly village markets, with their open stalls where riders sometimes came to deal and rub shoulders with townsmen, but shops with most of the goods indoors, requiring the buyer to commit himself and go inside. The nature of the buildings gave him no cue what business they did.

A woman passed near him, hatted and coated into shapelessness. "I'm looking for the bank," he said to her, and she evaded him and his question with a brisk thumping of thick heels down the walk.

He suffered a flare of anger, and half-smothered it before he remembered that Burn wasn't there to spread it around the area—but he couldn't *hear* a damned thing, either, not cues, not intentions, not directions to where money changed hands.

A merchant in thick sweaters was tending his out-front display goods, offering them to passers-by, woolens, as happened—fine knit-work in muted colors; and, offered inside (a sudden realization of the logic of such indoor shops), they'd smell better. He thought if the prices were reasonable, if he had money left after finding a gun, he might come back and buy one of those warm sweaters.

In that case, the man could damned well direct him. "The bank," Guil said, raising his voice to be sure he couldn't easily be ignored. "Sir, I'm looking for the bank."

A scowl, as the man arranged a sweater on a cardboard cutout of a man. A reluctant nod across the square to buildings on the other side. "Bank," the man said. That was all.

"Thanks," Guil muttered, jammed his hands deeper into his pockets and walked across the square, past waddling, gauze-masked children and clusters of their glum elders who stopped their gossip to stare. *God*, he wanted out of this place.

He couldn't swear to what building the man had indicated. He thought the likeliest candidate for a repository of money was the important-looking building with the bars on the windows: it didn't look to be selling anything, there being no displays, but there was writing on the windows and the door, and though he couldn't read, he'd never known anybody to write on windows of a private house.

The door was open, seeming to invite entry. So he walked in, onto a bare board floor, facing a grillwork, an armed guard, and a single young man at an undefended desk out front, while the rest of the employees sat at desks securely behind those formidable bars, which led one to wonder which ranked higher.

"Is this the bank?" he asked the guard.

"Seems so," the guard said, looking him over. Then the young man at the desk, a thin, nervous fellow, said: "Help you, rider?"

That was the most politeness he'd had in Anveney. He walked over to the desk, folded his arms, said, dubiously, "They say I can draw out money here I put in at Shamesey."

"Yes, sir. If you've the account number and proper identification."

You could have blown him over with a light breeze. It couldn't be this easy. "I know the number. I memorized it. My name's Guil Stuart."

"You're supposed to have a card. Do you have one?"

Yes, they'd given him a card. He'd very few places to store such things. He fished in his inside breast pocket, not entirely sure he had it, but he found a little white paper, a little the worse for wear. He hoped they didn't mind wrinkles.

The desk man looked at it and said: "Seems in order. Would you step through to a desk, sir?"

Sir, yet, from a townsman. Guil received the card back, decided he should keep it out, and as he followed the young man, heard a click that put him in mind of guns. It made his nerves twitch. But the guard had only opened the bars and let him in to the area where the men and women sat at safer desks.

"Help you?" the nearest woman asked.

"Yes, ma'am," he said, and came and offered her the evidently important card. "I'd like to take out some money."

"Certainly," the woman said as she looked at the card.

"I put it in at Shamesey," he said, still unconvinced the bank was going to work, or, more to the point, that it was going to work for a rider.

"That's fine, sir, the lines are up. No trouble at all." A waved gesture at the chair beside her desk. "Sit down. I'll be right back."

The woman got up, taking the card with her, which he didn't like, and walked back to a door she closed behind her.

Fancy townswoman. Nice clothes. Flimsy shoes that never saw mud. Behind that door was evidently the place of moneyed secrets and decisions, and Guil told himself that Aby had been right and this banking thing evidently did work. He'd personally had the feeling, putting hard-earned cash into the bank at Shamesey—a place where they took your money at an outside window, and you stood in the street—that he might be throwing it away. He'd never remotely thought that he'd be collecting it and Aby'd be gone.

He sat and he sat, feeling awkward, waiting for the woman to come back, and wondering finally if there was trouble with the phone lines. Wondering if there was some glitch-up, maybe the condition of the card—a few rainstorms had blurred the ink in spots, and he hoped it hadn't blurred anything important.

Finally, finally, the woman came slinking back, not so crisp, far from cheerful, and not alone. A frowning older woman walked behind her, an older woman who scarcely got rid of her scowl as she extended—as Guil was getting up—the offer of a businesslike handshake.

The young woman said: "This is Yolande Newater, Mr. Stuart, president of Anveney Trust."

"Ma'am," Guil said, and suffered his hand to be shaken by a cold, boneless grip.

"Mr. Stuart," Newater began. "There seems to be an embarrassing problem."

His stomach went sour. He recovered his hand, folded his arms, tried to keep his temper under control. "That's the card they gave me when I put the money in. That's my name. I put money in at Shamesey. They said I could get it anywhere there was a bank and a telephone."

"Yes, sir. It should be. However."

He frowned, not understanding this 'however.' Frustration boiled up, maybe too fast. He tried to hold it in. "I put in five hundred sixty and change."

"Yes. I'm not disputing your word, Mr. Stuart, or the card. Shamesey Bank confirms your deposit. I just talked to them."

Amazing idea. Just talked to a bank in Shamesey. He'd never been the subject of a phone call before.

He didn't think he liked it, in present instance. "So where's my money?"

"I trust—" Newater looked intensely uncomfortable. "I trust you know the co-holder was reported deceased."

"Dead." He didn't like vague big words for plain nasty facts. "*Dead.* I know."

"There was a new employee at the counter," Newater began. Then: "This is awkward."

"Just say it. You lost the money?"

"We don't lose money, Mr. Stuart. There was a legitimate claimant."

"What's a claimant?"

"A next of kin."

"Next of kin. *Hawley Antrim?*"

"Mr. Antrim came in with identification. He was listed . . . " Newater held out her hand and the other woman, silent, standing by her desk, snatched up a paper and handed it to Newater. "Right here, as Ms. Dale's next-of-kin."

She showed it to him, as if it was some special proof that cleared her. It was marks on paper, so far as he was concerned, and he wanted it out of his face.

"Hawley Antrim walked into this place and said he wanted the money. *He wanted the money?*"

"Either party can close the account. The right descended to Ms. Dale's legitimate heir. Mr. Antrim was listed on the appropriate paper—"

"The hell with any appropriate paper! He had no right!"

"As Ms. Dale's heir—"

"He's a cousin! *I'm her partner!*"

"It's not that way on the document, Mr. Stuart. There's recourse through the court, if you care to sue Mr. Antrim, but that's not our business. We have to disburse funds to the persons on the card."

"I gave you the damn card! My name's on it, right?"

"It is. But—"

"Then give me the damn money!"

The junior woman jumped. Newater frowned and said in a shaky voice, "Mr. Stuart, . . . this is clearly an emotional situation. I ask you—"

"I'm asking you for my damn money, woman. You had no call to give it to Hawley Antrim."

"Clearly the terms of your partnership weren't defined in our records. I'm in no position to evaluate the deceased's intentions in writing regarding another party. I can only follow what information Ms. Dale put on her card when she set up the account."

"Aby couldn't read."

"She clearly answered questions. One of those questions involves heirs and succession in the account."

"She didn't know about any succession. You and your words, they wouldn't mean anything to her, she wouldn't know what any succession was, any more than Hawley does. That son of a bitch just walked in here and said he wanted Aby's money, wasn't that what happened?"

Newater said, aside, hurriedly, "Lila, call Peter." And to him: "If you'll just sit down, Mr. Stuart, —"

As 'Lila' dived away like a scared cat, running for help: he had no trouble figuring, and he looked about to see where 'Lila' was going, jumped as Newater touched his sleeve—he wasn't *used* to being touched. "Look," he said. "Fair's fair. We can argue later. I lost my gear. I need a couple hundred. You just give it to me, and we'll talk when I come back. Minimum, I need a hundred. Rifle and shells."

"I beg pardon."

"I need a gun."

There was appalling, appalled silence from the woman. A shocked stare.

"I *am* a rider, ma'am. I need the gun to go up to Tarmin. Give me the hundred and we settle it next spring."

"Mr. Stuart, the right to the money passed to her next of kin. I can show you right on the authorization card—"

"Then some damned fool asked her the wrong question, that's what I'm telling you. They asked her her relations, they didn't ask her her partner who's sharing the account!"

"She had that option. She chose to list Mr. Antrim."

"She didn't damn choose!" A hand grabbed his arm from behind. He turned around with the simultaneous knowledge it was a man, and he didn't question whether the grip meant business: he assumed it did and he grabbed a shirt, twisted, stuck out a foot and the man hit the floor. Hard.

The man, the door guard, went for the gun at his hip from that disadvantage and Guil didn't stop to think—he kicked the hand before it had the gun clear, and the gun went spinning across the floor, the injured hand flew up to be cradled by the other hand, and townsmen were screaming and diving everywhere. Iron bars clanged and shut.

"Hell," Guil said, not pursuing anybody. The man with the sore hand was still lying on the ground, the barred doors were shut. Guil walked over where the gun was, figuring not to leave *that* in play, and the middle-aged fool scrambled up and tried to jump him from behind.

He didn't shoot the man. He didn't pull his knife. He didn't hit the man with the gun. He just dodged, the man being low to the ground in his dive, shoved him fairly gently as he passed, and the man hit the ground as all of a sudden a bell began to ring.

The man probably realized now he'd been a fool. He sat up on the board floor looking foolish, there wasn't a bank worker in sight except him, and Guil held the gun by the trigger-guard, so anybody could see he wasn't holding it on the man.

"I'd give you this back," he said, "except I'm tired of hitting you. You want to open the door?"

"Can't," the guard said sullenly.

"Then get—"

Runners thundered up to the open outside door, jammed up in the doorway and sorted themselves out with leveled rifles, aimed toward them through the bars.

Guil dropped the gun from two fingers. Thump, onto the boards.

Somebody, then, had to go outside and around back to get a key from Newater.

Ignoring the leveled rifles, Guil rested his rump against a table and stared glumly at the guard, who was getting to his feet, encouraged by the firepower.

Guil was mad. He was damned mad. He was scared, deep down. He had to get out to meet Burn by sundown, or Burn was going to get dangerously restless. He didn't think the guard was going to back his story. And it didn't look good from where he stood.

"He's got a knife," the guard said.

"You know," Guil said disgustedly, "you'd be a lot smarter to wait to tell them that, until they find the key."

"Hand the knife out," one of the uniformed police said.

"You can come get it."

"I said hand it over."

Hell, he thought, he wouldn't improve the ambient by arguing the point with four rifles aimed at him. He walked over to the bars and took out the knife, tossed it out through the bars.

"He's a borderer," a cop said. "He's got more than one."

"You want the other?" He bent and took it from his boot, tossed it out. "That's all."

"Don't believe it," the cop said.

Steps sounded fast behind him. He turned to side-step the fool rushing him, and something jabbed him in the back of the head. Stars exploded. The guard hit him, knocked him against the bars: hands grabbed him, held him.

Second crack across the head. He jerked to get free and more hands than two men had grabbed him through the bars and held him there. The guard hit him in the gut.

It was a stand-still when the man came back with the key. He didn't move and they didn't hit him until they had him outside the bars.

Then the guard thought he'd get one more in. Guil dumped the rightside man over his back, got a clear target with the guard staring stupidly at him and decked him.

Before an oncoming rifle barrel swung into his vision.

Chapter — xii —

THE PAIN BLURRED THE SKY. BUT THAT SKY WASN'T BLUE. IT WAS A wooden ceiling, a bare electric bulb for a sun. He had no idea where he was.

<Burn,> Guil sent. Always, on waking, the awareness of Burn, first reality of his world.

But Burn wasn't there.

And on that stomach-dropping realization, he panicked, staring into this electric, burning sun, trying to reconstruct his route to this place.

Aby was dead, up above Tarmin. That was how everything connected. He was lying on his back on a bare board floor with days-old pain in his leg and recently inflicted pain at various points about his skull.

<Moving darkness at Shamesey gates. A flash of fire, out of that crowd-shadow at the edge of night.>

He'd not realized what it was. Not until the second shot.

<Telling Burn to run away.>

He'd slid down, given Burn no choice . . . he'd thought.

But Burn had charged the mob instead of running away—gone at the townsmen mob dead ahead, and, dirty nighthorse trick, wasn't where he imaged he was.

He'd . . . damned well been where the mob had thought he was: third shot, and he'd caught it—it had knocked his leg out from under him and sent him sprawling downhill on the dry grass. He remembered.

<Lying there, hands burned on the grass, the camp gates opening . . . riders coming out—>

He thought they were coming to rescue him, he'd thought they wouldn't let the town take him: camp rights over town marshals—

<People shouting at each other, while he faced the down-slant of the hill, trying for his very life to get up. . . .

He didn't remember, after that. For a moment the next connected instant seemed here, under the electric light.

Aby was dead. More . . . more than that. Aby had died.

But he couldn't go into that pit yet. There was something in there he couldn't deal with, a darkness he couldn't escape if he went in there without understanding where he was now. . . .

He drew a deep breath, about to move.

And knew the smell. Anveney's stink.

<Desolation, bare, gullied earth. Himself and Burn, approaching Anveney. Meet—at the rider-stone. Burn waiting.>

How long ago? *God, how long ago?*

He rolled over fast, leaned back on his hands as the change of altitude sent pain knifing through his skull. Dizziness sprawled him back onto the floor, onto the lump on the back of his skull.

Stars and dark a moment. He tried it again more slowly, made it halfway.

No furniture in the room, except a bucket. Shut door. No window.

<*No window.*>

Didn't even know he'd gotten up. He was plastered face-to on the wooden wall as if he could pour himself through it, arms spread, shaking like a leaf—and deaf, absolutely deaf to Burn's existence. The whole world had left him: sound, sense, everything.

But the raw, rough wood under his hands was real. It proved *he* existed.

He could still smell the stench of Anveney around him. That proved something, too, but he couldn't hear a living soul.

His heart was pounding. Sweat stood cold on his skin. He couldn't let go of the wall. Couldn't keep his legs under him, otherwise . . . couldn't depend on his balance.

First thing a rider knew: panic killed. Panic led to crazy. Panic gave the advantage away, free to all takers. The sane, thinking man knew he was in Anveney, knew Anveney had no horses in reach to carry the ambient . . . but . . . God, he'd never in his life waked up deaf to it; he'd never been in a room without windows, he'd never not known how he got to a place. . . .

He persuaded his knees to hold him—edged along the wall, unsure even of his balance, to try the door.

Locked and bolted from outside. Of course.

He tried to shake it. He slammed the center of the door once, hard, with his fist, and heard only silence, inside his head and out.

Burn—

Burn would be in deadly danger if he came near the walls, and Burn would do that if he didn't get back before dark.

Burn would come for him, *knowing* the danger, within range of the rifles that guarded the town . . . but Burn wouldn't care. Burn would come in.

He didn't know how long he'd been out. He couldn't, in this damn box, tell day from dark, no more than he knew east from west, and he couldn't count on any rescue. There was no rider camp outside Anveney walls, no camp-boss to negotiate him out—in autumn, there probably wasn't another rider within 10 k of here, nobody to know if he didn't come out of this town.

Nobody but Burn.

Townsmen would know there was a horse out there waiting for him. They'd know the hold they had on him—that whatever they wanted, he'd do, rather than have harm come to Burn. That was surely why they'd shut him away like this; they surely had to want something from him, besides some stupid townsman penalty because a rider inconvenienced a bank that shouldn't have handed out money to a man that didn't have any right to it—

He remembered. Damn Hawley!

And to hell with the money. He'd have walked out once he knew they weren't going to give it to him—he'd have left their damn town. He didn't think he'd pulled any weapon on them. He didn't remember any. They didn't need to lock him up in a box and shoot at Burn, who was—surely—surely old enough and wary enough to give them hell without putting himself straight-off into some wall guard's riflesights.

But he couldn't depend on that. *He* hadn't done too well at escaping town guards, himself.

He staggered along the wall, one side to the other, wasn't sure what it contributed to the solution—his leg hurt, his head hurt. It seemed moving might clear his thinking, maybe; maybe hurt less than standing still. But if it helped, he couldn't tell it.

He bashed the door again, hammered it with his fist, in case someone could hear. He didn't think all that much time had passed, but he wasn't sure: it could be getting dark. Burn could be getting restless, waiting for him.

Saner to sit down. Didn't want to stop moving. Had to have something to do, not to think, didn't want to think. . . .

Damn, dead, stupid town. . . .

Knees ached and wobbled. He began to get up a charge of anger then, and braked it, in lifelong habit—

But it didn't matter. They couldn't hear that, either. He could wish them in hell.

He bashed the door with his arm. Twice. Kicked it, with the bad leg, because he could only keep his balance on the sound one; and that hurt so bad he had to use the wall to hold him up.

Hinges were outside. Door had to open out. No handle on this side. No hinges to take apart. But if the door opened out . . . maybe he could kick it open, maybe hit it with his shoulder until he split the upright.

He backed off several steps and rammed it. Once. Twice. Felt it give. Shake, at least.

He heard something then. Footsteps. He'd raised notice of some kind.

Voices outside. He tried to understand them, but his own heartbeat was too loud in his ears. He shoved back from the door, stood back as the bolt shot back outside and the door opened.

He wasn't at all surprised at the three badge-wearing marshals with guns leveled, reinforcing the guard who opened the door. He lifted a hand, palm out. "No trouble here," he said, trying to keep the ambient calm. And he couldn't resist it: "*Help* you with something?"

"Mr. Stuart." The man who'd opened the door indicated he should come out, so he came out. The men with guns backed up, maintaining their advantage. "Someone wants to talk to you."

"Fine." He hoped somebody wanted to talk to him. He hoped somebody had a deal to offer him to get him out of here, and after that, he didn't remotely care if Anveney burned down.

So he walked obligingly where the guard indicated and the man led, down a dingy hallway, through a maze of halls. He didn't put it past them to hit him on general principle; he was acutely aware of the armed men behind him, and acutely aware he couldn't forecast what way their minds were running—he *hated* the way townsmen dealt with one another. You could blame practically any craziness on the fact they didn't know, never knew, only guessed what another man wanted, or what he was about to do.

Hell of a way to live.

Meanwhile the man in the lead opened a door onto the daylight and Anveney streets.

He drew a shaky, ill-flavored breath, tucked his hands in his pockets, and amused himself, as they went out, seeking deliberate, surly eye contact with the rare passers-by, who, understandably spooked by the police armament, ducked to the other side of the street. And gawked, until they chanced into his angry stare.

Twice spooked then, they averted their eyes and found something urgent to go to.

They went halfway down the block like that, the guard in front, him in the middle, the police behind, until the guard came to what looked more like a house than an office, and showed him and their gun-carrying escort into a broad, fancy-furnished room with polished wood and fringed rugs.

Stairs went up from here, but the guard turned left. There were doors upon doors in the hall they walked. The guard led him past all of them, and through the double door at the end into a room where an overweight old man in expensive town dress sat in a green overstuffed chair roughly equal to his mass.

Smoking a pipe. God, did anybody in Anveney need more smoke?

"So," the man said. "You're Dale's partner."

First soul in Anveney that spoke sense to him, putting things like partnership in their right importance. His shoulders relaxed a little, guns or no guns, and he didn't care all that much of a sudden that the room reeked of smokeweed.

"Stuart," he named himself, and made a guess. "You're Lew Cassivey."

The man inclined his head, seeming gratified to be famous, at least to Aby Dale's partner. Head of Cassivey & Carnell, the man Aby would risk high-country weather to keep happy—his intervening made some sense, but it didn't guarantee his good will, or his good intentions.

"Sorry about Dale," Cassivey said, sending up a series of short puffs. "Real sorry."

The man wanted a reaction, Stuart realized, in a sudden new insight how deaf townsman minds had to work. The man didn't know. He prodded. He waited to *see* how he reacted.

Guil tucked his hands up under his arms, and in his best approximation of an outward reaction, shrugged and looked sorry himself. He felt the weight of the building on his back. He felt the scarcity of air. Smelled smells he couldn't identify. <"Rogue horse,"> he said. He couldn't stop expecting the man to see it, feel it, know it. "You heard that part."

"I heard how she died. Couple of the riders came in with the bad news. Lost a truck and driver, too."

"Sorry about that." He attempted town manners, town courtesy. He wanted help. This was the man that could give it—or have him shot, directly or indirectly. "I'm on my way to Tarmin."

"Alone?"

He shrugged, a lump of raw fear in his throat, because they'd arrived at the life-and-death points and he was feeling in the dark after reactions. "My horse. I need to get out there."

"Hear you had a real commotion at the bank."

What could he say? He hadn't intended it.

But no townsman knew that if he didn't say it.

"Didn't mean to," he muttered. God, he didn't know how to talk to these people. He didn't know what else they couldn't guess, blind and deaf as they were. "I tried my best to calm it down."

Cassivey seemed amused for a heartbeat, whether friendly or unfriendly amusement he couldn't tell. The amusement died a fast death. Smoke poured out Cassivey's nostrils. "I hear the bank gave her money to her cousin."

"My money, too," he said. "Everything."

"Your money?"

"Same account. They said it was town law."

"It's not that simple," Cassivey said. "But I doubt you'd want to sue."

"Go to court?" He shook his head emphatically.

"Not if it means staying around Anveney, is that it?"

"Weather's turning."

"Meaning?"

"Hard to hunt." He felt stupid, saying the obvious. He wasn't sure it was all Cassivey was asking him. "I have to get up there. Get it before the deep snow."

"With no help?"

"I need a gun," he said.

"Where's this man's property?" Cassivey asked the guards. "Who's got his belongings?"

"He didn't come with any," the one in charge said.

"No gun? No baggage?"

"Knives," Guil said. "Two."

"I'm paying his fine," Cassivey said. "Somebody go get his belongings. Stuart, sit down."

There was another chair near him, stuffed like the one Cassivey sat in. Guil put his hands on the upholstered arms and sank down gingerly, not sure how far he would sink. There was a sharp pain in his sore leg when it bent and his knees, now that he heard 'fine' and 'paying' and 'get his belongings,' suddenly had a disposition to wobble out of lock. The room swam and floated.

"You want a drink?" Cassivey said, as the guards cleared the room. "There's a bottle on the table."

"No," he said. It wasn't worth the risk of getting up. "Thanks."

"You need a doctor?"

"I just want out." His breath was shaky. He didn't intend so much honesty. "But thanks. What do I do for you?"

"Dale was reliable. You could trust things didn't get pilfered." Puff. Second puff. "What's your record on reliability?"

"Same," he said, embarrassed to have to make claims, when he didn't know how Cassivey should believe a man who'd come in with armed guards. "Mostly I work out of Malvey south," he said, and not sure Cassivey was remotely interested in his explanations, he remembered how the bank had phoned. "You could phone Moss Shipping in Malvey. They know me."

"I might do that," Cassivey said. "Dirty trick, what Dale's cousin did."

He shrugged. It was. But that was his business and he didn't answer.

"The job I have for you," Cassivey began.

"I," Guil interjected, fast, before the man committed too much. "I have to get up to Tarmin Height before the snow. I have to get that thing." Maybe it was stupid. From time to time since he'd left Shamesey he'd not even been sure he cared. But the realization—the reality—of Aby's death had made itself a cold nest in the middle of his thinking.

And she wouldn't rest until he'd cleared Aby's trail for her, mopped up all the loose business. Settled accounts to her satisfaction.

Which might make him lose this man's offer, when he was indebted for a fine he couldn't pay, with no gun, no way out. But that was the way it was; he hoped the man was reasonable. "I'm sorry," he said, "I have to go up there. Just get me out of here. I'll work it off for you next spring."

Cassivey stared at him, expressionless, the pipe in his hand. Then: "Don't turn down my offer until you've heard it. A commission. Enough money, supplies, whatever you need to go upcountry—the best commissions when you come to town again in the spring. Preference. Top of the list preference. What's that worth to you?"

It was beyond generous. It was Aby's deal with this man. It had to be.

"I still have to go up there. I have to hunt that thing. Local riders might get it. But they might not. You can't use that road till somebody does get it. It won't be safe."

"I don't argue that. You go up there, you get the horse that got her, and you do one more thing for me."

"What's that?"

"What kind of man is Jonas Westman?"

He didn't expect that question of all questions. He didn't know why Cassivey asked it. He was feeling in the dark again. And he didn't know how to put words around the answer that a townsman would understand. He drew a breath, said what said it all. "High-country rider."

"Honest?"

"Yeah." There were qualifications to that. "Enough."

"Honest as Dale was?"

He shook his head. Complicated question. He wondered just what shape of beast Cassivey was tracking with his question—or whether Cassivey in any way understood any rider. Sometimes he seemed to, and sometimes not.

"Aby liked you," he said to Cassivey, and still didn't know if Cassivey understood him. "Jonas Westman and his brother—they're Hawley Antrim's partners. Hawley's Aby's cousin. He'd do what Aby said, as long as she put the fear in him. So they might. On a good day."

"Aby wouldn't steal."

Steal. Pilfer. Town words, for relations between townsmen and riders. Different, in a camp, among riders—where some would and some wouldn't. "If you didn't cheat her," he said, "she wouldn't steal from you."

A pause, while Cassivey relit an evidently dead pipe. "Not even if she had a chance for real, *real* money?"

"How much?"

"Three hundred thousand. Maybe more."

He laughed, sheer surprise—tried to think how much money that would be, and it came up ridiculous.

"What's funny?" Cassivey asked.

Nothing, thinking of it. It was a townsman amount of money. A scary amount of money. It was an amount of money you found in banks.

And where would a rider come near that kind of money? More, what could a rider *do* with it if she had it?

Cassivey sent out another puff of smoke. "The truck that went off the road?" Cassivey said. More puffs. "Gold shipment."

Stunned comprehension. He stopped the breath he was drawing. Didn't move for a second. *Couldn't* reach after the ambient, much as he wanted to. It wasn't there.

But then, Cassivey couldn't know what he was thinking, either. Cassivey had just told him where enough money was that rich townsmen would kill each other in droves to get it.

Enough money that a rider, if he had it stashed, could take to the roads and the hills and never work again for the rest of his life—but he'd never sleep easy about it.

"Dale knew what was on that lead truck," Cassivey said.

Now he did. Townsmen would kill each other to know what he knew.

Except that townsmen, even heavily armed, even posting guards over their sleep, and traveling with more than one truck, weren't safe going up there into the High Wild to reach that wreckage.

Not safe from the weather.

Not safe from the rogue that could overwhelm all their defenses.

But somebody from the villages up there was inevitably going to get down to that truck. Its apparent cargo—what he'd seen in Jonas' image—had been lumber, which wasn't damn valuable on a forested mountainside, but just the metal in that truck had value. The engine parts. The tires and axles. Every piece of it was valuable salvage to a village. And if some village crew got to stripping it—

"Find the box," Cassivey said. "Turn it over to the head of Tarmin Mines, at Tarmin. That's Salmon Martines. Simple job."

"Simple."

"Truck went off on the downhill, on that bad turn—you know the road?"

"Seen it." He didn't say it he'd only seen it in Aby's mind. Cassivey wouldn't understand and it didn't matter. He'd seen it in Jonas' image. A rogue horse and that turn. Hell.

"Must be ten, fifteen trucks have gone down there." Cassivey puffed smoke. "There, and hitting the wall at the end of the grade. Rock's soft. Surface skids with you. Nasty, nasty turn."

"What's the weight?" He was suddenly in territory he knew, negotiating with a shipper, on technicalities he understood.

"More than one man can haul up a mountain. You'll have to bring it up part at a time. Hire an ox-team and drivers at Tarmin. It's going to take that. You ride guard on the crew, say it's company papers you're after, and make sure all of it gets to Martines. When the weather opens up next spring, and you're sure you can make it down with the load, you hire that same ox-team and bring it down to Anveney. Pay's equipment now, and a thousand in the bank. When we get that box back . . . I'll drop five more thousand into your account."

He saw why Aby had gone out of her way for this one shipper. And he knew, in one moment of revelation, *what* Aby had been guarding on these annual end-of-season convoys, and why Cassivey had gone out of his way to keep one honest, reliable rider very well paid.

"You're giving me the deal she had."

"I asked her once who else I could trust, if it ever happened she couldn't take a convoy through."

The air in Anveney suddenly didn't smell half so bad. "I need a rifle. Ammunition, blanket, carry-pack, flour, oil, burning-glass . . . couple of sides of bacon. Got to have that."

"You're a very modest man, Stuart. What in hell happened to your gear?"

<Gunfire. Hitting the ground. Burn.>

"No matter," Cassivey said. "None of my business. Six hundred do it on the gear?"

"Four. She said I was honest."

"Five. Get a pistol, too. A rifle's not always in reach. I want you *back* with my money."

The man wasn't just any townsman. He couldn't be a rider. Trucker, Guil decided. Maybe a high-country miner. At least someone who'd not sat behind town walls all his life. Aby hadn't said. Aby'd kept all her inside-buildings dealings at Anveney to herself, partly because he wasn't interested in towns. There was just the single surface thought urging him to join her on this run. The rest—he hadn't discussed.

This man was clearly a debt of hers. This man had asked her not to talk about his business. Somewhere, somehow, she'd owed Cassivey, in a major way. He understood it. He wondered if Cassivey did.

"Understand," Cassivey said, "you don't talk about what's in that truck. You don't talk about the thing those trucks sometimes carry."

"Aby never talked your business to me."

Cassivey nodded slowly. Made several slow puffs, staring at him. "A damn good woman."

He couldn't talk for a moment. He knew now. Aby'd not done anything out of order, hadn't changed, hadn't been other than the woman who'd grown up with him. Aby had pleaded with him to join her—and himself, thick-headed, he'd seen only the evasions and getting mad about it. But it was Aby. It was the woman he knew. She came back to him—dead, she came back to him the way she had been, she *hadn't* lied to him, and a weight went off his back.

"Yeah," he said finally.

"I'll make you out a contract," Cassivey said, and laid aside the pipe. "I'll send someone to the bank. One fine's enough."

He went out with what was newly his and with a contract in his pocket, riding in the open back of a Cassivey & Carnell truck, through the main town streets and down through the town gates.

One part townsman arrogance, he'd have thought it, without having met Cassivey, to send a truck outside Anveney gates with no horse to protect it, to deliver a rider back to the Wild.

He'd have taken it as an affront to his pride and his profession—under other circumstances; points for an old trucker, scored on a rider who ordinarily would watch over anybody going a stone's throw out past the gates of any other town.

Not at Anveney, the point surely was. At Anveney, armed guards weren't riders, and they didn't need help—in their grassless desolation.

Right now, with his leg hurting like unforgiven sin, he was just damned grateful that Cassivey took the trouble to save him some walking, and he was glad enough of that courtesy that he was willing to make idle conversation with the guard in the back of the truck, a guard who chattered about the weather and the coming winter and how he'd like to drive the long routes, but he wasn't sure his wife wouldn't take up with somebody else if he did.

So why didn't his wife drive or ride guard in the cab? Guil wondered, and remembered—he was more practiced at it than this morning—that the guard didn't remotely know what he wondered, no horses being near.

He was even moderately curious what the guard thought, after his experience with townsmen. He wondered to a greater extent than he ever had just what went on in townsmen minds—so much so that, on a further thought, he troubled to ask his question aloud.

"Yeah, but all those village girls . . . with my wife along?" the guard asked him in return, and laughed and elbowed him in the ribs as if he should understand.

But he wasn't sure he understood the guard's logic. He still felt dull and deaf to townsman cues . . . and he didn't understand 'wife,' he suspected, or at least, didn't understand Anveney expectations of wives and husbands.

But before he could ask into that odd remark, or try to figure where he and Aby had fit against that pattern in their own arrangement, they'd reached a turn-around at a fork in the dirt road.

The truck stopped, and the driver said that was as far as they were supposed to go.

So he climbed down—sore from head to foot, with a miserable headache and a spot on his temple that hurt like hell when he frowned into the evening sun. The stink was all around them, or he'd imagine it for days, and it clung to everything he'd gotten in Anveney.

But he wished them both a safe trip back, got information from them where the forks led, one to Anveney West Road—he'd thought he was right—and one to a mining pit he didn't want to visit.

They turned around and drove off in a cloud of dust, and he slung his new-bought belongings to his shoulder and walked, a little dizzy, limping, decidedly with more load than he had the strength to carry for very long or very far.

By stages and resting a bit he could, he told himself, walk to the junction of roads and the rider stone—he didn't know how he'd have done without the lift, but he was glad he didn't have to try, the more so since a bank of cloud was moving in, just the gray edge advancing from off the mountains over the foothills, promising weather before dark—cold rain down here and undoubtedly snow in the high country last night, he said to himself. A cold, damp wind, blowing off the peaks of the Firgeberg, fluttered the fringes of his jacket. Its occasional gusts bent the flat brim of his hat.

Before he'd reached the next hill the temperature had dropped several degrees.

Which said he'd better hurry, as much as he could.

Various parts of him might hurt—but he hadn't even marked down a grudge against the bank: thanks to Cassivey, who'd yanked strings on everybody including the bank, the marshal's office, and the town judge, he'd no record of any wrongdoing, he'd been able to buy everything he remotely needed in the way of supplies, money was, by arcane townsman miracles, back in the bank, under a new number with a new card that had only his name on it and no next-of's to enable anyone to rob him.

So Cassivey assured him, Cassivey having full confidence, Cassivey said, in the men he'd sent to make things clear to the woman at the bank. Cassivey'd paid the fine, the business was off, as townsmen called it, the books. All of which was, at the moment, more help than he'd remote interest in comprehending—if he survived the winter he'd be very interested.

But that was on the other side of winter.

He still wasn't sure if the bank business was going to work. He personally suspected it was a way contrived for townsmen to cheat riders, and the bank still held they'd been justified in dealing Aby's funds out to Hawley.

Which confused him—and which was the one reason he was remotely interested, right now, in what was the law with the bank. On one level he knew that he was right and that Hawley was wrong. But, town law holding to the contrary, and things having worked out in some kind of justice, by town law and townsman generosity—two words he hadn't thought possibly fit together—it left him in enough doubt about the right and wrong of what Hawley had done that he wasn't sure he'd even mention the transgression to Hawley, though he'd recently sworn he was going to get it out of Hawley, and then beat Hawley into horse-food.

He didn't, now, know how much fault was Hawley's and how much was because the bank women had suggested it to him. Hawley wasn't damn bright in certain matters, smart enough on the trail, as far as staying alive, but he could have let his wants and what the bank told him get ahead of his common sense.

He could understand that. He knew Hawley with all his faults.

But it would still be a good idea if Hawley and both his partners were out of Shamesey before he got back next spring. It would be a good idea if they just happened to find jobs elsewhere, but on roads he traveled, for a couple of years. A couple of years might be enough to let him cool down enough, and enough to let him figure what he thought about what Hawley had done—

Right now, still damn him to bloody hell.

Damn Shamesey and Lyle Wesson, too, who could have been a lot more helpful—a lot more forward getting his belongings to him outside Shamesey gate, for one thing. Getting his belongings was why he'd gotten shot, and getting shot was why he'd not had a chance to talk to Hawley and his partners.

And Hawley and Jonas and Luke hadn't been damn forward, either, to round up what was his and get it outside the gates, and maybe to signal there was more to tell him, and maybe, just maybe, like friends, to just camp outside the walls that night and make themselves available for talk, for errands, for whatever a man needed who wasn't steady enough to go into the largest camp in the settled world. Put themselves out? Make themselves available?

Hell, no, they headed for the bar and warm beds.

Nobody'd been a damn lot of help, once he started adding up what certain people should have done and hadn't. There was enough blame to go around in the situation as far as he was concerned—a lot of people in the class of riders that he wasn't damned happy with, which was *why* the business at the bank in Anveney had sunk away into cool indifference. Townsmen could be fools all they liked and you expected it. But *riders* had screwed him, people he dealt with, people with a history with him, and that made him damned mad.

Only Aby . . .

He knew, dammit. He knew the woman and he'd been the one to fail, thinking she'd changed. He didn't know what the debt was—he didn't have to know. She'd have paid it. If silence was what the man asked, regarding those shipments, and she owed Cassivey—

She'd done all she could to get him into Cassivey's employ, cajoled, pleaded. Truth be told—he'd refused to go up to Anveney for many more reasons than the smell on the money. He'd offered his own proposal: Come down to Malvey.

Why's it always your way? he'd asked, he thought, reasonably. They'd quarreled. He'd been mad. Aby'd gone off mad—and hurt, he'd picked that up in the ambient.

But nothing of her reasons. Aby could throw that anger up like a wall. And had.

They'd thought there was forever.

But she'd owed a man. And, damn, the woman he knew never betrayed a trust. Never. *He* had.

A sudden apprehension came shivering its way through his consciousness that he'd just slipped into Aby's last set of motions, working for the same man, following the same route—retracing, in short, everything Aby'd done down to leaving Anveney in Cassivey's employ, exactly where Aby'd wanted him to be when they'd had their last quarrel.

So he'd just taken that job Aby had wanted him to take—more, *he* owed Cassivey. It was her job he inherited, her obligation, her promises.

He wasn't superstitious like the preacher-men, but he kept thinking about that first step they kept talking about, the one on the slide to hell. He'd failed Aby; she'd have lived if he'd been there. He wouldn't have been riding at the rear, leaving Aby on point at the worst damn turn on the mountain. He'd sent her off to partners who'd failed her. He'd sent her off to die; and maybe, in the economy of the preachers' God, maybe he was going up where he was somehow supposed to have been in the first place.

Only this time Aby wouldn't be there for him. Turn about was fair play.

Got her back and the woman began to bother him again.

Got her back and he had to ask—where in hell did she spend the money?

Or had she spent it? She'd never said exactly what she'd had in the account. *He* couldn't read the damn card. No more than she could. And she'd never said.

How much did the bank *give* to Hawley, anyway?

His legs wobbled. The sky went violet and brass. His shortness of breath took him by surprise. The rifle, the pistol—a winter's ammunition, the food, all added up, considering he'd taken no few knocks. But he needed the gun. Needed the supplies. Couldn't lay anything down.

And Burn depended on him—Burn couldn't afford to have him go down on his face out here and freeze in the coming storm. He couldn't bet Burn's life that Burn would use the road to come looking for him. A nighthorse wasn't held to roads.

He couldn't faint out here, for Burn's sake, he couldn't faint and he couldn't quit. He set his goal as the next hill down the barren road and walked that far. Then he set his intention as another hill—struggled up to its crest, telling himself now that he'd done the hard part, he could make the downhill, at least.

But his breath was short and when he looked up his blurred vision was starting to give him two barren, eroded horizons, two road-traces among doubled rocks.

His head was light. His heart began to pound. Straight line was more efficient. Wandering used up his strength faster. Had to walk straight, had to stay conscious, above all else—if he was conscious, he persuaded himself, Burn might find him; if he wasn't, Burn might not hear him and go right by.

He walked the next uphill—and sat down at the top, in an act of prudence, to nurse his splitting headache at the road edge, rather than the middle of it, in the vague notion a truck *could* come along. Which common sense then told him wasn't possibly going to happen again in this country until next spring, but that had been his thought when he sat down—he didn't want to be hit by traffic.

He didn't want to freeze, either. He could sit here till winter snows covered him, the way he felt now. The pain shot through his skull from front to back and off his temples. He squinted and it was worse.

So he rested his head on his arms and sat that way to wait for his breathing to slow down. Raw air burned his throat. He coughed and coughing hurt his head. The cold of the bare ground had numbed his feet, and the bite of the wind that swept down off the mountain wall chilled his back. He wished he'd sent Cassivey's man after that sweater he'd seen. Rust and black one. Aby'd have liked it.

Then he must have shut his eyes for a moment—he couldn't tell whether the sudden darkening of the land and the advent of a brassy light was the thickness of the clouds overhead or the cumulative effect of blows to the head.

He heard the sound of thunder, and thought—damn!—with the kind of sinking feeling a man got when he'd realized a serious, serious mistake.

He knew he had to move. He sat there a time more, breathing deep to gather his strength, needing to be sure he could get up and not pass out; and while he sat, a colder wind began to gust along the ridge, raising dust. He saw it coming, adjusted his hat and scarf and pulled the cuffs of the sweater he did have down over his gloves as the first fat drops spatted into the barren dust at his feet.

That was it. God had decided. He had to move. He drew a breath tinged with copper and the smell of cold rain, and put an all-out effort into getting up.

Muscles had stiffened. He used the rifle for a prop—might not have made it to his feet, he feared, without it.

He used it for a support to bend and heft the two-pack, slung its not inconsiderable weight and the rifle-strap over his shoulder. Then he started walking, heavy drops spattering the powdery dust around him, making small red craters. It felt like liquid ice where a drop found its way past the brim of his hat, down his neck or into his face.

Then—fool, he thought, remembering in the general haze of his thoughts that he'd bought a slicker—he slung the two-pack around to get at it, and had to take his gloves off.

The slicker was one of those new plastic things that didn't hold body heat worth a damn, but he hadn't wanted to carry the weight of canvas, especially on the climb they faced; and the thin plastic at least kept you dry, life and death in the cold seasons, when a soaking and a cold wind could freeze a man faster than he could make a shelter. Cassivey's man had sworn it was tough—it could double as a ground sheet, and kept you drier than canvas.

If it wasn't flapping and cracking in the gale. If your fingers didn't freeze, finding the catches.

He had to drop the rest of the stuff to wrestle it as it snapped and fluttered in the wind, threatening escape from his numbed fingers, but he fastened latches one after the other and held it fast. It smelled worse than Anveney smokestacks, even in the gusting wind, but between that and the coat and the sweater and all, he had to own it kept the wind out. He felt warmer.

He put his gloves back on, gathered up his gear again, took the weight and walked all the way up to the top of the next hill before he ran out of breath and had to stand there leaning on the rifle and gasping and coughing.

But when he cleared the cold-weather tearing from his eyes, he saw clumps of grass around him, sparse, twisted, and brown with the season. He'd almost reached the junction with the boundary road. He was that close.

<Burn,> he sent into the silent ambient, knees wobbling; desperate for some sense of presence, feeling the wind cold against his legs as the slicker flapped open. He had to keep going, he said to himself, and walked, using the rifle for a stick.

A flash of lightning blazed through his headache, blinding him, making white edges on the rocks; immediately the thunder crashed around him, total environment, deafening, pain ricocheting inside his temples and behind his eyes.

Then the rain hit in earnest, a deluge so thick it made a vapor on the blowing wind. Rain pooled in the brim of his hat and made an intermittent waterfall off the edge. He kept moving, tightening his scarf about his neck to keep the water from going down his collar. His knees were soaked below the slicker. His feet were beginning to be soaked through despite the oil coating he maintained on his boots, and the last feeling in them was going—no help at all to his balance.

Then <wet horse> flashed across his vision, <mad, wet horse on one hill, Guil in flappy brown slicker.>

The whole universe opened up, a sense of location, a map of relationship to the whole landscape, and he looked uphill through the veil of rain and twilight. A dark shape was trotting toward him, brisk, angry, shaking itself as it came.

He didn't sit down. He wanted to collapse right there in the road, his legs were so weak—but he'd only have to get up again, and be all over mud.

<Bacon,> he promised Burn, but even that didn't prevent Burn from detecting the pain and the exhaustion, and didn't prevent Burn's growing agitation as Burn came slogging up in the mud, dripping wet and imaging <dark, fire, kick men. Guil on back.>

Burn stopped alongside him. He leaned against Burn's rain-slick shoulder, feeling its fever-warmth against his face, with the cold rain coming down on them—stood there, Burn smelling him over and snorting in disgust, finding <bad smell and smokeweed> despite the rain.

Burn was warm. Burn was a windbreak. Burn was solid. Most of all, his sense of the whole world was back. Burn didn't ask how he'd hit his head. Burn wasn't curious about done-things, just possibly-to-do things, and if Burn's rider was hurting, Burn was mad at the hurt and wanted it to go away. Burn wanted <kicking men,> if men were responsible, but <no,> Guil sent. <Man giving bacon. Three slabs of bacon. Man giving rifle and gear. Man in room. Guil in room. Nice man. With bacon.>

<Guil's face cut,> Burn insisted. <Blood-smell, bad-smell, Guil-smell. Kick and bite.>

He was too sick to argue. He just wanted up on Burn's safe back and the two of them away from here and under shelter of some kind, and he didn't think he could make the jump up—knew he couldn't, with the two-pack. He slung the weight over Burn's withers, wishing Burn not to object and still figuring to have an argument, with Burn in that negative mood, figuring possibly to be left in the roadway in the rain, <Burn shaking off the pack.>

Burn didn't sulk at all about the pack. Burn even dropped a leg to make it easier for a wobbly rider . . . but Burn's rider couldn't make it that way. He wanted Burn square on his feet again, and (the arm with the rifle all the way over Burn's withers and probably jabbing him in God-knew-what places) he couldn't do more than jump for it and land belly-down like a kid. He slithered a leg over with no grace at all, trying not to hit Burn again with the rifle barrel or knock the pack off Burn's shoulders—he caught it, squared it, pinned it with a knee and shakily tucked the slicker about him, wet knees and all, Burn standing still as a rock the while, for which he was very grateful.

Burn slowly started moving, testing his rider's balance. Burn's heat reached the insides of his legs, traveling upward under the slicker, wonderful, wonderful warmth. He could hug the slicker around him and hope for the warmth below to meet the lesser warmth he'd saved in his upper body, if he could stay upright so long.

He shivered, waiting for that to happen. His legs jerking in spasm bothered Burn, whose thoughts on the matter weren't coherent, something like <Guil falling,> and <this way> and <that

way,> because the twitches were signaling Burn directions he didn't mean and didn't want.

Burn figured it out, though, worried about it, and got mad, imaging <fire, and dark> and <kill.> But Guil imaged <log shelter,> and <rider-stone,> and Burn began to pick up his pace, imaging <grassy hills in twilight,> and <fire> and <fish.>

<Rider-stone,> Guil insisted, because there was a shelter where this road joined the boundary road. Intersections were places you could always look for shelter, and where there was shelter of any kind, riders set up a marker, be it wood or stone, in this otherwise desolate land, to carve or scratch over with messages to riders who came on the same road.

Burn agreed, finally, while the rain spattered about them and gullied down the hills. Burn had been waiting for him in that shelter, in a <barren, bad place,> and had only come after him when the weather turned . . . he already saw the refuge Burn was taking him to, <lean-to made of logs, next the stone. Barren land. Bad-tasting grass.>

Didn't have to say things out loud for Burn. Damn lot smarter than townsmen, Guil thought muzzily. Friendlier than bank-women.

<Handsome horse,> Burn agreed, splashing along the barren, puddled road, pace, pace, pace, pace, never missing a beat, strong and confident. All around them, water sluiced unchecked down the hills, remaking the gullies and washing at the roots of the feeble grass.

But at least the ground cover that held out grew more frequent.

Chapter
— xiii —

THERE WAS DAMP IN THE AIR, DAMP WHICH IN THIS UNEASY SEASON could be melting snow—or could herald another storm. The clouds which had in midafternoon wreathed the summit of Rogers Peak had moved on; and the departing sun, long slipped behind the mountains, had left a pink glow over the snowy rooftops and blued shadows along the snow-banked walls. Cookfires spread an upward smudge on the snow-blanketed evening, and the direction of that smoke said quiet winds, change pending.

"Early winter," Tara said, on the porch of the rider quarters where, the light being better and the wind being still, she'd pulled the table outside, and she and Vadim diced potatoes for their common supper. She hashed one to bits and lost three pieces overside onto the porch. "Damn." It wasn't a good score she was keeping.

"I can finish," Vadim said. "Take it easy, Tara. Go sit down."

"I'm fine."

"I know you're fine. You need your fingers."

It made her mad. It shouldn't. She knew it shouldn't. She

chopped away, hacking at the job, trying for self-control. The horses were out of range, collectively, in the den. Flicker was 'taking it easy.' Flicker was sore as hell, and had earned her rest and care, having saved both their necks.

The knife slipped. She swore, sucked at a nicked finger.

"Tara, for God's sake—"

She evaded Vadim's attempt to see it, or to hold her, kept sucking at it. The taste of blood somehow satisfied the gnawing unease. It was real harm. You could taste it, smell it, feel it, you didn't have to imagine it. She stood there as Vadim, with misgivings evident on his face, set back to work. For a moment, inside, the world was white. White was everywhere and her heart was pounding.

"Trust you with knives," Vadim muttered. "I told you—"

She snapped, "I thought Barry and Llew would have started back. They ought to have started back."

Vadim didn't look up. A single peeling spiraled down from a potato in Vadim's strong, capable hands. Finally Vadim said, "They're big boys. They'll manage the same as you did. If there's something out there, they have as good a chance as you did. More. There's two of them."

"Bunch of skittery townsmen on their hands," she said in a low voice. "Oxen. God knows what they'd do. The townsmen damn sure don't know. There's that wrecked truck out there. The damn convoy could have told us. Aby could have *told* us."

"They phoned."

"From Shamesey! They let us sit here—"

"They were just four riders, that's a big convoy, and the horses were already under attack: truck transmitters would have sent them sky high and attracted the trouble to them. God knows what else. Aby did right."

"They could have tried somewhere on that road!"

"It might have followed them. They couldn't lead it to a town, and it'd go straight for a transmitter. That's thousands of people down there. If it fixed on Shamesey—they just couldn't risk it, Tara. At least they didn't lead it here."

"Well, it *came* here, didn't it? God, she let us deliver a work crew out there, she let us leave Barry and Llew out there—"

"The rogue could have been anywhere on the mountain. You don't know it was ever even near you."

"The hell."

"You don't know. Unless you saw it next to you, you don't know."

"Well, how do you know, either? You never dealt with one. You didn't feel what I felt out there. You didn't even know it was out there until I got to the gate, so tell me who was close to it!"

"I don't know," Vadim confessed, concentrating on the potatoes, and she hadn't meant to raise her voice. Or to say what she said. She was embarrassed.

"I'm sorry," she muttered.

"No offense. I wasn't out there."

"It scared me," she said—stupid, obvious admission she wouldn't have made, except she regretted going at Vadim like that. "I'm still spooked."

"Yeah," Vadim said, "no blame from me. I'm only sorry I didn't hear it."

"Believe me. You aren't sorry."

The sending had fallen back before she got to the gate. He'd heard it only from her memory—and she didn't want to go spreading it, recreating it, carrying it like a contagion in the camp.

Potatoes went in pieces. She was still mad. She couldn't say why. Every nerve was raw-ended. She couldn't stand still. She didn't want to go down to the den, near the horses, but Flicker didn't understand the reason for that reluctance, Flicker needed her, and she had to go down and rub down Flicker's sore legs and try to keep a cover on her anxiousness. She'd rather peel potatoes, only she couldn't do that right, either.

"You didn't get any kind of shape on it," Vadim said with a look under the brow. It was a question. Three times now, it was the same damned question. "You still don't know if it had a rider."

"I didn't get any shape," she said—snapped, and didn't mean to. "Flicker was too strong. I told you. I couldn't reach past her." She'd said that over and over. But she hadn't said, and she did say, "Truth is, I didn't ever think of it."

"Under the circumstances," Vadim said. "Yeah. No question."

Another potato went to bits under her knife. She didn't look up. Vadim said, "Just thank God Flicker *is* a noisy sod. She kept it out. Whatever it was, she kept it clear of us, if it ever did come close last night."

Come up to the walls? She hadn't thought about that, either: her impression of distance and location of the danger behind her at the last had been so absolute she hadn't questioned it. She'd feared it—at the gate. But everything had threatened her, then.

And with Flicker down, trying to get Flicker's mind off it—she hadn't had time for questions.

But she'd had to call and call for Vadim's attention. Pound at the gate, while no one in the camp or the village was aware of the danger—God, for the same reason they wouldn't have heard the rogue—because Flicker hadn't relayed anything. Flicker had shut everybody near her down cold, sending <white-white-white> to everyone in her reach until midmorning.

"Flicker shut us out," she said. "You couldn't hear it, either."

"The thought crossed my mind," Vadim said. "Flicker could have blocked most anything from us in the den with her. The village didn't spook, at least—so it didn't come closer or it was quiet except for someone *listening* for it. But there's no point looking for tracks. The snow didn't stop till dawn."

That was true.

"Hell," she said.

"If it had a rider," Vadim said.

The whole conversation was sending chills down her nerves. She didn't know who'd started it. Vadim was camp-boss. It was his job to find out things. He was doing that. He'd already reported to the marshal and the mayor what she'd encountered in the woods. The marshal said don't tell the town anything: the marshal and the mayor were afraid of panic and had kept the phone call quiet. But she couldn't fill in more detail than she'd given. "I don't think so," she said. "No."

"But you never did see it. Never did even imagine seeing it."

"I'm not one of the kids," she said, again too sharply. She was disquieted by the thought of touching anything that wild, that unstable. It hadn't gotten past Flicker's determination. But a nighthorse was the most powerful thing on the planet.

A nighthorse was . . . far and away the most powerful thing.

"Could be one of the wild ones," she said. "A fall, a fever."

"And it could be anywhere in the hills," Vadim said.

"It was here, I *felt* it. It was behind me. I *know* where it was. No, it didn't come to the gate. I was scared, was all."

She remembered <the woods, the rogue's position shifting>—she hadn't let herself think of it, however fleetingly, in her long hours in the den watching over Flicker. She hadn't let her mind stay on that dark thought for two consecutive seconds, since. It was still dangerous to think of too vividly. A going-apart, was how she'd heard it described. A mind going in fragments, bits of it coming together at random—tenderness, hatred, desire, sexual arousal, rage all combining and separating at total random. She didn't know. She couldn't swear what she'd heard. But Flicker hadn't *let* her hear. That was the point.

"The wild ones will go down to lowland pastures any day now," she said. "If there should be something with that band—maybe it'll go down, too. Or maybe it'll follow."

"They'd try to drive it off. They'll kill it if they can. They won't let it follow them."

She didn't think Vadim knew any more than she did—what the wild ones might do or be able to do against a threat like that. Vadim had grown up on Rogers Peak, born to Tarmin; she'd been a free rider, but only on Darwin Peak, ranging between Darwin settlements, and they were both guessing, she knew for a fact. The long riders—they told such stories, around safe firesides. That was collectively all they knew.

"It'd go for people," she said. "That's what they say. I don't know if that's always true, but, God, if it does, there's all the villages around the loop, besides Barry and Llew out there in that damn road camp. —Vadim, —"

"You made it in. They can make it in."

"I was lucky!"

"You make your luck. If you heard it, they heard it, and they'll take precautions."

"Fine. Fine. But what if it's smarter next time? What if the thing shows up on—"

A bell rang—the one at the village side of the Little Gate. Some villager was coming to request something of the riders, God knew what, maybe another trek out to the road crew. Maybe the marshal with worse news—maybe with a notion the weather was going to turn. She hadn't looked at the glass since noon.

She watched as the blacksmith passed through the gate and shut it. His name was Andy Goss. His teenaged sons trailed him as he made a straight line for the porch where they stood. It sure didn't look like a delivery.

"You seen my daughter?" the blacksmith asked, coming up out of breath.

"Not since morning," Vadim said. And Tara remembered Brionne Goss coming into the den this morning—the kid never had understood No or Don't or Leave my horse alone. Wonder that some horse hadn't bitten hell out of her. Then let the father howl.

But not since morning—

"For *what?*" the blacksmith asked, still hard-breathing, sweating despite the cold.

"She brought a biscuit for the horses. Wanted to talk. We said it wasn't a good time. She left."

"Then where'd she go?" The blacksmith was angry. "We got the whole village searching, door to door. When was she here?"

The outside gate, Tara thought with a chill. The spook in the woods. The kid's hanging about the horses . . . "Crack of dawn." It was approaching twilight. "You've searched the village? You've searched all the village?"

"Everywhere."

"Rider gate," Tara said, and ran the steps, struck out past Goss and his sons, down across the snowy yard and toward the den, Vadim hurrying to catch up, the blacksmith and his boys close behind.

The snow between the village wall and the exposed side of the nighthorse den hadn't melted that much during the day. They didn't go to that side of the den unless they were going to the outside gate and nobody'd been out, none of the horses had been stirring out—truth to tell, they *and* the horses had slept the whole afternoon.

But somebody in small-sized boots had gone past the corner of the den and along the wall, and not come back. The pointed-toed footprints led up to the camp's outside gate, and the gate had been dragged open and shut again—enough, one was sure, for the owner of those boots.

"Those your daughter's tracks?" Tara asked, indicating the prints, but the horses were near enough she was already feeling the father's rising panic.

The father didn't know the half of it.

"Chad and I had better go look," Vadim said.

"The hell," she said, imaged <Tara and Vadim riding out,> imaged <guns.> And <long shadows on the snow,> which was the reality out there. It was close to evening.

"You're not up to it," Vadim said. "Flicker damn sure isn't. We'll look as far as we can follow those tracks."

She didn't want to stay and wait. She knew the search wasn't going to turn up a live and happy girl, and that conviction in her mind might have been what agitated the blacksmith: they were next the den wall.

"What in hell'd she do it for?" the man asked as Vadim went off quickly around the corner, <getting Chad,> and the ambient flared with her distress, her resentment of villager stupidity, villager demands. The blacksmith caught her arm, hard. "I'm talking to you, damn it, Tara Chang! Why in hell didn't one of you put her back out the proper gate? What in bloody hell was she doing here in the first place?"

"It was a dare," one of the boys muttered, and an image flashed into Tara's mind: <Brionne slipping through the village side gate.> "They dared her do it."

"Who dared her?"

<Kids watching, from the village side.> "The kids. But she was always coming here. She said she could hear the horses." <Brionne in a village house. Brionne at a fireside. . . . >

But it wasn't anywhere Tara had ever seen. And dammit, Brionne *didn't* hear the horses. <Snatching the young fool out of

harm's way,> she remembered, precisely because the girl didn't hear—or hearing, refused to believe that any horse refused her insistent attentions.

But she was seeing <Brionne in the village, Brionne next the forge, her face glowing> and it wasn't her doing it, it was the blacksmith and his sons too near the horses.

"My girl's been coming here?" the blacksmith cried, as if it were *her* fault. "She's been in and out of here and you didn't report it? Damn you!"

They were townsmen unused to the images that came thick and fast next the den—<Brionne with biscuits, Brionne running out the door of the den>—and Tara felt panic rising in the ambient. "She came here. I told her go home. We all told her go home. It didn't take. She—"

She couldn't focus on it. She was seeing <Vadim and Chad getting supplies. Restless horses, waiting.>

<Mina and Luisa wanting to go.> The argument had broken out on that score before Vadim had exchanged words with Chad inside the den. Hell, Tara thought in the eyeblink give and take of the ambient, and caught a breath on: <Chad angry. Long shadows. Clouds. Twilight behind the peak.>

<Vadim wanting Mina and Luisa with Tara. Flicker upset.>

—and glared in startlement as the blacksmith for a second time caught her sleeve. <Scared. Wanting daughter.> Then images from some other near source boiled up: <Hating Brionne. Brionne in house. Rage.>

<Goblin cat crouching, ears flat, over bloody rags, red coat—satisfaction, pain, *wanting* this with a fevered, angry ache—the man at the forge, hammering glowing iron—wanting him, *wanting* him to look at him—>

God, <the kid, the boys—> She couldn't get a breath past the hate in the spiraling ascension of tempers, and the blacksmith rounded on the kid with <*beating* boy,> his fist cocked. The boys were on the retreat along the wall, the shorter dragging the taller, whose fists were also clenched. Hate flooded the ambient. Anger. Pain.

<*Village. Gate.*> Tara couldn't find her faculty of speech. She

threw force into the image, shoved at the blacksmith, wanting <*Goss leaving, boys leaving. Camp gate shut.*>

"Don't you push me!" the blacksmith yelled.

Flicker's temper hit the ambient. Flicker was on her way outside.

"Get out of here!" She found the words, scarcely the breath, and hit the man with her fist. "You're upsetting my horse! We'll find your daughter, man, just <get out of here, dammit! *Now!*">

She shoved him as Flicker came around the corner of the den, a shape of anger and night. It was a cul-de-sac between the den, the palisade wall and the camp's outside gate, with a mad horse occupying the only way out, sending <anger, danger, kill, flashes of light> as Tara ran and physically pushed at Flicker's chest to restrain her from a charge.

"Get past!" she shouted over her shoulder, leaning all her weight and will against Flicker, making her <back up,> wanting her to calm down. "Get past, dammit!"

It was an eternity measured in breaths. Goss and his sons eased past them. Her arm shook against Flicker's strength, Flicker's anger—but then Goss and his sons, Goss shouting recriminations at the boys, headed back along the wall. Goss opened the Little Gate and went back to the village side of the palisade, mad, scared, with something maybe broken forever between him and his sons.

The Goss boys had let loose more truth at their father than they'd ever intended. The boys hated Brionne: the father was overwhelmed with panic and the boys with hatred of their sister. The images as they faded in distance from the wall were of rage and outrage, and a rider couldn't judge what the right of it was, or who was justified.

Brionne was the youngest, Brionne was a pampered, headstrong brat. Given, she didn't like the kid, but she'd never in her life shared a moment of such hatred among strangers—sendings going wild, sendings of a frankness that villagers weren't used to, minds cycling wildly over thoughts, darting after known soft spots and old faults as unerringly as willy-wisps to ripe carrion, horse and human tempers flaring completely out of bounds.

Shaking, she leaned on Flicker's shoulder and tried to calm Flicker down, telling herself she didn't remotely know why

Brionne had gone out this morning, or what Brionne thought she was doing—but if she had to lay a bet on it, the young fool had thought she'd heard a horse.

She didn't like that thought. God, she didn't like it. And she hadn't handled Brionne's father well. She was painfully aware she'd set up the encounter, not remotely suspecting more than concern on their side until they got near the horses.

She stood, still shuddery, with her hands on Flicker, whose mind she did understand, and kept imaging <quiet, quiet water> and <still trees and sunshine,> patting Flicker's neck to quiet the violence she still felt in the ambient.

She told herself that Flicker was still on edge from a brush with disaster; or Flicker was reacting to villager hysteria—Flicker shivered and snorted and worked her jaws, <wanting bite, wanting blood>—she was still trying to haul Flicker down from her fighting mood when Vadim and Chad came riding around the corner with the kits they always kept ready against a sudden call—outbound.

Bound outside into danger she'd ridden through last night, for a damned spoiled brat who'd killed herself in one willful push of a latch.

<Goblin cat,> she imaged, and felt Flicker jump under her hands. She had a leaden weight of apprehension in her gut. There was no *use* in what they were doing, this late in the day. Vadim was having a crisis of guilt, Chad was going because Vadim was dead set on it; and she was *mad,* dammit. They were running a risk and they knew it, but they weren't listening to her.

Mina and Luisa arrived from around the same corner, their horses trailing behind them—but being nearer the outside wall than they were, Tara found it her job to walk along in the men's tracks, unlatch the gate for them and fight it wide against the snow piled up inside.

"Back before dark," Vadim said, from Quickfoot's back, "unless we do find her trail. We might have to make a camp. I don't think she got far."

"She couldn't," she said, and clapped a hand to Vadim's leg, trying to still the ambient. "Don't be a fool, God, don't either of you be fools. You know what's out there, the damn kid's gone to it—"

"I'll turn him around before dark," Chad said, meaning Vadim. "Don't you open that gate, Tara, don't open that gate, unless you know it's us or it's Barry and Llew."

"Get back before dark!" Mina said from behind her. Vadim was Mina's lover and hers, from time to time, as Chad was Luisa's—or hers, from time to time, but not so often as Vadim. She caught the imaging from Mina and from Luisa, both her own most-times partners—and for a moment it was an intimacy rider with rider and horse with horse that took the breath and scared hell out of her. It was love, it was friendship, <vivid and warm and smelling of straw and sex> and the boys were about to ride out the gate.

"You're senior," Vadim said, and Chad's Jumper passed by her with a whip of a well-groomed tail.

"Latch down tight," Chad said.

Then Vadim and Chad passed the gate with a pelting of trodden snow from their horses' heels, and rode away on a trail of young girl's footprints.

They wouldn't find the hope the blacksmith wanted to find, she was well sure of that.

Worse, the first hint of sunset color was already in the sky: light didn't last long in autumn, on this eastern face of the mountains—they had a treacherously short while they could ride, to find what an uncompromising Wild might have left of Brionne Goss, and to get back again safely.

She dragged the gate shut. Mina helped. Luisa dropped the latch and shoved it down hard, to be sure.

<Rider-stone in green grass,> Guil remembered. <Trees.> But Burn remembered not. The accompanying rider-shelter as Burn had it in his thoughts had not even brush around it, with precious little grass at all, a desolate place with <bad-tasting grass.>

And when, as they rounded a bend of the road around a long hill, Guil saw the rider-stone with his eyes, not his mind—he rubbed them to be sure.

Indeed the image, wrapped in the murk of rain and twilight, did stop when he pressed his fingers against his eyes.

Burn was right. There was no pasturage worth considering. The stone stood in a widening mud-puddle filling a slight depression—a sight that afflicted Guil with a shiver of some kind, be it chill of weather or doubt of the future he'd bargained for, listening to Cassivey, committing himself to the man's employ.

Anveney was death. He didn't know how he could have forgotten it, talking to the rich man, taking his hire. It didn't matter if Cassivey was affable and convenient and talked an extravagantly good deal—Anveney was still death.

And when they reached the stone and he chanced to glance at the signs scratched on it, old marks and new—the first thing his eye fell on was a plain circle with a crescent.

Aby and Moon.

<Us on the road,> he urged Burn, unreasoning, spooked. He wanted nowhere near this place. He wanted no part of this trail, this direction, this chain of events.

But Burn thought, <warm log shelter,> and carried him willy-nilly along an eroded rising trail until the dark, rain-dripping shadow of the log shelter was in front of them.

<Aby staying in this place,> Guil thought, and ducked reflexively as Burn passed under the roof edge, into almost-night, into an east-facing recess where the wind had to come clear around three walls to enter, and where the rain had to ride those gusts or seep weakly through cracks in the roof in order to fall on them.

Something small skittered past Burn's feet, out into the rain. Burn stamped at it, imaging <nighthorse> and <fire> until whatever it was vacated the place glad to be alive.

All the same, the jolt of that move hit Guil's nerves and sent him light-headed. He had to lean on Burn's neck until he could muster the strength to slide off under the weight of the rifle and pistol and the rest that he carried.

He committed himself finally, leaned and swung. His feet hit the ground at the same moment he shed the rifle strap into his hand. He stood very precariously for a moment, sight and hearing fading.

Then he saw and heard the rain falling in a night-lit curtain outside—felt random drops dripping through the absolute black of the chinked logs onto their heads, and breathed the mist gusted in from the open side, but the air inside the shelter felt breathlessly warm and strange to his cold-numbed skin, all the same, after the rush of wind-borne water outside.

He dragged the pack down from Burn's shoulders and wobbled over to the wall, wet below the knees and around the cuffs of the sleeves. He couldn't just sit down and wait to dry out, when rain could easily turn to sleet or snow and temperatures could drop below freezing with no more warning than that mountain wind out there already gave him.

He felt along the wall and leaned the rifle in the corner, then dropped the pack in what he hoped was a reasonably dry spot. Then he unbuckled and shed the weight of the sidearm to pegs he felt, some rider's thoughtful addition to the accommodation.

Lastly, light-headed, he sat down on the damp earthen floor on the spot to strip off the wet boots and the trousers, wrapped himself below the waist in a dry blanket from the canvas pack, still wearing sweater, coat, slicker and all, because the plastic was holding in his body heat and he needed everything he had that was remotely dry to keep that heat around him.

He knew one thing for dead certain: he wasn't moving on in the morning. If a man got soaked at the edge of winter, a man already possibly concussed, to judge by the hellish headache he carried behind his eyes, then that man if he wasn't a total fool didn't travel out of shelter till fire or sun had dried his clothes.

And Burn's better night vision, in the black inside of the shelter, told him that a fire wasn't an option. He sent Burn out into the rain, <looking for woodpile against shelter wall,> but Burn didn't find one, came in wet and shook himself.

Nobody'd restocked the shelter. Wood wasn't available in the land any longer.

No wood. Aby'd been the culprit, maybe Hawley and Jonas. Couldn't blame them, damn their lazy hides. But if it had been woodless when they used it they'd sure not ridden after any, either. *He'd* have restocked the damn shelter unless there was a life-and-death hurry about getting out, and he didn't think there had been. If it were anybody but Aby he'd have said careless.

But maybe with the weather changing, and a need to go on a schedule that couldn't, by Cassivey's whim, and needn't, by Aby's judgment, wait for spring—he could forgive her.

Still, —damn—

He began to shiver. He huddled there shaking his teeth out, took his hat off, put the blanket over his wet hair, wrapped his arms about himself under the blanket and slicker and tucked his feet up—he couldn't feel his toes, but he didn't think he'd been out there long enough for frostbite, thanks to Burn, all thanks to Burn.

<Bacon in dry bright sun,> he promised Burn, clenching his teeth to still the shivers. <Burn coming over the hill in the rain. Burn carrying the packs. Handsome, splendid, shining in the sunlight nighthorse.>

Burn lapped it up like cream; and Burn began to think of <fire, and dry bedding and bacon cooking,> which wasn't as good as edible supper, but it was far better than the drip of rain in the real world outside.

<Wet, dripping wood,> Guil thought, there being very little convenient way to image a complete lack of any given thing—and Burn wasn't much on the technicalities of fire-making. Burn knew it was raining, of course, and Burn hadn't found a woodpile, or any trees, but Burn was hungry. There were three slabs of bacon in the supplies Burn's rider had lugged an agonizing long way from Anveney—and that of course changed all logic. Bacon was here. <Fire> happened in Burn's mind when Burn thought of it.

So Burn thought of <fire.> Burn did his part. Burn *expected* it to happen.

Well, so the one of them with fingers bestirred himself, teeth chattering, and, for a peace offering, took some beef jerky out of the pack, only then and shakily remembering that food hadn't crossed his path at all today, either.

So it wasn't bacon, and it couldn't be bacon until the rain stopped, until he dried off, or unless a woodpile miraculously appeared, but Burn took the jerky as the best he could do under difficult circumstances, and simply thought <bacon.> Burn chewed the first piece, then heaved a gusty sigh, circled, Burn's habit when he was tired, and sank down, precarious process in the cramped space between him and the storm, narrowly missing a vertical support pole, arranging himself so that Burn's rider, who insisted on sitting, could feed him bits of jerky, two, of course, to the human's own one, considering Burn had a far bigger appetite.

Burn was, overall, mollified.

Guil cut his thumb, he was shivering so, but, hell, there were worse fates. He had something to keep his stomach quiet, he was reasonably sure after a few bites that the food was going to stay down, which he hadn't been sure of when the first bite went past his teeth, and his situation tonight, give or take the blinding headache and a slight nausea, was improving. He gave Burn less than Burn wanted, of course, but then, Burn was bottomless, and the supplies had to last a lot farther than Anveney Stone.

<High country,> he said to Burn, <snow and ice. Us walking.>

<Snow falling,> Burn agreed. <Rider shelters. Hunting spooks, playing in the snow.>

<Traveling the ridge. Snow and fireweed thickets, bright red in the sunlight.>

But he didn't want to think where they were going first, or why, or searching for what. He shied away from that.

He thought of <here> instead. Aby had slept in this place. He'd suffered that one crazed impulse to bolt, before Burn had brought him here and come inside, all the same, leaving him no escape.

Except freezing to death in a rainstorm. He was saner than that. He'd not acted like it, spooking out, out there, but Burn had known he wasn't rational, and Burn had duly taken him where he had to go.

So I'm here, woman, he thought in distress. What more do you want?

God, I should have heard you. Should have heard, when you said you couldn't say your reasons.

It wasn't easy to hold back with the horses involved. They'd met as juniors, they'd been naive, having no idea how to deal with people, how much to give away, how much to deal for—at least he, personally and sometimes painfully, had had to discover the rules.

He'd run whenever she came too close to him, he'd stayed whenever it looked comfortable. He was ashamed of it—but he was a skittish sort. He just didn't know how to tell right and wrong even with her, let alone with riders he didn't know, least of all with townsmen; and he supposed now in hindsight that he'd sensed for four years that Aby had something going in the Anveney business. When she'd been snowed in up on the heights last year—he'd wintered down in Shamesey alone; hell, he'd been mad, Aby'd tried to talk to him—he hadn't seen it. He just hadn't seen it.

Maybe she'd thought he was cleverer than he was. She always gave him too much credit. And she'd gone off this summer more than mad—she'd gone off hurt.

Burn, half-asleep, jerked his head up, shifted a foreleg, licked his face once, twice, urgently, until he elbowed Burn off.

Burn always had had a jealous, protective streak.

Burn had, he recalled of a sudden, interrupted him and Aby on their first night together, at a very personal moment.

He'd been a kid, embarrassed at his horse's manners and mad as hell. Aby'd been helpless with laughter—able to laugh, when he couldn't find it in him.

Aby'd ever after stood between him and quarrels he'd otherwise have had. Aby could generally calm him down. Guil, she'd say, you're being a fool. And, Down, Guil. You're wrong. You're outright wrong. Listen to me.

Suddenly it was that year again, that giddy, all-or-nothing time, the moment, the night, the place, an open-air camp in early autumn, with the chance of frost. Two fool kids had started out in all good behavior trying to keep warm, they'd built a small fire under a cliff, on rock that turned out to be less than comfortable. They'd shared a blanket, chastely watching leaves from quakesilvers higher up the slope drift down into their fire and go in a puff of fire. You could see the veins in fire before they went to ash—quakesilvers were tough.

He'd said it was like seeing through the leaves. She'd always remember the image, because she thought it wonderful; veins of fire in a leaf gone invisible. It was their secret. It was the image she'd cast him . . . whenever she wanted him.

The horses had set at their own lovemaking, autumn being wild in the air—and two chaste fools had gotten, well . . . warmer under their blanket, and more reckless.

And at the worst—or best—moment Burn had just gotten curious and hung his nose over them to watch.

God. He'd chased Burn clear across that mountainside, swearing and bare-ass naked and embarrassed as hell—while Aby had rolled on the ground laughing and laughing.

Two fool kids, in a place and a raw edge of weather no little dangerous. But they'd been only kids, and invulnerable, and they'd had Burn and Moon with them for protection—what forethought did they possibly need?

First love. Never faded.

He dreamed awake: he drifted in that time, before quarrels, before mistrust or a promise ever passed between them.

In the mating season, when desires ran high and thinking was at an ebb.

The rain drizzled down, dripped miserably off the firelit evergreens, and the smoke of the campfire collected under the branches, whipped this way and that by mist-laden winds, stinging eyes and noses. They sat in slickers, black and brown, glistening with rain and firelight. Drips from the overhanging boughs scored on Danny's neck no matter how he shifted his position at the fire, and Cloud sulked, standing off from the Hallanslake horses' position under the trees.

Hallanslakers, it turned out, felt perfectly free to get into somebody else's supplies, saying they'd pooled everything.

Which meant they were common thieves, in Danny Fisher's thinking, and his displeasure had to come through to them—if Cloud's continual sulking didn't smother it.

Nothing like his contempt seemed to bother the Hallanslakers, who were evidently used to being thought badly of.

And that left not a damn lot a sixteen-year-old could do, his gun and ammunition having been pooled, too, along with items of his personal gear he was sure he wouldn't get back until he could physically beat the man who'd taken them, not a likely prospect, counting the man bulked like a bear.

<Cattle,> was Cloud's constant impression. <Dung-piles.>

Danny thought so too. He wasn't even sure they were going to feed him once they'd made supper with his supplies. He and they hadn't been at all pleasant with each other.

But when they got down to handing it out, he set his jaw, got up and made his move for what he figured was a fair share. Nobody stopped him from filling his plate.

He ate a spoonful. *He* was a better cook than that. He didn't care who heard the thought.

<Hitting kid,> was the thought in a nearby mind, though the man didn't take the trouble to get up and do it. Danny took it for a warning, kept his head down, and thought about <wind moving green grass. A sulky, stormy wind. With thunder.> He learned from Cloud.

He had his biscuits and sausage—or half of it. He saved half for Cloud, who otherwise was making do on the sparse, edge-of-the-road grass pasture, in the dark and the rain. The Hallanslakers took shares out to their own horses, which was at least decent behavior; Danny slipped Cloud a biscuit and half of the sausage.

The other horses thought they were going to push in for Cloud's dinner. Danny took his life in his hands and swatted one nighthorse nose that came far too close—dodged a kick and bumped into one of the Hallanslakers, Watt, who grabbed him, sent a surly <behave!> to the horses in general, and told him, aloud, "You keep your hands off my horse, kid."

"Then keep him out my horse's face," he answered Watt back, in the same mood he'd swatted the horse.

And got spun around by another hand, face-to-face with Ancel Harper.

"I'm not going to stand there and get bit!" he said to Harper.

"You . . . " Harper said, "be careful how you carry yourself, kid. You could have a serious accident."

The man meant it. Danny had no doubt. Cloud meant the anger *he* sent, too.

Danny struggled for calm, said, on a breath, "Yeah, I figured," and shrugged his arm free.

He went over then to stand in the rain in Cloud's close company and think about Shamesey, because Cloud was mad, and Cloud could get hurt—<gun firing,> Danny sent, and stroked Cloud's shoulder and neck and held on to him tightly. <Quiet grass. Quiet water.>

But Cloud thought about <Ice and Froth,> and even of <Shadow,> which he thought might be Cloud's way of saying they'd been much better off where they'd been, and if Cloud's rider hadn't lost his temper they wouldn't be here.

Danny tried not to think about the camp. He thought instead about the mountains where they were going, and high-country cold, and tried not to think about Jonas, or guns—they'd pushed hard and late in their traveling and still not managed to catch Jonas and his crew. They'd found Jonas' abandoned campsite with no trouble: the horses could smell <smoke> even when a fire was dead and buried.

But they hadn't caught Jonas and his company, and Danny wasn't at all sorry about it. He feared there'd be shooting if Jonas and the Hallanslakers met, and he didn't want himself or Cloud to be in the middle of it. He skittered nervously around the thought that maybe Jonas and his friends could win a shootout, if one happened; or that Jonas might lie in wait for Harper; or that Jonas being out ahead of them might warn Stuart and team up against the Hallanslakers.

Most of all he tried not to think about Stuart, since he'd as good as told Harper aloud what way Stuart had gone, and by that, how and where to lay an ambush.

Ambush was very much what Harper intended. He gathered that from the lot of them. They wanted no fair fight. And he didn't know why—except they hated Stuart because of a dead man whose name he didn't know, and because of a quarrel they'd had when they'd worked together. It seemed to him a thin reason to want to kill somebody, since by what he could gather, Stuart hadn't killed the man he'd fought, and it had been a fair fight—but that didn't matter to them or to Harper.

And the Hallanslakers in general kept imaging Stuart and the rogue as one and the same, as if—as if somehow they'd become the same thing in the Hallanslakers' minds, an ugly thing, a tricky, shifting thing in their thoughts. They wallowed in their notion of Stuart as the enemy and their image grew and grew even off things *he* knew and *he* brought to the ambient: they caught his image of <Stuart on the porch> and twisted it until it was an evil, cheating man, giving a kid bad advice. They caught his memory of <Stuart shot on the hill> and twisted it around until it was <riders defending Shamesey gates> against <man meaning harm to them.>

He felt sick at his stomach with the shifting-about they were forcing on his memories. They didn't beat him, and on the evidence of tonight's camp, they didn't intend to starve him. They just thought their skewed thoughts at him so insistently and so often and so vengefully he felt the edges of his world curling up, as if the images he cherished of Stuart were about to peel away and show something else underneath.

But when the Hallanslaker images came thick and fast, Cloud just imaged <dung-pile> and <white, crawling maggots,> continuing surly—a noisy horse, Jonas had said of Cloud.

And Cloud was. The ambient several times in the afternoon had gone crazed with conflicting images and Cloud's disgusting commentary, until the man who'd appropriated his supplies had started calling him names of a sort he'd never in his life tolerated, and then threatened Cloud.

That was Quig, no other name, Quig. There were three of them, counting Harper. Quig and Watt—he gathered they were cousins. Harper's horse was an image of shapes and dark—Spook was how he thought of the beast, but he never heard Harper call its name; Quig's horse was flashes of light; and he didn't even catch Watt's big horse: it just slipped around in the ambient. Watt had a hellacious scar running back into his hair, and a dent in his skull where it looked like he'd been kicked once upon a time. They all carried rifles. From what he could tell they'd rather shoot from far off than confront anybody on equal terms.

He heard movement. He felt it, simultaneously, from Cloud:

<Harper walking,> and looked behind him, where Harper stopped, hat brim dripping with the rain. Harper was mad.

"Smart-ass kid," Harper said. "Damn troublemaker. You don't know all you think you know."

He didn't want to listen. He turned his face away to avoid a fight and Harper punched him in the shoulder.

That got his attention, and a move from Cloud that he stopped with a shove of his hands.

"Smart-ass, I'm saying. Big threat, kid. The Wild doesn't give a damn."

<Dark. Separation. Forest, trees thick-shadowed with night. Body in the shadows, lying on the leaves, bones broken, face mottled with shadow and blood, bone bare on cheek and forehead. Body in the woods, gunshot in the forehead—>

Harper's thought. Cloud shied off, the horses around them shied, catching the rogue-feeling implicit in the sending, and Danny didn't know when Harper grabbed him. Harper was suddenly holding his arm so hard the slicker clasp parted at his throat. They were together in a woods where it wasn't raining, and this . . . *thing* was around them.

"You don't like it?" Harper asked him. "Don't like it?"

Harper had cared for the dead rider; Harper had felt pain and guilt then that Harper felt now, and it was all one thing with Stuart, <Stuart with a knife, Stuart inviting attack, a different Stuart than he knew, angry and deadly serious.> And <the woods and the rogue and the hillside above Shamesey—> Everything was muddled up together in Harper's mind, and <rider and horse going off a road> and <blood on the rocks> and <body in the woods> were all together with <rogue-feeling.>

Danny couldn't breathe, couldn't think straight. <Quiet water!> was all he could fight with. And it *was* a fight: Harper was angry and Danny used what streetwise and campwise skills he had, twisted at Harper's grip, insisted on his own thoughts—but Harper twisted back with a stronger grip and imaged gruesome detail of the battered, dead face.

"My brother," Harper said. <Dead face. Gunshot between the eyes.> "My *brother.* You think you're going to go up there on the mountain, facing that thing, and be a hero, kid? You think it's all that easy? You think you'll sleep easy after that?"

He began to be afraid, afraid Harper was crazy, afraid that Harper was going to spook Cloud into an attack and they'd shoot: he kept sending <no> to Cloud as hard as he could, aware of Cloud's anger, Cloud's revulsion and the spillage of thoughts of violence all around him.

"I've *seen* it," Harper said, up in his face. "It wants you, that's what it does, it wants you so bad, and it'll get right up to you and you'll let it, you can't help it. It wants you, and you can't hear anything else. And that's when you've got to hold firm, that's when you've got to want to kill it, you got to want to kill it before it kills your horse and it kills you, you hear me, kid? You shoot it fast, because you want it so bad it'll haunt you, it'll be back in your brain every time you put your head down to sleep, it'll be there behind your eyelids every time it's quiet. It'll be there. It's always there. I've seen it. I've shot it. I shoot it every time it comes back to me, because I won't let it near me, you hear me?" <Man shot between the eyes> was the image. <Rogue-sending> was the feeling.

"Yessir," he breathed, "yessir," because it was the only way he knew to get loose. He felt sick at his stomach. He wanted <free of Harper.>

Harper shoved him away so hard he struggled to keep his balance on the wet leaves, and that set him free of the images, just <wet leaves, here, dark, rain> and <Cloud> the instant before he staggered into Cloud's shoulder.

Cloud was shivering, twitches of Cloud's skin up his leg and onto his shoulder, muscles jumping, but something else was going on, too, association with the horses around him, a sense of <us> that Cloud hadn't had on the road with these horses, instinct, whatever it was . . . it was suddenly <*us*> against <scattering-feeling>—

But in the instant of his panic, Cloud traded it for <us-Danny-Cloud,> the way it always was, the way Danny expected it to be, wanted it to be, insisted, dammit, Cloud listen to him. Cloud wasn't theirs.

He was shivering. The ambient was still rattling and shaking to the feelings Harper had let loose. He had no doubt that Harper had dealt with a rogue before, and Harper still had dreams about it. Harper had scared the whole camp. The Hallanslakers were afraid. They were bigger than Harper, stronger than Harper, but neither one of them was smarter, neither of them was more in possession of the ambient. Only these two had come of those who had stood with Harper in the meeting, but these two did what Harper wanted and resonated to Harper's hate and fear.

Noisy, Harper was that. Harper was always There, when you were near him. And nobody could argue with him. Harper knew what he knew and you weren't going to change it.

He hadn't liked them in the meeting. He truly didn't like them now. He traced a finger over the softness of Cloud's nose, told himself he should think about <quiet water> and notice the firelight on the puddles and the firelight on the beads of water falling from the evergreens and not think about any damn thing else—but he didn't know who it could fool. He couldn't be invisible and he couldn't persuade them he liked them at all.

And as for why they hadn't shot him, or beaten him—they wanted the same thing Jonas had wanted: they wanted him to find Stuart for them. They probably had the idea he was stupid enough to go on giving them what he knew, the way he already had. Jonas said that being noisy like that wasn't unusual in kids who hadn't gotten a hold on their sendings, or learned to be polite—and Cloud being young, too, it made it worse.

So the Hallanslakers counted on him being a stupid kid who'd think about what he tried not to think about, and give away everything he knew if they just kept him rattled with their lies—

Only—*they* didn't think they were lying. They believed what they thought about the world and about Stuart, which meant *they* were the stupid ones; they only thought they had the straight of things.

And having no other defense, he decided to think so as often as possible.

Chapter — XIV —

THE FIRE IN THE HEARTH HAD BURNED DOWN AGAIN. TARA GOT UP and put another log on, but the chill was more than in the air of this night. Vadim and Chad hadn't come back.

So what could they do but wait and go on waiting, she and her partners? The shelter ambient was full of floor-pacing and frustration—they couldn't go kiting off after Vadim and Chad, because they couldn't leave the village undefended, especially since they had reason to fear there was something out there dangerous enough to put two riders in trouble.

They could only cling to what Vadim had said about maybe staying out if they found something—they told each other that, as hope of things going right grew thinner and thinner.

By now they were on the third big log of the night; and while they agreed that Vadim and Chad wouldn't have any trouble camping out on a clear night, no one could sleep, no one was quite on her best logic, and no one was talking with any clarity. Anxieties were too high. Words were too unreliable. They kept the horses away in the den, out of range of the shelter—they hadn't precisely consulted about that decision, but Tara had wanted the horses there, and Luisa and Mina, whose thoughts already were too dark and too disturbed to make supper sit well, agreed.

"If there's any chance the girl's alive," Luisa murmured now, breaking a long, long silence, "if she'd gotten somewhere she could hole up and stay there . . . and if they found it, they could have tucked in there, waited for a shot at it . . . "

"A kid's not going to resist," Mina said. "A kid's not going to hold out, whatever it is out there. That kid couldn't fend off a newborn willy-wisp, let alone—"

Mina's voice trailed off. They weren't thinking that thought with any clarity. Weren't using that word.

Luisa said: "If she just wedged herself into the rocks and stayed there, I mean, kids panic, that's all, they'll freeze up, go still when they're scared. A horse can't get through that. The kid could actually be safer than—"

"Let's not talk about it," Tara said.

"The boys aren't fools," Mina said. "The likelihood is, they tracked fast and found something nasty and they're going to hunker down the night—they're not going to come running back here for us to hold their hands. I mean—what could they do? We have to have at least two of us here all the time. How else can we sort it out?"

"I said let's not talk about it."

"Well, the kid could actually have gotten a wild horse," Luisa said. "I mean, there's always the chance. There's been a herd at the water meadow . . . "

"The kid's a damned fool!" Tara snapped. "The kid's something's supper, if she's wildly lucky, which I think she wasn't; and the boys are riding around out in the dark risking their necks for a spoiled brat who's already *met* what she bargained for! It's not damn worth it! The kid batted her eyes at Vadim, the kid sneaked out of here when she damned well knew better, and they're off being damned stupid *men*!"

She didn't need to have said that. She immediately wished she could call it back. The chill in the air after that was immune to a fever-heat fire.

So the night wore on in interminable minutes and eternal hours, while two grown men who'd gone out to play hero because *they* couldn't say no to a kid who simpered at them . . . were out there in mortal danger.

The kid could hear the horses—hell, *any* villager could *hear* the horses if they stood next the wall—hear *and* be heard, at close enough range: that was why there were walls, for God's sake, that was why townsmen didn't go walking out in the woods without a rider—because they *heard* too damned well.

But Brionne was so self-sure that what she heard was ever so much more than a horse's own rider did, some flaming miracle of special sensitivity and understanding of the horses—

God, the kid had probably been listening out into the dark for years for what she *wanted* to hear . . . and she probably hadn't realized the defense Flicker had been sending out into the storm was even going on, because <white-white-white> *was* the snow, *was* the storm. The blacksmiths' house was far enough away from the camp that the kid might not even have heard Flicker at all or been within Flicker's defense. She might have heard something beyond the *other* village wall.

And then because stupid damn little girls who thought they heard the horses and didn't even sense when one was backing up and about to trample them didn't the hell comprehend that what precious oh-so-talented Brionne wanted didn't damn matter to the laws of nature and the inclinations of a crazed killer—precious Brionne took a walk.

"You know," Mina said, "they could have gone on to the road crews and tried to find out about them."

"Will you the hell *let it alone?*" Tara said, and hadn't meant to say that to Mina, either. "I'm sorry," she said. "I'm sorry, Mina."

Mina shrugged, looked elsewhere, hurt—not at her, just hurting, without an ambient to carry it, that was why the rider quarters sat the measured distance it did from the horses, but, God, she could see it. Luisa and Mina were partners. They were best friends, together and with the men.

And because she was the know-it-all newcomer, it didn't call on her to curse at Mina—she hadn't access to the ambient to say <I love you> or <I'm scared, too,> and she couldn't say what she thought aloud—words sounded stupid and lame when the ambient wasn't behind them.

But she was their senior in years, with Vadim out of the camp. She was supposed to lay down the laws, she was supposed to keep them from driving each other off the edge. She was supposed to keep the camp in order and the village safe—but that hadn't meant yelling at Mina.

"Mina," she said, feeling the shakes nudging at her arms—"My fault. Sorry."

"I don't like this," Luisa muttered. "I don't feel good. Nothing feels good."

"None of us feel good!" Mina snapped. "None of us *feel* good. Can we just not go for each others' throats?"

Tara was seeing <white> again. She was back in the forest.

Then an ember snapped, wood they'd carried in out of the snow-covered woodpile: it spat sparks and snapped and spat while it dried. But her nerves were raw-ended. She jumped and twitched, and couldn't for a moment get her breath in the sickly closeness of the air.

The main room was log-walled, chinked with mortar. The corners were refuges for shadows, places the light didn't reach, and they'd not lit the lamps. The firelight cast their three shadows large on the walls, on the rafters, and the interlocked shadows jumped with the gusts that bested the chimney's updraft.

Another snap, not as loud as the first. But the nerves still jumped. She'd put off her jacket, but she was all but inclined to put it on again and go out into the yard and touch ambient one more time tonight.

They ought to go the hell to bed. Luisa was right: the boys were surely holed up somewhere and weren't going to stir out again until the sun came up and they could face the unpleasant job of reporting back a grisly find which had to be the story out there.

If she hadn't snapped at the kid when the kid had come into the den—

Probably with wonderful, special news to tell them. And they hadn't fallen down admiring her. If there was a bad horse out there, it was enough trouble. If a bad horse had a rider when it went, the after-midnight lore held that the rider who didn't shoot it fast went with it, and whoever was his good friend had better shoot him equally fast.

If the rogue snared that kid, then it could get from her what horses got from human minds—an outright addiction to the complexity of human images and an ability to remember and stick to a task until it was finished.

Until it was finished.

And Brionne, precious Brionne, didn't *think* what anybody else wanted. When Brionne got an idea—nobody counted but what Brionne wanted. Did they?

She had gooseflesh on her arms. She *didn't* need to turn over that mental rock and examine the underside.

She found herself on her feet and pacing again. Mina was standing, arms folded, staring at the shuttered window. Luisa was whittling something. Luisa was always making wooden animals—she had a collection of them on the mantelpiece, real ones and fanciful ones. Tara couldn't see what Luisa was carving. Didn't want to guess. She ought to set an example and go to bed, but the thought of going off to a separate room and lying in bed alone with her thoughts was not at all attractive.

And maybe it was after all a good idea to check outside again before she tried to rest.

It was something to do, at least. If she just found silence out there, it was some reassurance; and she felt steady enough to look in on Flicker. So far the ill effects added up to a little swelling and soreness in the legs, nothing rest wouldn't cure. Flicker could lie down and get up at will now, no worry about her going down and her lungs filling; but Flicker's rider wanted to be sure of that from hour to hour, especially when she was staying a little outside Flicker's range.

Surely the boys were all right. God, they weren't a pair of juniors. They could take care of themselves. Fears spread, was all.

Hell, she said to herself then, and got up and went for her coat.

"Where are you going?" Mina asked.

"Just to take another listen," she said. "Be right back."

Mina looked worried. "You don't go *out* anywhere," Luisa said. "You want me to come with you?"

"Better just one of us. We're too noisy tonight. I'll check on the horses. Get a grip on my temper while I'm at it." She shrugged into the jacket under two worried looks. She slung on her scarf and went out, not dressed for a long stay in the winter night, not even putting her gloves on.

The first breath of cold night air was a relief. She went down the wooden steps, crunched her way across a new film of ice on the tracked and hole-riddled yard, and trekked out toward the den under a starry, cloudless sky.

But there wasn't peace. She felt, even at distance, a sense of unease among the horses, even before one of them came out of the den, a shadow in the low, earth-banked entry.

The second horse that showed up was definitely Flicker. All of them were in a surly mood. The first out had been Mina's Skip, and Luisa's Green turned up at Flicker's rump—Green nipped at Flicker, and Flicker returned the favor with real temper.

<Quiet trees,> she sent. <Deep snow. Snowflakes falling softly.>

<White,> came Flicker's chilling echo.

Then something got to her, a quickness of breath and a speeding heartbeat where everything around her said there was nothing wrong.

<Behave!> she sent to Flicker, and the horses sent a shivery, angry impulse back, on edge about a feeling she couldn't see in the sky or hear in the air or smell on the wind.

<Vadim,> she sent out into the ambient as strongly as she could. <Chad!>

Then—she was being crazy. She wished she hadn't made that noise in the ambient—in the remote case the horses together *could* carry it—in case the boys might hear it and do something foolish in the mistaken notion that the camp was in distress.

<Safety,> she thought, and wanted Flicker to carry that idea far and wide. <Forest. Village walls.>

But Flicker was skittish as she walked up. Flicker kept doing a nervous <white> sending and shifted about uncooperatively when she bent to lean against Flicker's side and listen to her breathing.

Just the harsh, regular breathing of an uneasy horse, heartbeat a little fast, but it kept up with the breathing, and Flicker kept shifting about with her, quarreling with her den-mates.

Tara gave up, since Flicker was healthy enough to be difficult—ears up, nostrils working, disturbing attention outward; but she couldn't get any sense of direction about it, just a general distress. She went from one horse to the next, patting necks, dodging shifting, restless bodies and swatting Green, who came just too close with a snap of her teeth.

<Inside the den,> she ordered them. <Flicker inside, Green inside, Skip inside.> She got that occasional <white,> and then a grudging compliance when she seized Flicker by the mane and pulled and argued with her.

Then the report of a gun echoed off the mountain—stark, sudden, close. Flicker jerked free of her hand. All the horses were looking toward the palisade wall, not the outer one, but the one that divided them from the village.

A flare of light touched the tail of her vision—she turned her head briefly, saw the shelter door open, a coatless Mina and Luisa standing on the porch.

"What was that?" Mina called to her.

"It came from the village side," she said. It was all she was certain of. The rogue might be across the village, next the wall—that was her first clear thought. She went for the narrow gate, the gate no horse could pass, and she began to run, her feet cracking the frozen, pitted crust.

"Tara?" Luisa called out. And Mina: "Wait, dammit! We're coming!"

"Stay there," she turned around to shout. "Stay with the horses!"

She wasn't the only one who'd taken alarm. The village bell began to toll the three-stroke that called Assembly.

The village didn't know what it was. She guessed that much before she even reached the gate. She lifted the latch, went through, aware that Flicker had followed her, aware of Flicker's frustration at the gate Flicker couldn't pass.

She didn't have her gun. She hadn't even brought her gloves—fool, she said to herself when she checked her pockets. She was damned little use. But she found herself in a flood of villagers in nightclothes and robes and boots and carrying guns and even axes, all streaming toward the common hall, to find out what no one knew and what the ambient, even reinforced by the concerted effort of anxious horses, couldn't tell her.

But before she ever reached the hall she was hearing rumors—the blacksmiths' neighbors, Vonner and Rath, came running up saying it was the blacksmiths' house the shot had come from.

The crowd surged in that direction then, unordered, unruly—she was uneasy, walking deaf in a group of people who didn't read the ambient, either, unless that feeling of unease she had now was coming from elsewhere.

One of Andy Goss' kids was on the doorstep. The other came out with a gun dangling in his hand. And *she* feared she knew.

In the next moment the village marshal came up and took the gun from the boy without resistance.

Andy Goss' wife, Mindy Rath, was safe. But Andy Goss wasn't.

Dead, the marshal's deputy reported with a grimace, on a quick glance inside the door. Bad in there, Tara thought.

And the marshal took the boys away, both of them. Tara caught whispers of dismay, whispers that the Goss-Raths were an upstanding family, and nobody could imagine what prompted it.

She didn't know what to do, what to say, how to explain to them. But half the crowd went away, shivering in the cold, and the marshal took the boys away. And she didn't know what she could say that would make it better.

So she went back the way she'd come, through the rider gate, and found Mina and Luisa, dressed for the cold, out in the yard with the horses.

She told them. She said, remembering Andy Goss and the boys beside the den: "They loved him. I think they killed him."

<The porch, the boys, the gun, the wife. Herself, watching from the crowd.> She remembered from their meeting beside the den <the boys hating Brionne, wanting their father.>

She added, in a feeling of utter shock: "I think that was why they did it."

The day came up still misting rain, a gray drizzle outside the shelter. Guil lifted his head, and pain like a knife went from one point to the other of his skull and bounced. Several times. He let his head back, eyes shut.

He didn't want to move after that. He just wanted to lie there and breathe until his head mended or he died.

But Burn got up, slow shifting of a heavy body, a second imperilment of the roof supports. He heard the timbers creak.

Then a breathing horse-smelling shadow came between him and the daylight, and Burn nosed his face, puffing warm horse-breath on him. Persisting at it. Guil pushed him away with a none too coherent <Guil hurting.>

<Bacon,> Burn imaged, as if that cured headache.

And nosed him in the face again.

It took him a moment more to muster reason, and a moment after that for coherent images. <Wet wood,> Guil thought, <fire.> If he could possibly sit up, which his dizziness and the pain in his head made a nauseating prospect, he was resolved that Burn should have bacon, if there were any wood to be had.

He'd never asked Burn to do the job. It seemed worth a try. <Burn finding wood. Burn dragging it back to the shelter, wood making fire, fire with bacon.>

<Cattle,> Burn thought. Burn didn't believe fire made bacon. Or didn't think wood made fire. At this point in the morning, Guil didn't know what he believed, either.

But he groaned, and shifted in his cocoon of blanket, slicker, sodden coat, and sodden shirt. Which reminded him he hadn't dried out during the night, and he needed fire for more reasons than bacon.

"Hell," he moaned, tried to reckon in fact where he was going to get wood. <Burn on grassy hills. Finding wood. Guil hurting. Fire. Big fire. Trees. Wood. Burn dragging wood with his teeth.>

Burn didn't think so. Burn imaged <bacon> and <Guil riding.>

<Burn *outside.*>

The last made his head hurt. It upset Burn, who went out imaging <fire> and <dark> and <fight.> And there wasn't a damned thing out there. Guil could see it in Burn's images as if he was seeing it with his own eyes: <eroded stone, bare rock, puddles and more barren hills with tufts of grass . . . >

<Burn.> Guil wanted him back now, and Burn came back under the roof.

<Fire,> Burn imaged, imaged <heat,> which was some help. He could actually halfway feel it, illusion that it was; but wood was nowhere outside, from horizon to horizon—thank you, Aby, thank you, Jonas and Luke and Hawley.

And if he could somehow persuade Burn to go off hunting the nearest dead tree, it left him sitting alone in the Wild with a rifle and a handgun—no more than the Anveney truckers had, to be sure, and they were still fairly well in the die-off zone, but there'd been vermin last night, and he wasn't sure he wasn't going to fall on his face and pass out.

Which could mean coming awake with willy-wisps swarming over you, no, God no, there were ways to go, but gnawed half to death while he was passed out wasn't one he'd choose.

Lying here wrapped in plastic, waiting for some sunny day to dry his trousers wasn't a choice, either. He couldn't depend on a sunny day coming along before snowfall, in which case, also thank you, Aby, he wanted dry clothing.

That meant firewood.

And since one of them couldn't leave the other, it meant moving. He wasn't sure he could get on Burn's back without falling on his face, but if he did fall, Burn wouldn't desert him.

Which meant at least willy-wisps wouldn't come near him. So he was safer going with Burn, if he didn't break his neck falling off. His head ached so—he really, truly, please God, didn't want to fall on it again.

He made it by stages to his feet, splitting headache and all. He couldn't see for a moment, couldn't find his balance, caught himself against the shelter wall—which reminded him, lucky thing, that he had gear to take with him.

So, knowing he wasn't tracking mentally at all, and in a gloomy shelter with his eyes not working reliably, he leaned against the wall until he could list very carefully what he had hung where and what he'd brought in.

Then he gathered up his belongings. He folded the blanket, which was still reasonably dry, and put it in the two-pack. He found his trousers and his boots, which were colder, if no wetter, than they'd been last night.

Burn was worried. Burn kept nosing him in the arm, in the back, which didn't help his balance at all. Burn licked him on the ear.

<Burn carrying two-pack,> he imaged at Burn, figuring he'd get away with it or they weren't going. He put on the ice-cold and sodden trousers, as something Burn's body heat and his could somehow warm, at least: warm, wet clothes were better insulation than dry, exposed skin, and the slicker could make a tent, of sorts, on Burn's heat-generating hide.

Then, leaning on a post, and on the same logic, he forced one foot and the other into cold, soggy boots, hoping blood moving would warm them and hold that warmth as long as the wind stayed still. He just, half wet as he was, couldn't afford to fall.

<Burn outside,> he imaged, last of all, and when Burn did leave, out into the drizzle, he buckled on his sidearm and put his scarf and gloves and hat on, picked up the gear, occasioning a moment of visual blackout, and walked through that dark out to Burn—a direction he couldn't lose even without his eyes, and he realized he was in fact walking with them shut.

He slung the two-pack across Burn's back, put the rifle over, and made his best effort first, belly-down, at getting on.

<Truck going off a cliff. Guard trying to exit. Fear in the ambient. Horror. Riders unable to move—logs scattering like straws down the rock slide. . . . >

He just lay there a moment belly-down and crosswise on Burn's back while his headache left him alone with the images, not quite sure where up or down was, except <Burn> was in contact with him and <Burn> was usually down. . . .

The fog cleared. He could see the ground. He thought for a precarious, strengthless moment that he might throw up, but Burn wouldn't like that. He rested as he was and breathed hard for a minute or so. Burn, <wonderful, handsome Burn,> stayed rock-steady under him, so eventually, still in the red-pulsing dark, he dragged his right knee over the bump that was Burn's hipbone, lodged his heel over the hollow that was Burn's sensitive flank, trying not to send Burn sky-high, and leaning one hand on the leather flat of the two-pack that was across Burn's shoulders, used the weight of the rifle in his right hand and the pistol on his right side to drag himself square on Burn's backbone.

Burn sidestepped. Guil swayed like a sapling in a windstorm, and the whole blurry, double-imaged world swayed out of balance as gun-side and no-gun-side refused to find center. Burn moved across under his center of balance, and got the idea, he thought, that his rider wasn't at all interested in a run right now.

Burn walked, so sedately a baby could have stayed up. Burn compensated when the world swayed out of balance, which occasionally required a drunken sidestep. The wind blew cold on Guil's face and his double-vision and the dark traded places occasionally, aftermath of exertion—but the blood pressure finally evened out between his head and his feet. He discovered that a curiously comfortable convenience—he never had appreciated how nice it was that was usually taken care of.

Forgot where they were going at first. What they had to do. Then he remembered he was in wet clothes and wanted a fire; and he remembered about <wood> and <mountains> and <Tarmin village.>

Eventually his legs grew warm on the insides, but his feet remained chilled. He bore with it. He imaged <wood> and <trees> and Burn kept a pace that didn't jar too much, because <head hurting> afflicted Burn too.

Then after what seemed most of a morning, he saw trees growing up against the rise of a rocky face. The road, on which the rain had filled all the old tire-ruts down to a gentle high center and two long puddles beside, tended in that direction.

It dawned on him then, perhaps a sign his brain was less addled, that he had a medical kit. He recalled he'd some bitter-root for tea, which was good for headache. Water certainly wasn't any problem.

Pans weren't, either. He had a pan. He'd bought it. He told himself he could have hot tea if he didn't fall off and drown in the puddles.

If he got a fire built. One damn thing after another.

The world shrank away to toys when you looked down from the mountain. The world faded to pale colors, and the mountain became vivid, rocks and evergreen, and more rocks, as if the two worlds hadn't a chance of existing together, and you traded one for the other. All of Shamesey would have been thumbnail-sized if you could see it from here—but Danny couldn't. A piece of the mountain was in the way.

And they had to walk a lot more. The horses couldn't carry them as fast as they could walk. Cloud's back got tired, and Cloud like the other horses let a rider know when he'd had enough.

So they hiked, carrying the baggage, which the horses wouldn't carry. The Hallanslakers might be scum, but there was no way even stupid scum could argue with their horses.

An elbow arrived out of nowhere, knocked the wind out of him for a second. He bent and Quig gave him a knee for his thoughts—<mad Quig> and <Harper mad> was all through the ambient of a sudden, then <bite,> as Cloud let out a fighting squall and lunged at Quig.

Quig's horse—then *all* the horses—dived at Cloud, pushing him to the edge as he fought back.

Then: <*Quiet water,*> somebody was sending, and <*blood*> was equally strong in the ambient—the Hallanslakers grabbing horses by mind and mane as fast as they could, as with his feet on the eroding road edge, he got a grip on Cloud's mane and got through Cloud's anger in a frantic effort. <Danny falling. Danny *falling,* Cloud going forward a step. Breathing quietly. Danny and Cloud. Danny and Cloud. . . . >

His heart was going like a hammer, altitude and panic balled up together in his chest. Air came so short his vision went black at the edges. Couldn't get a breath. Couldn't do anything but hold on to Cloud, unsure where his feet were, how close they were to a fatal fall.

Harper was sending <anger. Gun firing.>

Then Harper said, with absolute coldness, from where he was standing, between them and his own horse—"You keep that horse in line, kid. You hear me. You keep your damn noise *down,* and you keep that horse quiet or I'll shoot him. No warning next time. If he starts a fight I'll shoot him."

Cloud was mad enough to go at Harper's throat—Danny felt the muscles bunch, and he leaned against Cloud's chest, got a hand on his nose and pressed on the nostrils the way a senior rider had told him was a last-ditch way to get a horse's attention. Air was short enough as was—he shorted Cloud what there was despite Cloud's instinctive duck of the head, kept a hold so Cloud had to drag him or listen, and, panting and shaking, <Danny scared,> he sent with no effort at all. <Cloud stopping. Cloud standing with Danny—edge of road. Rocks below. *Edge of road, Cloud standing still!*>

Cloud quieted, slowly, and Danny let up the pressure on his nose. Cloud felt <pain> at his shoulder—the skin was torn there, black hide glistening with blood, and Danny hugged him and got him to stand still. He was shaking so he could hardly get his own breath. He believed <Harper shooting. Nighthorse falling in rocks. Narrow road. Men with guns.> Nighthorses didn't do well with future ideas. <Men shooting> hit Cloud's mind and meant a fight, Danny began to figure that, and held on to a fistful of mane with all the shaky strength and breath he had.

"No. *No,* Cloud. Quiet down. Quiet." The rest of the party started on their way, <men walking with the horses. Cloud walking with Danny, quiet clouds, white, peaceful clouds . . . >

Jonas had tried to tell him he was being a fool. He hadn't listened. He wasn't doing things right; at some basic level he wasn't doing what the other riders did. <Cloud in danger.>

Cloud believed him, and threw his head and snorted, looking for <men with guns. Wanting fight, wanting kill—>

Harper looked back at them, and Danny pressed his hand hard on Cloud's nose, saying aloud, "Quiet, quiet," because he couldn't think straight through his panic.

Everybody else had their horses quiet. They were scum, but they got their horses quieted down. It was just him and Cloud that stayed on the edge of violence. He didn't know why. He wanted to know, but Cloud couldn't tell him. Cloud was barely willing to stay with him.

"Come on," he pleaded with Cloud. <Cloud with ears up. Cloud cheerful.>

Not likely.

He carefully let go of Cloud's nose, wanting <Cloud walking quietly, easily beside Danny.> He walked, kept imaging it, tried to remember <Jonas talking to him.>

<Jonas talking about elbows and knees.> That was when you were riding. That wasn't any good, and he couldn't remember the rest of it.

He tried to slow his breathing despite the thin air. He tried not to shake. That was harder. But Cloud didn't do anything else rash, at least—Cloud had calmed enough the bitten spot was hurting, one of those spots Cloud couldn't reach to lick, so Danny got into his pack while he walked and found the drying-powder, took his glove off long enough to pat a little onto Cloud's hide.

It made a white and red spot on Cloud's shoulder and, dammit, it was going to scar. It made him <mad.>

And Cloud got upset.

Shut up, he said to himself then, desperately wanting <quiet.> Jonas had said it was *his* fault Cloud got upset. And he'd just done it; he'd just set Cloud off.

So he concentrated on being quiet, on <Cloud walking quietly. Jonas saying, <Elbows not moving. Knees quiet. No extra motions.>

Hard to do when you were walking with a batch of scum, but he could, he had to. . . .

Quig didn't react. It was stupid of him: he had to stop thinking thoughts like that—but Quig didn't hear him: the horses up ahead were noisy in the ambient, still <mad,> and Cloud's contribution was all <Danny on road, Danny upset. . . . >

He walked with his hand on Cloud's shoulder, fervently thinking <spring grass, evergreens. Nice-smelling evergreens> and then not touching Cloud at all, trying to hold him just by thinking of trees.

Their own share of the ambient stayed quiet, Cloud just thinking about <road ahead, nighthorses, strangers,> and Danny: <evergreens.>

Then: <Danny being quiet. Danny's body walking, no more motion than walking needed, just enough motion, no more, every step quiet. No elbows. No bad-boy stuff, not Shamesey street-stuff. Just walking on gravel road. Machine shop: Papa's grease-stained fingers lining up the gears of a machine, no wobble, no play, everything right in line and smooth, the way papa knew it had to go. Efficient, papa saying of an engine. No work but what produces power. Kitchen: mama's brushwork on a chair arm, laying down paint, the outermost few hairs on the brush making the line right down the edge of the design, absolutely calm and sure in mama's thin fingers. One long stroke. Mama's little finger, bracing the whole hand so the brush could only stroke so far at a time, mama's hand knowing just exactly where to touch to make the next stroke. Papa's hand turning a set-screw, feeling exactly how far.

He couldn't do what mama's fingers did. He couldn't feel the set-point that papa felt.

<Papa saying, "You're rushing it. Feel the wear-point. Listen to the motor. Listen to the motor." Papa hitting his ear, enough to sting. "*Listen,* Danny. Hear it? Hear it change?">

He hadn't heard it then. He'd lied and said yes. But he listened instead of talking. That was the best he could do, then.

<Jonas saying, "*You* keep him agitated. Don't twitch.">

Burn got him there, bit by slow bit—Burn even managed not to drop him in the mud, passing by the isolated brush as the land began to look healthier, higher up, westward along the road: the wind blew too strong and too cold for open country, even with the slicker and a dry blanket to break the cold. Guil held out, much as he longed just to stop and rest and try an open-country camp; he told himself he could hang on, he could make it, he could last just another hour on Burn's back—Burn hadn't complained yet of carrying him, and Burn would let him know when he'd become a load.

Then the topping of a hill showed them not just scattered brush but real trees where the rougher ground began and where the road began to rise. Even Burn thought he could hold out longer, for <big fire> and <bacon> and <sweet grass.>

Burn got him to a place deep in the dripping shadow of evergreens, next a stand of quakesilvers and the edge of the wood where redleaf grew, gone to hollow, pithy stems in autumn, the seedpods all scattered.

Those stalks were what he wanted. He slid down, sat down, unplanned, in a hard landing on his backside on the needle-carpet, with the rifle and all the gear. It sent a jolt from his tailbone to the top of his skull and down to his eyes, and blinded him for a moment.

Unfair, he thought. The pain was entirely unfair, after all the rest. But he was here, he'd seen what he needed to see, even if it took a moment for his eyes to clear and bear the daylight again. He sat still, tucked up into a huddle of knees and slicker and pack, the rifle tucked up with him, and imaged, amid the pain, <redleaf stalks, Burn bringing redleaf stalks,> which he could have gotten up and done, as soon as his head cleared, which might happen in a while—but, hell, Burn could have <bacon> soon. There'd be <fire in the redleaf stalks.> Burn could do it. <Wonderful horse. Beautiful horse bringing redleaf stalks to Guil.>

Burn went over and got <nasty, mouth-prickly brown stalk,> and brought it to him and dropped it on the ground in front of him. Burn pawed it with a three-toed foot, head lowered, <looking for fire in the stalk,> but Burn didn't find it.

<Burn bringing another stalk,> Guil imaged. God knew what Burn thought in Burn's different world, maybe that he was looking for the right stalk, so Burn went and dragged back another of the man-tall stalks. And another.

And another, under Guil's insistence. His head had cleared enough that he could see. He broke them up in chunks, split them with his thumbnail to expose the pith, not trusting himself with the bootknife. Burn nosed into the pile of stalks, still doubtful.

Guil got out the pocket lighter, flicked the wheel, far faster than the burning-glass, more reliable with the broken cloud overhead—and Burn jerked his head back as a little flame jumped from it to the redleaf pith.

He fed his tiny fire more redleaf pith, and then redleaf stalk, and a small pile of only moderately wet evergreen needles swept from off the ground around him.

<Burn breaking down quakesilver deadwood,> Guil sent, imaging the quakesilver grove near them. <Burn dragging deadwood back to Guil and fire.>

The headache was still killing him. The pants hadn't dried, he was icy chill from the hips down, he hadn't felt anything at all in his feet in at least an hour and the wind was kicking up. But it helped to have something to do. And his fingers at least could be warm in the tiny flame, so long as the wind didn't scatter his work, or another spate of rain come and drown it.

Burn knocked the deadfall down. Burn was good at destruction. Burn forgot what he was supposed to do—enjoying destroying the tree, Guil supposed, and re-imaged <bringing the wood,> and <bacon.> As the preachers' tempter to evil and corruption, Guil thought in the extraneity of delirium, Burn was remarkably easily distracted. <Wood,> he imaged, "dammit. . . ."

It arrived. At least half of it did, the stick Burn carried dragging other brush with it in a haphazard string. He wanted Burn to trample it where he dropped it. Burn wouldn't. Burn went back to get more wood, having figured the rest of it belonged with this part.

So Guil cracked up the sticks he could reach and stuck them in the feeble fire. And cracked others, the bark, the ragged pieces, whatever there was.

Burn brought him a live quakesilver branch with the last sodden autumn leaves still on, but, hell, by now the fire could handle the sap-rich wood. He threw in whatever Burn brought and the fire grew. The heat grew. He felt it against his soaked knees.

And faithful to his promise, with <Burn bringing wood,> Guil hauled out <pan> and <bacon,> and put it on to cook. He needed more wood. Burn wanted more than one bit of bacon. It seemed a workable bargain.

A second supper—was baked potatoes and sausage, which took no thought, no effort, and nobody in Tarmin camp was much interested in food. Tara ate. She didn't taste it. A quiet, worried day, it had been. She supposed that she ought to report to the village that Chad and Vadim were still out, but the village was wrapped up in its own grim business over the blacksmith's murder, and there was still the chance—still the chance—that the boys would turn up before she had to explain to the marshal.

She took potato and grain mash with sausage bits out to the horses and listened into the gathering dark, standing between Flicker and Luisa's horse, patting Mina's Skip on an insistent nose as she set down the pan.

Then she did something she'd never willfully done, and drew Flicker's attention first—that was effortless. But she wanted to hear <outside,> and asked for it.

Flicker heard the usual little spooks around the edges. Tara kept listening, putting her attention out to the ambient, and nudged into Green; and still it was spooks, a lorry-lie, maybe.

Skip's attention came in without much noise at all, and of a sudden they were reaching far, far out, listening for <Quickfoot and Jumper, Vadim and Chad.>

What came instead was a disturbance of other minds, and she tried to shut it out, but it was noisy, much too noisy: <Boy with gun. Crowd in the village.>

She didn't know what that was. She didn't like it. She didn't want panic in the village, some villager picking up on her query outside the walls.

She drew away from the horses, wished <silence, still branches,> and walked completely out and away from the den.

Not a ripple in the ambient from Vadim and Chad. But, she said to herself, the likelihood was that the boys would come riding back with some gruesome story they truly didn't want to take to the grieving family. That in itself could keep the boys out a little longer—if they found something they couldn't get quiet in their own minds: a rider didn't put as first priority the friends waiting and worrying about him. A rider had loyalty to his horse first; his actual working partner second; his partner's horse third; his responsibilities to his hire somewhere after that; and his lovers wherever they crossed the ranks of partners or friends—

Which meant neither Vadim nor Chad would desert the other

out there, where two horses might stand off what one horse couldn't, and where two minds might find a calm one mind couldn't recover.

But it damned sure left three women in Tarmin camp pacing the floor and sweating out the hours, while reasons for them to hold back bad news at least from the Goss family had evaporated on a gunshot: the Goss family was shattered. Chad and Vadim couldn't know that unless they heard her sending. And there was no sign they had.

The sky was headed for its second full dark, and cloud was moving in, girding Rogers Peak now with a gray, impenetrable ceiling—heralding earlier dark, the chance of snow, and a chance of storm, if that cloud just kept coming, as well it could—this eastern face of the mountain had better weather, but it gave you surprises you didn't take lightly.

The shadows had already gone blue and vague. Tara took the by now well-worn trail toward the porch, not quickly. But the feeling of harm was in the air.

She walked as far as the wooden steps, had her foot on the first when the summons bell rang a gentle request for attention on the village side, and the rider gate opened.

Townsmen came in, the mayor and the marshal.

Mina and Luisa had heard the bell. They came out onto the porch, hugging sweatered arms against the cold as the delegation trudged closer across the cracking, potholed ice.

"Need to talk to Vadim," the marshal said.

Tara took a deep breath. "Not here."

"Where is he?"

"Out looking for the Goss kid."

"He didn't say—"

"There wasn't a need to say."

"Not a *need*!"

"He's doing his job, that's all. He and Chad. They're looking around out there. What can I do for you?"

"Talk," the mayor said. "Inside."

Light was fading fast. A wind was getting up. Tara nodded, uncertain in her capacity as senior rider—it was unprecedented that village authorities should ever have the urge to cross through that gate unless it was something involving the whole village-rider agreement, but she nodded, and Luisa and Mina went inside as she preceded the mayor and the marshal up the steps and into the lamplight.

"Tea?" Mina asked.

"We'll make this brief," the mayor said. Bay was his name, and by his manner he didn't intend to sit, take off his coat, or ask any hospitality. "We've got a meeting going on right now. Judicial meeting. Andy Goss' son shot him. The older boy. Carlo. He doesn't deny it."

"There were circumstances," Tara began, but the mayor cut her off.

"The whole village knows the circumstances. The boy hated his father."

"Loved his father," Tara said, though she wasn't quite sure she understood love as villagers had it. It *felt* the same. "It was his sister he hated."

The mayor and the marshal didn't look impressed, just nervous.

"This is a bad time to be down to three riders," the mayor said. "This is a real bad time."

"You can't find anything out sitting inside the walls." She found herself unwillingly defending Vadim's decision, and had a sudden dark thought: Damn. *Damn!* They're hunting it. *That's* what they're doing.

"No word of the road crew either?"

"No word," Tara said, "no word from Vadim and Chad, either. I've listened."

The mayor looked as if he'd swallowed something unpalatable. The village *couldn't* tell the riders how to run their affairs. They weren't obliged to like it. Or to accept *how* riders knew things.

"Is there a possibility," the marshal, Delaterre, asked, "that the girl was murdered? That the boy had something to do with that?"

"Absolutely not." Tara was appalled. "The boy's not a killer. I can swear to that. Brionne, on the other hand—"

"Possible that the boy enticed her outside, knowing the danger out there right now, in the hope she wouldn't—"

"Marshal, the girl's a spoiled brat—she sneaked out the gates.

She knew the danger out there same as anybody over five. The boy and Goss himself were in our camp looking for her."

"Goss hit the boys," Mina said. "Goss beat them."

She was twice shocked. Mina *never* spoke her mind in front of villagers.

"There's no evidence," the marshal said. "The wife is testifying against the boy—"

"The wife helped," Mina said shortly. "They beat *hell* out of the boys. Brionne could do no wrong."

The horses weren't anywhere near. The ambient through the camp was all but dead still, quiet, hushed. Even villagers might feel it.

"Will you give a deposition to that effect?" the mayor asked.

"I swear." Mina held her hand up. "I swear right here. You're witnesses. You can swear for me in court. A rider doesn't need to go there."

There was silence in the room, just the crackle of the fire. The rattle of a shutter in a rising wind.

"They'd no business," the mayor said, "the senior riders going off the way they did. The village is their first job."

Tara frowned and plunged ahead. "I'll tell you something, mayor Bay. There's something out there scared hell out of my horse. But the Goss girl went out on her own, looking for a horse *she* heard. That's what happened."

"We're not sure," the marshal said. "You said it. The boys hated the sister."

They were wanting to think ill of the boys. They had their case made. She didn't need the ambient to see that. And it turned a corner she hadn't expected. She stuck her hands in her pockets and waited for clarification.

"You saw the girl leave?" the marshal asked. "Or not?"

"Didn't see, didn't hear," Tara said. "We had a sick horse. Mine. It was too noisy to hear anything in the camp. Not in the village. Not if that kid was listening to the Wild."

The mayor and the marshal looked uncomfortable—villagers didn't want details about the horses, or anything else in the Wild. They wanted their walls to prevent that.

"Meaning you wouldn't know. You're guessing."

"We wouldn't know," Tara said. "That's the point. But footprints went out the gate."

"Alone?"

"Goss and his kids all accepted it was the girl." She remembered queasily that they didn't immediately see in their minds what she saw. She tried to build the picture for men that didn't see. "The snow hadn't been tracked. Just the ice-melt from the den roof. The tracks. The gate being pulled inward made a scraped mark. About as wide as a girl needed. Tracks going out, about her size feet, no tracks going back."

"Where are these tracks?"

"Gone now. Horses tracked over them, all over out there."

"That's real convenient," the mayor said.

"Mayor Bay, there's one way out that gate. Horses had to take it to go out to look for her. And that's what the boys are doing—looking for her."

"Single tracks?"

"Pointed-toed boots." She had a good mental image of the boys' feet. Their tracks. Her brain saved things like that. "The boys' boots are square-toed. The blacksmith's—his were round. These tracks were smaller and lighter. No rider wears boots like that."

"Andy Goss identified them?"

Absolutely no doubt in her mind. "The father had just found out," Tara said reluctantly, "how much the boys hated the sister. They were standing near the horses. They heard more than they wanted to hear about each other. I was there. I heard it. I couldn't help hearing."

"You'd better come across," the marshal said. "Give a deposition, too."

"I've sworn to things before," Tara said. She didn't like village justice. And it didn't take a rider's word. "I saw what I saw. And heard what I heard. I agree with her. Write it. I'll sign your paper."

"Better you should swear to it over village-side," the mayor said. "Tonight. Where the village can hear. We want this case disposed. Feelings are running high over there."

A damned hurry, Tara thought, and looked at Luisa and Mina,

and drew shrugs there. But the Raths, the mother's family, were damned well-to-do. Deacons of the church. Pillars of the village council.

"All of you," the mayor said.

"Got to get our coats," Luisa said.

"All right," the marshal said and, with the mayor, headed for the door and out, no hesitation.

"What did you mean," Tara asked Mina, an urgent whisper, "the wife helped, the *wife* beat the boy? For God's sake, you don't know that for a fact! —Do you?"

Mina shrugged. "Goss is dead. What good's it going to do to shoot the boy, too? He's not a bad kid. Goss beat the boys—and what was *she* doing for sixteen years?"

It was logic. She had to admit that. Save the salvageable. Villagers couldn't tell truth from untruth in a rider's mind. They *could* save the boys. And the Raths weren't going to like it.

She grabbed her scarf and hat, and went out with Luisa and Mina, the three of them resolved on a lie, and no horse near to tell the mayor or the marshal.

No horse near to tell them what was going on outside, either. They crossed the icy yard behind the villagers and entered together through the village-side gate . . . it was farther than they liked to be from the horses, Tara felt it and she felt the same from Luisa and Mina.

But they walked, all the same, and heard a commotion out in the winter cold, saw lanterns lit, and a steamy-breathed crowd gathered under the lanterns.

They proved more conspicuous than they liked, as they walked into that crowd in the mayor's wake, and followed (Tara supposed they were to follow, and nobody stopped them) all the way to the porch of the marshal's office and the village lock-up, which was mostly for midwinter drunks, if they got to breaking up the village's single bar.

This time, though, there was a gathering of the village officers, the clerk and the justice in front of a lot of the village—men, women, and children—and now the mayor and the marshal and, lastly, themselves, up the steps and onto the wooden porch that fronted the marshal's house and the jail and the court office, that being all the same building. They'd hung lanterns from the porch-posts and set a table and a chair between them. The judge sat at the table. The village clerk sat at a right angle to him, to do writing.

"Say what you said to us," the marshal said, and Tara couldn't feel Mina panic, but she saw the flinch. Mina said it again, in a quiet voice:

"The kid had cause."

"Louder," the mayor said, and shouted for quiet, and the judge bashed the table with a metal hammer and said he wanted quiet in the hearing. There was the hammer on the judge's table. Lying near it, jumping when he hammered for order, there were two large-caliber bullets.

That was the way it was. Tara was appalled; and she nudged Mina, saying: "Tell it good."

So Mina spoke up. "Goss and his wife beat the boys. He could have killed them. It was real clear. They didn't want Brionne back."

A woman's voice—Goss' wife, Mindy Rath, Tara saw, off to the side of the porch: "They did it!" the woman shouted. "They were always bad boys! They were always a trouble in the house! I want my Brionne! I want my Brionne! What have you done with her, what have you done with her, Carlo? You put her outside the gate, didn't you? You lied to her, you made her go out there!"

"That's not so," Tara said. The magistrate was pounding with the hammer, and the bullets fell off onto the porch. The clerk scooped them up again and put them on the table.

"Say it again, rider Chang," the marshal said. "Say it louder."

"I'll say it," Luisa said, and raised her voice. "She's wrong. There were tracks going alone out the gate! Tara saw them!"

The crowd broke out in murmurs, in calls of "Liar!" from the wife, and "Hearken not to the beasts!" from one of the village religious enthusiasts.

"Say what you know!" the mayor said. "Rider Chang?"

People were shouting. The elder boy shouted, too, all but crying, "I didn't want to shoot him, he made me shoot him!"

Right then Tara got the same impulse Mina had confessed to;

and drew in a guilty breath, and remembered at the same instant that nobody could hear what she thought.

The judge pounded the table, to no avail, until the marshal fired off a gun, into the air and off over the walls.

"Rider Chang," the judge said. "Ordinance of Incorporation, Article Twelve, a rider can't take oath. But you can give an unsworn deposition. What did you observe?"

"I talked to Brionne Goss in the horse den this morning. I saw her tracks, alone, going out the gate. I saw, at sunset, Andy Goss, Carlo, there, and Randy, coming in to ask about her whereabouts."

"Fornicator!" the religious yelled.

"—and those tracks." Tara raised her voice, thinking only of the boys now, the way Mina had thought, and with the queasy notion that she could lie or tell the truth on this side of the wall and the minds in front of her wouldn't hear the difference. "Were only of the girl. Goss identified them and I personally heard Goss threaten the boys, I personally heard the boys complain of beatings and blame unfairly placed on them."

"Liar!" the wife shouted.

"Mr. Goss agitated my horse with his behavior. I advised him and his sons quit the camp for their own protection. Vadim and Chad went out the gate in search of Brionne Goss. They aren't back. They'd promised to come straight back. I can personally report—" There was a rising murmur and she outshouted it with what she'd decided the town had damned well better know, and she needed to be *sure* the town knew. Two nights and no word from Vadim and Chad meant the odds weren't in their favor, and the Gosses had already made fatal mistakes. "I can personally report, there's something out there that scared my horse *and* me. Evidently Brionne heard it and didn't have the sense to be scared."

"You liar!" the mother started shouting—and nothing came through the ambient. It was a curious numbness.

"She wanted the horses!" Tara shouted back. "And thanks to the fact she *didn't* tell us, and she went out that gate *on her own*, and without our advice, she's probably met something we could have wished she hadn't. It wasn't the Goss boys' fault. I *saw* the father beating the boys; I saw it in his mind and I saw it in theirs!"

"Blasphemy's not court evidence!" the religious yelled. "You can't blaspheme against the almighty human God and call it evidence!"

"God," Tara muttered in disgust, and cast a look at the judge, who hammered the table furiously.

"She is a liar!" the mother screamed. "She was luring our Brionne to perversions! *They're* responsible!"

"Then you can go to bloody hell!" Mina yelled. "There's a rogue horse out there! Your precious Brionne went out to it! If she's lucky, it didn't take her! If she's not—God knows what we're in for! So if you want to winter here without riders, you're on your way, woman! The road crew's not back and the two that went out looking for your daughter were supposed to be back in a couple of hours—yesterday! So go to hell! We'll take care of our own, if that's where we stand!"

People were shouting over the last that Mina had to say, people who were scared about the rogue and scared as hell to have the riders offended, people yelling about God and blasphemy, going quickly from words to shoving and pushing—the judge was getting no attention from anyone with his hammering; and Tara grabbed Mina by the arm to get her away from the edge of the porch before rocks went flying.

"Take it easy, for God's sake!"

"I'll *be* out that gate! I'm not trading *us* for these fools!" Mina jerked away, headed for the side porch steps, and Tara grabbed her again.

"Mina, use your head!"

"I've used my head, I've waited. If you're with them ahead of us, maybe that's your choice, Tara, but it's not mine."

"Mina!"

Mina had jerked to be free, and Tara jerked hard back, realizing in the moment she did it that there *was* an ambient now. It had come flooding around them subtle as body-temperature water—you didn't know it was there, and it was, and it ran over the nerves and stole the breath. "*Mina*, dammit!" Crowd-noise was everywhere. Minds were everywhere. A gunshot went off, right next them, but that was a gun on their side, the marshal firing his pistol off.

"Shut up!" the marshal yelled into a sudden silence, and Tara dragged Mina back to Luisa's spot near the rear of the porch. The marshal was yelling about law and order and how they'd better listen to the judge or he was going to start making arrests.

"You can't argue against almighty God," somebody yelled; and the judge ruled the man in contempt and fined him fifty on the spot. Other howls went up over that, and the mother started yelling about justice again—

"Shut up!" the judge shouted, and banged the hammer, until it had to dent the table top. "It's clear we've got witnesses missing."

"You can't take testimony—" —from riders, the religious was clearly about to argue, but the hammer came down again.

"Another fifty! I say I'm not finding cause for a trial until after we've got all the principals, and they're not here. Marshal, lock these boys up until somebody—"

But the words faded out. There was just <dark, snow, wind.>

Tara felt <Mina slipping from her hand,> felt <Skip and Flicker and Green> in angry distress . . . felt <hundreds of minds . . . shooting and not-shooting, panic and dark and screaming . . . >

"Mina!" Luisa screamed, halfway down the steps, in pursuit of her partner, but Tara grabbed the railing and got focus enough to will <calm water. Quiet water. Flicker. Quiet water. Quiet. Quiet air.>

"Damnation!" a resisting mind cried, but the ambient was gibbering nonsense, <fear-fear-fear> and something more.

Tara needed the railing to keep her balance, and she fought with that noisy mind, with a deliberate *<behave!>*

A scream. Shocked quiet, after. She could feel the railing wobble under her gloves. She looked up at the marshal with a sense of desperation, her partners having cleared a space for themselves in the yard. The ambient was complete chaos.

"Something's wrong," she said, maybe louder than she should—her ears weren't hearing: her mind was, and she felt she had to shout. "Keep that gate closed. If the kid comes back and wants in—don't listen. *Keep that gate closed!*"

Her partners went toward the camp. She had to be there. She was the only one who might argue Mina out of doing something foolish, but they were <wanting the camp, wanting quiet dark, wanting Skip and Green,> and she suddenly could hear Flicker—<wanting Tara. Wanting fight, wanting kick.>

Bang! something went at the Little Gate. *Bang!* of nighthorse hooves.

She didn't know what the marshal answered. She overtook her younger partners on the run, the crowd seething with questions and fears of the unknown outside—more than one voice was raised in screaming panic.

No comfort existed in the ambient.

<Dark. The going-apart. Flicker wanting through gate. Wanting Tara. *Danger! Now!*>

Chapter

— XV —

THERE WERE STORIES—HOW SOMETIMES IN SPRING THEY FOUND people frozen on the mountains, just the way they'd sat down, and when the wind blew the fire out, Danny began to fear some party coming up the road with the thaw would find them all that way in a melting snowbank, still huddled around dead sticks.

"Maybe the son of a bitch froze," Quig said, hugging one hand under his arm for protection.

But Harper swore at everybody and Watt kept working, using a lighter, the lot of them using their bodies and holding a tarp to shield the fire until it took.

Stupid place to camp, Danny thought, while he contributed his own skinny body to the effort and held a corner of the tarp.

They'd found a less windy place a little downland, and thanks to Harper's pushing everyone, they'd ended up at the edge of dark camped in hellish cold, on the high uphill of the road, where the wind could get a run at them and the horses had no grazing.

They'd run both late and tired, slogging ahead at a pace that taxed both humans and horses, walking and riding by turns—the last had been walking, the Hallanslakers' horses and Cloud alike simply refusing to carry weight any farther on the uphill.

And finally their road had met another road at a rider-stone, way, way up in the windy cold, where—contrary to expectations of shelter one ought to find at a rider-stone—there wasn't.

There might still be one fairly close. Maybe even a village—he wasn't so clear on the distances up here. But the Hallanslakers either knew there wasn't a shelter—or they had some reason not to go find it. Danny didn't ask. He didn't ask anything or question anything since they'd hit him for no more than thinking. He'd found he could tuck down and be quiet—and he was so cold he was brittle. He truly didn't want to be hit right now. He just kept his grip on the tarp edge and kept as quiet as he could while Harper and his friends from Hallanslake did whatever seemed reasonable to people who couldn't go into villages.

The rebel thought didn't get him hit. He didn't entirely understand why not, except maybe they didn't want to let go of the tarp to do it.

And that thought didn't get him hit, either.

He supposed what he thought wasn't going into the ambient with any strength at all because the horses were tucked together at more than a stone's toss distant, in a clump of old bearded evergreen, where the wind was less—except Cloud, who sulked apart, but on their lee side, so he had them for a windbreak, Cloud being no fool.

There was a phone line near them—they were making the fire near a telephone pole, so he knew they were on a main road, maybe the Tarmin road itself, and definitely, in that case, not far from real shelter. He hadn't seen phone lines all the way up, and he remembered the Anveney road was the one—

But he didn't want to think about that road. He just wasn't sure what road they'd picked up, but there were the phone lines, and it did go off into Wild in either direction.

Stuart might be real near. But he didn't want to think about Stuart at all, except he hoped Stuart had met up with Jonas and they were all out there in the bushes this very moment setting up to blow Harper and his friends to hell in a crossfire.

He really, really hoped Jonas wasn't too mad at him.

He cast a furtive look at Harper, wondering that nobody had heard him, himself and Watt being in body contact at the moment. Maybe they were all thinking about the fire. Maybe everybody was too busy. Maybe Cloud was too cold to image. He hoped Cloud was all right out there in the cold.

But certainly he'd gotten away with more than he had this afternoon on the trail when Quig had elbowed him for thinking Quig was stupid.

Quig *was* stupid.

Quig was *really* stupid.

Still no notice.

Maybe they were just all too tired.

Maybe God was going to freeze them to death for punishment. He was in what his mother called bad company, he'd had no question of that, and it wasn't God's fault—stupidity had gotten him here.

Papa would be disgusted. Papa would have no respect for any of these men if they walked into his shop, loud and obnoxious, let alone the fact that they were riders. The men with Harper were scum. Nobodies, real nobodies. The Hallanslakers—who Harper was (by what Danny could gather) somehow kin to, or leader of, or both—thought a lot of things were funny that weren't—and they were stupid.

Just damn-all mean, papa would call it. Anybody who was an outsider to them, like him, was a target, the way Stuart would have been a target when he'd worked with them. He understood now how that long ago knife-fight could have started. Stuart wouldn't have backed down.

He didn't want to know what they'd think up to do to *him* now if there wasn't Harper's glum influence, and if there wasn't Harper to knock heads when things got too rough. He couldn't figure what hold Harper had over these men, except they'd *wanted* to go up that mountain: they'd egged each other on until they were blind, stupid tired and the weather turned on them. They'd challenged each other up that mountain because there was mischief to do, and they thought it was fun. They were men on the outside, but inside they were a nest of willy-wisps, all fangs and claws, all mean—he'd known boys like them in town, and he'd avoided them even before his father'd yanked him sideways, knocked him on the side of his head and said he expected brains in his sons and he expected his sons not to die stupid.

He'd never heard his father talk like that before and never since. But he'd remembered.

Then he'd gone to be a rider and his father didn't talk to him about virtues at all now.

He'd not known everything before he left home—but, damn, he knew his father would have had the insight to have pitched any of the Hallanslakers and probably Harper out of the shop on first sight. He didn't know where his father had learned about people like the boys his father had found him with, but his father had had them pegged, all right, and he'd gotten the measure of the Hallanslakers in the same way: eager to go up that mountain to do all the harm they could to Stuart, who'd, by all he could figure, never done any harm to them personally. About Harper's motives—he didn't want to think.

They just had to have a target for their meanness, he guessed, because if they didn't have one, they just had each other to pick on.

And that wasn't much fun, since they were too damn stupid to feel pain.

He could think that, with his knee right against Quig's. That was really odd. He thought: Quig's a pig, just to see—not wanting another elbow in the ribs.

But he was quiet and secret now—mad; but he'd grown far more canny in the passing hours. He'd had to be hit a couple of times, like with papa and the boys—and then, damn, yes, he did learn. He could keep his thoughts quiet.

Or Cloud wasn't paying real close attention right now.

He stole a glance sidelong, saw Cloud about his own business, nibbling the weeds that still poked up above the snow at road's edge.

But Cloud didn't look up.

<Cloud,> he thought.

But he didn't move his elbows when he thought it, and Cloud still didn't look up—didn't seem to notice at all.

Maybe he had a lot better luck being quiet if he wasn't right in Cloud's convenient view, attracting Cloud's attention. There were trees in the way. He'd made himself ever so quiet, even wrestling with the tarp.

And that led him suddenly, while Watt was swearing at the tarp and Quig was a slightly less bearlike mass beside him, to the basic fact that he'd heard a hundred times but never, somehow, gotten through his head in reality—that he could think anything he liked if Cloud wasn't in range, and he suddenly realized—astonished—that the fact that he heard uncommonly far wasn't necessarily all Cloud's doing. Cloud certainly didn't seem to hear him right now.

And with that, he acquired a notion of *how* he got a constant flow of images from farther than he was supposed to—dimbrained kid that he was, he naturally assumed when people called him noisy that it was some marvelous special gift he and Cloud had that nobody else did.

Special, hell. He fell off his horse and Cloud got into fights: it wasn't exactly a shining performance on this trek. He'd annoyed two groups of seniors and nearly gotten shot on the last set-to because he couldn't calm Cloud down.

Noise wasn't exactly an advantage if you hadn't any choice about it.

And Jonas had said that kids did it—and seniors didn't—except Wesson, who needed to because of who he was.

So it wasn't exactly a special gift, it was a special problem kids tended to have.

And if it ever was useful, this getting Cloud's attention at a range at which most people didn't have constant talk with their horses, it wasn't *always* useful, witness the situation with Harper this afternoon.

When he was on the outs with people, he wanted Cloud's attention; he just—wasn't comfortable with people the way he was with Cloud, not even with his friends anymore, since the new had worn off him being a rider. Cloud was his friend. Cloud didn't carp and criticize—

Maybe Cloud ought to criticize. Maybe somebody should have done what his father did and what Jonas did and what Quig had done—like tell him he was fouling up, mad as it made him. He was doing wrong with Cloud. Jonas had tried to tell him, but he'd been too righteous then to believe it.

Elbows still, Jonas had said. Knees still. Quit *looking* at Cloud, which he began to realize was almost impossible for him—every two seconds he was reaching for Cloud, wanting to know where Cloud was, like a toddler running after his mother.

Which kept Cloud's attention all the time on him and nervous. Other riders had seen it. He'd been the only one not to see it—and it turned out so damn simple: if he could just hold his body still and not demand Cloud's constant attention, he could hate the sons of bitches as hard as he wanted. Horses could hear humans, just barely, but humans didn't hear well enough to hear each other—he'd known that, sort of, as a townsman kid knew anything, even before Wesson had told him. And what that *really* meant had just slid off him as one of those details like long division, which he never liked so he never bothered to think about.

Stupid kid, he said to himself. Smarted himself right into a real mess. Didn't *need* to know things. Didn't *like* to know things. Real damned bright—now he was in a situation where he wished to God he had listened to everything his seniors had tried to tell him. He swore he'd go back to mama, if God gave him another chance, and ask her to tell him again about long division. And he'd ask Jonas Westman to tell him all the things he was doing wrong, if God just let him and Cloud get out of this.

But thinking all those things, he didn't move. He didn't twitch. The tarp fluttered, but he didn't bob around controlling it, he just bit his lips and tried to keep his arms still as if he had the same strength as Watt beside him.

The fire caught, streaming sideways in the wind. "Hold the damn tarp," Watt ordered everybody. "Hang on, damn you."

On one level he was fascinated with what Watt was doing. He'd never seen a fire built in a gale-force wind the way Watt was doing it, with a hastily thrown-up wall of wood, to which he figured the tarp was a help, not a necessity—and he wanted to see the technique. They'd failed it once and had to take it apart; but Watt, now that his inside kindling was set and lit, started assembling his small-grade wood inside his three-sided shield of bigger pieces, working fast so that the fire would stay lit—he stuck tinder and smallest kindling in out of the wind, shielding it with the edge of his hand the second after he set in a larger stick. There was never a hesitation in what he picked next, as if he'd had the sizes of the sticks in his head all along. Fast as he was working, every stick fit as tight as could be to its neighbor, so that, just with the irregularities of the wood, the fire could breathe; but the wind couldn't get at the fire to blow it out.

Watt stuffed his next grade of sticks in with one hand while with the other hand he began to take bigger wood from the stack—he'd built the inner frame, and it was burning. The outer frame was a chimney now, and the fire held—until, Danny thought, the really big, last-an-hour stuff could go in after the firepit was full of coals and able to handle it, and when it wasn't so prone to throw sparks on the wind. They were scum, but they were careful scum: *nobody* burned a forest down.

Watt was scum. But he had an amazing skill.

"More wood," Watt said. "That wind's going to burn a pile of it tonight."

The others grumbled about it, but they moved off. Danny, being still, followed them with his eyes, thinking—

But Harper hadn't gone. Harper sat with his arms on his knees staring at him, and it was Watt himself who went to gather wood with Quig.

"I really wouldn't," Harper said darkly.

"Get more wood?" Danny played stupid. Harper didn't buy.

"You know what I mean. Go ahead. Run. See what happens."

He didn't want Cloud involved in his thoughts. Not moving at all took willpower. He stared at Harper, thinking that Harper might be asking himself why Danny Fisher was so quiet this evening.

He wasn't faster than a bullet in the back. That was certain. And Harper had served notice he was watching.

But he got up slowly after a moment, left the fireside and joined the men gathering wood, choosing at the same time to move as far away from the horses as he could, into the teeth of a freezing wind. He started gathering up deadfall, to prove his honest intentions.

But he knew now, all but bubbling over with the discovery, that he could keep quiet enough to have private thoughts, he *could* do what the senior riders did—and he resolved then and there that he was going to leave these men in a snowbank if he got a chance.

He didn't know woodcraft the way the long riders did, that was his most serious handicap—like, right now, he would dearly love to know whether, say, common wood fungus was at least moderately poisonous. He could get plenty of it off the deadfalls, and he'd, oh, so gladly put it in their tea, and fake drinking his.

But if it turned out to taste too strong or if it wasn't debilitating fast enough, they'd shoot him; and they'd shoot Cloud, because Cloud would go for their throats in an eyeblink if things blew up.

So that wasn't a good idea. Whatever he did, he had to make good on fast, and it couldn't give them a target. Like maybe if the snow got worse.

Maybe if a blizzard came. The middle of the night. He could slip away.

There had to be riders up here, maybe riders who wouldn't take to what Harper or Jonas or anybody intended. He wasn't alone up here. There were whole villages full of people up here—and they had to be close now that they'd come up on the phone lines, where Stuart had to come—

God, shut that thought down. Fast.

But that the Hallanslakers were willing to camp out in the cold like this, when there were supposed to be shelters with free food and firewood, as he understood it, argued to him that they were scared of Jonas. Harper or somebody had been thinking about Jonas earlier—even seniors were sometimes noisy. Harper had been thinking about Jonas and about Stuart—and it hadn't been pleasant thoughts.

If Harper thought Jonas and his friends *were* holed up in a shelter for the night, or, probably worse from Harper's point of view, if Jonas had gotten up here first, he'd have gotten to shelter. *That* could be the reason Harper had them out here shivering in the cold: they were scared to shoot it out with Jonas at a shelter where Jonas had cover, and maybe get shot at themselves. That was too much like a fair fight.

And they were going to go on skulking in the brush and the cold until they did find a place Harper didn't mind shooting.

He wasn't acutely scared anymore: he'd reached a stomach-upsetting kind of terror he could live with—but trouble was, now that he'd figured out how to be quiet—he didn't know how to do anything else but be quiet without giving everything he thought away; and he didn't know at what moment something was going to scare Cloud and upset the balance.

At which point Harper might decide he wasn't any use finding Stuart, and that he was a liability among them if they ran into Jonas.

He stayed out at the perimeter as long as he dared, so long his fingers were growing numb through the gloves. He gathered up a fair armful of wood and followed Watt back to the fire. He dumped it down and squatted down on the edge of the wind-blown heat, chafing warmth back into his fingers, avoiding Harper's eyes. Harper had never left the fire.

In the same moment he felt Cloud's attention skitter over him—Cloud just brushing by his thoughts—and he thought of the fire and of <Cloud resting> and <them making supper. Biscuits.> He liked the biscuits. They weren't as good as mama's. But they were going to taste good on a cold night. Cloud was going to like the biscuits. He ought to tell them use less soda. That was the taste they could use less of. He'd asked his mama, on one of his visits home, and she'd been making biscuits at the stove and he'd stood right there and paid real careful attention to the measures and everything she did, because he really missed those biscuits.

He stuck a little wood in the fire, not too much. They wanted less flame than coals in this wind. Nothing to carry into the trees. Hope they had a decent meal tonight. Watt scorched everything.

Always on the edge of catching the pan afire. He was better. <Mama saying—>

Close, close, close, he mustn't look up. Little nervousness among the horses—they could solve it. He didn't need to look up.

<Mama in the kitchen. Smell of bread and paint. Home smells.>

<Mama saying everybody needed to know how to cook—"You might marry somebody who can't," mama'd said.

<Them eating their own cooking. Burned.> Mama said they'd have to. So they got better at it. Even Sam.

<Baking and paint smells, all mixed up together.> Mama would buy some scuffed up table or chair from a shop or another household and do a little sanding and fixing and painting.

Then she'd trade it to a store or direct to an individual for more than she paid for it.

Or sometimes she just did refurbishings for the same owner—any of which paid money that came in handy before he started bringing in money and fixed the place up.

Mama would be sitting there with the bread baking, all the while she'd be painting flowers on a chair—she liked that part—or sanding and swearing—she always swore when she sanded—<her hair trailing around her face, and flour on her chin.>

There was always some piece of furniture in the apartment that you weren't supposed to touch or sit on, and it always made his nose run when she'd been painting.

But the bread-smell was over all of it, <smell of home. Smell of comfortable things.>

Harper never stopped watching him. Just watching.

They'd warned the village. They'd advised everybody lock the doors and the shutters and stay inside no matter what. People had guns. They had their storm-shutters locked.

The rogue-feeling went away and it came back, maybe two, maybe three hours into the night, as if it was feeling them over, and it wasn't a thing anybody could catch with human senses. You didn't know when you'd started being afraid. You just knew by the prickling terror behind you that it was there again. A shutter banging in the wind. Rattle of sleet against the roof. A sense of presence . . .

Something was near the walls.

"It's Vadim," Mina murmured as the three of them, sitting by their fireside in the shelter, listened. "God, it's Vadim."

"No!" Tara said sharply, because it was coming by way of their own horses now, she could hear them, could hear Flicker take up that <white, white, white> refrain. Mina shoved her chair back and Luisa grabbed her arm, arguing with her not to go outside, to stay with them.

"That thing could be anywhere on the mountain. It's no good going out there. God, it's echoing in every creature in the woods, can't you hear it? That's what it's doing—that's why it's so damn loud—"

The whole mountain seemed to echo it, loneliness, mourning over something lost. It echoed failures, or things undone, a terrible melancholy. It gnawed, it burrowed, it ran, it flew, it crawled—it slavered with winter-hunter and ached in rut and leapt along the ground, aching with loneliness and fear—

Then it dissolved, flew apart in screaming rage.

<White-white-white.> Flicker was still there. Skip and Green were, Tara could feel them through Flicker's noisy presence and, Luisa's advice to the contrary, she went and snatched up her coat.

"Tara," Luisa protested.

"I'm fine, dammit, Flicker's not. I'm going out there."

"We'll all go," Mina said.

So that was the way it was—they went out to the porch and down into the nightbound yard. Snow was gusting on a fierce and biting wind.

Then a presence came to them, <running, running in the wind. Holding tight. Snow stinging the face.>

<Damned fool,> Tara thought. <You little, damned . . . *fool.*>

She lost her balance—slipped and skidded on the ice. Mina had her arm.

A presence so . . . lost . . . so idly strayed from reality . . . came flitting through her senses.

<Flowers and snowflakes,> it imaged. <Sugar lumps. Biscuits.

Brionne with the horses. All the horses loving her. Brionne in the moonlight, in the snow . . . the numbing, gentle snow. . . . >

"Get away from us!" Tara shouted into the dark.

<Wanting mama. Wanting papa . . . mama listening. Mama sitting with her Bible . . . thinking of Brionne. Papa . . . papa . . . *papa—!*>

<*"Tara!"*>

Luisa hurt her arm, she grabbed it so hard. She slid on the ice and Mina grabbed both of them.

<Papa!> went out across the ridge. <*Wanting in. Wanting in—*>

"It's her," Tara said. "It's the Goss kid—God, stay here. Keep the gates shut."

"Where are you going?"

<Marshal's office.> The ambient was so live it didn't need a horse near. <Luisa and Mina taking care of horses. Gates shut. Gates *slammed.*>

<*Mama,*> the voice cried on insubstantial winds. <*Mama, let me in . . .* >

Tara ran, sleet stinging her face—she ducked through the village gate and let it slam behind her; she ran not for where instinct or whatever drove her told her to go: instinct was screaming at her to go the other way. She ran against it—ran for reason, ran down the center of a deserted, sleet-hammered street, all the way to the end of the street, her throat hurting with the cold air. She ran up the wooden, icy steps to the marshal's office and pounded her fist on the door.

She heard someone coming, footsteps inside. The feeling of presence behind her all around her—was overwhelming, a wave of living anger rolling toward them, from all around the walls.

"Who's there?" the marshal called out. "Who's out there?"

"Tara Chang!" she shouted back, holding to the rail—resisting the impulse to look back and see if anything was in the street. "It's *here*—" she said, and got a chill breath as the marshal opened the door. The marshal's wife was holding a pistol aimed at her: she paid it only passing attention. "It's the rogue. It's the kid. Brionne. She's with it. She's wanting her mama and her papa. You've got to send word down to Tuck—keep those gates shut. No matter what!"

"It's a *kid* out there," the marshal began. "We've got to shoot that horse."

"It's *hell* out there." She found herself shaking. "It's my partners out there. It's our men. It's that kid. We can't help them. We can't do anything but *hold that damned gate,* do you hear me? Get out there! Keep that gate shut, I don't care who wants in! That horse comes with her and everything in the woods comes next! *Keep it out!*"

The marshal went for his coat and his scarf and his shotgun. "Watch the boys!" the marshal said to his wife. "If it's the Goss kid—she might try to get to the boys! Keep that door locked!"

Tara stood there shivering in the wind, trying to keep her hand from freezing to the icy porch rail—trying to be deaf and blind and numb to the ambient. Mina and Luisa were with the horses. She knew.

She knew that the Goss boys were still in lockup.

She knew that Brionne was with the rogue.

She knew that Brionne was calling to all that was hers—her mother, her father, her brothers, her friends and acquaintances . . . every one.

Brionne had never gotten on Flicker's good side. But she was calling to <Skip> and <Green> in the lame way she'd always imaged their names.

She called to <Mina and Luisa.> But not to her. *Not* to Tara Chang. Brionne hated her. She felt the lost presence flit past her in anger, and she ran for the camp, assaulted by the <lost, aching> ambient.

<"Papa!"> it wailed.

Shutters were opening. Lights from those windows flared out onto the snow, here and there down the village street. A door opened, a larger spill of light.

Answering that voice.

That was the way they heard it. The town was ready and armed for a rogue.

They heard a lost kid. They heard Brionne Goss wanting in, wanting rescue.

"Stay inside!" Tara screamed at the tanner, who came out on his porch. "That's *it,* damn it! *Get that door shut!*"

She didn't know whether he listened. She ran for the only source of help, half-blinded by the sleet, through the narrow gap of the Little Gate, into the rider camp—and had a clear sense of Flicker's sending, that <white-white-white> shutting out the world.

But Skip and Green were absent from the noise. There was only a darkness wanting <out,> wanting <running, all running.>

"Mina? Luisa?" She ran for the den, skidding on the uneven ice—caught herself on the corner post as she came inside, unprepared for the darkness that rushed at her—<nighthorse,> was all she knew.

It flared past like a black rage and she pasted herself to the wall, blind and deaf to everything but <kill> and <bite> and <shoot> as it passed—

<Rider,> she realized then, and <Mina,> and she heard <white-white-white,> so intense and so close a sending that she couldn't see where she was.

Gunfire, then. In the village, outside, she wasn't sure. Shots were going off, echoing off the walls.

<"Luisa!"> she yelled, trying to get through the ambient, but <white-white-white> came down like blizzard. She wasn't sure of Luisa's whereabouts. She wasn't sure of Green's. She only knew Flicker's, and she didn't want to lead Flicker to disaster.

<Flicker standing still!> she sent and felt rather than saw her way—as if the whole world had gone to snow.

She reached the open air and the blast of the wind, she wanted <Mina,> and she went the way she'd sensed Mina go.

But she heard someone screaming then, into an ambient gone red and black amid the white, a voice beyond the village wall, a voice near the village gate.

<"That's my daughter!"> it cried—and she saw <Brionne standing outside the village gate, Brionne afraid, *Brionne, Brionne, Brionne—wanting mama—*>

An image of <gate opening> as <desire> and <killing anger> and <hunger> came flying together in the air, assembled itself in a rush that reached the heart, the mind, the gut, one creature, one self, one mind—anything else was <Enemy> and Tara was <Enemy.>

She thought she saw—sight came fleetingly through the <white>—the outer gate of the rider camp standing wide against the dark.

She thought she saw snow whirling about her—white, thick snowfall, and wind so loud she couldn't hear the screaming or the howling it made. It just was, and the snow was, and the cold was.

<White> came up beside her, it brushed against her, it called to her, and her hands knew its shape, found its mane to clench onto, and her body knew where, as she launched herself, she would find <horse> and <strength> and <warmth.>

Then—then she was <astride> and <with> and, blind and deaf as she was, she became the whiteout, she became the blizzard—blind and deaf and <killing cold . . . >

Nothing could touch her. If she'd had another purpose she'd lost it. If she'd had another destination she didn't know.

She was in the woods again, sweeping through the trees, <white> and nothing more.

Harper hadn't moved. Quig had come back with another load of firewood and dumped it.

But suddenly something was wrong—Danny felt it, just as the firewood struck the ground and scattered, like something witnessed at that half-aware substitute for sleep, a thing of strange importance and insignificant aspect. He felt a jolt, just the faint brush of something like horses, running horses—and acute fear—like Shamesey streets, when the horses imaged together—

The horses were in it—they snorted and milled about. But that wasn't the only source. It was coming from somewhere completely opposite. It was huge, and full of anger, and it had a thousand feet. It moved—

<Cloud!> Danny sent. <Quiet water. Quiet.>

"What in hell is it?" Quig asked the air in general.

"Could be a cat," Harper said.

"Cat, hell!" Quig reached for Danny's arm. Danny hadn't expected it, and scrambled backward from Quig's hand, hit on his rump as Quig scrambled after him—and he scrambled away, scrambled up, turned and ran.

A weight hit from his back—he fell, skidded on the snow with that weight on his back trying to pin his arms. He spat snow from his mouth, dug with his knees, to get to <Cloud. Getting to Cloud—>

"Back that horse off!" Harper yelled from somewhere, and he panicked, wanted <Cloud running!> wanted <Cloud gone! Guns!>

He felt the jolt of nighthorse feet on the ground, sharp pivot, and <Cloud running, breaking branches, gun firing—>

But none fired, or he'd gone deaf. He was still spitting snow when whoever had fallen on him hauled him up by the scruff and shook him, and somebody else grabbed his arm and cuffed him on the ear.

He could see Harper then. He knew where he was, in camp with the Hallanslakers, in the dark, in front of Harper, and Cloud was <in the woods, in the dark, running and running—>

Cloud had left him. He didn't know what could make Cloud leave him—Cloud never had, never would, but he felt something so scary, so dark, so threatening in the ambient—

Then he felt as if the mountain were flying apart, as if the ground were dropping out from under all of them, as if the trees were about to fall on them.

"It's the damn kid!" somebody yelled.

<Quiet water,> somebody was sending. He thought it was the man who was holding him, but he didn't feel calm—he felt as if he were drowning in ice water, sinking and sinking in it, the whole world gone from flying apart to folding in on him, pieces coming together, heavier and heavier, the red-haired rider, and Stuart—

"Kid!" Someone cuffed him hard, across the face, and in that moment's shock he tasted blood.

Blood was part of the ambient.

Blood was the smell, was the wind, was the air, was the taste on the tongue—blood was the anger and the envy and the hate and people were shooting—

"Get that horse back," Harper said to him, holding his face in a hurtful grip. "You hear me, kid. *Get that horse back!*"

He tried. <Wanting Cloud safe. Wanting Cloud quiet, not fighting. Quiet water. Guns.>

"It's his horse," Watt said out of the dark behind him, and Harper hissed:

"It's the rogue, fool. That's what it is—watch the dark! Watch the dark, dammit, and hold on to the horses! Keep them here!"

But more real than Harper's voice came something moving and dark—an ambient full of screams, cold of snow under Danny's hands—he tasted blood and sprang up and ran, with <Cloud running, Cloud safe. White, and snow, and blood. People. People running in the streets, buildings, people screaming—>

"That's Tarmin," Quig said. "That's Tarmin gates, damn, that's Tarmin, do you see it? *They're shooting each other!*"

"You got to catch him, you got to, you fool! Stop him! He's doing it!"

<—fire blazing up, firelight on snow. Gunshots. People yelling—people falling under him—>

He couldn't hear. Somebody hit him across the face. His head snapped back and then he was in the woods again. His right ankle had folded, but the hands that held his arms had held him up, dizzied as he was, and cut the blood off from his lower arms.

He felt the entire side of his face hot and numb, and he was <darkness in the streets,> he was <going apart,> he was <killing the voices, killing the staring eyes, killing the silence—>

He wanted his family. His. Now. And they were <going apart, flying into the winds—mama—papa! *Papa!*>

A second time a blow landed across his face. Second time someone shook him.

"God, shut him up!" someone yelled, and he saw <horses spooking, running through the trees, branches coming at faces, branches breaking—> "He's spooked the horses, shit! *Stop!*"

<Riders wanting them, light blazing and fire breaking out and gunfire echoing all around,> but he was <lying on the ground, head exploding, watching the legs of men running past him—>

He had no other chance. He got his knee under him, he lurched to his feet, branches breaking—immediately recoiled from a sheer drop, and ran along the edge. <Wanting Cloud, now, quick, Cloud coming back through trees!>

<(Voices—screams in the houses. Fire reflecting on window-glass. Embers glowing on the wind.)>

He ran and ran, breaking through branches, plowing through thickets, blind, desperate. His side caught an agonizing stitch and the world was still churning with images, <streets and fire and anger.>

But snow began to muffle the shouts and the screams, as if the wind-driven white that skirled through the dark had deadened the pain and smothered the fear.

He walked, breathing through his mouth, holding his side, knowing he was free of Harper, but equally well aware he had no gun, no supplies, no idea where he was going.

<(Log walls and fire. Gates open. Going through streets, on horseback.

<(Looking. Searching.

<(Days-old ice crunching under three-toed nighthorse feet.

<(Everything the same as she remembers, all the street the same, but windows reflect orange with fire. Fire through veils of sleet, sleet flying out of the dark, touching face, making stars in nighthorse mane—

<(Gunshot. Horse jumping forward, horse wanting fight, wanting her, wanting—what horse can't find.

<(Red-haired woman.

<(But she can have red hair like that. She can be grown like that. No one can ever stop her again, no one can tell her no.

<(Wanting what horse wants. Wanting what she can't find, a mind she doesn't hear, but listening, listening, all up and down the streets she knows, because it might be here.

<(Faces come. Voices come. People walking about their daylight business as if they'd forgotten the dark.

<(People buying and selling.

<(Old woman making soap—telling her go away, don't bother her.

<(Riders with horses—telling her go away.

<(Girl with baby—blond braids. Pretty clothes. Kick and bite. Nasty girl.

<(Her hair . . . red like the autumn leaves. Fringes fluttering about her. Her horse going where she pleases.

<(Horse trampling over something in the street. Not caring.

<(Buildings reflect fire on window-glass. Fire shines paler on the snow.

<(White drifts down. Ash. Or snow.

<(Riding, searching, still, for what she can't find.)>

<"Cloud!"> he shouted out loud, desperate. The other sending was pouring over him, overwhelming all sight, all sense of direction.

<Cold, white coming down. Snow falling thicker and thicker.

<Branches raking, breaking, breath harsher and harsher, stitch in side, long pain, can't remember from when, scrapes on face, cold skin, numb fingers, numb toes—>>

<(The dark is all, dark streets, new snow falling—)>

<An edge, then.>

<Heart jumping. Arms catching. Foot on slick ground, sliding.

<Sailing through dark space . . .

<*Thump.*

<Flat on his back.>

Ahead turned to up, fire to night, ash-fall to snow-fall, thick white puffs fell in a stillness of the wind, on his sweating face, into his dry mouth.

The world was strained to the limit. He felt half of him missing and he desperately wanted that piece of him, stretched thin into the dark—

Not she. He. Him. Here. <(She)> screamed out into the dark after what she was missing.

But he was alive. Breathing. And the strain grew less. The missing part drew near to him. He'd dropped off a ledge. He'd fallen in a snowbank. He'd had the breath knocked out of him.

He lay there, got his breath back, relatively undamaged—too stunned to be alarmed at the moving of the brush on the ledge over him.

Not surprised, either, at the <presence becoming Cloud.> The missing half of him had shown up and Cloud wanted <downslope,

now, nighthorse feet probing the ledge frantically for a way down to him, but Cloud couldn't find it—> Cloud was going to jump.

"No!" Danny found self-awareness at least to wish <Cloud still, Cloud standing—>

Then before Cloud tried it again, he had to move an arm, a leg—finally to turn on elbows and knees and crawl up the snow-chill slope, past the screen of thorn branches—

<Cloud walking dark, fire-windowed streets.

<Cloud afraid and angry. Looking for Danny.>

He hauled himself up by the brush that overhung the last of the slope. He was on his feet then, couldn't remember getting up, just <on his feet, hugging Cloud's sweating neck, two of them, here, in this dark, snowy place, Danny and Cloud.>

Cloud made a sound between a cough and a snort and shivered up and down his shoulder. Cloud wanted <us.> Cloud wanted <kicking and biting,> but Cloud didn't know what the enemy was. Cloud was as lost as he was in the battering of sendings; and Danny spared one frightened thought for <lost supplies, lost gun, lost fireside and lost Hallanslakers—>

But after that Danny just thought <us,> and heaved himself up, belly-down and grace-be-damned, to Cloud's snowy, willing back.

Cloud moved, walked, not sure where they were going except <us.>

Danny rode, not at all sure where he was going, except that, for the hour, he was where that *thing* wasn't, that *thing* that he'd felt and had no question—

—no question she was a killer.

He heard too much. He didn't want to listen anymore. He just wanted Cloud; he wanted to drift on through the dark and the downfalling white. He wanted <quiet,> and <escape> from the things he saw, that still careened centerless about his memory.

He rode until he was keenly aware of the snow and the cold.

He rode until his hands and feet and face were numb.

He rode until he found himself in <forest> and knew that <fire-windowed streets> was a place he'd never, ever been.

Then he was afraid to go farther. He'd been following the beacon of that place—but it was nowhere he wanted to reach.

Nothing stirred. Nothing dared. The air felt warmer than it had. The wind had stopped blowing. The snow fell, real snow, in thick, fat lumps.

<Evergreens,> he thought. <Wide, protecting evergreen boughs.>

Because he remembered <Stuart on the porch, Stuart in the rain,> and somehow it had come up in what Stuart had told him, about having a knife, and how a knife should be last of everything you lost, because with that, no matter how desperate you were, no matter how much of your gear you'd lost, you could make a den, keep warm, get food, stay alive.

He hadn't even the knife. They'd taken that.

But he had his bare hands. In everything about him, even, if it got to that, tearing the fringes off his jacket for bindings, he had the makings of shelter, of tools.

He slid off Cloud's back, imaging <shelter made of evergreen,> and Cloud hovered about him as he set to furiously, tearing at branches with his hands, leaning his body against them to break them free.

Cloud tore at a few small limbs, using his teeth. <Bad taste,> Cloud thought, and spat out bits of bark.

But gloved hands jerked, ripped, twisted until branches splintered, until muscles ached. He tore at the trees, sweating and gasping for breath, until he had a pile of branches he thought was enough.

With them he made a bed, and he had <Cloud lying down on it.> Then, pulling branches over himself, he lay down on the edge of their mat, himself tucked against Cloud, warm on one side, keeping Cloud's side warm because in that horse-smelling pocket he could make of his body and Cloud's was the only warm air, and his chest ached and his gut ached with the fall and with shivering. A long, long time he lay there and shook, until Cloud's warmth seeped into him.

Then Cloud himself sighed, gentle movement against his shoulder.

Snow fell on him, but that was all right. It could do that. Snow was an insulator, wasn't what he'd heard?—as long as he had Cloud's body radiating warmth into his.

Snow was warm, if it kept away the wind, if it kept away the dark.

If it didn't let him dream of streets and fire reflecting off glass, and if it didn't let him dream, sweating warm despite the cold, of dark and something more terrible than the preachers' devils—

He wanted daylight.

God, he wanted the day to begin and this night to be over. He tried not to image, but kids, Jonas had said, couldn't keep from noise. Kids couldn't shut down.

(Kids in that village, oh, God, they'd have been close to that thing. Mamas and papas couldn't do a damned thing to help them—they'd have been the first, they'd have gone to it.)

He kept seeing <fire on windowpanes. Kids running. The devil loose in the streets, and the innocent all running.

<Preachers in Shamesey streets—crying, Follow not the beast, hear not the beast—

<Denis screaming, "God's going to send you to hell!">

Cloud snorted, shifted, settled. The whole woods was so scarily quiet you could almost hear the snowflakes land. He'd not realized that until now: the whole woods was hushed, and Cloud was part of that silence.

They're born to this world, Stuart had said to him. They hear the Wild first. If you can't hear what's going on, listen to your horse. Always remember that.

Cloud's rider listened.

Cloud's rider lay still, noticing only the trees, only the wind, only the snow, until he was as quiet as Cloud.

He wasn't there. For any number of very long hours, he wasn't there.

Chapter
— xvi —

THE ROAD UP FROM ANVENEY WAS THE SHORTEST, FASTEST WAY UP to the High Wild—a good idea, Guil thought as the morning brightened to warmer daylight, good idea, considering both the season and the condition of the rider, because he and Burn weren't going to make any record time; and he damned sure didn't want to trek all the way back to the main road and then take that ascent: speed was everything when the weather was chancy, and when you had to factor in that long trek even to get to the other road. He didn't mind camping on the main road in clear weather. But he didn't trust it would stay clear of snow long enough for him to get over there and get up the mountain. Its gentle slope was treacherous, piling up snow in overhangs—and the chill was definitely in the air.

Whichever route you chose, the long, avalanche-prone ridge to the south or the steep, icy climb he was on, you didn't want to be on the ascent or the descent once the snows started in earnest: once he made Tarmin Ridge he had choices and shelters—which in the high country didn't mean any shabby lean-to: the high-country riders took their storm shelters seriously and stocked them reliably. Get just that far and he could survive the worst the mountain could throw at him.

There was even a shelter at the halfway point of the climb he was on, so he'd heard, but by all he knew it was just a shack, no regular maintenance, no store of food, and he wasn't going to push himself beyond reason to reach it or stop early to use it. Nothing in the world cost more than an hour or two delay when you were reckoning the weather by the minute.

The ill-famed Anveney service road looked easy, at least the rolling part of it, that went through the sparse, bad-grass hills—but that, he knew, was the gentle prelude. One had only to look up at the towering northeast face of the mountain to see that what the south road did by gentle turns, this road did on the most hellacious grades trucks or ridden horses could manage.

And increasingly as he rode, the mountain took on the appearance of a sheer wall. A series of hairpins, on the most meandering of which he began to realize he'd already embarked, laddered the same steep face that, you had to remember, ten k north, plunged away into river-cut Kroman Gorge, a view straight down for most of a mile. It was a famous sight, it was certainly worth a ten k ride to look at—and he'd seen that vertical slit in the earth at least in Aby's mind as <grand and amazing.> But Burn imaged it nervously as <falling into darkness> and he wasn't sure himself if he went there that he wanted to stand anywhere near that edge.

He wasn't sure, facing this upward perspective, that it was going to be much better up there.

But the road he was on still looked to be faster than the other from bottom to top, maybe even by a couple of days, even with the road in the condition it was in. He'd lost precious time, two whole days he was relatively sure of, drying out his clothes and his gear and nursing his headache, or his several headaches, counting the knots on his skull.

He'd been concussed, he was almost certain—not thinking too clearly for a day or so; and concussed meant, if you talked to doctors, lie down, do little, eat and sleep, if you had somebody to wait on you.

Fine, he'd rested, between the necessity to get a fire going and to fend for himself. He'd used up money-bought supplies he'd rather not have touched, but a forced lay-up was what such supplies were for—he supposed they were well-spent. He was alive.

He'd done some fool things—but close as he was still to Anveney and doctors, rational or irrational (as he'd been when he'd taken that ride after wood instead of going for an Anveney doctor), he'd turned out all right. He didn't need any townsman doctor, one he couldn't talk to, understand, or deal with. He wasn't going to have any strangers, however well-intentioned, poking around at him while Burn fretted at the gates. He'd known, when he waked that morning with the headache that didn't go away, exactly what he had, at worst, unless his skull was fractured, which time proved it wasn't. He certainly didn't need any high-paid town doctor to tell him that his head hurt, and not to walk any distance in that condition.

So he'd won. So he'd been able to lie about feeling his head expand and contract, and watching the colors come and go behind his closed eyelids, wanting occasionally to pass out until it was over—

Eventually you died or you got better. And since he hadn't caught pneumonia, and he hadn't gone into coma, and since the leg the bank guard and the marshals had banged about didn't seem infected, just ached like hell, swelled, and hurt when he walked on it—he guessed he'd saved himself and the town doctor the bother, and he was still going to make the Ridge before the snows came down. He was going to deal with Aby's problem, and finish Aby's business up there. Money was hindmost in that calculation: the doctor would have cost time and kept him off the trail; and the snows would have beaten him.

And by the time they'd gone up a distance, with him walking and limping on the steep grade, he began to fear they weren't going to make the speed he would have wanted today: his sore leg was aching, his good one was burning, his head was splitting, and his breaths came as if he'd run a race. He leaned on Burn's side and stood there a while staring up at the first true hairpin before he could find it in him even to consider going on up the grade.

He walked as far as he could: Burn wasn't going to make any speed, either, slogging along under his weight at the angle the road climbed.

A turn or so higher, Burn took him up, and when Burn tired again—where they stopped for breath and for him to get off—the view down, where the edges had eroded in a series of slides, was absolutely spectacular: raw rubble spiked with trees that had found a foothold on the slopes; while the view up from there was enough to give a man or a horse serious doubt whether they were sane to try this road at all. He couldn't see some of the roadway, the angle was so steep—what he could see of the zigzagging trace of back and forth hairpins and phone lines was daunting, entirely.

But underfoot, tribute to mechanical persistence, he could still see the scarring that trucks this summer or last had made on the road, such tough, small trucks as ran emergency supplies and phone lines for the line-riders.

The modern log and lumber monsters, and the tankers, couldn't hope to take even the lowest and easiest of the turns to get up here. It was risky, his eye could well judge, even for the line repair trucks, and they couldn't go all the way up these days.

<Truck going over. Tires over the rim.>

Once that happened you hadn't a chance, no way to recover your traction.

He pulled back from that thought, heart pounding as if he'd been *on* that edge. He started walking, diverting himself with the pain in his leg and the search for breaks in the phone line, not that he could do anything about them, but Cassivey had promised him to call Tarmin and warn them if the lines were up.

If he knew a call *could* get through—that would take at least some weight of necessity off his mind. But it looked chancy. Watching where the line climbed, ahead of them, he saw poles braced up with rocks—some of them leaning in impending breaks. Wait till the winter winds, he thought. Wait till the ice. They wouldn't hold. They might not have held on the road above.

No phone line at all on the main road—that was why they'd

kept maintaining this old run on Anveney West, specifically because the phone lines were already here and because avalanche was constant hell on the other one in winter, sweeping poles and all away, more than they lost here to slides. So Aby'd said. And they kept the phones going.

Fifty years ago, when the gold fever had been rampant in the hills and speculators in every sort of vehicle had made Anveney their base of operations, this ill-conceived switchback had been all the road that served a network of mining roads and little, isolated camps. Most who had tried winter camp, with just their guns and their gold-fever to insulate them from the Wild, hadn't made it through the first winter, but by the second winter, the survivors had clumped in larger camps and the survivors of those had made a dozen villages up on the Ridge, only a few of which still held out—compared to those that had once been. That, also, Aby had said: her man in Anveney told her so.

<Come on, Guil, you'll like it up there. . . .>

And, headache and all, he looked for line-breaks. But you couldn't, as the inside edge of the road grew more wooded, always see the poles, let alone the lines. Thickets of greenwood and shag had grown up around them, unrestricted.

Worse, washouts were multiplying, eroding away the outside edge of the road in graveled gullies that were a real danger to the trucks. Weeds, untouched by trucks' undercarriage chains, had grown up on the center ridge. Scrub leaned well over the wheel tracks, and grass had grown up in the tracks themselves. It had to have been some time since the last line repair truck had come up here—let alone the road crews it badly needed.

And that neglected road repair, it took no intelligence even for a lowland townsman to guess, increased the frequency of spooks along the way: like weeds, spooks were, no single breed, just vermin, prolific and nuisanceful to humans. Hunted out of any traveled territory, they expanded right back into any territory where brush provided adequate cover. He heard them as he rode: a constant shifting image of giant grass and the noise of something large and the fear of something <formidable> nearby—which was, of course, themselves, and the grass wasn't giant except to the creature doing the sending. Burn heard them very well, and occasionally sent out his <nighthorse> and <eating willy-wisps> image, which cleared the area in short order.

The little spooks were no harm to a rider, or anyone a rider escorted. But once little spooks grew plentiful, they made rich hunting for midsized spooks, which would happily add the vermin-rich offal heaps of villages like Tarmin and Verden to their hunting range; they'd dig and gnaw and try the defenses of supplies in the rider-shelters—and clear out fast if riders showed up.

One had to know, though, that after the middle-sized spooks like nightbabies and lorry-lies moved in, serious trouble was right behind: goblin-cats and spook-bears and bushdevils and every other sort of creature that could make a village's dreams uneasy. Tarmin and the rest of the high-country villages in Anveney's mining union should have raised hell about the washouts and the brush. It was a steep, steep face, and if it grew brushy and the road got beyond even riders, then there was a breeding area and hunting ground for things the villages up on the Ridge might not like for neighbors.

But figure it, too, that Anveney with its smelters and furnaces was the chief customer of the mining camps, chief user of the phone lines between Anveney and the camps, and while the mining and logging camps had riders encamped and accessible, even semi-permanently resident, Anveney, alone of towns, didn't have riders, especially in the current feud with Malvey, to maintain those lines.

So blame the want of action on the camps and the villages, he decided, who might regret it once their politicking with Anveney or their neglect had let the whole east face of Rogers Peak go back to the Wild.

Two more turns and the road grew worse, with washouts trenching the whole road surface, with rockfalls lying in the roadway some rocks of which were considerable—if you met that kind of thing with a convoy you stopped and with shovels you filled the washes and fixed it as best you could—

Or you hoped you hadn't gone too far from a truck turn-around.

With a horse—and no trucks to worry about—you rode past and hoped it didn't get worse up above. But he had faith in Burn.

<Cattle,> Burn thought. Burn didn't approve of the road.

But Burn didn't argue to turn around, either.

Burn had the high-country wind in his nostrils. Burn thought <mountains> and <snow> and <females.>

The way-shelter that was supposed to exist at sundown turned up well short of that—not that he was ahead of schedule—but that the shelter was a collection of scattered logs and scattered rags several turns below where it was supposed to be. He saw part of the foundations further up: a boulder had swept it right down the mountain face.

It left a flat camping area, once he did reach it, at the edge of night, but not one he was tempted to use. He cast a misgiving eye up at the sheer face of the mountain, wondering what other brothers those boulders had poised and waiting up there, and kept moving until dark dimmed the road too much to see.

Then he camped in a little stand of brush as sheltered from the wind as he could manage. There were spooks—he thought one was a nightbaby, by the distressing <lost-lost-lost> images it sent.

Something evidently believed it. Whether it caught supper or whether it became supper, it went silent, and the ambient was quiet for a while.

He'd collected dead wood for some distance along the roadside before he camped, as much as he could conveniently carry—and now sheltering his little construction with his body and Burn's, in this wide spot among the rocks where saplings clung, he built a tiny, well-protected fire, not easy when the wind searched out every nook and cranny.

So there was <bacon> for Burn, and cakes for them both.

Not so bad, he said to himself, snugged down dry and warm with Burn for a backrest. He had his single-action handgun resting on his lap beneath the blanket—hand on the grip but his finger prudently off the trigger, ready, if Burn heard something that Burn couldn't scare.

He heard only nuisance spooks, all during supper.

They sang. They imaged their fierceness. He settled to sleep against something that, if Burn roused and grew annoyed, could send <mayhem and anger> louder than the lot of them.

Which Burn did from time to time, though not troubling to get up, when the ambient grew noisy with the nocturnal pests.

Guil sighed, imaged <Burn sleeping quietly,> and shut his eyes in all confidence of Burn's hearing the ambient even when Burn was asleep.

<Wind,> Danny decided, huddled in the lee of tumbled rocks, as another night came down. It had to be <wind moving the boughs.>

Cloud hovered close, hungry and in an ill mood, but Cloud had kept that uncommon quiet, taking no chances, and imaging <snow> and <snow on branches> so consistently Danny could hardly, at times, realize he was hearing Cloud and not seeing <snowy branches.>

He'd never known Cloud to do that before. He sometimes feared that something was wrong with Cloud's mind; but Cloud grew disturbed when he tried to get Cloud's attention—Cloud imaged <hungry horse> and then went back to his <branches> so loudly he couldn't *see* anything but that.

He didn't know what they were going to do about food. He'd gone to sleep hungry one night, now it was the second, and he didn't know where they were going to get food for either of them. He was mad at himself for not thinking to grab his packs, or anything—but he hadn't been thinking at all when he'd run from the camp, and not thinking a lot today, in their forest of <snowy branches.> He was mostly scared.

They'd moved, today, and they'd seen game, but Cloud hadn't wanted to hunt and he had no gun.

He could at least have made a fire. He had his burning-glass in his pocket, he'd some wrapped, waxed matches on him, but he was scared to do it for fear that Harper or a horse he didn't want to meet or even think about would smell it on the wind, in this place where smells you didn't notice downland were very, very obvious as man-made. So he'd made his bed with evergreen, the same as last night, with less desperation, with more care. And he really truly hoped Cloud would find them <breakfast.>

But that wish got him nothing but <snowy branches, snowy against the clouds,> so persistently it upset an empty and already chancy stomach.

They'd found a berry bush with berries still left out of reach of smaller creatures, and Cloud could eat the berries, so they were probably all right, but that wasn't always true: human beings weren't of the same earth-stuff as horses, and you couldn't always rely on the safety of plants horses could eat—so once he'd seen Cloud go at them, he'd tucked handfuls of the autumn-dried berries in his pockets and eaten just one of them, figuring to test if he got stomachache or went strange afterward.

He hadn't, and they were still in his pocket, so he nibbled a few. They were sour and set his teeth on edge, but they were better than an empty stomach.

Cloud found a few sprigs of dried grass that grew about the rocks, and licked lichen or some kind of fungus off the stone; at least it looked as if Cloud was getting something to eat out of all that effort—the image was now <lichen on stone,> for variety, instead of <snowy branches and dry grass above the snow.>

Which was probably smart to do, this <branches> business. But it made thinking and planning hard.

He watched Cloud for a while, wondering if the stuff on the rocks was edible—but he wasn't greatly tempted to peel it off and have a try at any scummy fungus, no more than he was tempted to abandon the little warmth he'd found to go collect it.

He didn't know where he'd go next, or, more to the point, where Cloud would be willing to take him. He was, he had to admit it to himself, lost—not *lost,* in not knowing where down was on the mountain, any fool could tell that, but lost because he didn't know which side of the road he was on, and he didn't know whether the nearest village was behind him or in front of him, above him or below him on the mountain. They hadn't crossed a clear-cut, or seen any other indication of a road in any place they'd crossed.

Most disturbing—he figured that Cloud was imaging <snowy branches> so fervently because there was a good reason for hiding.

Which made him, unwillingly, think about the <fire on windows> and that <presence> he didn't want to feel.

Cloud snorted and shied away from him, with <snowy branches> louder than ever until he stopped and plunged his head into his hands and swore to the God back in Shamesey town he was through being a hero: he wanted <finding the downhill road, going down to lowland pastures.> Cloud would have his winter in the Wild, just not in the high country—

Because Cloud's fool rider, having gotten them into one human mess after the other, had now lost all his gear and everything he owned. Cloud depended on his rider to see ahead and think ahead, and understand the Wild, and his fool rider hadn't even understood human beings. He wasn't any help to anybody, and the best thing he could do was get them off the mountain alive and get Cloud fed and safe.

<Snow falling. Snow drifting down in the dark.>

<(Desire,)> came a thread of feeling. <(Bodies together, dark nighthorse bodies, feelings intense as the dark . . .)>

Danny caught a breath, roused out of sleep, suddenly beset by feelings he didn't know where they'd come from—out of control, but he wouldn't, he wouldn't, he didn't understand what was happening to him. . . .

<(Wanting—wanting closeness, wanting—)>

<Snow> came down on him, cold and quiet, poured down until he was lost in a breathing, snowy night. That was Cloud. He knew it was.

<(. . . bodies merging, tearing, ripping apart—)>

<< . . . Watt, running through the dark, running and running—chest aching, breath coming edged with cold and terror, not enough air, branches breaking against arms and face, jabbing at eyes, branches crashing and breaking—>>

Stuart on the porch. "Stay with your horse." Jump across time. Another moment. "Stay with your horse." Danny and Cloud at the fireside. "Stay with your horse, whatever goes wrong, stay with your horse."

<<Man running in the dark, something behind him, branches

breaking—he won't turn, he won't turn and look, just running, sound coming closer with every stride—open ground, and steep rocks, and empty, dark air—>>

Danny gasped, jerked, caught at the ground, couldn't get breath, couldn't overcome the falling-feeling—

<<Snow. White everywhere. Heart slow, so slow his blood can't move. So slow he can't breathe—>>

Then could. Danny sucked in a breath, his ribs able to move.

He got another, and another, and his gloved hands knew the solid ground was under him, he hadn't fallen. He wasn't falling. That was somebody else—somebody was dying.

<Cold on his face, chilling cold against the sweat.> He sat there with his heart pounding, sure he'd been somewhere else—that he'd been *somebody* else. He was sure that something had been behind him, but when he looked he saw only the night-shadowed trees and the solid stone of the mountain.

A presence went past them then, fast, like a blink of starless dark—it swirled and it reeled dizzily, it wanted, it fell, it rose, it was a man and it wasn't—it was lost and it was angry and it was looking for someone, it lusted after sex, after touch, after feeling, after something it had <(lost and couldn't find)>—

He suffered a spasm of chill, then of arousal, but he held himself still, too wary to catch. He felt <drifting snow> on his face, and after a time of harsh, measured breathing the lust and the hurt and the wanting went away, sucked away into the dark farther and farther and farther, faster than any horse alive could run.

He thought at first it was another kind of falling, and clung to the rocks, shaking and afraid that the whole mountain would dissolve around him—straight outward into the air.

<(Hunger. Fright. Pouring through the woods—something chasing it. One and the same, predator and prey, feeding and fed upon. Pain and hunger embracing each other, tearing and biting—)>

<Blood on pale skin. Knives flashing. A man Harper loved—>

—and shot dead. <Face pale in the dark woods. Hole in the forehead. Staring at the sky. At Harper.>

<Cattle,> Cloud thought, telling him he was stupid. <Dungpiles.>

He felt his fists knotted up. Every muscle was stiff. He was dreaming, he said to himself, remembering with eyes wide awake—he didn't know for sure it was Harper. Things you heard in the ambient sometimes didn't come to you full-blown until later, sunken things rising to the surface of your mind with more and more detail. He kept seeing that dead face—

<Harper shooting—horse, at a fireside. Man and horse coming into firelight.

<Harper shooting: they had to die.

He was holding evergreen bits in his hands. He was sitting on the ground, on his evergreen bed, testing whether he could breathe on his own, and whether the ground would stay still and the rocks not fly off into the night—his brain knew better than to trust what he'd just lived, but he couldn't let go for a long while, couldn't understand what had just happened, until he suffered a panicked fear and found Cloud nuzzling his cheek.

All right, he said to himself, all right, Danny Fisher, that was the rogue. You found it. That's what you wanted. It's up here. No gun. Nothing. Cloud's got to get us out of here. . . .

A rogue could send far, far across the mountain.

But if it wasn't near them it couldn't hear them, because sending that far, that was what *it* did—but it couldn't hear farther than *they* sent—and they weren't nearly as strong or as loud. Except—

Except the creatures near them. It picked that up, the same as they could, only maybe—better than they did.

It had been near Watt. He'd heard—he'd *been* Watt: the dark and the falling-feeling came back to him, the mind-taking pain of branches gouging an eye, tearing across his face—

Harper might still be alive. Quig might. He didn't think Watt was. Somewhere on the mountain, Stuart might be alive. They might get the rogue. *They* might shoot it.

He had no gun. He sat and shook in the dark, and fished a berry or two out of his pocket to take his mind off his fear.

Cloud came closer to him, hungry and <wanting the berries> Cloud could smell.

And suddenly he realized Cloud wasn't stuck on the <snowy

branches> image any longer. Whatever Cloud had been saving them from—was gone from the ambient.

So Cloud got the berries. All he had. They weren't much for Cloud's big body, but Cloud got them, and Cloud's rider had only one last one. Cloud was due that much.

Cloud would find more berries tomorrow, and they take the chance they had and go down the mountain, please God. He'd been stupid. He'd run off from his parents and come up on the mountain where a stupid kid hadn't any experience or any business being. God punished people like that. But maybe they had one more chance to get out of this.

Cloud snorted, mad. Cloud didn't understand God. But if that was God that was out there in the dark, Cloud took exception to his thinking about God: Cloud came between him and the wind and licked vigorously at his face, making it wet in the cold air. He tried to shove Cloud off, but Cloud wouldn't leave him, Cloud pressed in so he had to tuck up tighter in his nook or have his face scrubbed raw.

He was warm, though. He shivered, and whenever he thought—as he had to—that what he'd felt was real, and Watt had run through the woods, and Watt had fallen off the edge of some cliff—he disturbed Cloud, who didn't want him to, and who thought about where they were and about <snow,> until he gave up trying to think of anything else.

<Snow sifting down on them.> He thought it was Cloud's imaging. But he opened his eyes and felt it on his face when he looked up. It whitened the evergreen that made their blanket. It stuck to Cloud's back.

The terror didn't come back. Maybe the rogue was asleep.

Maybe it had found what it was hunting. But he hadn't felt it satisfied. It had just—flown away, not finished with what it was doing.

<Harper firing—on a man and a horse, firing until the gun was empty.>

—until the man was dead.

He squeezed his eyes tight, not wanting to think about that. So he thought, like Cloud, about <snow and branches> and bore down on that thought very hard.

Chapter
— xvii —

THE AIR AT DAYBREAK WAS QUIET, LADEN WITH MIST THAT MADE the woolen blanket damp. Guil folded it up, wet though it was. He had two blankets. He'd felt the moisture in the air last night and not taken the other out of the pack. If the sun came out today he'd wear the one cloaklike a while and let the wind work on it; but it could only get wetter, as the morning promised to be, with a veil over the road.

Today, he expected a harder trek, and maybe one more night on the climb; he hoped to God not, mistrusting the clammy mist that meant a lot of moisture in the air. It was a treacherous kind of weather. All it took was a front coming over the mountains, and they were in heavy snow—or a freezing mist. Aby had indicated in vagrant images of her high-country treks that the high end, beyond the shelter, was far steeper—more than a twenty-five percent grade in places.

Ravines.

Bridges.

Loose fill where the roadbed was sure to have washed out at the edges. The number of trucks in the old days that had lost their brakes and taken the straight route down was legendary.

With frozen sheen marking the edges of leaves this morning, it wasn't a road to like at all—but that was the situation they had, and they walked, both of them, for an hour or more, with only hazy rock at one side to tell them where the road was bending, hazy gray at their right to tell them where empty space was, and the grade of the road and their own burning lungs and weary legs to advise them how high and fast they were climbing. At least once the sun was lighting the mist, the frost on the rocks slowly turned liquid.

By midmorning a mild breeze began, and as dry cold scoured away the mist, the world below appeared in pastel miniature, a memorable view down the series of switchbacks and slides.

There were fewer rock falls: a falling rock wouldn't *stay* on this steep, he swore. Earth-slip had skewed a whole section of phone poles, the line not yet broken, but the poles wanted resetting. He vowed to tell Cassivey next spring in person and in no uncertain terms that if they wanted these lines to stay up, whoever was supposed to be responsible for them, they'd better hire riders—and get a road repair truck up here next summer, or not even a line-rider with a wire-cutter and a roll of tape was going to be able to get up here in another year. Damned stupid economy—to wait until they had to blast a new roadbed out.

It only got worse. In one place, erosion had cut away half the road. It made him give anxious thought to the ground under their feet, which was shored up by timbers the slide had compromised. Badly.

In another turn he met the first of the high bridges: the road was climbing by a rugged set of switchbacks and going further and further back into a fold of the mountain, and where the roadbuilders hadn't found a way to blast away enough mountain to make a roadway past the slip-zone they had evidently just bridged the gap and hoped.

But with the fresh scars of slides going under the bridge, he got down off Burn's back, climbed down at least far enough on the rocks so he could take a look at the underpinnings; and it did look to be sound.

He climbed up then and walked across the boards ahead of Burn—as Burn trod the weathered boards imaging <boards shattering> and switching his tail furiously. <Sharp rocks,> Burn insisted, <far, far, *far* down in the gully.>

It wasn't that far down. But, give or take the missing tie-downs that made no few of the warped boards rattle and rock—and thunder like hell under wheeled traffic, Guil could well imagine—it forecast nothing good ahead.

The next such bridge they reached was worse—two boards were actually missing in a span above a higher drop. Hope, Guil thought, that the villages had done better with the bridges up near the crest.

Another short span. Burn had to cross over more missing boards, easy stride for a horse—but Burn was, by now, not happy with bridges in general.

Then they caught sight of the big one Aby's images had foretold they could expect, over a gorge by no means so large as Kroman, but impressive, the longest bridge yet—and as Guil looked up from below, it showed sky through its structure.

Guil gazed up at it in dismay, and Burn outright balked on the gravel road, catching the image from his mind and dizzily lifting and turning his head to have his one-sided horsewise view of it. Burn immediately ducked his head down and laid his ears back, shaking his neck.

Nothing to do but have a look, Guil thought, and nudged Burn with his heels, twice, to get him moving up that steep gravel incline.

The bridge looked no better when they came up on a level with it, a long span over a rift in the mountain flank, a cable and timber structure far more ambitious than any they'd met.

It wasn't wholly suspension, thank God. The rails as well as the roadbed were missing pieces, and four and five of the crosslaid planks were gone at a stretch. He counted four, five such gaps in the bridge deck, so far as he could see from this side, gaps exposing the underpinnings. The boards had probably, Guil thought, sailed right off in the storms, considering the cold gusts that battered and buffeted them, sweeping unrestricted along the dry, slide-choked gorge on the one side and dizzily out into open sky and the whole of the plains and the distant haze-hidden Sea on the other.

He jammed his hat on tight and slipped the cord under his chin before he walked out on the span to look it over, and the look he got sent his heart plummeting. The gaps were big enough to drop a horse through, and the winds that swept across that span could rock a man on his feet.

Burn didn't like that idea. <Guil coming back,> Burn urged him anxiously.

Days—*days* to go back down and across to the other route. With the weather about to turn. If he went back now he wouldn't get up to Tarmin Ridge until spring—and that left him sitting in Anveney territory all winter, with nothing done, nothing but using up his supplies, his account—granting money was there, of which he was not entirely certain if he failed Cassivey's commission now. If the villagers found that shipment up there in the rocks—Cassivey and a lot of Anveney folk weren't going to be damned happy with him.

He didn't like losing, or explaining to a shipper why he'd failed; and failing what he'd promised himself and Aby, hell—it wasn't why he'd come this far already.

He walked back off the bridge. <Sharp rocks,> Burn imaged as he made a risky, wind-battered descent off the roadway, holding on to rocks to take a look underneath at the supports. <Burn standing. Guil standing on road. Guil standing on ground.>

The supports were sound enough, run through with iron rods and huge metal plates bolting the whole together.

He climbed back up to the road and walked out on the bridge as far as the gaps. He stood looking at the far side, then shut his eyes a moment, and made his mind as quiet and confident as he could.

<Burn walking to Guil,> he sent. <Burn standing on bridge with Guil.>

<Burn in meadow. Burn eating green grass.>

<Burn on the bridge. Strong thick boards.>

<Sharp rocks. Holes in bridge.>

"Come on, Burn, dammit. It's too far to go back." He looked up at gray-bottomed clouds scudding above the peak. <Snow clouds. Burn. Burn walking. Now.>

<Guil with snow on him.>

"Burn, dammit! Come on!"

<Thicker snow. Guil in snow, standing on bridge.>

"Burn. Get your ass out here. *<Now!>*"

Burn moved, came step after slow step, the wind whipping his mane upward, trying each plank, imaging as he came: <Cold belly. Tail tucked. Fire and dark. Weathered, split boards.>

"It's all right, Burn. Come on."

Burn came up beside him, at the area of missing boards, stopped, and lowered his head to take a long, unhappy, dizzy look down into the depths below.

<Burn standing still.> Guil patted Burn's shoulder hard, to be sure he felt it, laid his rifle and his gear down on the bridge planks, and with a hand along Burn's side and rump, walked Burn a little distance out to where a number of planks were loose.

It wasn't easy to free one. It was a plank sized to support a small truck. It weighed like hell and he could only lever it up from the end, looking out over a sheer drop down the face of the mountain, and the wind blasted his hat off, left it spinning and jerking at his back, held only by the cord. He got the plank up, turned it, dragged it back past Burn and, with slow maneuvering and a final, satisfying thump, installed it in the gap.

Burn leaned forward in curiosity and peered over that edge. Didn't trust that board. But Burn was amazed, preoccupied with the gap, when Guil walked back by him, hand on Burn's side.

He worked and worked, freed the next plank, and dragged it along past Burn.

Then Burn caught on what he was doing, <planks missing behind him.>

Burn backed up in a panicked rush. Guil let the plank fall crashing to the deck and grabbed a double fistful of nighthorse mane to stop him. <Burn backing, putting foot into gaping hole. Burn with cattle tail!>

<Kicking Guil,> Burn sent, <biting.> But Burn didn't do it.

Burn stood there shivering, with a clear imagination of the bridge unraveling behind him.

"You don't move!" <Burn standing. Guil fitting plank.> Guil hurried as best he could, picked up the plank and dragged it into place.

He went back and got another one. Burn was still standing, shivering. Burn could cross a single missing board. Guil dragged the third board up to Burn's position.

But Burn was far from certain that any board he'd just seen moved was going to stay put. Burn grew confused about directions, and started to back up in great haste.

"You fool," Guil swore, threw himself under Burn's rump and shoved with all the strength he had. <Gap behind us,> he argued, until Burn bent his neck around and took a confused, misgiving look back.

Burn didn't trust <migrating holes.> Burn wasn't going back. Burn wasn't going forward. No.

There were two of them shaking now. Guil retrieved the plank he'd dropped, a quarter over the edge of the decking where it had bounced. He jammed his hat back on and swore and wrestled it up to the two-plank gap.

He dropped it in. He was exhausted and his headache had come back, but he wouldn't ask Burn to accept a hand-span gap in the planks that were there—Burn's estimation of gaps wasn't so reliable at the moment. He dragged and wrestled with it and got it butted.

Then he got up and stamped loudly over the repaired section, while Burn watched in horror. Stepped across the single missing plank. Did a kickstep across it, back and forth and twice more, like a lunatic.

Then he went back to Burn, and with his hands constantly on Burn's neck, patted and cajoled and argued, with the wind blasting up out of the gorge at both of them, rocking even Burn on his feet. He imaged <Burn walking on bridge.>

When that didn't work, he tried <Burn standing on bridge in snow. Snow falling thick.> He was cold. The wind cut like a knife. Burn was cold. <Frozen Burn. Ice crystals on hide. Guil covered in

frost. Boards falling, carried away on winter wind. Us standing on the last few lonely boards.>

The last was only half a lie. It spooked Burn. Burn jumped forward, <going forward> with a thunder on the new, loose planks, imaged the gap as <gaping hole,> and spooked across it.

Right for the next gap.

<*"Burn!"*>

Burn cleared it. *Thump-bang*!—and stopped, scared and confused.

Guil grabbed up his gear and ran, heart pounding, as far as the gap Burn had jumped, before his knees wobbled and gave out.

He squatted down. Burn was standing sideways on the bridge, looking back in distress.

It took a considerable while of catching his breath before Guil slung his rifle to his back, threw the two-pack across the gap, and crossed it, astride the support boards, with the wind out of the gorge blasting up under his coat and whipping his hat this way and that.

<Guil on bridge,> Burn imaged to him, wanting him safe.

<Burn standing still!> he flung back, scared, and with his teeth chattering. He was mad, he was furious with himself for going ahead, but back wasn't any easier than forward right now.

Something white flew across his vision. Several more followed.

Snowflakes, scattered, few, and from a partially cloudy sky. But it was a warning. It was a clear warning.

<Snow.> Burn saw it. <Cold wind.>

"I'm trying," Guil muttered, and tried to will the headache into some inner dark. Let his temper and the headache go off together and trade insults. They'd this bridge to cross. He didn't know how many more. He didn't know this road except by Aby's image, and that was the way an experienced rider killed himself and his horse, just too damn good, too damn cocky with the weather and an unknown road a junior wouldn't think of trying.

Burn deserved better. Wasn't going to leave Burn to freeze on a gap-toothed bridge.

Two more gaps. More laborious board-movings, a twice-mashed finger, a bashed knee, a splinter through his right glove, that he couldn't get all of with his teeth and he didn't want to take the glove off for fear of losing it, the wind was blowing so and his fingers were so numb. Cold helped the headache, only thing he could say for it.

Don't do anything, a doctor would say—and the wind blasted at him at the worst moments of his balance, so he lost one plank that caught the wind, spun him around, and off his balance. He let go and fell, it went sailing off into the gorge: he didn't follow it. The pistol damn near did, spun past his face to the gap: flat on his belly he grabbed that and recovered it as something else, small and shiny, slipped his pocket, skittered across the wind-scoured boards and over the edge. He'd saved the pistol, but the lighter was spook-bait.

He got up and got another board.

He didn't want Burn to try another jump, even if he could talk him into it. A nighthorse walking the old timbers was one thing. A nighthorse landing on them was another. He didn't trust the wood. But the far side hove closer and closer, plank after laboriously gained plank, and Burn crossed the next to last gap when he told Burn it was safe.

<Burn standing,> he sent. But once Burn was across that, Burn realized <solid ground ahead,> dismissing the intervening gap as <small hole.>

"Burn!" Guil yelled, at the same time Burn gathered himself for the charge, hoof-toed feet thundering down the board.

Burn sailed across the gap, landed. A board broke—Burn went in halfway up to his hock, and Guil stared, heart stopped as Burn clambered across the last few boards to the solid bridgehead.

Guil took a wobbly few steps forward, remembered his gear, gathered it up and followed, far more scared than Burn was. Burn stood on solid ground again. Burn was pleased with himself—raised a hind foot to lick a scrape, but that was all.

Burn's rider crossed the last gap above sharp rocks and mountainside and tottered to a rock-sheltered spot to sit down, dizzy, dry-mouthed with exertion, and feeling his skull trying to explode.

Which wasn't something he'd regret at the moment.

But they were safe.

And the smells on this side of the gorge he suddenly realized were evergreen and not chemical smoke—clean, pure evergreen, rocks, nighthorse, and the tang of snow on the wind. . . .

<Guil riding.> It was a feeling as much as an image Burn sent him: Burn's feeling, Guil's sensations when they were touching, the working of muscles in unison, the warmth in his body and Burn's at once. They could do that, when they touched, could be one mind now if he let go and let Burn have him.

And Burn lipped his ear. His hands met a soft nose, velvet nudge at his cheek—Burn's tongue licked the side of his eye with utmost delicacy and tasted salt.

The taste came into Guil's mouth, too, and identity melted. He scratched Burn's chin where Burn liked to be scratched, he shut his eyes and saw through Burn's, <the mountain, the sky, the snow making white caps on the rocks.>

Not a full-out storm, only a spat of snow. Not thick enough yet. Burn stood there, a barricade against the wind. His head still reeled, and he thought it hurt: it was one of those ghosty kind of headaches. Half-blind, feeling the altitude after his stint in Malvey and Shamesey lowlands, he uncapped his canteen and took a sip of water to ease his throat.

<Guil riding,> Burn sent, *wanting* him, wanting reassurance he was all right. <Guil riding in sunlight. Evergreens. Sweet smell of evergreens and horse.>

It took maybe a half an hour for him to get to his feet, and to climb, belly-down, onto Burn's back. But on this side of the gorge the wind was less, and the next switchback came up among sizeable, snow-blanketed evergreens that cut off the sight of the valley.

They'd made the Height. They were on the lower loop of the Tarmin road.

<Snowy branches> had long since given way to <cold nighthorse> and <hunger.> That was the only assurance Danny had of safety in the woods: Cloud was complaining about the game, which they hadn't seen (another bad sign, Danny thought: something had scared it) and the lack of berries (which argued game had recently been here).

And, no, lichen wasn't edible—or it was, but it wasn't something a human palate or a human stomach wanted to try again. He'd chewed evergreen trying to get the taste from his mouth. And it had mostly worked.

Cloud imaged a better taste for the stuff. Cloud didn't believe his.

And his gut hurt, since he'd eaten the stuff, and his heart had raced and his vision had tunneled for at least an hour afterward, which wasn't at all a good sign. That had scared him off further trials of anything fungus-like.

The effect had finally passed. The stomachache had eased, and become the stomach-empty feeling that had gone past mere lightheadedness. He wasn't near starving to death. He knew that. A human could go a whole moon-chase with nothing at all to eat, he'd heard of people doing it who broke a leg or something where they couldn't get help, and who had to crawl for days.

He thought about warm beds and his mother's cooking.

And maybe Cloud interpreted that as a wish Cloud should do something about, because he felt a fairly purposeful change in direction.

Within a few minutes Cloud came down a steep, snowy slope onto a clear-cut that extended in either direction, a track across the Wild.

More—he saw phone lines.

Chapter
— xviii —

THE EVENING SHADOW ROLLED DOWN EARLY, THICK WITH CLOUD, and the black, bristling evergreens were white with snow. Snow made a fine dust in Burn's mane and in the folds of Guil's coat—still a spat, not a storm, but advising a traveler it might be well to think about camp: it was all too easy if a real blow came up—as well could happen with the weather like this—to stray off the road in the dark and the snow, and right off the edge of a cliff.

But there was due to be a shelter ahead, down what was, so far, a well-defined road—a clear-cut marked by the solitary phone line.

And all the while that thin thread of human talk and commerce, he supposed, could have let him call the villages ahead. He'd thought once of buying a handset and learning how to tap in; those who rode the lines said it was stupid-simple, and all you needed was tape and wire-cutters besides, but, hell, he'd never needed a phone—until now. There was a stop-start way you could send a message without a handset; but the authorities put out warrants if you ever cut a line purely on rider business, and besides, he didn't know the code: he couldn't spell any more than he could read. And a handset? It was weight and cost, and Burn had enough to carry, Burn would tell him so.

Burn had been damned forgiving this trip. Burn was a <fine horse,> and he was sorry he'd made Burn's back ache, which it did. There'd be <bacon> when they got to shelter, there'd be <liniment and warm water—Guil rubbing tired nighthorse legs, rubbing sore nighthorse back—>

Burn was immensely pleased. Doubly so that Burn's rider opted to slide down and walk; Burn was concerned about his rider's limp and sore leg, and wanted to lick at it—attention he had as soon not—but Burn was very glad not to have <heavy, pack-laden rider on tired nighthorse back> and wanted to be generous.

You certainly didn't push yourself at this altitude if you weren't acclimated, and neither of them were acclimated. You didn't press beyond sensible limits—his own chest ached with the thin air, and persistent headache rode just at the back of his eyes, not, he thought, entirely due to the concussion.

But the thought of a solid shelter and a wood fire was a powerful incentive: there was supposed to be one fairly close to the ascent and one more before Tarmin. It was encouraging that there was no sight nor warning of trouble so far—but he didn't take the High Wild for granted—he walked with a loaded rifle and a sidearm ready, at the pace he felt like maintaining, which was a leisurely limp that didn't hurt beyond what his nerves could bear; and he'd much rather have solid walls around them tonight.

The two of them trod knee deep in snow that showed no disturbance but the occasional footprint of some spook or other, delicate imprints written in white, in that strange glow a nighttime snowfall had.

And if the little spooks had moved about in the open not so long ago then they were the biggest threat abroad. Lately they'd heard a wally-boo call out to the woods at large, soft, silly cooing that belonged to a little spook, all whiskers and ears.

Burn wasn't sending out his <nighthorse> threat. But as they came down a slight decline in the road Burn suddenly lifted his head, switched his ears about and sniffed the dark with that curious

<on the edge> feeling that went with winter winds and the chance of meetings.

<Females,> ran under that train of thought. <Snow and females.>

<Wild ones,> Guil thought anxiously, not wanting to think about the rogue they'd come to hunt: it came to him now and again as <dark and danger> when Burn grew too fractious, or too scattered from what they'd come to find.

Burn worried and gazed off into the woods with misgivings, thinking of <willy-wisps> and <lorry-lies,> which was sometimes a goblin-cat's camouflage: a horse above three or four years knew that spook trick, and Burn was well aware there was danger up here. A lot of things imaged what they weren't. Some had the knack of making you see things that had nothing to do with the ground you were walking on. The dangerous ones had worse tricks. You'd see people in the woods. You'd hear them call to you. They'd wave. A spook-bear could give you anything, any image it had ever seen.

A horse was a lot worse than that. A horse could convince you of anything.

Burn wasn't sure, himself, of whatever he heard—he shook himself, started moving again, treading carefully for a space, then gradually warming again to the thought of <safe den, nighthorses, bacon.>

<Bacon,> Guil agreed. Granted they got to shelter before the night grew too thick or his legs gave out, there would assuredly, he promised, be <bacon.>

<Guil riding,> Burn thought then. <Burn walking fast.>

"Silly ass," Guil muttered, patted Burn on the shoulder and intended to keep walking. He wasn't willing to wear Burn down, or have him sore tomorrow.

But Burn nudged him in the back and wanted insistently to go faster, and he couldn't, counting a bullet-grazed leg and a bashed knee, sustain the pace Burn wanted. Burn was skittish and full of notions this evening, thinking of <nightmares> one moment and <lorry-lies> the next, switching his tail and wanting to move, wanting <fight,> wanting <us on road.>

So he arranged his gear and made the weary effort to get up—aching in the arms, and the hand he used to grip with hurt like hell: probably, he thought, he hadn't gotten all the splinter out.

But he was glad not to walk, truth be told. Much as he'd tried to ignore the leg—his eyes watered once he'd gotten up and gotten relief from it. Burn struck a quicker pace than he could have held, and he let himself relax while Burn moved—in such intimate contact he heard the ambient as running through his own flesh and bone. He felt Burn's muscle and movement, saw and smelled the snow thick on the evergreen boughs, white on dark, sweet on bright; heard fat flakes changing to sleet that rattled against the branches.

Soft, soft sounds, cold, strange smells. Winter in the High Wild. The night was home and safe when he saw with Burn's eyes and heard with Burn's ears—they were one creature, the human drifting on a river of nighthorse senses, the horse remembering where he was going with human tenacity. Burn had struck his staying-pace, uncommonly determined, uncommonly spooky and . . . the feeling crept up Guil's backbone . . . suddenly, strangely focused on something in the dark.

Then, expected and unexpected in the night, they came on a structure of logs—deserted, by the feel of it: it was the shelter they were looking for.

Thank God, he thought, as Burn walked up to it, ears forward. <Bacon,> was definitely in the ambient now.

Nobody home. Burn would have known. Guil winced his way down to the ground and, rifle in hand, waded through a shallow drift to the door, stiff now that he'd been off the leg for a while. He set the rifle against the wall, seeing that the latch-cord was out as it ought to be. He drew his pistol, he pulled the cord, the bar inside came up, and he kicked snow aside and dragged the door open—outward, as the latch-doors always opened.

The dark inside was as cold as the snow-glow outside; but it *felt* empty. Burn put his head in past his shoulder and gave out his <nighthorse> warning, to scatter any sleeping vermin that might have burrowed a way in—but what they were hunting, although it could mask itself as <deep shadow> or even <human occupant,> couldn't manage a shelter door without human hands.

No occupants. No pilfered supplies. He put the gun away and felt after an electric switch beside the door in the small hope one would be there—lately lowland shelters had installed batteried lights at the entry.

No such luck.

But the fireplace was always on the right of the entry, and he slung his gear aside, took out his waxed matches and sacrificed one in order to see the state of things in the fireplace.

There was indeed a fire laid, stuffed with kindling—he spotted a slow match hanging from the mantel before his wooden match could die, snatched up the tarred braid and touched his failing light to the end before the heat got to his fingers.

He unhooked the slow match from the nail then, bent down with a wince and a grimace and touched off the tinder, which was, thank God, dry. He pulled the chain to open the flue, and the gust from the door swept in along with a moving shadow and a slow thump of nighthorse hooves as Burn ambled into the shelter. The door banged back all the way, threatening the fire. Guil sprang up to reach outside, grab his rifle, grab the door and haul it shut against the wind.

The latch dropped. The door sealed out the wind, but the single room had taken the cold into its wood and stone from long vacancy, and every surface was frozen cold, not tempting a man to take his hands out of his pockets or risk his nose above his scarf.

In the light of the burning kindling Burn clumped over to the nearest bin, nosed it up, already looking for <grain.>

<Burn swelled up like three-day carcass,> Guil imaged back, and squatted down by the fire to warm through his gloves and his layers of leather and wool.

<Bacon,> Burn insisted, gulping down grain, impervious to insult.

He stayed where he was, finally feeling a little warmth through the chill. He knew that Aby had been here a number of times—he looked up at the rider board on the wall, an old and extensive one, and there, sure enough, were Aby's marks among the others. She hadn't been the last to visit here—the filled triangle and the X were probably the riders who'd regularly refurbished it: they were the most regular. But she'd been familiar with this place, very definitely, even from years ago when she'd first used to come up this way, a kid escorting the small supply missions and the phone crews.

Her earliest jobs, the years they both had scrounged what hire they could.

Then they'd gotten downright prosperous. They could turn down jobs. All but the best.

If her presence lingered about here, he'd wish it could talk, or that she'd once, just once unbent and told him the few important words that would have made him understand the things she'd done.

But what in *hell* was she doing with Hawley and Jonas? Leave Luke out of it. Luke was whatever Jonas wanted. But why tell the bank woman that Hawley was entitled? Had to have been the wrong question they were asking her.

Burn brought his head up, came over and nudged him hard. "What was that for?" he asked. The sound of his own voice startled him. He didn't use it often—only as often as Burn's behavior defied imaging.

Burn nudged him again, decided he was going to lick his sore leg—"Hell!" he said, fending off the help. Burn left wet, sticky grain on his trousers. And wasn't helping.

<Guil and Aby,> Burn imaged to him, then. And as sloppily licked his cheek. So Burn thought he was crazy. He rested his head against Burn's neck, arm on his shoulders, really, really wishing he could fall into the icy-blanketed cot over there and not move for two days.

But a man—or a woman—paid out promises, or lived a liar.

So supper and bacon it had to be.

The snow came down in puffs and stuck, thick on the tall trees, making precariously balanced loads on branches that dumped down on rider and horse when they brushed beneath.

Maybe they should camp for the night, Danny thought. They couldn't see where they were going. He didn't know what was behind Cloud's insistence on moving. Trust your horse, he kept telling himself—and telling himself if there were anything out here in the dark he would know it through Cloud's senses; but the tales he'd heard around the camp firesides said there were exceptions, that horses could be tricked, too, and walk right into traps, a sending so seamless and on so many levels that even a horse couldn't see the lie in it.

<Cloud stopping,> he thought, but Cloud kept going.

<Cloud stopping. Danny getting off.> Cloud paid no attention.

He shifted his weight then, intending to make Cloud break stride, then to slide down. But Cloud gave a pitch of his hindquarters and imaged something so strange, so disquieting an impression of multiple minds that it sent chills down Danny's back. He lost all inclination to get off.

<Cloud stopping,> he insisted, but that feeling only grew, more and more distinct, like a swarming of half-crazed animal minds, <food, fight, gnaw.> Cloud hadn't been carrying it on a conscious level: it was out there, and Cloud had just sopped it up and not reacted to it, not passed it even to the rider on his back. Being transparent, that was what the seniors called it. The predators were good at it. And he'd startled Cloud into at least a quiet, body-touching-body sending.

"I don't like this, Cloud. Wait. Stop."

<Tumbling over one another. Logs. Jumble of logs. Big, little images, high and low. Smell of smoke. Logs. Gnawing at wall. Taste of flour. Taste of blood. Tugging at human hand.>

"Cloud, *stop*!" He grabbed at Cloud's mane mid-neck and pulled up, signaled <back up> with his legs, but Cloud ducked his head, jerking the mane out of his hand, and plowed ahead.

<Rogue,> Danny thought, and helplessly remembered: <Fire on glass. Log buildings. Village gates. —Cloud stopping. Cloud stopping.>

But Cloud sent <blood> and <fight> and carried him willy-nilly toward the chaos in Cloud's thoughts.

Maybe the rogue was calling to them. Maybe Cloud was going crazy himself. He didn't know what to do. If he got off he couldn't hold Cloud back at all. Cloud would be helpless, prey to whatever Cloud believed he was seeing.

<Men taking Danny's gun,> he sent. <Harper taking gun. Cloud stopping.>

Suddenly walls appeared through the veil of falling snow, walls at the side of the road—<log walls, a bell-arch, standing hazed in falling snow. Gates wide open to the night—the main gate standing wide.>

And rising from inside those walls: <eat and gnaw. Blood and flesh. Sugar and salt.>

<Nighthorse,> Cloud sent of a sudden. <Angry nighthorse.> And charged the open gates so suddenly that Danny scarcely grabbed a handful of mane.

They burst through into a street still reeking of smoke, a street where vermin by the hundreds, black against the snow, swarmed from under Cloud's charge, snarling and spitting and squalling as they fled the street for the porches, the porches for the shadows. Vermin poured over walls, ran down the street ahead of them, a hissing recalcitrance all up and down the street.

Something sizeable went over the porch of a house near them, a house with what looked bodies lying on the porch. Scavengers scurried across the unmoving shapes and into the dark between the houses.

<Nighthorse,> was all Cloud's sending. <Angry horse. Dark and blood. Clouds and lightning.>

Danny sat paralyzed on Cloud's back as Cloud paced down the street. There was no real defiance, no <fight> coming back at them—the scavengers rolled back like a black tide in the force of Cloud's warning, willy-wisps running for cover, lorry-lies clambering up over the walls, flitting shadows diving off porches and under them and down the spaces between the houses.

There was no horse present. No answer to Cloud's challenge. Charred, skeletal timbers that had been buildings. The stench of smoke. A burned building standing next to a stone one that wasn't touched at all, its windows appearing intact.

Bodies—thick in some places, bodies and what was left of them, sometimes just gnawed pieces, animal or human, he wasn't sure.

A backbone that small teeth hadn't taken apart turned up in the snow where something had dragged it and left it. For a second he wasn't sure what it was. He'd not thought before what pieces would resist the scavengers longest—if a human or a horse went down out here. He'd not seen anything to match this destruction, not even from the images seniors carried with their stories—nothing, nothing this complete.

"Anyone?" he called aloud, scared to make a noise. His voice sounded thin and strange in the snowy silence that had succeeded the hissing.

He sent <horse and rider> into the ambient, but he feared no villager holed up in any refuge would dare put their head up until they heard a human voice. "Hello! Anyone hear me? Call out! You don't need to come outside—just yell! I'll find you!"

There wasn't any sound. Scared, he thought, if anybody was alive—he'd endured only a few minutes of the scavenger babble before Cloud had sent them running; and he'd had a horse under him.

Any survivor would have had to hold out sane—God, since he'd *seen* the images of the attack. The village had cried out into the ambient for help—with only the rogue to image for them. No one had come. No one had answered. There were supposed to be riders here. And they hadn't saved the village.

"Anyone?" he called out, louder. "I'm a rider up from Shamesey! Do you need help?" Stupid, stupid question. "God, —can anybody hear me?"

He thought then that he did hear something, thin and far, he couldn't be sure, except he thought he heard it through Cloud's ears, too, and Cloud's ears had pricked up.

Then Cloud quickened his pace, imaging <disease> and <fear> and <fire> as he went—Cloud went as far as a building at the end of the street, and stopped, a shiver going up his leg, his head up, his ears up—<disease,> Cloud maintained. <Blood. Vermin.>

But something else came through: <room with bars> and <dark> and <fear> and <cold,> all jumbled up together.

"Who's in there?" Danny called out. "Come out! I'm right outside. It's safe."

"We can't," a voice cried from inside. "We're locked in. God, oh, *God*, get us out of here."

He wasn't sure. He had no gun, he had no advice; he only had Cloud to keep vermin from going at his legs if there was anything lurking under that wooden porch, and if the rogue should come back—God knew what they could do, at this bottled-up end of the street and with the wide-open gate and escape far, far off at the other end.

He was scared to go up the steps—he was scared to open the door; but he was scared to linger here, either, dithering while trouble could be making up its mind and coming toward them. He leaned on Cloud's withers and slid down, climbed the snow-blanketed steps and tried the door.

Latched. The paint was raked off the door and the door-frame, down to bare wood, the same spreading out over the wall and the storm-shutters. Several of the claw-marks were head-high, and deep.

"Get us out! Please, let us out!"

He didn't know what to do. He didn't want to raise a lot of racket. He called out, "Can you unlock the door?"

"No," one voice said, and, "Break it down," the other called out. "Please. God, please! We're locked in!"

Images came at him, <gunfire outside the windows> and <woman with gun. Them shouting. Gun going off in the woman's hands. Spatter flying—red on walls, on bars, on floor—<rogue-feeling> in the ambient—>

It was so real, for a moment Danny's heart reacted. He cast a look back at Cloud and down the street to see if any other source of that feeling was out there. Cloud snorted, circled out and back, fretting; but there wasn't anything; it was Cloud hearing it and carrying it to him from inside the building.

"Hell," Danny muttered between his teeth, checked which way the door hinges were set—inward opening, which was only safe inside towns; and it was the only break he'd gotten. He rammed the door with his hip and felt play in it, hit it with his shoulder and finally, holding to the rail outside, hit it with his hip again, above the doorknob, over and over.

Wood splintered. The door flew back too fast and banged half-shut again.

"Oh, God," a voice said. "We're here! We're *here*!"

It was a house, maybe. But, walking in, he couldn't see where he was. He took a match out of his pocket and lit it—saw bars in the back, two haggard faces behind them.

God, it was the village jail.

He didn't want to let loose criminals—but—

Did you leave anyone—any living creature—in a cage like this, to be eaten alive by things small enough to swarm through the bars?

The match burned his fingers. He dropped it—saw it burning on the wooden floor and stamped it out.

He saw in the last impression on his eyes, the lump that was a woman's body. The sheen of gunmetal, all in the same memory of matchlight.

Cloud was insistently <wanting Danny on porch,> and he imaged back, teeth chattering, <Cloud in doorway, coming inside.>

"There's a lamp," one of the voices said. "On the table by the door."

"It went out," the other said. "It burned out."

"It's probably the wick. Try the wick!"

He was far more interested in the gun he'd seen lying on the floor. But he wanted light to see what else he might be dealing with, and where shells and maybe food might be, if the vermin hadn't gotten into this building, and by the evidence of two people alive, they hadn't. He stripped off his right glove, felt after the lamp and, finding it, shook it.

There was a little slosh left, a very little. He shook it and tipped it to get oil up onto the wick—took the chimney off and, blind, turned the key to raise the unburned wick—a lot of it.

He spent a match. The dry, charred end of the wick went in a tall, extravagant flame, and the oiled part stayed lit as the rest fell away in ash.

He looked across the room—saw a woman's body, grisly damage to the jaw from a gunshot, blood and bits of flesh spattering the walls.

Rifle on the floor, under her. <Moaning on the floor. Bleeding to death. Rogue-feeling. Gunshots in the village. Woman aiming at *them* and them yelling and screaming don't—>

Not men. Two scared kids behind the bars—kids maybe not as old as he was, no coats, clothes blood-spattered, faces gaunt and eyes bruised from want of sleep—<wanting out, wanting, wanting, *wanting*—>

"There's a key!" one told him, teeth chattering, and pointed through the bars. "In the drawer. In the desk drawer, get the key—"

"We told her come in with us, we begged her lock the door and get behind the bars, but they were all over the porch—"

The kid lost his voice. The other babbled out: "They kept jumping at the door, trying to get in—"

<Fear, scattering-apart.

<Fire on window-glass. Rogue-feeling, outside the building—in the street.>

They began babbling, trying to tell him something, he couldn't even track what it was, except desperation to be out of there. He searched the drawer, and the key they claimed was there—wasn't. He found a box of shells, and set that on the desk. He kept looking, disarranged the desktop clutter, and found it.

"That's it, that's it!" the boys cried, and the younger-looking started sobbing—then yelped as a heavy body trod the steps outside and stopped as the steps creaked.

<Thin boards,> was Cloud's opinion of the porch. Cloud didn't want to risk it, and Danny didn't want him trying: <nighthorse foot going through boards,> he thought; and with a shudder he bent to take up the rifle from under the dead woman. He had to tug the stock from under her leg.

"Who was she?"

"Peggy Wallace," one answer came hoarsely. And: "The marshal's wife," the older boy said. "Tara Chang—one of the riders—she came. She wanted the marshal. Then—there were shots outside. There went on being shots—"

"It was a rogue," the younger said, between chattering teeth. "Rogue horse."

He was increasingly uneasy with every passing moment he was

out of Cloud's immediate reach. He had a gun in one hand. He picked up the box of shells, checked the caliber, found they matched and stuffed them in his pocket.

"You've got to let us out!" the younger said.

And the other: "Look, look, —I'm the one who belongs in here, my brother doesn't. He didn't do anything. *I* did. God, he's only fourteen. Get him out of here."

"You're both going," Danny said, before the younger could set up a howl. "Wouldn't leave a dead pig for the spooks. But you listen to me, do exactly what I say, and if I say move, you move, and if I say shut up, you shut up, and you don't mess with my horse. He'll kill you quicker than you can see it coming, you hear me? He's not used to strangers. So you be real quiet and real fast to do what I say. Or you're spook-bait. You got that clear?"

"Yes," the answer was, both of them shaking-scared and throwing off <fear, fear, fear> that didn't have a source or a point—it washed out their thoughts in a jumble of <scavenger> images and the <gun going off> and <nighthorse outside, and somebody they knew, but twisted, and wanting something, wanting someone, angry—and wanting to kill.>

His hand shook shamefully just getting the key in the lock. He shoved it in, turned it, and as he pulled the door open, the boys came pushing each other out—neither of them having a coat against the winter around them, no sweaters, no gloves, no light or heat. They'd had two blankets and each other, that was the only reason they hadn't frozen when the heat died. Their shuddery breath frosted in the air.

"You get those blankets," Danny said. "You'll need everything we can find. I'll get you out of here."

"The rogue's out there!"

"It's not out there—but the gate's open. It could have come in here any time it wanted. We've got my horse with us. We're all right so long you do what I tell you and do it fast."

"We got to find mama," the younger said. "Carlo, we've got to find mama—"

"No chance," Danny said brutally, but there wasn't any faking it. He thought about the street and it probably carried. The kids reflected something back so scared, so full of blood and terror and sense of being stalked that he couldn't get an image through it and didn't have time to try. "Everyone's gone or dead. We can probably find things the spooks didn't get, but it's not safe out there. I don't want to get boxed in this far down the street. I want nearer that gate—if we can find anything left."

"It couldn't get in," the older—Carlo—said. "It went all around the place—"

"It's Brionne," the younger broke in. "It was *Brionne*."

<Blond girl, younger than either boy. Blond girl by the fireside.

<Man and woman and the boys angry and yelling.

<Gun going off. Carlo holding the gun. Anger. Hate. Man hitting Carlo. . . .>

"Don't tell him!" the younger cried, shaking at Carlo's arm. "Don't tell him, don't think it, don't think about it! He can *hear* you!"

"Kid's right," Danny muttered. He didn't like Cloud outside alone right now the way he didn't *like* the idea that Carlo'd shot a man. "What you did to get locked up—I don't give a damn. We got to get a place we can hold out." There had to be a lot of supplies and equipment in the village that the vermin hadn't gotten. Guns. Shells. Knives. All the resources a village had inside it were still here. Had to be. He didn't like taking stuff from dead people—but he wasn't riding away from guns and shells and food that could make a difference in their survival, either.

And if they could find a hidey-hole he liked the look of, they could tuck into it until he could get sorted out. The village gate out there hadn't looked to be damaged—just standing open.

Spooks could go over a wall. A horse couldn't. A horse could trick you and spooks calling to you could make you open a door—but the rogue for all its strength couldn't get in and it couldn't for all its power make these kids open the bars without a key. *That* was why they were alive.

"Woman saved your lives," he said to them, searching the cabinet for shells. And found another box. "She could've been a fool and opened that front door. Bars wouldn't stop the little ones. They'd have got you. She knew she was going to do it and she shot herself instead. You don't ever forget that woman's name, you. *Hear me?*"

The older one held onto the younger. The younger kid was crying. He guessed by that he'd scared them enough—but she'd been a woman with the guts to stop it all when she started going under its influence. The only better thing she could have done was come in with them, shut the doors and throw the key out, if she'd had her head clear.

But no question, once the spooks started clawing at that door, she was lucky to have found the trigger once.

With the time the spooks had had to do their work, not likely that the marshal or anybody else in this village was going to turn up out of some similar hidey-hole—the luck to have a door you couldn't open yourself wasn't going to be general. He didn't know about this Tara Chang the kid talked about, <woman in fringed leather. Dark-haired.> Senior rider, if he had to guess. No sign of her or the rest of the riders—no help from that quarter. Not if that gate was standing open.

He brought the kids outside—they balked when they saw Cloud waiting, and Cloud snorted and laid down his ears.

"You be polite," Danny said in as stern a tone as he had. "He's not used to village kids. His name is Cloud. You let him smell you over. You think *nice* thoughts about him and me, you hear? Hold out your hands, let him smell them. That way he won't mistake you for spooks."

They were scared to death. They thought <Cloud biting fingers,> but they came down the steps and, the older boy first, held out their bare hands. Cloud sniffed and snorted, threw his head away from them, and wanted <Danny riding.>

He wanted <finding food.> But he didn't think, on a second, queasy thought, that he wanted to let Cloud do the guiding—Cloud having no fastidiousness about some things, and there being pieces of human beings in the streets. He thought instead about <store> and <cans and flour,> hoping the vermin hadn't gotten everything, and a thought came into his head—he was sure it was the boys—telling him exactly which building would have that kind of thing.

Most urgent of everything—<closing the gate.> Once they did that, inside, they could get some distance from the walls, at least, with Cloud's help, enough to keep from mental confusion coming at them from the spooks outside.

He didn't know, as tired and sore as he was, if he could get up to Cloud's back on one try, with the rifle and all. But he wasn't giving the only gun to two jailed kids to hold. He wanted <Cloud close to the steps> and he cheated a mount off the bottom step—made a fairly senior-style landing on Cloud's back, rifle in hand and all.

Then he told Cloud <closing gate> and Cloud set out at a fair pace down the street. The boys hurried after, wrapped in their blankets, having to run to keep up—and by the time they'd reached the gate and he'd slid down again to heave the huge door shut, the boys were still halfway back along the street.

He shoved the gate, the truck-sized door needing no small push against the accumulation of snow. He brought it to, and the bar dropped, comforting thump.

They were in sole possession, he supposed. He had a look about the gates, checked the latch—felt Cloud bristle up with warning as the boys came running up, gasping and terrified.

"We're all right," he said to them. "Gate's shut. If we don't open it, nothing can. We just stay far from the walls. What village is this, anyway?"

"Tarmin," Carlo gasped shakily. "This is Tarmin village."

The biggest. The most people. The place you'd run to for help. All dead.

But maybe *not* all dead. Other, awful possibilities came to him as he looked back along the snowy, devastated street.

"Can you think of any other places where somebody couldn't get out?" Worse and worse thoughts. "Any sick folk? Any old people, crippled people—any babies?"

There were. There had been. The boys were well aware who and where—they were worried, they were sickened at what they saw, and scared, not feeling like outlaws and killers at all; he, God help him, didn't want to do this. He really didn't. But when they started telling him where people lived, and thinking of houses, it was clear they knew their village: <wanting people,> came to him in confused fashion, an aching fear for specific faces they knew and feared were <bones in the street.>

At least it wasn't hard to find a sidearm—he could take his pick, once he began to walk about among the remains. People had come out with guns, they'd died with guns in their hands, all up and down the street. He kept his rifle in the crook of his arm, and walked back along the street with the boys in tow, Cloud following close. He scavenged a pistol and holster just lying in a bloody jacket.

He gave the jacket to the older boy. He kept the pistol. They found scarves, hats, a lot of them chewed. A coat for the younger kid—and a gun. The older boy hesitated at it, afraid to make the move. Danny took it, checked to see it was loaded, and gave it to him.

"Don't make a mistake. Hear? I'll nail you."

The kid didn't say anything. But the boy wasn't thinking hostility, either. He was <scared,> thinking mostly about his kid brother, and <vermin under the porches.>

They went from house to house, after that, and they called out at every house. Danny imaged <rider with horse, rider with boys. Rider looking for people in houses> as loud as Cloud could make him; but Cloud didn't smell anything he liked in those houses.

<Human baby,> Danny imaged, <human baby, old people—> but he didn't get answers.

They'd done all they could, he told himself. They forced the door to the village store open, and it wasn't touched. He got a flashlight and some batteries, and he kept thinking about <babies in houses> and the couple of places they'd tried the hardest.

So he went out again, took the boys with him for backup, and with the boys staying on the porches, he went into open doors with his torch in one hand, and a pistol in the other, went into upstairs halls while Cloud was sending his <nighthorse> image downstairs. He looked in the shut rooms—in one house where the boys said there was a sick old man who couldn't get out of his bed.

That was bad. That was really bad.

And inside one after the other of the houses where they said there were babies—he saw enough to last him. Parents had run to hold their kids when the panic hit. They'd opened the doors to help their neighbors. That was all they needed to do.

You learned to damp things down when you worked with the horses. You learned just—see colors. Patterns. No emotional stuff. You could see anything. It didn't kill you. Blood was blood, you had it, they had it, bone was bone, everybody was made of it.

He went down the steps, of the last one, the one he'd had to talk himself into—cold, numb. Cloud wanted <Danny coming back.> Cloud wanted <fight> because Cloud's rider was upset; but there was nothing available to fight.

A support post got in his way as he came out onto the porch. He swung on it with the flashlight hard enough he bent the barrel at an angle and killed the light. The boys didn't ask what he'd found.

He walked. He didn't want contact with Cloud for a while. Cloud walked near him, mad and snappish. The boys must have sensed it, because they trailed along out of reach.

They went back to the store. That was the best place. The only one with no bodies and no blood.

Chapter
— xix —

THEY WERE THE BLACKSMITH'S SONS. THEIR NAMES WERE CARLO and Randy Goss. And beyond that it was hard to get all the story. They brought Cloud up the low porch of the grocery—the flashlight, by some wonder, still almost worked, at least so they could get an oil lantern lit, and by that light they started a fire in the ironwork stove. It had been dark when the trouble came, the store was shut—the grocer lived next door, the boys said; the door over there had been open, but this one had a keyed lock, and there was no need, Danny agreed with the boys, to open the door into the house.

The awful thing, where they'd been and what they'd seen, was having an appetite. But Cloud wasted no time—Cloud was interested immediately in the cold-locker, not an ears-down kind of notice, but <ham> was in his thoughts, and Danny held the pistol on the door while Carlo and his brother opened it.

It was hams. Hams and packets of other stuff. Cloud started imaging <ham frying,> and Danny didn't think he could stand it, but Cloud wanted it, and with the whole store filled with supplies, they didn't have to save anything. There were unseasoned iron pans the store had sold. There was the makings for biscuits. Danny stirred up soda biscuits and had the boys slice up the ham and put it in the skillet so they could at least make a start on Cloud's appetite.

And by the time the biscuits were cooking on the edge of the stove Cloud was completely occupied watching <ham frying.> No extraneous thoughts from Cloud—Cloud dominated the ambient, Cloud wanted <ham, food, warmth> and that was what was *in* the ambient—Cloud's stupid rider finally figured out why they were ravenously hungry and why he found himself heaving a tired sigh and why the boys had tried to nip a little scrap of ham that floated free in the pan. *Cloud* had no squeamishness and no remorse.

And no fondness for thieves.

"That's Cloud's," Danny said. "Cloud gets peeved if you steal his supper."

That brought a sullen look.

"You want a mad horse or a happy horse inside this little place with us?" Danny put it to them. "You cut some more ham right now. We'll get ours."

Carlo took a cue fast. The younger kid whined. Carlo hit him with his elbow, said, "Man's telling you," and sliced more ham.

Man, Danny thought. *Man.* Was that what he looked like to these kids?

Damn fool, if he let that reaction get into the air. He checked on the biscuits, decided with Cloud involved, he'd better make more biscuits. It wasn't real good for Cloud to eat nothing but ham, Cloud's ambitions to the contrary—it was a lot of what the horse doctors called foreign stuff for him. But Cloud tolerated biscuits just fine.

Cloud didn't mind <biscuits.> Cloud thought they were good with <ham.>

So they settled down on supply sacks in a fire-warmed room and cooked panful after panful of ham, stuffed themselves, stuffed Cloud (harder task) and washed it all down with lowland draft beer, which the boys had never had. The older was smart with it and sipped.

The younger, Randy, gulped his like water and passed out on the sacks after one mug.

Carlo said, after a moment of quiet,

"Got to thank you."

"Couldn't leave you," he said.

"You didn't say your name."

"Danny—Dan Fisher." He'd lost *that* chance. Damn. And he needed authority with these kids, for their collective safety. "I felt the rogue attack. Long way off. But I couldn't tell where it was, or even what it was, at least when it started."

"My sister," Carlo began, and trailed off into a long silence, something about a rider den and a stocky man and a leather-jacketed rider that looked like this Tara Chang that Carlo had already talked about.

"Your sister's a rider."

"No. She *wanted* to be. She ran off. And it was her with the rogue. I know it was her. I could feel it. I could see it, right through the walls. She was looking for papa. She kept calling and calling for papa—"

"A rogue horse is apt to *want* people. And they're loud." He was on the edge of what he knew about the subject, but the kid wanted comforting. "It could take an image right from your mind. It'd feel like somebody you knew. People paint their own images—the one they want most, the one they're most afraid for. And a predator will pick it right up and give it back to you."

Carlo gave a fierce shake of his head. <Girl> came into the ambient. <Tracks leading along the snow. Gate with fan-trace in the snow.>

Danny let out a slow breath, decided maybe after all Carlo knew what he was talking about.

And he didn't know why he'd found <Carlo in jail.> Didn't understand Carlo <shooting man.> Things were getting tangled. And he'd like answers.

Carlo flinched, tucked his knee up fast, rested his chin on his hand and didn't look at him. Lamplight glistened on Carlo's eyes. Chin wobbled.

"You have a good reason to shoot somebody?" Danny asked.

<Man with stick raised—headed at him and his brother. Woman screaming. Hate, wanting, fear. Shouting>—But you couldn't tell what in a sending. Cloud couldn't carry human voices yet in any way you could hear it, just the noise.

But it looked like—house and family. It *felt* like house and family. He knew the scene when his own papa hit him. He flinched the same as Carlo and Randy flinched—but, damn, —he'd never shoot papa, he couldn't do that—he loved him.

Carlo got up in a hurry, scaring Cloud, who snaked out his neck and grabbed a mouthful of coat.

<*"Cloud!" Letting coat go. Boy standing. Still water.*>

Carlo didn't stand. Carlo made it away into the shadows, to sit down on a coil of cable. He crouched there with his head in his hands and cried, great noisy sobs.

<Blood,> Cloud thought, confused, thinking <fight,> but no longer mad. Cloud knew he shouldn't have hurt the boy. Cloud was upset, and stared at the boy, wide-nostriled, remembering <Danny making that sound,> because, dammit, he'd soaked Cloud's shoulder a couple of times since they'd teamed up, especially when his father had announced to the neighborhood he was going to hell.

Carlo—had done the unthinkable. No knowing why. Carlo was hurting—he was hurting all over the ambient, aching for what he'd done.

"Calm it down," Danny said. "You're near a horse, dammit. Calm *down*."

"I shot him," Carlo stammered. "I shot my f-f-father."

What did you say to a statement like that? What did you follow it with? He knew Carlo didn't want to have shot anybody. The moment was there over and over again, <the fireplace, the man, Carlo with the gun.

<Two-sided anger. Flying every direction.>

<*Quiet.*>

He scared Carlo. Carlo looked up at him, stunned and shaken.

"Horse," Danny said. He was all but sure of it. "The horse was sending."

"What horse?"

"The rogue. It was spooking around out there near the village when you had your quarrel. It was there. You *know* it was, but you don't know you know. I'm hearing it in your memory. Only *I'm* a rider. I know what a horse sounds like. *I* know what I'm hearing in what you're sending *me*."

Carlo wiped his face, still staring up at him out of the shadows, <wanting, listening, pleading with him.> "I can't send!"

"You hear me real damn good," Danny said, knowing he was laying it on thick and knowing he was out of his depth, but he couldn't afford a kid going off the mental edge in this place. This was a kid who'd listened to the preachers. He'd been there, once, and he knew how to make it sound better, at least. "People don't ever really send, you know that. Not even riders. We all say we do, but really only the horses hear us and pass things back and forth. Some people can hear better, or they think images better, or maybe they're just quicker to put things into shape. A rider's brain just sorts pictures out better than some—something like. That's what I've heard, anyway. I'm not as good at it as some. But *I* can talk in words. I know riders you don't hear two words out of in days. And I know how to pick out a rogue-sending. Trust me in that."

"My sister could hear the horses." Carlo's voice shook. <Fear> was very strong. "She could hear them at night. She could hear spooks in the woods. Maybe it runs in the f-family."

Carlo didn't *like* this sister, this sister <wanting horse.> There was a lot of anger there. A lot. And he had a damn scared kid on his hands.

"I hate to say your sister was wrong," Danny said. "But *I* don't hear the horses all the time. If I'm far from Cloud—I don't. She may have thought she did. If you hear one across town—that's a real upset horse. A rogue—she'd maybe hear. But so did you, that's the fact."

"I didn't hear it when she left."

"Yeah, but you heard it later. And she was *trying* to hear, what I pick up from you. —Listen to me." The kid was close to panic. His own nerves were shaky. He wanted it <quiet.> "Listen: that horse was hanging around. She left, right? Your family was upset. *Nobody's* going to think straight when a crazy horse is pushing temper into the ambient. Listen, down in Shamesey they were shooting at people when the horses got upset, and there *wasn't* any rogue, just a report of one being up here. I'm not saying there wasn't any fault. I'm saying it went crazy like it did because you got a crazy horse sending like hell out there. It couldn't hear *you.* But you could hear *it,* no trouble at all, and you could hear anybody who was *with* that horse. Sending's the same as hearing. The *same* as hearing, do you hear me? You're not going to hell."

Carlo's jaw worked. Hard. Carlo took another swipe at his eyes with a hand shaking like a leaf. <Listening. Cautious. Wary.>

You couldn't push the argument too far. For what he knew the kid was guilty as sin. But the hazard of the kid blowing up was an unease sitting like lead at the pit of his own stomach—and the ambient began to ease.

"Want another beer?" Danny asked, and got up and filled Carlo's mug from the keg.

Carlo came and took it. Cloud came up behind him—<close behind him. Boy turning quietly. Quiet water.>

Cloud gave him a sniff-over, trying to figure what was the matter with him. Carlo held his beer and stood very wisely quiet.

Cloud went back to his ham-grease and biscuits.

"Cloud protects me," Danny said. "He's making sure you're not sick. They don't understand everything we do. He wouldn't like it if you were sick."

Carlo was shaking so he spilled beer on his hand.

"You're all right," Danny said. "We'll get out of here. You and the kid each with a rifle and a sidearm and supplies and all, I'll walk you out to somewhere."

"There's Verden."

"No village up here is real safe right now. This place at least isn't real noisy in the ambient. The rogue may go for something louder. Or easier. We're not going to open the gates."

"Our mother did it."

"What?"

"Opened the village gate. She heard Brionne. She wanted Brionne." Carlo sipped his beer, staring unblinkingly into it. Swallowed hard, as if that wasn't all that was going down. "Brionne sure came home, didn't she?"

God, Danny thought, and didn't say anything. The ambient for a second was full of <Brionne at the breakfast table. Papa at the forge. Kids playing in the blacksmith's shop. Throwing snowballs. Laughing.>

Danny shoved at the ambient. <Boys walking, Danny riding on Cloud down a sunny, snow-covered road. Blue sky.> "If we don't hear anything, I figure we'll go out tomorrow. I got a friend I'm trying to catch up with."

"From where?"

"Shamesey."

"That's where you're from? Clear from there?"

"Yeah."

"Him, too?"

"Know it's a him? Know it's a rider?"

"Yeah." Carlo looked puzzled. "I mean, I guessed."

"What color's his hair?"

Carlo looked entirely uneasy. "Blond," he said.

"See?"

"I don't want to. God!"

"Yeah, I figure you don't want to, but there isn't any choice—if you come near a horse, you're going to see things. You prime yourself to go *toward* my horse, you got it? Not away. If anything goes wrong, you don't spook off on your own—it'll get you sure. Same with Randy. You better listen real hard to the ambient and don't be afraid of it. Drivers with a big truck around them, they can sort of ignore it and follow the rig in front, but on foot, you're down there with the spooks and the vermin. —Hey. You got your brother for a responsibility. You'll do it. You *have* to."

Carlo didn't feel sure. Carlo stayed scared. But he looked aside at the sleeping boy, and said, finally, "Yeah."

"I got a kid brother, too," Danny said, which was about as sentimental as he meant to get. But Carlo Goss was pulling together real well. Real well. He hoped it lasted.

"Yeah," Carlo said again, and went and got another beer.

Couldn't blame him. Carlo was getting wobbly on his feet with two. But there wasn't damned much—

Cloud's head came up. Stark, concentrated look toward the wall. Toward the outside.

Not a sending. <Creak of hinges.> Somebody was out there, or the wind was moving a door in all that quiet.

From *up* the street, not down. But nobody could be stirring out there. It *felt* like a presence. It kept shifting.

Shifting. A horse. A rider. Side of the camp.

<Rider gate, human coming through where the horse couldn't—>

Shit!

He grabbed his coat and hauled it on in feverish haste—the coat first, because you couldn't aim worth a damn shaking your teeth out. He pulled on his gloves, he grabbed the rifle.

Carlo and Randy were <*scared.*>

"You got a handgun," Danny said. He was scared himself, but he had to move too fast to think on it.

"Don't go out there," Carlo begged him. "Please don't go out."

"That's a gate open. Somebody's out there. If they open the big gate, we could have the damn rogue in our laps. You stay here. The kid's passed out. You stand over him. You know what the marshal's wife did. Just don't be too early—or too late."

"Yeah." Carlo's teeth were chattering. Danny went to the door and Cloud followed him, ears up.

It didn't feel like <Cloud being mad.> Cloud was <hearing the intruder and wary.>

<Man,> Cloud saw in the ambient. <Man in the dark street. Man with gun.>

<Stuart,> Danny thought, and with his heart in his throat opened their makeshift latch and went out onto the porch in the dark.

<Jonas> was standing in the middle of the street. Pistol levelled at <Cloud and Danny.> The gun lowered. Slowly.

"Everybody all right?" Danny asked. He thought there might be more <horses> than one in the ambient—he wasn't sure.

Jonas had been scared. Jonas Westman—had just been <sur-

prised and scared.> Jonas walked across the snow-covered street toward him, <mad and madder.>

"There's ham and biscuits," Danny said, very pleased to be able to say that to this man, coolly, in full ownership of the premises and the situation. "It'd take me about fifteen minutes, supper in hand. Or if you'd rather—"

"You left the rider gate open."

Trust Jonas to land on the one mistake. "Hope you closed it."

"Stuart with you?"

As if he couldn't be where he was without senior help. "Haven't seen him. You?" <Harper's camp. Men scattering. Rogue in the ambient.>

"No luck," Jonas said. <Partners at the main gate. Cold, worried partners. Jonas opening gate.>

<Jonas latching gate.> He hadn't quite meant to let that insolent query hit the ambient. But there it was, edged with hostility.

<Man in doorway.> Jonas didn't take alarm. <Man with gun.>

Carlo was behind him. With that three-sixty degree, back of his head surety of multiple riders restored to him, Danny thought about <drinking beer.> About <sleeping kid.> About <stove> and <cold-locker full of hams,> and Jonas walked on down the street to let his partners and Shadow in. Jonas went out of Cloud's range and into Shadow's, he was sure by the way Jonas vanished into there-and-not-there presence.

He hadn't thought <Carlo in jail.> He resolved he wasn't going to. He picked up Carlo's confusion, turned and pushed Carlo back into the warmth and the light.

"That your friend?" Carlo asked.

"Did it feel like it?"

"No," Carlo said.

"Friends of my friend. Real sons of bitches. But they're all right sons of bitches. They're high country riders. Borderers. We've got help."

Carlo didn't quite seem to trust it. Carlo stayed scared, and worried about <jail.>

"I'm not going to tell him. It could slip—won't guarantee that it won't. But village law's not rider law." He had a thought and got

Carlo's attention with a knuckle against the arm. "These guys? Don't let them bluff you."

Carlo didn't like to hear that. He cast a nervous glance as if he could still see Jonas.

"They'll try," Danny said. "They're not leaving you and the kid here. Or if they do—depend on it, *I'm* not running. Think of <them running away> if they think about it. You don't have to say a thing. Think <scared riders.> They'll hate it like sin."

They made biscuits—Carlo had never cooked in his life, but he tried; Randy waked with all the commotion and sat up bleary-eyed.

"Riders are here," Carlo told him. "We're going to be all right, Randy. You hear?" Randy sat there looking numb and shaky, maybe a little sick from the beer—the ambient was queasy and scared, but Cloud wouldn't put up with it. Cloud thought <horses with cattle-tails> and <horses standing outside in the cold> and Cloud wasn't happy with the arrival.

Going to be all right was a little early, too. Cloud's rider didn't count on it, because Jonas was an argumentative son of a bitch and Cloud's rider wasn't going to take it.

Well, Cloud's rider thought—maybe Danny Fisher could tuck down a little and listen to Jonas, whose disagreeable advice had kept him alive. He'd learned a bit. He'd been desperate enough to learn, and he could try being—not ducked down and quiet, but maybe not quite so touchy.

He didn't have to feel as if Jonas was threatening him. He'd had guns aimed at him. Jonas was a lot different.

Jonas, who was coming in asking for supper and shelter in what was, Jonas could figure, *his* camp, which he'd set up and where Jonas was asking charity.

Cloud was first in. Boss horse. Cloud should be <nice,> but the store was <Cloud's den> and <Shadow-horse standing on the porch in the snow> if Shadow had <fight> in mind.

He'd fairly well built the picture when assorted footsteps arrived on the porch and Jonas' bunch knocked, wanting entry.

Danny opened the door. "Pretty crowded in here. Room and food for your horses if they're quiet."

<Cold horses smelling ham> came back to him, from at least a couple of the horses in the street. Heads were up and nostrils working, in that veil of snow. Jonas was his sullen self, but Luke and Hawley looked exhausted.

"Come on in," Danny said, and held the door, imaging <sacks to sit on, horses lying down. Ham and biscuits.>

"Were you here when it happened?" Jonas asked, taking off his hat.

"They were." Danny nodded toward the two boys, and made the introductions: "Jonas Westman, Luke Westman, Hawley Antrim—Carlo and Randy Goss. Only ones alive. Their sister Brionne's on the rogue."

That got attention. Hats that had been coming off in courtesy to the house got tucked in hand and everybody stared at Carlo and Randy for a heartbeat, then wanted <girl on horse.>

He filled in the blonde hair, the red coat, the fact it was a kid looking for dead parents.

"Shit," Hawley said. Hawley was upset. Something about <trucks and rocks and a rider,> that went blurred as Hawley's thinking skittered away to <rocks.>

Jonas bumped Danny's arm. "Kid opened the gates?"

He didn't want to think. He didn't. He said, "Carlo, ham's burning." It wasn't. But it was close. Cloud was on the far side of the room, by the cold locker door; Cloud was closest to the stove, and put his nose out, smelling <ham.> The other horses were near the door, crowded in the narrow room, growing argumentative; but human presence gave them no more room.

"Kids are upset enough," Danny said under his breath, and Jonas didn't push it. "Bad time," Danny amplified the image of <dead village. Pieces of bodies.> But Jonas had seen it.

"You shouldn't have left that side gate. The outside rider gate was standing open wide."

Damn. But he had it coming. Jonas was telling him what he had done that was stupid. That wasn't an unfriendly act in this country.

"Yeah," he said. "I didn't think. I knew it the second I knew somebody was there. Scared hell out of me."

Jonas was standing close in the crowded quarters. Jonas laid a hand on his shoulder, squeezed it. He wasn't sure he liked it, wasn't sure what it meant. Jonas had turned his back and gone over to investigate the stovetop cooking, where Carlo looked to have too few hands available for too many pans and Danny still wondered what that had meant—from Jonas' disposition. Hawley was sitting on a barrel, the source of a glum pressure in the ambient: upset with what he'd seen outside in the street and trying to keep it quiet.

Luke—Luke was sitting on pile of sacks talking to Randy, asking him questions in Luke's quiet way. Randy sneezed, exhausted, probably sick from the beer, and stared at Luke somewhere between reassured and scared: too many horses, besides which Shadow and Cloud together weren't an easy presence in a confined space.

But four horses, four armed riders and two village boys, well-armed and fed, holding a wide walled perimeter with a lot of fuel against the cold were much better odds than he'd hoped for against the rogue. They didn't *need* another village until spring, if they had to hold out.

"Is there a phone?" Jonas asked. And it was like the business with the gate: he just hadn't thought—they were still in the process of getting a camp in order. But he hadn't thought.

He said, calmly, "Carlo, where's a phone?"

"Mayor's office," Carlo said. <Dark streets. Snow and dead.> Carlo didn't want to go tonight. It was one too many dark buildings, but Carlo was willing if they had guns. "Don't know if it's working."

"Do what we can," Jonas said. "We're all right. But villages up on the High Loop need to know."

"Yeah," Danny said. He was embarrassed about the phone. But he didn't know how to use one, anyway. It wasn't quite as bad a mistake as he'd made with the gate. "I'll go see about it. What building and what do you do with it?"

The morning came crisp and clear, sunlight striking the tops of the evergreens—Guil put his head out of the shelter, shut the door and took his time in the warmth. He had two dry blankets, dry fire-warmed boots, everything warm from the fireside, and Burn and he had breakfast on the bacon they'd brought and on the dry supplies the villages supplied the riders that served them: biscuits and sugar syrup, firewood already cut, an assortment of small blades and cords and such that riders might need—you took out, sometimes you put in, if you had a surplus; it was just an oddments box, always on the fireside. They made the shelters so much alike on purpose—so you didn't have to wonder. There were bandages. There were matches. You left them alone if you didn't need them.

He sterilized his own needle in the lamp-flame and got a nasty splinter out of the heel of his hand, a few minor ones out of his fingers. He'd lantern light and firelight this morning, the room was warm—he'd had time to warm himself and his dry blanket last night and even wash off before he went to bed on a decent supper. Then he'd gone out, just out, until he waked with the fire gone to coals and staggered out to put a couple of more small logs on.

Quiet, quiet morning. He was tempted to hunker down and stay another day, at least: he had aches and pains enough to justify it—he'd do it if there weren't so urgent a reason to move on, at least as far as Tarmin, where he could find out from the local riders what the situation was and pass the warning of the situation. Tarmin could advise the High Loop villages of the danger if the phones were working—or if very brave riders wanted to try to get through.

There was one more shelter between here and Tarmin if he needed it: he knew it from Aby, and the map painted on a board nailed over the hearth advised the same, in a system he couldn't doubt. There were the sideways crosses for the shelters; there were the dashes for the phone lines, with a circle for where you were, at this cross, and the triangles for the villages. Reading might tell you more, he guessed, because there were some letters on the board; but you didn't need to know so much which village was which, if you were on this road. All you needed to know was that there was a village ahead and not just a mining camp. The marks always told you that, triangles for a village, stars for towns (there weren't any on Tarmin Height) and squares for the camps. Trails were dot and dash, roads were wide solid lines. It always made sense.

Not to Burn. Burn believed that it was <villages and roads> where people and horses were, right down to the shingles and the walls and the horse dens, but Burn never believed that the circled cross was where *he* was. Burn knew where Burn was: he was, of course, in a shelter with walls this color and a fire and bins of grain. *Burn* wasn't in any mark on the board, Burn was where Burn clearly saw Burn was, and the ambient was all <warm, content nighthorse, Guil sleeping.>

"No," Guil said reluctantly. <Burn and Guil in snow.>

Burn was *not* happy. Burn sulked. <Guil walking in snow.>

"Come on, Burn. Cut it." Guil gave a slap on Burn's shoulder and got snapped at by strong nighthorse teeth.

But he packed up. <Guil walking outside. Goblin-cats sneaking through snow.>

<Snow on Guil's head.>

He kept packing. He put out the fire, put on his coat and hat and scarf and gloves. The shelter was fast to chill with the fire out. Much less comfortable. Much less inviting. He gathered up the two-pack and his rifle, and opened the door. Cold air wafted in.

Burn shook himself, imaging <fire> and <smoke.>

Burn was sulking as he came outside. Guil latched the door.

Guil started walking. Burn followed, still sulking.

But after a little Burn's gait grew more cheerful, Burn's nostrils worked on the cold mountain air. Breaths frosted. The snow made that sound underfoot that came of profound cold. The light sifted through the middle branches now, shafts of light on the snow-frosted boughs and spots of light on the snow.

Burn grew bored with slow moving on a cold morning. Burn was sore, but Burn wanted <going faster> and couldn't arrange a compromise between that and <Guil walking.> So Burn danced along, taking two and three steps for every one he needed.

Burn ran for silly long bursts and circled with a spray of snow and came back again. And started to cough from the dry air and the altitude.

Guil didn't ask to ride. Burn's back was probably sore: Burn had put some few knots in it carrying him up the mountain. He still had a headache, but not so bad this morning. His legs were sore—too much sitting about camp, he said to himself; about time he stretched the kinks out.

So he walked a good distance, until he was limping and beginning to think about <numb feet.>

Burn had worked off his little coughing fit. But it was too bright and clear a morning to laze along. Burn was in a good humor and wanted <Guil riding> for no particular reason Guil detected, except that Burn probably wanted warmth on his back.

There wasn't an apparent threat in the morning—a dry powder snow scarcely supported the little spooks, making strange plowed tracks in the deep places. It flew in clouds from under nighthorse feet. The air was clean-washed and clear.

The eye that took in constant information from such tracks could say there were a lot of them, and they were all nuisance-spooks, nothing serious.

The mind—understood a threat in that pattern: there should be bigger hunters abroad, even with a local number of horses in the ambient. A horse wouldn't drive the hunters out. Compete with them. Annoy them. Yes.

But not interfere with a hunter's predations among so many, many small spooks—unless human riders wanted to clear the area. That would be the obvious conclusion—if this rider didn't know there was another, more ominous possibility.

The predators gave each other as much room as they needed, unless hunger or human presence drove them into a fight that neither ordinarily would pursue: their sign and their sendings defined where that back-to-the-wall point was, so they passed with bluster and bluff; the life-and-death struggle was all with prey, and prey never lacked predators.

Never lacked predators.

It didn't make either of them comfortable, the horse-image in his head when he thought that.

The ground showed occasional tracks, never enough of them. The ambient held the occasional spook-image from the bushes. They walked along together, or Guil rode, and walked again, as Burn pleased. They had the morning's biscuits as bacon sandwiches, had a couple of targets if he'd wanted to hunt, but they had supplies enough and he could get a good meal at Tarmin this evening. He didn't want to shoot off a gun and spook everything into behaviors that said everything about the gunfire and nothing at all about what he was hunting. And he might not stay in Tarmin after he got there. He might sit out and listen—if there was a place he could fortify and quiet enough near the village to sit out in the dark and listen.

Because he never forgot what the job was: he just broke it up into smaller pieces that never left him daydreaming his way across the mountain—quick way to disaster, that was; of all mistakes Aby had made, he knew it wasn't that one—she'd been too long in too many bad places to get caught napping.

The phone lines and the clear-cut were a guide along the easy way—no need to worry about pits, rocks, and hidden holes: Burn was willing to move—Burn had <village at evening> and <females> in his head, and wanted <moving fast> again now that Burn had caught a breath and rested his back.

Guil took a fistful of mane and was about to do that when he saw a strange growth on the mountainside above them, like slats or a curiously regular weed growing out of the rocks. That was the first blink.

Then he realized it was bone supporting a coating of snow. A rib cage, or a part of one, and large. <Horse-bones,> he thought, and Burn flared his nostrils and looked, sniffing for <trouble.>

Guil swung up. Dead horse up there. Possibly a wild one. Hard to say how long dead, but the very fact the bones were hanging together—though they might have frozen in that state—made it worrisome.

<Shelter,> he thought. He'd ridden all along with a shell in the chamber, not a practice he'd have recommended to juniors—but juniors weren't riding where he was riding, with maybe a hairbreadth margin of decision between himself and something that could take a nighthorse.

A fall was always possible. A broken leg, a stone-edge gash, a death by freezing or blood loss or even old age. But that was the way you'd explain a horse death on mountains where you didn't have other, worse, possibilities, and he listened into the ambient, in case there was a rider stranded and dug in somewhere.

It was very, very quiet in the area—which wasn't unusual in areas of the deep woods. But it wasn't an ordinary area, in which a nighthorse had met with something it couldn't deal with. He could wish it was the rogue and that whatever injuries it had had just caught up with it—but he didn't bet their lives on it.

Burn didn't take great upset at the sight at all. <Bones> were <bones> and the woods were full of them, few hanging together for any length of time—that a few did argued that the horse hadn't died too long ago; and that made Burn prick up his ears and sharpen his other senses into the ambient, not recklessly: Burn listened, and Burn's rider sat astride and listened, in as close a borrowing of nighthorse senses as a human being could use.

All around, just a sense of life, little life, distant life, a whisper in the ambient, the awareness he'd dropped out of only in the desolation as Anveney.

That hush, everywhere about the mountainside. The rogue, if it was within reach, was quiescent for some reason.

Sleeping, maybe.

Or involved with something near and preoccupying to it, if it shared any traits of sane horses.

<Shelter,> Guil imaged, thinking of riders potentially in trouble. Burn made no objections to that idea. <Shelter> was a very good idea with <danger> in the area, but the danger was all <Guil danger.> Burn didn't find a source of it in the ambient.

Burn picked up his pace, hit his meaning-business gait and kept at it, whuffs of breath and hoof-falls in the snow assuming one quick rhythm. Over close to an hour, the road led down across a rough spot in the mountain flank and around into a climb to a place protected by trees and the angle of the mountain.

It was a place a rider would look to find a shelter built, if he knew one was due; and Guil had no trouble spotting it among the evergreens a little above them on the mountain.

But there was a darkness about the door. It was standing wide; and when he and Burn turned off the road and went higher on the slope to investigate the place, vermin scurried madly and darted from the open doorway.

<Rider opening door,> Guil thought uncomfortably, and sat astride Burn and called aloud, "Is anyone here?"

There was no answer. Not a one. A last willy-wisp racketed about the interior and ran out in desperation past Burn's feet.

<Horse bones,> Guil thought, and Burn snorted the scent of the place out of his nostrils and turned his head without Guil asking, going <downslope> and <toward the road> and <toward den and females.>

A restocking of the supplies in a shelter didn't accidentally leave a door unlatched. A rider wasn't that careless or he was dead in his first year.

<Horse bones,> Guil thought, and probably <human bones> not far from the others. Opening a door under attack was the last thing a rider would do, except maybe to save a partner, maybe to get off a shot at the attacker—but, first off, there was a gun-port; and second, if you did go out, you latched that door. Leaving that door open behind one's back was a mistake only a fatally confused rider might make, under circumstances when places of safety and places of threat might trade places—when even a rider used to sendings might not be sure what he'd done and not done, or where the enemy was.

They turned back down to the road and found, as they went, supplies strewn along the ground, a blanket hanging in a bush, a big tin of what had probably been flour, very clean, shiny, dented and scratched, and missing both flour and lid, lying in the roadway. It had snow inside the open end and a deep blanket of snow lying undisturbed on the upper surface.

That also said something about when the occupants had died.

It wasn't the last of the debris. Rags turned up here and there, a few bones hanging together that didn't look to be horse bones. The scavengers were quick and thorough. There'd been one at the bones only a moment ago, but it fled into the bushes.

Burn maintained a very close, very soft contact with the ambient, listening, lowering his head and smelling the bones and the vermin-tracked snow—but only briefly, obtaining nothing definite, from what Guil could detect, besides the expected blood and animal smells. There were many more ways to reach that cabin than from the road, given the surefootedness of a horse.

There were more ways to die in the Wild. But none more sure than what those riders had done—under what pressure he didn't hope to guess. He'd never met a spook he couldn't resist. He was still alive. And he didn't call them fools for having died. Fools didn't get past their first season up here.

The deep snow in the tin said the deaths had happened before the snowfall quit—last night or before; and he hadn't heard a thing in the ambient. Nothing.

Possibly it just hadn't had the range a rogue was credited to have. Possibly that was exaggerated—he didn't take everything he'd heard as truth. *He'd* never dealt with one. But granted the range of its sending *wasn't* exaggerated—then it might have been as much as two days ago, before he'd arrived on the Height.

Grim as it was, his mind was working on details like that while he went, and confusing Burn, who was thinking <bones> and trying to figure the smells that came to him. Burn didn't understand past things as relevant; Burn wanted <travel fast,> with a vague notion of <eaten horses,> and hit a gait not kind to a sore leg and an aching head.

Guil made no complaint.

The sun had passed overhead and westward, behind the mountain wall, putting the snowy woods in the blued shadow which was the story half the day in the mountains, in any season; afternoon clouds formed above the peak—formed and drifted on with a little spit of snow, to drop rain on the lowlands.

Demi-shadows lengthened with afternoon, evergreens grown near-black against the snow. Thunder rumbled and echoed among the peaks.

That was a serious, imminent warning, not of the afternoon snow-flurries that were a daily event once autumn began, but of the truly dangerous storms that swept winter in their wake, that dumped snow nearly waist-deep to a man in a single night. The wild nighthorses fled the mountains with the coming of the first winter fronts. The spook-bears took to digging, and with their long, long claws made tunnels out again after such storms ended, retreating more and more until, when hunting grew sparse, they slept the deep sleep and waked again with spring.

There was that feeling in the air, worse than Jackson Peak, which he'd served out of Malvey—six days south and a thousand meters lower made a great deal of difference in the weather. Rogers Peak was that much farther north, Tarmin Ridge was higher than the villages on Jackson, Konig, or Darwin, and a man or a horse who disregarded that difference was in for trouble. Not a night on which he'd sit out and wait—not if a major storm was moving in.

<Burn walking,> he thought, and when Burn slowed, coughing in the bitter, thin air, he slid down and carried the packs himself. <Guil walking side by side with Burn, Guil riding, Guil walking, Guil riding—>

It had taken him years and argument to get that simple sequence of events notion through Burn's present-time attention—now, soon. But Burn understood him now: Burn walked along with him, head lowered, coughing, as Burn's rider struck the fastest walk a two-legged creature could sustain on other than level ground. Legs burned, lungs burned, sore leg hurt like hell, but it gave Burn the interval to catch his breath.

Then it was Guil up to Burn's back again, another stint as fast as Burn could take it; and walk again. <Village gate at sunset,> Guil kept thinking, and <us walking, us riding, going fast.>

Burn understood. It wasn't the worst or the first time they'd made time like this: it was <go fast,> that was all, and Burn was completely in agreement, feeling a storm wind and smelling <snow.> The tops of the evergreens sighed with a breath of wind and with successive gusts—then whipped over and tossed in a sudden knife-edged gale that dropped the temperature by tens before they'd passed the next winding of the trail.

A dry wind, at first, and they could be glad of that—but Guil swung up to Burn's back and Burn struck his staying-pace again.

Hope, Guil thought, that the rogue found similar need of shelter—or, best for everyone, that in its demented state it just stood still and froze to death.

He walked again. And in that stint at walking he came on a

strange thing—a child's coat in the snow, and not just lost—gnawed by vermin teeth.

A short time after that he found rags of cloth and leather, stiffened with ice. And vermin that, despite the weather, scampered down the mountain face below the trail.

Bones, then. Small, unidentifiable bones, recent, half-lost in the snow and the rocks beside the clear-cut and fill.

Snow was starting to fall. He thought, <us coming into rider camp, sunset in the sky. Village gates. Snow falling on us,> and took a skip and a bounce for a junior's belly-down mount onto Burn's weary back.

Burn was thinking <bones> and <dark.> Burn moved the moment he felt his rider's weight, and struck a desperate pace through the gathering chill.

There wasn't a phone working. No way to warn the other villages. "Lines must be down," Carlo had said, when Danny reported back; but Luke had had to try it, saying he must not be doing it right; and Luke had had no luck.

Luke had also seen enough by daylight to convince even a senior rider he didn't want to go into the other buildings. Luke came back and had a beer and stayed quiet for a time. Jonas thought he might go try the phone, and asked if they'd cranked it—"Yes," Luke said testily. "I'm not a fool, brother."

It seemed to Danny it was time to keep his head down and argue nothing at all—argue when it mattered, yes, but if the Westmans wanted to accuse each other he had ample patience to wait in a corner of the store beside Carlo while the Westmans sorted it out.

The horses had wanted out, weary of the inside, accustomed to freedom to go where they liked as they liked, but not leaving their riders, either, in a place that smelled of <dead things> and <fight.> Cloud snapped at Shadow, Shadow snapped at Cloud, but all of it was horses insisting they were staying close to the store—all of it horses worried with <dead village> and <vermin.>

Danny just sat on a heap of flour sacks and listened to the ambient through the walls.

And more than the ambient. A wind rose. Something loose was

banging repeatedly, somewhere down the street—but weather be damned, the horses didn't ask to be in again, not minding the wind—he heard Cloud's <wind, cold, smell of snow> in the ambient, and the spookiness that was Shadow. Ice and Froth were there, too, skittish, smelling <dead bodies> and <evergreen.>

"It's going to storm." Randy came and sat down with them, huddled up close against his brother's side. There was a little silence. The weather was worsening—the night was coming. It was one more night in this place, waiting.

"She's coming back, isn't she?" Randy asked finally, sum of his dreads.

"We don't need to be afraid," Carlo said. "There's a lot of us now." Carlo put his arm around Randy's shoulders. "Don't think about it. All right?"

<White streets,> came from outside. <Snow coming down thick. Wind blowing.>

<Skull.> One of the horses had found a curious object. Thought it might have something edible about it. <*Horses near porch,*> came a severe order—specific to the horse, and Danny thought it was Jonas ordering Shadow to leave it alone. The boys were upset, and there were faces and people in the ambient, village folk Danny didn't know.

<*Still water,*> Danny sent, occupying the ambient with a rude, strong effort that seniors might have slapped down, but he had help then, Ice's rider, Hawley, thinking <freezing water, rime of ice on the edges,> so that the very air seemed colder, right next to the stove.

"Stuart better make it fast," Luke said, dealing cards to Hawley. "That's getting mean out there."

"Can't have gone past," Hawley said. "He'd at least check it over."

Danny didn't want to think about the wreck, but suddenly it was there, <rocks, truck falling,> and Hawley's glum mood: he didn't want to think about the wreck, but it nagged the ambient, a before-snow impression of rocks and empty space under the riders' right hand—Jonas had gotten testy with Hawley's brooding and told him have a drink, so Hawley had had several.

Hawley and Luke resumed play with Hawley's frayed pack of cards.

They were safe enough. Jonas had taken exactly the position that Danny hoped he would, that they shouldn't have to move again, that Guil Stuart would come to them, because from the direction Stuart should be coming he had to pass by Tarmin gates.

So they'd get Stuart to join them, and shelter here until they'd rested up—

And wait until the rogue came to them, he supposed. That made sense. It made a vast amount of sense if you didn't think about the other villages up on the road, higher on the mountain, or if you just took for granted the rogue would stay around the area—

He didn't understand what Jonas planned to do besides wait for Stuart—he wasn't altogether easy with the notion of them being fast friends. But he didn't think they had any mischief in mind. He wished Jonas would hint what they were going to do about the coming night. Or what precautions they were going to take.

And maybe Jonas was just a son of a bitch who didn't explain his plans, ever; and maybe Jonas had the notion he'd had—that if there was connection between the rogue and the boys, there was every chance it would come back to Tarmin rather than go to the villages up the mountain. Bait.

That kind of thing, he understood with no trouble: hard choices, greater and lesser risk, foolhardiness and courage—there was a dividing line. Papa had always said so. In that sense they were protecting the villages on the High Loop just by sitting here and protecting themselves, and he supposed that was good and he was on the right side.

But he didn't understand the dying. Didn't understand the bodies out there—nor why a reasonable God let it happen to people who'd, in the preachers' economy, had no defense but not to listen, to shut their ears, inside and out. These were people who'd paid their tithes and gone to church and not been riotous and drunk too much and danced. And they were dead.

His own mother and father and Sam had bought that life for themselves. They believed in it. They believed righteousness made you safe.

But, God, it was all so fragile. It was all so terribly fragile. Five riders hadn't been enough—the way he understood the boys' image of the situation: five in town, two out on road repair—and none of them had stopped it.

In that thought, too, Jonas was doing absolutely right, holding them here. But the man was so damned cold. As if—

The ambient changed. Something more was out there than had been—he couldn't define the change, he didn't know why he was suddenly feeling the mountain more strongly, just that background noise that was always there—that now was more to the fore of his mind.

He didn't know what else had come in, but he wasn't alone in perceiving that something had—every rider in the room had gone still. The card game had stopped—Luke and Hawley looked toward the wall, toward the outside and the east. Jonas, who'd been cleaning and oiling his pistol, hesitated just ever so slightly, then snapped the cylinder into lock, a sound that made the boys jump, the general spookiness in the air surely having its effect on them as well.

"What is it?" Randy asked. <Terrified,> came flooding through from both the boys. They had guns. They'd at least had Luke's short version of how to aim and hope to hit something, and how not to empty the gun, ever, until you were down to the thing coming dead at you with no way to miss: they'd found the boys simple revolvers, single action, no rounds to lurk in the chamber and no safety to remember to take off. Pull the trigger and they went off—a danger to themselves and everything around them if they spooked.

"Could be Stuart," Danny said. He couldn't tell even yet what it was. It was far or it was quiet, and he suddenly suspected that if it was in fact Stuart, it could sound like that. Stuart and Burn wouldn't necessarily be a noisy presence.

A horse had come up onto the walk outside. Cloud wanted <Danny,> and Cloud wasn't alone in signaling human attention to the sudden change in the air.

Jonas went and opened the door—Jonas didn't tell anybody what he thought and you didn't get it even now through the ambient, not past Shadow's blurred images—but Cloud came in, snow-blanketed, with thunderous steps on the boards.

Knocked into a stack of pails as he dodged past Jonas. They fell and rattled. Cloud spooked another couple of feet and stopped, shedding snow with a whip of his tail.

Danny found himself on his feet, not alone from the snow-shower: Carlo and Randy were beside him. Hawley's cards had scattered on the floor. Horses outside and inside were feeling an undefined presence in the ambient, the echo of living creatures out in the woods, all reflecting what the creature in the next territory over had heard in its range.

Something large was definitely out there in the woods. Maybe *more* than one.

"Is it the rogue?" Randy wanted to know, picking it up himself, or reading the distress in the room.

"Hush," Carlo said. "They know. Let them alone."

Carlo had the right of it: they didn't want distraction—but they *didn't* know, that was the trouble. It might be any large creature—several of which had gone over the wall last night, and might have grown braver during the day: autumn brought voracious hunger, hunger that outweighed fears and better sense. The little slinks were back in the upper end of the village, around the marshal's office, Danny was sure of it—fast-moving scavengers that would be over the wall or into the cracks before a horse got up the street. There was no good chasing them and they did no harm with the horses here.

They might well be the source of some of the alarm, although he had a strange conviction it was generally eastward—like waves rolling on the sea, one to the next, to the next hearer.

"If it's Stuart he's on his way here," Jonas said. "He'll hear us in good time."

"Weather's one hell of a mess out there," Hawley said.

"Doesn't keep this from being the safest place in the district," Luke said. "Just sit still. He'll hear us. He'll want shelter tonight. You *hear* that out there?"

Cloud was dripping puddles onto the board floor, snow melting off his back. The view outside, beyond the porch, had been snow-veiled, enough to haze the buildings across the street. Danny wanted <going to the gate,> and Luke agreed with him. That was two.

"But we don't know it's Stuart," Jonas said.

"I'm going," Danny said. "You can do what you like. He's close. Whatever it is—he's close—" Because that was suddenly the feeling he had. It *was* Stuart.

But he got a <Danny stopping> from Jonas, so strong he did stop and look back.

"I came here by myself," Danny said. "I make my own choices."

"That's fine. Use your head."

"I am using it. He might need some help out there."

"He could," Luke said, redeeming himself in Danny's sight, right there, clean and clear.

Jonas wasn't happy. <Cold, snow, and vermin> dominated the images. But Jonas thought about <Stuart,> too, or somebody did. Jonas, still frowning, picked up his jacket. "Fisher," Jonas said, "you stay with the village kids. It might not be him."

"Then you need—"

"I said—stay with them. Do I need to explain? You've been *wanting* Stuart into the ambient for an hour, Fisher. Use your head." <Rogue and panic, Carlo and Randy afoot among the horses, down at the gate. Guns and gunfire.>

It wasn't a slur, he heard that. It was even good sense, keeping the boys out of the range of trouble—he understood it; and Jonas was right; he might have given the rogue an image to use on them. He'd been stupid. He just didn't want to be the one staying in the store.

But there wasn't another likely choice to guard the boys. And 'Fisher' wasn't 'boy.' He didn't protest when the Westmans and Hawley picked up their winter gear and their guns and went out to the porch.

He went outside himself, just far enough to see it was a real blizzard developing, worse than any storm he'd ever seen come down in Shamesey district. You couldn't see across the street in the blued twilight.

If it was Stuart out there in that whiteout, they might have to guide him in. And that was dangerous, because they didn't know what they might be calling to in the ambient, or what might come back at them out of it.

Didn't need a junior to go calling out into the storm wide-open, he said to himself. Jonas had been polite when he'd suggested that village kids were a liability and hadn't included him in that number. It wasn't safe to go bunch down there by the gate and listen into the storm for whatever happened to image back at you. Jonas had a reason to be hesitant just to go out there, that close to the wall.

A lot of reason. He went back inside, shut the door before they lost all the warm air—stamped off the snow.

"What *is* it?" Randy asked, and his older brother elbowed him with,

"Shut up, for God's sake, they don't know."

"It's all right," Danny found himself saying. "These guys—if you had to be in this situation, they're as good as you could hire anywhere. They won't open that gate until they're sure."

<Guns shooting> was in the ambient. And, with an edge of anguish that turned to a darker, more desperate feeling, from at least one of the boys:

<Brionne.>

He couldn't answer that hard problem for them—not with anything they wanted to hear. <Men shooting,> he thought before he could stop it. Because they would—without a question their survival was at stake.

Because by now if their younger sister wasn't bones in the forest out there—she was half of the rogue. If she wasn't dead—and the boys thought not—she rode it; she made at least half of any decision to run, to fight, to kill the village, to kill even their mother.

With her brothers in the ambient they'd have her attention, that was what he guessed. They were all the reference points the girl had now. The rogue was going to come back sooner or later. He had no question of it.

Just—if it *was* Stuart, if they could get Stuart in with them, along with Jonas, then the odds began to shift the other way.

* * *

The snow came down so thick there was no telling they were on the road, except the lack of trees in front of them, and that could almost as well mean a drop off the mountain if they missed a winding of the road.

It wasn't a time to hurry, no matter how cold. It was a time to have made camp, if they'd planned to spend the night in the open.

There couldn't be that much farther to go to Tarmin. He wasn't completely sure of his distances, but they ought to be there by now. They hadn't seen further signs of destruction. The snow was too thick and coming down too hard, now—but the ambient had been damned quiet. Damned quiet.

<Village,> he insisted to Burn. <Warm den.>

Burn thought, he would have expected Burn would think, <females.>

But Burn was as confused as he was by the silence, and thought instead, <dead things in village.>

And the ambient was cold. So cold and still.

Then—*wasn't,* quite.

<Riders,> he said to himself, spirits lifting. Somebody else was out in the hills, on the trail—or maybe in Tarmin itself, where he'd promised Burn they'd come by nightfall.

But he still found himself shying off from the thought. He wasn't sure. He *couldn't* be sure. The ambient, vague and strange and silent as it generally was, began to conjure thoughts of a warm fire already made, and a *company* of riders. Too good to be true.

It didn't make sense with what he'd seen, evidence of dead riders—at least of a dead horse.

But riders might well be out hunting the rogue. Riders out of Tarmin village might be looking for it—and a bunch of them, in this storm, might be sitting safe behind Tarmin walls, trying to beacon him in through the whiteout of the blizzard, sensing a sane rider and a sane horse, and not the threat the rogue posed.

Maybe Cassivey had even done what he promised and called up to Tarmin to warn the villages. Even Shamesey might have. One lowland agency surely could have had the basic common sense to phone a warning of what the villages up here faced; and if that was the case, even if there'd been trouble here, then he could hope he came welcome, at a fire he didn't have to build, and a sane barrier between him and the dark.

He *wanted* that. He was in one hell of a fix if Tarmin was shut to him—or lost.

He was spooked, was all. He'd spooked badly at Shamesey gates, and he hadn't any patience at all with himself—he couldn't afford it in the Wild, with the snow coming down in what was unquestionably now a full-scale, high-country blizzard—and a rogue somewhere in the question. Damned sure that there was trouble on the mountain, but *he'd* better sound sane to Tarmin riders, or they wouldn't let him in. They'd leave him outside till they could get sober sense out of him, and that risked Burn. Calm down, he said to himself. Calm *way* down.

A couple more rises and falls of the road, a bending against the flank of the mountain ridge—and he could smell wood smoke in good earnest. It wasn't at all as noisy as he thought a village Tarmin's size should be—but it was all right, he said to himself: the heavy fall of snow and maybe a bad night last night could have sent a lot of the village to bed early, and left the rider camp on watch.

Burn saw <horses.> Burn was picking up something that came through to him as a liveliness in the otherwise silent ambient.

Burn called out suddenly, that sharp, high challenge to another horse that shook Burn's sides, and there was a <darkness, instantly turning toward them,> instantly in the ambient as Burn imaged <Burn and Guil.>

Something came back to him—a familiar echo, he wasn't sure from where or when, but he'd known that feeling. Burn said <shifty-image horse> and answered it <fire, dark, and pain.>

A shot came off the rocks near him, ricocheted and whined. Burn jumped in utter startlement and a second shot splintered bark off an evergreen.

Instant, too, the image that came back, <shifting shadows, changing shapes,> <foam on water> and <ice-glisten.>

Damn, he *knew* those horses.

Jonas. Luke.

Hawley.

He didn't consciously think. It hit his gut and it hit Burn's simultaneously, and Burn slid immediately into fighting mode, ready to settle accounts.

"<No!>" Guil sent, and Burn shied away from the challenge—imaged <*gun!*> and jumped into a run as a gunshot echoed off the mountain and shattered bark right next to them. They were *at* the village gates—snow-hazed, shadows of men and horses were there. It was <Jonas and Shadow.>

Burn took him past. He ducked down and hung on, trusting Burn to get them clear.

"Guil!" someone yelled, far behind him. "Guil, damn your stupid hide!"

He didn't look back. He rode low and Burn ran hellbent for as much distance as he could put between them and ambush—raced panting and reckless through the deep white of the road.

Signal shots, had been Danny's first thought when he heard the gunfire—

He'd run out onto the porch, and then—then heard what sounded like an exchange of fire.

<Harper!> he thought.

Harper. Nobody else. Harper was up here on the mountain for one reason, and he hadn't given up his hunt—it *was* Stuart; and it was Harper, too.

"What's wrong?" Carlo and Randy were on his heels, coatless as he was as he ran down the street, rifle in hand, Cloud running along with him, and past him.

But he couldn't answer, he was hearing <Jonas mad,> he was hearing <Jonas on Shadow,> taking off into the blizzard, he was hearing <Luke chasing him> and <Hawley holding Luke> while <horses> were headed for <fight.>

"Damn," he said, and spun about and yelled at Carlo: "Get your coats. Get *my* coat! Come on!" He could see <Cloud getting into it.> Cloud *was* into it, <wanting fight> because there was <fight> in the air, and Danny didn't wait for coats or the boys or a second, reasoned thought. He put on a burst of speed with the cold air burning his lungs, the pistol trying to escape its holster, and the snow hitting his eyes so he couldn't see. The street was a straight line—if he stumbled over things in the snow he didn't want to know what they were. He ran until he was close enough for Cloud to have to recognize he was *in* the situation. He wanted <*Cloud!*> loud and clear.

Luke and Hawley were mounting up to ride out. Right in the gateway he grabbed Cloud first by the mane to stop him from going out with the other two, then got a hand against Cloud's chest and shoved him back.

"Dammit!" he yelled at Luke and Hawley. He meant two senior fools going out into the whiteout and leaving the gates open on him and two village kids. He was mad. He wanted <hands on them.> He wanted <beating hell out them.> They had no right, dammit. Harper was out there in the whiteout. Harper was near the village for all he knew.

But he couldn't catch them. He couldn't leave the boys.

The two boys came running up out of breath, carrying their coats, and his, and rifles. He was too hot right now to need a coat, but he put it on anyway, put on his scarf and hat that the boys had brought, and took the rifle they handed him. Cloud was fidgeting back and forth, wanting <chase horses,> but his rider wasn't about to go off into the whiteout to find a pack of double-crossing sons of bitches.

Stuart—God knew what Stuart thought.

Or what kind of line *he'd* fallen for from Jonas.

Stuart's friends. He couldn't swear it wasn't Jonas who'd fired.

"Our riders," Carlo panted, <scared,> "didn't come back."

"I know, I know." He wanted <gate shut. Jonas and Luke and Hawley begging to be let in again.>

Then he had a cold, clear impression they weren't alone. <Horses, to the left,> and before he could say a word, he knew it was <Hallanslakers.> Cloud went on guard facing that direction, projecting <fight> and <shooting guns.>

What came back was <Harper and Quig> and what came shadowlike out of the blowing white right in front of them was two riders coming to the gate.

<Shutting gates!> Danny sent, and the boys moved while he put

a round in the chamber and lifted the rifle to his shoulder, shaking in the knees, but not in the steadiness of his aim, which was right for center of the shorter one he mentally labeled <Harper.>

<Rogue in the woods,> he got back. <Quiet water. Quiet grass. Us coming in the gates.>

"The hell—*shut it*!" he screamed at Carlo, and kept his aim while the riders moved for the gate and two scared kids shoved the heavy gates shut and dropped the bar.

"Kid!" he heard Harper yell, the other side of the gates. "Kid, open up. Open it, or we'll leave you for the rogue!"

<Harper frozen sitting at fire. Quig with icicles. Us warm. Ham cooking.>

"Son of a bitch! *Open the gate!*"

"You had your chance, Harper! You want supplies, we'll give you supplies, right over the wall. But hell if I owe you anything but a cold bed in hell! Go find a shelter. You and Quig go tuck in for the winter and hope to hell I don't come after you myself!"

<Rogue in the ambient. Bones breaking. Watt falling.> He sent that to them. That was what he remembered. And they didn't like it.

Stuart had been there. Stuart had been that close to the gates and spooked off. He'd felt Stuart's presence and Stuart might not know anything right now except someone here had shot a gun off at him. Jonas and company had gone after Stuart and might not intend to come back—which left him with Harper and Quig, sitting here in the biggest, most attractive stationary target the rogue had, if the Goss kids were right about their sister.

In that light he could *use* Harper's help. He could use a couple of good shots and he didn't want to think of anybody dying out there in the Wild the way all Tarmin village had died.

But Harper wasn't interested in anything but Harper—Harper was damn crazy, dead set on shooting Stuart, for reasons that had gotten further and further from any reasonable fear of Stuart's going rogue. Harper wanted into Tarmin gates because if the Westmans came back Harper might shoot all of them and have the supplies, and spend all winter hunting Stuart, if Stuart didn't get him in his gunsights first.

There was no dealing with this man.

<Harper talking to Westmans,> came back through the gate. <Harper and Quig riding with Westmans through the snow.>

<Cattle,> Danny sent. Cloud added, <Cattle dung.>

"Who are they?" Randy asked. Randy's teeth were chattering and he tried not to show it. Cloud was sending into an angry ambient, <bite and kick,> and violence shivered over his skin and down into his gut. "They're not who we're looking for. Are they? Where did Jonas and them go?"

"These two are thieves." Danny said. "Damned *bandits*, is all. They're up here hunting Stuart for some crazy grudge. I hope to God he got away clear." It dawned on him Jonas might have kited out like that in honest fear that Stuart or his horse might have been hit and need help out there in the storm. Luke would have gone after his brother—no fault in Luke for that, or Hawley for going to protect him. But right now he wished Tarmin had a gun-box the way Shamesey had, because, damn, he'd dust Harper and Quig right off their doorstep.

"Kid," Harper said, from the other side of the gate.

"My name's Dan Fisher, Harper, get it straight."

"Look—" Harper said. "Call yourself anything you like. One horse is no match for this thing. Who's that with you? *Kids?*"

"You just camp right there, Harper. We need bait."

"You're real damn brave on the other side of that gate!"

"You're real damn stupid, Harper. That's why you're on the other side of that gate." God, he hadn't lost a bit from his bad-boy days and Randy thought it was wildly funny. Harper clearly didn't. Carlo looked a shade more maturely worried.

But Cloud sent <cattle rear ends> into the ambient, loud as Cloud could be.

"You damn fool!" Harper said.

"Camp out there. Be our guests." He was thinking, <Jonas and his friends coming back, guns firing.> And wasn't altogether confident of that fight going the way he'd like.

"You listen to me," Harper said. "You listen. I know what I'm talking about. My own brother—my *brother* went that way. You hear me?" <Man and horse coming into firelight. Harper shooting.

Shooting. Shooting until there weren't any bullets.> "You son of a bitch, you hear me? Your friend Stuart knows about it. *So* damn righteous!"

<Weather coming down, clouds over the mountains. Men and horses in whiteout.

<Stalled-out truck. Riders and truckers struggling with a truck on the edge, trying to winch it—

<Winch cable snapping—

<Recoil through the air, hitting horses and men—

<Man with bleeding face, horse knocked down—men over the edge as the truck falls—>

"Maybe you can talk to Jonas," Danny said. "Convince *him* you're a good guy." Give the son of a bitch at least the idea of talking it out, if it didn't naturally occur to dim brains. "He might think you were worth it. Or he could let you camp out there. Who knows?"

"My brother, kid. His name was Gerry Harper. You hear me? Took that hit in the head, him and the horse— 'Oh, we can make it through the pass, yeah, we can make it.' Stuart talks a good game to the truckers, but he's never on the end of the cable when it breaks. —*Gerry Harper*. You hear the name, kid?"

"That's a real sad story, Harper, but it doesn't get you in here."

"You listen to me. I shot him. *I* shot him. Who's going to pull the trigger on this one? You better get a *man* in there—you hear me? You hear me, kid? That thing'll have you for breakfast."

"Hasn't yet. If you want to shoot it, shoot it from out there where *it* is! You don't rough me up and threaten my horse and ask my charity, you damn jerk! —And Watt's dead! You hear *me,* Harper? Watt's dead out there. If you want to do something really useful, ride up to the High Loop villages and get some help down here!"

"Quit being an ass and *<open this damn gate!>*"

"No." He was shaking. Shot his brother, it was now. He was dealing with a crazy man.

"Kid, —"

"You're losing ground with me, Harper. I said I had a name. You keep forgetting it."

"Fisher, then." The ambient was wholly uneasy. There was complete lack of worry in the voice. "You can be a fool if you like."

Damn, he thought, realized he'd gotten caught up in the images and dived into the <quiet water> image to mask himself, signaled the boys away from the gate, farther and farther. Cloud drew back with them, mad and still wanting <fight.>

<Cloud at gate,> he sent, and Cloud stopped following and willingly turned back to <fight.>

"I'm a fool," he said to the boys, not trusting his ability to keep his intentions and his worries out of the ambient. But he had Cloud's attention occupied with a nerve-jangling flare of <angry horse. Bite and kick.> He looked at the guard-post, where, if he climbed it, he might get a shot, but he couldn't go thinking about it. "Rider gate, Carlo. *Fast.* Can you get a shot off from there?"

Carlo looked mortally scared.

"*I* can't do it," Danny said. "Cloud and I'll keep him talking. Scare them off. Put shots around them. Whatever. Fire fast. Spook them out away from the wall—I'll get up there—" A cut of his eyes to the guard-post aloft—and down, as he grabbed Carlo's arm. "Don't for God's sake get shot. Or let them in."

Carlo didn't want to. Danny jerked his arm. "They can *hear* me any second, dammit! *Do it*!"

"Yeah," Carlo agreed then. "—Randy, stay with him."

Carlo didn't stop to argue: Carlo went—Randy tried to run after him, but Carlo grabbed him, jerked him hard and sent him back.

<Carlo shutting the village-side gate,> Danny wished, but Cloud wasn't in position to carry it to Carlo—he wasn't getting this organized; he had Randy in his charge—he had to hope Carlo remembered.

Then he thought of vermin maybe occupying the rider camp—vermin a rider took for granted would clear his path. Carlo *wasn't* protected that way, Carlo was a damn brave village kid—with no horse to *see* what was going on before he opened that outer gate. Hell with his plan for climbing the gate-tower: if Carlo went down on any account Harper and Quig could take the rider camp and *have* Tarmin, with just him and Randy left.

He grabbed Randy by the coat and didn't wait to explain—he

dragged Randy with him half the distance to the rider-side gate, until they were far enough from the front gate he knew Cloud couldn't hear—"Don't think about Carlo!" he said. "The horse carries it! Stay here! Dammit, don't budge!"

Randy was trying to get a breath, trying to get words out—Randy grabbed his arm and hung on and Danny swung and knocked the kid across the snow. He didn't have words, didn't have time—he aimed his rifle skyward and fired off two rounds <warning Jonas, scaring spooks> and the shots echoed off the mountain above, shocking the silence.

He didn't hear Harper and Quig now. But something else was coming through the ambient—something ominously considerable.

Damn, he thought. Damn! His heart was speeding. Now he didn't know where Harper and Quig were. Cloud had left the front gate. Cloud was coming—but there wasn't a damn thing Cloud could do from midvillage, and he'd not used his head, God help them.

He raced down the village street with Cloud at his heels and cut over to the camp gate—Carlo had shut it. Give the kid credit—he'd shut it. He flung the latch open and dived past the centerpost, leaving a mad, frustrated horse behind him trying to get past a barrier that made that door human-only, Cloud making panic-sounds, sending out <anger and fear> into the ambient as Cloud's rider chased down Carlo's rapidly filling tracks, white on white, past the horse den, breakneck through the blowing snow. He let off two more rounds at the sky to warn Carlo and Jonas at once, saw Carlo at the rider gate, just then opening it wide to the driving snow.

"Carlo!" he yelled. *"Get out of the way!"*

Carlo turned, confused—looked at him and started to shut it again.

In the same moment a snow-hazed figure showed up in that gateway and Danny skidded to one knee, brought the rifle up and fired without stopping to see who it was.

Stupid, *wrong*, his brain told him. It might have been Stuart. Jonas. God knew. He'd probably missed. He'd scared hell out of Carlo, and the gateway, after his one shocked blink, held only blowing snow. He knelt there sighting down the gun and shaking as Carlo, only belatedly realizing he wasn't the target, had the presence of mind to grab the gate and shove it to.

A shot from past Danny's shoulder hit the log wall by Carlo and splintered the wood.

He knew it was Randy even before Carlo yelled at the kid, "Don't shoot, don't shoot, dammit! God! What are you doing?"

Randy didn't fire another round. Cloud was making a sound he'd rarely heard Cloud make, a squalling, spitting fit. The den wall thumped to Cloud's temper as Danny used the rifle butt to get his shaky legs under him.

His lungs were burning. Carlo was yelling against the wind at his brother, something about Put the damn rifle down, it was all right. Carlo was coming toward him and Randy was spooked, he got that in the ambient along with Cloud's temper.

He didn't know how his knees were staying under him. He bent over, rifle and all, leaned against his knees and tried to get his breath, short of wind in the high altitude, aware of Carlo coming past him, Randy running to Carlo, betrayed and scared and hurt.

"I hit the kid," he gasped, straightening up, and threw the situation into the ambient, <Randy and Cloud, Harper at the gate> because he didn't have the wind to talk and he was hearing Cloud all too well. He went into a coughing fit and got it under control. He had a stitch in his side. "Did the man go down?" was what he wanted to know, whether the man he'd shot at had dropped, whether he'd killed somebody—whether they still had Harper to contend with—

But the pressure in the ambient, that *thing* he'd been feeling, was gone. The gunfire might have spooked it off.

"Did he go down, Carlo, dammit?"

"I don't know," Carlo said. "I think you got him."

He couldn't hear anything but Cloud's panic and outrage. If there was a rider down, his horse should be doing something, feeling something. Harper's horse should. He had a bad feeling about things out of control in every direction, and walked back where the kids were and where Cloud was, Cloud on the far side of the camp gate and mad and scared.

Carlo had Randy by the shoulder, <scared, mad,> too, saying

something about "Told you to stay put, dammit!" and Randy was paper-white and on the edge: Randy had been <scared. Danny hitting him—>

"Kid," Danny said, and lost his voice again. He clapped Randy on the back. "Danger you'd leak Carlo to the bad guys. —Sorry. Sorry I hit you. They could have heard you—understand? Sorry."

Randy had a hand to his bloodied mouth, tears freezing on his white, cold-blotched face. He still looked to be in shock, but the ambient eased.

"Did you shoot him?" Randy asked.

"Dunno." He still couldn't breathe. He was getting the shakes enough for them to notice. "Pretty sure I missed. Damned mess. Sorry. <*Cloud, dammit, quiet.*>"

Cloud was trying to shoulder the obstructing gate-post down. But there was only Cloud out there on the village side. Danny went through the gate and moved Cloud back with a push on his chest.

<Mad horse. Frothing-at-the-mouth horse.> Cloud had blood on his shoulder where he'd tried to force the narrow gate, and his breath steamed in great puffs on the bitter wind.

Danny flung his arm about Cloud's neck and apologized in a cheek-to-cheek way that didn't need the kind of confused, angry force Cloud was sending out, just <quiet water, very quiet water, still, still, reflecting us, reflecting Randy, reflecting Carlo, all quiet.>

Cloud had never found himself on the wrong side of a barrier like that. Cloud was so scared he was trembling, too, and he was spitting froth mixed with blood—he'd bashed his lip on the post, Danny decided, and was sorry. But he couldn't have done anything else—<Man at far gate,> he told Cloud, <Danny shooting. Man running.>

Big shiver out of Cloud. The boys had come through to the camp side behind him. They could get the side gate shut and latched on *this* side, then, but the main gate still scared him. He wanted <them and Cloud guarding gate> and walked in that direction, shaking too much to run.

He wasn't in the least cold. He was sweating, and his chest burned from the thin winter air. He could get <up on that tower

with rifle, him above, Cloud below, boys with thick coats and blankets, shooting Hallanslakers.>

Cloud didn't disagree.

Then somebody fired a shot that rang far off across the mountainside, and they stopped still.

Second shot, from out there.

Distance made them blind and deaf to the origin—the mountain echoed it until even Cloud didn't know where it was.

He waited for a third shot. It didn't come. The boys were <scared.> But <rogue horse> was in Randy's thoughts. <Shooting at horse. Shooting at scared blonde girl.> The brothers didn't want that. The darkness that had been around the <Brionne> image last night wasn't there, this time.

<Shooting father,> was there. <Gun going off. Woman screaming and screaming. . . >

"Cut it out," Danny said sharply, "shut down. *Quiet*, dammit. It's probably just Jonas signaling he's coming back. Maybe he's bringing Stuart."

He fervently hoped so. More, he hoped they'd just shot the rogue, and that the boys' blonde sister was coming back with them, and they'd find Stuart, and they'd tell Harper go to hell and take his sad stories with him.

Cloud stayed beside him as they went to the gate—closed and latched the door on the store while they were at it, because the boys had left it wide open, let all the heat out and burned up a load of wood besides endangering their supplies—"Sorry," Carlo said. But he didn't blame the boys, and latched it and went on.

They didn't go into the gate house. Randy thought they should go in where it was warmer, and set up a fuss about it—but Danny said a flat no, and tried not to image what was in there. He climbed up to the tower and down again when he found he couldn't see anything better in the blowing snow—if he'd gone up there he couldn't have gotten a clear target anyway; so everything about his plan was stupid, and he came back down to Carlo and Randy fast, before they got to investigating anything in the gate house.

He tried not to think about <bones under the snow> while he was doing it. But there were. Bones and dead people were all up and down the street. The snow was just covering them, that was all, burying them <deep, deep and quiet.>

And he wished—he prayed to the God who didn't hear riders—that Jonas would find Stuart and get him back here so they could all be safe and the senior riders would know what to do to save their lives.

He'd only covered his mistakes. He didn't know who he'd shot, he didn't know anything: he was down to admitting that, even to himself.

Chapter — XX —

THE AMBIENT WAS CLEAN NOW. THE SNOW AND THE TREES WERE A silence no other presence breached.

<Riders hunting through the woods,> Guil thought. He'd long since slid down from Burn's back and walked beside Burn, Burn with head hanging, still coughing occasionally from the cold air. Moisture from Burn's jaws, frozen on his chest, glistened in the blued grey of the snowfall. Burn still kept expecting <guns behind them,> his rider's expectation to the contrary.

But there wasn't any safety in lingering. Guil kept a hand on Burn's side, <us walking,> he imaged. <Us moving through the storm, us walking through the woods—> and he tried not to think beyond that, or to wonder about human motives, because Burn was taking in everything and he couldn't stop it.

They'd gone off the road. They came down to it again, both still walking. It didn't take hard guessing—just careful footwork on the steeps, and down again in the same direction. No knowing whether Jonas was following them or not.

But he'd heard faint shots back in the direction of the walls, and another couple closer, that he thought might be the searchers signaling each other—they weren't close enough to be firing at him, but that didn't mean safety.

Jonas had yelled at him to come back, called him a fool.

And maybe he was. Maybe there was a real good explanation—like a nervous guard. But shooting at him wasn't confidence-inspiring.

Most of all, he didn't know what in hell Jonas was doing sitting in a village surrounded by tattered scavengings, after he'd shown no sign of coming up here.

He damn sure wasn't going to risk Burn going back to give them another try. And considering things Jonas hadn't told him about Aby's dealings back at Shamesey gate, he wasn't at all sure what had made Jonas take another trip up the mountain.

Jonas had gotten his convoy to Shamesey. He was free to go back with no one knowing—or giving him specific orders, unless he'd *also* gotten them from Cassivey; and he didn't think so.

Jonas was much more distinguished by what he *hadn't* done: Jonas hadn't come out that night to bring him what was his at Shamesey gate.

Jonas hadn't said—I'll go with you up the mountain, Guil.

Jonas hadn't said, in sum, anything about his gear, the bank account, Hawley, the gold shipment, or his own intentions to be here.

Jonas had wanted <quiet> around him, and not given him damned much at Shamesey—just walled himself off and tried to bottle up the rogue-feeling so it didn't spread: that was a service, but it was, as they said in the hills, a real cold supper. He didn't say he'd have been more in control of himself at Shamesey if Jonas had given him even an I'm sorry; but Jonas hadn't buffered anything he gave him: just—flung it at him. "Aby's dead, Guil.'"

Now did Jonas come to help?

Hell.

Jonas knew about the gold, was one good bet.

But—that came back to the same question: what in hell did a rider do with that kind of money? A village could steal that much. A village could loot the truck. A rider couldn't find anything to do with it, couldn't be *safe* if he had that kind of stash, couldn't keep from rousing curiosity if he didn't work—and had the better things that money could buy. There was no damn *way* he could use the pure metal for one thing. He'd have to fake nuggets or corrupt an assayer, —or somebody he'd forever be vulnerable to. It wasn't something a rider would do.

Get himself in good with Cassivey? Get Aby's job? *That* was much more likely.

That was a rider motive.

He checked Burn over head to hoof and head to tail once they reached the level ground of the roadway, in case Burn should have been hit or cut in their mad dash away from Tarmin and neither of them know it. Burn was his only worry. Burn's welfare and the quiet of the mountainside was the only thing that occupied his brain: they were all that had to make sense at the moment.

Burn was <mad and wanting to go back, wanting fight,> wanting <bad fight,> but Burn was running on fragile strength right now, too, having carried him much more than Burn ordinarily would. They'd gone since dawn; they'd had one real night of rest since the climb up; somebody, most likely Aby's summer's-end partners and the cousin who'd raided their bank account, had shot at them for reasons he still didn't figure; and until things made better sense to an aching head and a tired body, he figured to stay ahead of the questions and just take care of the business he'd come to do: get the rogue that was surely responsible for the scavenged remains and dead horse he'd seen back there at the rider-shelter, and *then* figure whether or not to talk to Jonas.

Then let Jonas keep Hawley Antrim out of his reach. *And* let him explain the situation at Tarmin village.

There were, in his mental map of the lower side of the Tarmin road, two shelters available, one midway, one just short of the Climb that went up the steep to the High Loop. The middle one they could make. They could do it, just hit a staying pace and keep moving.

Meanwhile the snow was coming down thick. It melted on Burn's overheated back as fast as it fell, sticking on Burn's mane and making a fair blanket on his black hide in only the time he'd stood still being checked over. The track they'd plowed downhill was fast vanishing under new snowfall.

He walked, Burn beside him.

<Truck going off the edge.

<Aby dead on the rocks.

<Cassivey in the big green chair, surrounded in smoke. Bathed in smoke. Backed by men with guns.>

<Jonas at Shamesey gates, refusing to look at him. Jonas with his edges crimped in real tight, same with Luke, and Hawley a lump of grief behind him.> Hawley was the one who'd *felt* something when they broke the news. Hawley at least had cared.

Hawley hadn't said about the money. Though, granted, Hawley wasn't damned bright: Aby's mother's half-sister must've screwed a post to get Hawley—he'd maintained that for years. Aby'd argued he wasn't that dim, but, damn, he'd far undershot it. Hawley pulling what he'd pulled at the bank—God, what did you *do* with a man like that?

He wanted to pound Hawley's head in right now, if only because Hawley was the easiest problem to puzzle out, and probably the one of the three with no malice: Hawley got ideas and got himself in trouble, not thinking things through, not remotely adding it up why he was going to make people mad. You wanted to beat his head in, but you didn't somehow ever get around to doing it, because to make it worth a human being's time, Hawley had to understand why you were mad at him—and, dammit, you had a better chance explaining morals to a lorry-lie.

At least you knew where Hawley was on an issue. You could even call him honest, he was so stupid about his pilfering.

Jonas, on the other hand—if Jonas was coming up here with honest intentions, meaning nothing else on his mind than paying debts to Aby, it needed more reasons than he'd ever pried out of the man. Shadow was a spooky, chancy horse, and Jonas was that kind of a man—you had to get *Luke* alone and a few beers along if you wanted the truth. Jonas and that horse were both spooks. In a minute and twice on a weekday, yes, Jonas would opt to keep the truth to himself. Jonas, even to his partners, especially to outsiders to that threesome, parted with information the way a townsman parted with cash money, piece at a time, and always, *always* to Jonas' advantage.

Jonas always did his job. Letter of the contract. Depend on it.

Jonas come up here out of belated remorse? Loyalty? —Friendship? Not to him.

And where was Hawley, if Jonas was involved?

Hell, ask Jonas what Hawley thought. Hawley always did.

<Horses> crept up into Cloud's awareness, <Froth> first, a noisy presence through the palisade walls and the gate.

<Harper shooting from the hill,> Danny imaged hard, the instant he picked up Jonas' party at all. <Hallanslakers in the Meeting in camp.

<Harper on his feet yelling. Harper shooting. Harper shooting. Harper shooting—Harper and Quig at the gate—

<Danny shooting at a man in the blowing snow.>

<Ice> appeared almost immediately after <Froth.> <Shadow> had to be that disturbance around them. Cloud snorted and wasn't sure he wanted them back, but the boys were glad enough to realize they weren't on their own any longer. And—which he had trouble admitting—he was.

"Is that the riders?" Carlo wanted to know without his saying anything. "Is that Jonas? Are you warning them?"

"Yeah," he said, trying to steady down his images *and* his nerves before he had to deal with Jonas.

"Are they coming back?" Randy wanted to know—Randy had a sore cheek, but Randy wasn't hurt otherwise, and Randy had maybe learned to stay away from a horse when there was something you didn't want shouted to minds all over the area. Randy had figured a number of things out, maybe, and at least wasn't mad at him anymore.

"Yeah, they're coming in. I don't think Harper's stayed around in range, or he's real quiet out there." He put a hand on Randy's shoulder and squeezed, feeling the shivery excitement in Randy's mind. "Just calm down. If you want to go around horses you have to keep it down all the time, all right?"

"Yeah," Randy said; and took a deep breath. "Are they going to shoot? Are they going to find this Harper guy?"

"Just be ready to open the gate," Danny said to the boys; he kept thinking of <Harper> and ambush. "Fast."

But <Harper> was gone from the ambient and had been since the gunshot at the gate, spooked out, elusive as any four-footed ghosty.

"Have they found the man?" Randy asked. "The man Harper was shooting at?"

"Stuart?" he said. "No, the blurry one's probably Jonas. He's not real noisy. They're coming up on the gates. Be ready. They'll come in and we shut it behind them fast as we can. Harper's a coward. He'll lie low if he's outnumbered. But he could try shooting at them." He was sending <Harper with gun. Harper's face,> as clearly as he could—he couldn't put any time sense with it, he couldn't *tell* Jonas it was now and not then he was worried about. <Man with rifle. Shooting at gate.>

Randy handled the latch, and he and Carlo hauled at the door, moving a blanket of snow along with it. They hauled hard, making a horse-wide fan of it as Luke and then Hawley rode in, their faces stung red with cold above their scarves, snow thick on them and their horses. Then Jonas came in last and <not happy.>

"Harper was here!" Danny said. "Harper and Quig. We shot at them."

"Explains the gunshot," Jonas said, and slid down.

"What about Stuart?"

"Man's a damn spook," Jonas said. "Couldn't stop him. Wouldn't listen."

"He thinks *we* were shooting at him," Luke said. "Lit out up and over a slope somewhere—couldn't track him in this stew."

<Steep rocks, brush, blowing snow> came through. So did the fear of <Stuart shooting from ambush.>

And from Hawley, Danny thought, the more pleasant image of <ham and biscuits and a warm fire.>

<Danny shooting at Harper?> Jonas asked.

<Harper at front gate, gate shut, Jonas and Luke and Hawley off on road. Danny talking to Carlo, Carlo running for rider gate—>

He didn't want to confess how entirely stupid he'd been, but <Harper or Quig maybe being shot, thick snow, gate coming open> was something Jonas needed to know.

"Hit him?"

"Could have. Could have hit Quig. That's the other guy. But I'm not sure."

"You'd know," Jonas said matter of factly, and the ambient went queasy with <pain, anger, horse going crazy> while Jonas' personal shell around it was cold as ice. Jonas took his hat off and dusted it against his leg. "Get us inside. Damn near frozen."

<Cattle,> was Burn's judgment on the situation, and Guil patted Burn on the neck as he walked beside him, too numb and too sore to be coherent.

Snowed on. Shot at. Chased. Yelled at for a spooky fool. His feet were numb. His head hurt.

<Box on the lead truck. The truck that had gone over the edge.

<Hell!

<Hell!>

Burn snorted, shook his neck, throwing off a warning to the neighborhood—a dangerously loud sending out into the ambient, considering the danger they knew was on the loose up here.

But Burn always thought he owned the territory. Guil caught a fistful of mane in the middle of Burn's neck and yanked it to distract him from challenging everything in reach.

<Shooting at him.> He was *still* damned mad.

Wouldn't really have thought it of Jonas—wouldn't have thought that Jonas would miss, for one thing, but the snow had been blowing hard. Gust of wind, snow in the eyes . . . nobody was perfect.

Or it *could* have been an overexcited villager, thinking that he was the rogue: spooked villagers could shoot at any damn thing they thought they saw.

Could have, could have. The fact was Aby was dead and he didn't know he was in any sense justified in his increasingly dark suspicions of Jonas—but somewhere between the headache and the ache in his leg, he was on the irrational edge of very damned mad.

Give Jonas credit—he'd lay odds Hawley hadn't run straight to inform his partners about the bank. On a day in town with the horses a long way off, even dimbrain Hawley could conceivably have done something Jonas and Luke didn't know about.

And ask where Hawley *put* the funds—maybe the cold air was waking his brain up—but he bet to *hell* there was another bank account. Hawley Antrim could have one. The bank women didn't ask about brains, just if you had money. Hawley could have put most of it right back in *his* account, right there in Anveney.

And ask why Aby had used a bank at Anveney—and why Hawley knew it.

She hadn't been able to level with her partner—that was what. She'd hammered home to her partner that the account existed and he should use it. He hadn't known—God!—that it was in event of something happening to her, as if she'd *known* she ran risks more than the ordinary. Just so casual—Use the bank, Guil. It's safe.

In the absence of her partner on her end-of-season run, she'd had to get a crew she could trust not only not to make off with the cargo but not to spill every damn thing they knew in village camps; granted there wasn't anybody closer-mouthed or closer-minded than Jonas and Luke. Hawley—Hawley was moderately discreet because he didn't have two thoughts a day—but he supposed, hell, he'd probably have picked Jonas and his lot himself, given Aby's situation and Jonas showing up.

Jonas in breaking the news to him had told him about the rogue, imaging just <Aby dead.> That was how he'd gotten it. The <trucks racing down mountain> he'd gotten from Luke, but no real chain of events from Jonas. No side information—and that was typical Jonas: you got things through that horse of his that flitted, that shifted, that you just couldn't quite focus on. A nest of willywisps wasn't as echoey as Jonas when he and that horse shaped you something out of memory. Clear and crisp-edged—Shadow wasn't. Shadow enjoyed <blood,> Shadow enjoyed <fight.> You didn't want to linger in Shadow's ambient in a situation like that with Burn in striking range.

Two damn dominant males, Burn and Shadow.

Burn took high offense at the mere comparison with Shadow. <Biting and kicking. Females. Autumn and snow.>

"Easy." He gave a tug at Burn's mane, set his hand on the back of Burn's neck and shook it as Burn sucked winter air into his nostrils, <looking for females.>

God.

<Nightmares,> Burn imaged happily, sniffing the wind and looking for mates while the wind blasted at them cold as the floors of hell. He was trying to figure who'd just tried to kill them, and Burn skittered off onto <snow> and <autumn,> running on nervous energy by now—while his was flagging. Hell, he thought, maybe he and Jonas *were* crazy as the horses.

God knew if Aby and Jonas had had anything going between them. He couldn't imagine it. But maybe there was *that* in the ambient. He'd not picked it up.

He wouldn't be offended—he didn't think he was. Jonas was potentially more *serious* than Aby's occasional others.

But—no. He didn't think so. Not Jonas. For the damn-all major thing—Jonas wouldn't do it. He wouldn't put himself that close and that off-guard to Aby's questions.

A wally-boo called. He took it for reassurance. He had the rifle slung to his shoulders, his hands stuffed into his pockets. He took one out, in the wicked gust of snow-laden wind down a fold of the mountain, to pull his breath-sodden scarf up around his nose. It was freezing with the moisture of his breath and sagging down to his mouth. He jerked it behind his head, tugged it down tight inside his collar, thinking about that sweater he could have bought in Anveney—thinking about frostbite, and asking himself whether the oil on his boots was holding out.

Maybe some sense of obligation had actually gotten to Jonas, Aby having paid her life for it.

Or maybe—maybe Cassivey had talked to more than one man, made a deal with more than one man regarding that cargo.

Damn.

Damn!

That distracting notion took the trail-sense out of his legs. His foot wobbled into a hidden hole. He recovered himself a few steps, but he'd hurt the sore leg. The cold had clearly gotten to his brain. He was frozen between the consideration that maybe he ought to go back and find out what Jonas wanted—and the equally valid thought that that had been no signaling shot that had blasted bark off a tree. Jonas *hadn't* fired at him when he'd chased him. . . .

Burn swung his head around and bit him above the knee, not hard, but enough to wake him up. <Guil riding,> Burn insisted. <Warm Guil on warm nighthorse back.>

Wasn't fair. Wasn't fair to weight Burn down. <Guil walking,> he thought: the shelter couldn't be far. He'd cut across the mountain where a horse could go and a truck couldn't, and he didn't know how much time he'd taken off the trek, but he had to be far closer now to the next way-stop than he was to go back to the village.

Didn't dare to do it again, how-so-ever. Shaky legs had no business on a mountain. Damn near killed themselves doing it once.

And there was a chance of coming down to the road a second time some distance past the shelter. A chance, if the storm worsened, of freezing to death on the mountainside.

But he was limping. And speed was harder and harder.

<Burn carrying baggage,> he imaged; and Burn didn't want to. Burn would carry *him* carrying it. Burn didn't like the pack. It tickled.

He argued, he imaged <bacon and biscuits in the baggage,> but Burn, remembering that, just wanted <bacon cooking> right then.

<Shelter,> Guil insisted. <Burn carrying baggage. Us walking,> and Burn still wouldn't.

He stopped. <Guil sitting down.> Burn offered to bite him on the leg again and he offered, <Guil walking. Burn carrying baggage.>

Burn wasn't happy, but Burn finally carried it—<nasty ice lumps bumping at cold nighthorse ribs. Us in snow. Us in dark. Snow on us.>

<Warm fire in the shelter,> he sent back, <bacon frying in the shelter.>

For a considerable distance further that even dominated <females> in Burn's searching the scents the storm brought. But

<evergreen and ice> was what Burn smelled. <Willy-wisps> once. The ambient was healthier where they were.

But night was also coming down fast. The sunglow was leaving the sky behind the mountain wall. The temperature was dropping fast and the wind had a shriller voice as it howled among the evergreens.

<Nasty willy-wisps,> Burn imaged. <Nasty falling-down lean-to.>

But a high-country shelter was, Guil swore, going to be there—ransacked like the last one or whole, he didn't care, as long as it was whole walls, a door that would latch, and a supply of wood.

Jonas would probably be after them; Jonas could show once the weather cleared and they'd talk and have some answers.

They'd talk with him behind a wall with a gun-port and Jonas out in the yard telling him what the deal was with Cassivey, that was how they'd talk.

But he had to get there. Had to get there. Legs had to last. Lungs had to last.

As the light dimmed and dimmed, until they were walking in a murk defined by tree-shadow and the ghostly white of the clear-cut.

There was ham, there was yeast bread. Danny knew how to make it, and nobody else claimed the knack. He hoped Harper could smell it out there on the wind and Harper was real, real hungry.

He truly, truly hoped Stuart had made it to the next shelter.

Jonas thought something he couldn't catch. Luke had another slice of bread.

"I'll bet," Luke said, "that Harper's pulled back to the north-next shelter."

"Could," Jonas said.

The boys just ate their supper.

There wasn't a sign of Harper, though he thought they all kept an ear to the ambient. He ate his supper without a qualm.

It was only afterward when he began to think again about <man in the gate, snow blowing> and that man vanishing in the jolt the gun made—that he really worried he'd hit Quig.

He didn't think he ought to worry. But he did.

He sat in a warm spot near enough the stove it overheated his knees. He rubbed the warmth of overheated cloth into his hands, and didn't want to move.

"You think you did shoot him after all?" Carlo asked, squatting down near him.

"I don't know. I could have."

Carlo didn't say anything else about it. Carlo was thinking about his father. About <gun going off.> About <anger> he couldn't deal with. Carlo was quiet, and Randy came up and sat down by him, all of them scared. The banging went on down the street, where the wind hadn't yet hammered whatever-it-was to flinders.

"When the snow stops," Carlo said, "are they going to go after this Stuart guy again?"

"Probably." He rubbed his knees again. The heat was back. It was almost too uncomfortable.

"What happens to you," Carlo asked then, careful around his edges, "—if you go with a rogue and they shoot it?"

"Dunno. I really don't."

"Do they know?" A slide of Carlo's eyes toward Jonas and the others. "I mean—"

Cloud moved in, put his head on Danny's shoulder, and Danny scratched Cloud's chin without thinking about it.

"Yeah," Danny said. <Blonde girl in red coat> was insistent in the air. "It's not a good time to think about it, all right? I don't know what happens. Harper isn't any genius. He just got spooked bad." <Man Harper knew. Rogue in the ambient. Shooting man.>

<Shooting Brionne> came through, and upset ran the whole room, horses shifting, heads coming up.

"Go to sleep," Jonas said, and it was like a bucket of ice water on the ambient. Things just—stopped, the way old Wesson could get your attention.

But it scared everybody. Cloud had jerked his head up, too, and Cloud was surly, feeling it as <attack.>

Jonas got up and walked over to the stove, towering over them, his face and himself half in shadow from the flue pipe.

"No gain," Jonas said, "to some questions. She could freeze. She could fall off. Could be she's sane. Could be she isn't. But if you get her back she won't be the same as she was. Plain truth."

The air was cold around the fire. Just—cold.

"She's thirteen," Carlo said in a shaky voice. "She's just thirteen."

"Horse can't count," Jonas said. "Rogue doesn't care, mountain doesn't care. Storm out there doesn't care. And we won't know."

"Ease off him," Danny said. "Jonas, it's their sister, for God's sake."

"No difference."

"Maybe riders get dropped under a damn bush, but village kids come with sisters, Jonas—sisters and brothers and <family,> and damned right it matters! You grow up with somebody and you got 'em even if you don't damn well like 'em!"

<Sam. Sitting at the kitchen table. Having a mouthful of beans.>

<Wrench, settling on a thin, crooked pipe fitting. Open air. Cold air. Gravel underfoot.>

Didn't know who that was. Jonas all of a sudden flared up—was just <there,> and <mad> and they were <on the floor>; Danny couldn't make sense of it, but his heart had jumped.

"Clean up," Jonas said.

"The hell. *You* clean up. I cooked it."

Horses were <upset.> <Fight> was in the ambient.

"Hawley," Jonas said. "You want to pick up the site?"

"Yeah," Hawley said, and the air was quieter.

Carlo had gone tense. Randy was stiff and scared-looking, huddled against him. Danny felt a flutter in his heart and got up from where he was sitting, went over and calmed Cloud down, trying not to think real-time, thinking about <flour and biscuit's and how long the wood stack was going to last.>

<Wrench on a fitting. Brown metal and cold.

<Papa and the shop, papa fixing engines. Pieces all over the table. Papa's hands all over grease and black from his work.

<Papa washing up in the sink.>

But papa never got his fingernails clean, never bothered too much because it was back to the shop after supper. Papa worked real hard.

<Papa in the blacksmith shop. Sparks flying. Iron glowing in the heat.>

That last was Carlo. It was Randy, too. They'd gotten up. They came over to join him, still <scared,> but picking up on it, maybe, that when the air went like that in a camp you left things alone, really alone, fast.

The ambient grew quieter and quieter, as if the whole world was freezing. Even the hardier creatures on the mountain had sought shelter from the storm, and the nightly predators had evidently decided on a night to stay snug in their burrows.

There was a time you thought you had to give it up and try to tuck in somewhere, and if you didn't, you somehow kept going. And after you were mind-numb and still walking on that last decision there came a time the body kept working and the brain utterly quit: Guil caught himself walking without looking, a second after he slid on a buried rut and had the bad leg go sideways. Burn just forged ahead.

The leg could be broken, for all Guil could feel—it was numb from toes to knee, the knees and ankles were going, and Burn, damn him, just kept on plowing through the snow.

<*"Burn!"*> he yelled, straining a throat raw with cold, thin air. That started him coughing, and still Burn didn't stop.

It was a betrayal he'd never in his life expected. Burn had never left him.

Females, maybe, delusions of females—only thing that he knew would distract Burn to that extent.

Then: <Shelter in the dark. Logs covered in snow, snow piled high. Bacon cooking.>

He got up, he slogged ahead in the trail Burn broke for him. He stumbled and he used the rifle for help staying on his feet, but, damn, it was there, it was solid in the dark, he could see it with his own eyes, tears freezing his lashes and his lids half-shut. Burn was a <splendid horse. Strong, admirable horse.>

<Wonderful horse,> Burn agreed, pleased with himself. Burn was already up at the entry to the cabin, nosing the door, having

gotten, over a lifetime, damned clever with latches and latch strings.

"Hell, Burn, you'll ice it breathing on it, you fool—" He could hardly talk, but he set the rifle against the wall and squeezed up beside Burn, got a grip with stiff, gloved fingers on the latch chain, and pulled.

The latch lifted. Getting a snowbound door was a matter of kicking the snow clear and the ice clear, getting a grip on the handle and pulling the door so you had a crack to get your hands into.

Another tug outward and Burn got his jaw into the act, stuck just his chin through the door and started pulling back, working his head in and forcing it wider.

Outward-opening. Always outward opening, all the shelters. You had a snow door, even a roof trap you could use if the snow piled up and you had to, but outward gave you better protection against spook-bears, who always pushed and dug.

"Come on, Burn, Burn, give me some room, you fool, it's still blocked—"

Ice broke. It moved, and Burn wasn't taking any nonsense. Burn got a shoulder in, and more ice broke—Burn's rider's foot was a narrow miss as Burn shoved his way in with thoughts of <supper> and a warning of <nighthorse, fierce nighthorse. Eating willy-wisps cooked in grease.>

Clean shelter. No vermin. Nothing moved in the dark inside.

He had an idea how the locals set things up now. He retrieved the rifle, got the door shut—pulled his right-hand glove off with his teeth and put his fingers in his mouth to warm them.

They hurt, God, they hurt so much tears started in his eyes and added to those frozen to his eyelashes. Burn came and breathed on him, that was some help when the shakes started, enough that he was able to get into his pocket and get the waxed matches.

He got one lit—the thumbnail still worked, even if he couldn't feel the thumb.

Better yet, he was able to hold onto the match as it flared and showed him a cabin like any rider shelter—showed him the mantel, and besides a charred slow-match, a lantern with the wick ready and the chimney set beside it.

He lit it on one match, blinked the tears from his eyes and felt that one little flame as a blazing warmth in a world gone all to ice and wind.

The fire was laid and ready. He lit the slow-match from the lantern, lit the fire from the match, and squatted there fanning it with his hat until he was sure beyond a doubt he had it going. The wind was all the while moaning around the eaves like a living thing and thumping down the chimney. He chose to take a little smoke until the fire was strong enough for the snow-dump that sometimes came when you opened the flue—there was almost certainly a snow-shield on the chimney, but when he finally pulled the chain, he still got ice. It plummeted onto the logs, hissed, and knocked some of the inner structure flat.

It didn't kill the fire, only flung out a white dusting of ash. He stayed there in the warmth and light with Burn going about sniffing this and that—he pulled off his left glove and checked his fingers over for frostbite—felt over his face and his ears, which were starting to hurt, with fingers possibly in worse condition.

But he wasn't the only one cold and miserable. He put his fire-warmed gloves back on, wincing with the pain, wrapped a scarf around his head and, taking a wooden pail from the corner, cracked the door to get snow from outside, packed it down with his fists and came back to the fire to melt it. While he waited for that, he delved into the two-pack and got out the strong-smelling salve that by some miracle or its pungent content wasn't frozen solid.

Burn was amenable to a rub-down, even if it took precedence over bacon, and Guil peeled out of his coat, called Burn over near the fire and rubbed on salve barehanded, chafed and rubbed until he'd broken a sweat himself, despite the cold walls and floor.

Burn was certainly more comfortable. Both of them were warmer. He thought his fingers might survive. He pulled off his boots and the cold socks, and applied the stinging salve to his feet, relieved to find the boots hadn't soaked through, that feeling was coming back, at least an awareness of his feet, and a keen pain above the ankles. He wasn't altogether sure he hadn't gotten frostbite. Couldn't tell, yet. And the toes wouldn't move. Couldn't afford to go through life with unsound feet. God, oh, God, he couldn't—limping along on the short routes where the horse could do all the walking.

He didn't want that for a future. He was more worried about his feet than about gunfire—so anxious that Burn in all sympathy came over and breathed on his feet, licked them, once, but the salve tasted too bad.

He'd have been safer and smarter, he thought now, to have camped in the open. He'd have been warmer sooner. A blizzard like this could pile up snow in drifts high as a shelter roof—it might not let up with morning or even next evening. The wind screamed across the roof—there was a loose shingle up there or a flashing or something that wailed a single rising and falling note on the gusts, a note you either ignored or let drive you crazy; but he was so glad of warm shelter tonight he told himself it was music.

Burn made another try at his feet. Burn was half-frozen and had a fearsome empty spot inside. <Miserable horse. Hungry horse. Looking for crumbs on floor. Hoping for pack to be open.>

"Hell," Guil moaned, and crawled over, stretched out an arm as far as he could reach and dragged the pack up close—fed Burn and himself jerky and a couple of sticky grain sweets, the kind he kept for moments like this, except his mouth and Burn's had been too dry too long out there, and Burn's throat was too raw, his tongue too dry to enjoy it.

But maybe, maybe there was a little bit of feeling in his feet. He tried moving his toes. Couldn't quite get all of them to work, but some did that hadn't—and finally, finally, he got movement out of them all.

Guil sighed then, with vast relief—took a pan out, thinking of other comforts, took his knife to thoroughly frozen bacon, having to lean on the blade to get through it.

There was water, finally. There was oil for biscuits—Burn got the bacon squares; he nipped a couple for himself.

By then his feet and hands had begun to hurt. Really hurt.

But the toes wiggled quite nicely, and he sat there content to watch that painful miracle while the biscuits nearly burned.

Meanwhile Burn, with water to drink and with the ambient a lot less <Guil scared> and <Guil hurting,> had his head blissfully in the grain bin, fending for himself in the absence of more bacon.

<Beautiful horse,> Guil thought, and offered Burn the first biscuits out of the pan.

They disappeared without hesitation. He made more, got one for himself out of the next pan. Burn got six. He found he hadn't as much appetite as he had thought—but before he lay down he stood up, hobbled painfully over to the door and pulled the latch-cord in to protect their sleep.

Then he stirred up more biscuits for the morning, put them on to bake over the coals; and after what felt like a second, Burn had to wake him up off the warm stones to get him to take them out. Burn knew <scorch> when he smelled it.

He ate one more biscuit then, put the rest by, and in shaky self-indulgence, made hot tea, assured now his teeth wouldn't crack if he drank it.

Among his Anveney purchases was a little metal flask of spirits, for steeping medicines, as he intended, not the luxury of drink.

But the shelter came, courtesy of the maintenance crews, for which he blessed their kindness—equipped with a bottle on the mantel, and he poured about a third spirits into his second cup of tea; sipped it ever so slowly, letting it seep into dry mouth and dry throat and burn all the way down.

It was the first time he'd looked at the rider board, up above the mantel. His heart nearly stopped.

Some not-so-bad artist had filled a large area of the board with a horse head, all jagged teeth, staring eyes, wild mane, ears flat to the skull.

Rogue horse. A warning to anybody who came here.

And he knew the sketch artist beyond a doubt when he saw, above it, the mark that was Jonas Westman.

Jonas had been in this place, on his way to Tarmin, Jonas and his partners—sitting here where he sat. They'd laid the fire he'd used.

Made that ghastly image.

But that wasn't the total source of disturbance. He was feeling something—faint, dim sense of presence.

—Something in the ambient, no image brushing the surface of his thoughts, just a whisper of life outside the shelter that sent his hand reaching for the rifle.

It had Burn's attention, too—head up, ears up, nostrils flared, as he stared toward the door.

<Jonas> was the first thought that came to him. <Jonas, Luke and Hawley coming through the snow and the dark.>

But the sending didn't seem to come from several horses. It wasn't strong, it wasn't loud and it shifted and eluded his conception of it, at times completely disappearing.

Shadow could feel that way—alone.

But Shadow wouldn't *be* alone. And he wasn't sure what it was. He wasn't sure it wasn't some passing cat—but no cat in its right mind would be out in a blizzard.

And it didn't travel. It strengthened, there and not-there, consistently strengthened, while he and Burn stayed still.

Horse. Horse, he was almost certain. Strengthening presence meant it was coming straight toward the shelter.

Single horse.

He grabbed up the rifle, cursed himself as he checked its action—long overdue precaution. He'd used the piece for a walking-stick. God knew what he'd done to it the time he'd gone down and bruised his knee. But it worked. He had a bullet ready.

He waited, conscious of that sketched image staring out across the room over his head. He felt the tension in Burn, felt—now and again—the sense of something reaching out blindly into the dark, feeling about it, looking.

A lonely something. A desperate someone. Burn didn't make the young-horse mistake of reaching back. They waited, quiet for a long, long while, anxious—but he began to want the thing, began to think about <Aby> and <rocks> and wanted that thing to come in, come to the gun-slit at the front of the cabin; get it over with, get it finished, the first night he was on the ridge.

He got up from the floor. He stood listening into the ambient, quiet, careful, not wanting Burn to commit too far, too dangerously out into that dark.

But it knew now that they were there. It skittered across his mind, canny, and scared, and desperate. He wanted to use his ears—hear it coming toward the door—but the wind screamed that single note across the roof, covering all sound else. He could feel it coming closer, and closer, and filling all the ambient, there and not there. He went to the wall, where the gun-port was—hesitated to unlatch it until he was reasonably sure what he was dealing with.

<Cold,> he felt it. <Hungry. Very hungry.> Then: <female horse.>

Burn made a strange soft sound. <Female,> entered the ambient. <Female wanting in. Male here. Male horse.>

Another thump. Hard. Two. Burn immediately grew excited, throwing his head and imaging back <male, male, male> as, over the shriek of the wind came an unmistakable nighthorse sound outside the door, a female's sound. Burn did a little sideways dance as Guil left the wall and grabbed a fistful of mane with his free hand.

"Burn, *dammit*, shut up." He got a breath. <Burn *quiet*.> God, <Burn quiet, quiet, quiet.>

"Let me in!" It was hardly a voice. It was maybe a rag of a human voice past the wail of the wind. The ambient was howling <female.> "Open the door. Open the door, do you hear me?"

Burn jerked the mane out of his hand, <wanting female.>

"Open the door!" the voice outside cried, thin and breaking. "Dammit!"

A blow thumped against the door. He saw <horse and rider, snow blowing. Snow on them.> He saw <shut door> and <fist hammering it.> Most of all he felt <desperate fear. Wanting in. Wanting *in*, something behind them—>

"There's a rogue loose!" he yelled back. "How do I know it's not you?"

"I'm not, you damn fool! God! Open the door! I left my camp, I smelled the smoke—I'm freezing out here, we're both freezing. Open the damn door!"

<Numb feet, numb hands. Cold horse.> They didn't feel insane. Bush wisdom held that sometimes a rogue seemed entirely normal. Then wasn't.

Burn was going crazy behind him, on totally different grounds, Burn was <wanting door open, door open, wanting out—>

But that was the mistake every victim made in the Wild. The voice outside, someone in desperate, mind-shaking need—the reason to open the door.

"God! Let me in! I'm not any damn rogue! Let me in, you damn coward! Open this door!"

Burn believed it. He began to believe it, telling himself it was still early in the season, there could still be a rider out, and he could find somebody frozen to death on his step.

It was a woman, he was sure it was a woman, by the horse and by the pitch in the voice when it cracked—and he'd no wish to deal with female horses or female riders; Burn was going crazy on him, Burn was going to go for the mare if he let them in—

"Open up!" Another thump of a fist. And he didn't see what else to do. He set the rifle aside, drew his pistol for closer range—then lifted the latch, gave the door a shove, and put his shoulders against the front wall.

The door dragged outward with a gloved hand pulling it. Then a horse, as forward as Burn, forced her head in—surged through, a snow-blanketed darkness that met Burn in the middle of the room and dodged him in a perimeter-threatening dance around and around a second time as Burn sniffed after <female> and the mare gave him a surly, <cold, hungry horse> warn-off.

He'd glanced at *them* like a fool—anxious about the horse. He glanced back a confused eyeblink later face to face with a muffled, snow-mantled and angry rider—as the mare shook herself from head to tail and spattered the whole room with snow and icewater.

"Who are you?" the rider demanded to know, and slammed the door shut. A gloved hand pulled off the hat and ripped the scarf off a head of dark hair, a pair of dark eyes, a wind-burned and pretty face—which was no comfort to a man hoping he hadn't just let two killers into the shelter with him and his horse. "What are you doing here?"

"My name's Stuart," he said, and didn't put away the gun. "Out of Malvey district. Who are you? The proprietor?"

"Tara Chang. Out of Tarmin village." Teeth were chattering. Hard. "Malvey's a far ride. What are you doing up here?"

"The rogue killed my partner. I'm afraid it's got your village."

A tremor of distress hit the ambient, but not strongly. The situation at Tarmin was no surprise to her.

But it was about all her constitution seemed able to bear. The <anger> bled out and she walked over to the fire—sank down on the hearthstones in a precipitate collapse of the legs, head down, gloved hands in hair. "Hell," she said, and the pain in the ambient drew the mare over to nose her rider's back.

The gun didn't seem so reasonable as it had. He wasn't sure. He kept expecting an explosion, a sudden shift into insanity. But with none in evidence, he put the gun back in holster, carried the rifle back to the far side of the fireplace, the side he determined to sit on—and thought of <biscuits> and <tea.>

"Yeah," she said. <Hungry.> Her eyes were pouring tears. She hadn't gotten her gloves off. God knew about her feet. Or her horse's.

<Salve,> he thought. <Warm nighthorse legs.>

She approved of that. She leaned and got the bottle of spirits—uncorked it and took a swallow.

You weren't supposed to do that. It was stupid when you were cold, but she didn't take another. He put on another pan of water to heat, and with a wary glance at the woman sitting on the hearth, eyes shut, cradling the bottle in her lap, decided he'd better fill water buckets again—his and the horses'.

Which meant the door opening, however briefly, and a cold gale swirling for a moment about the room while he packed one and then the other bucket with snow.

Burn didn't care. Burn was nosing about the mare as he came back in, pulled the door shut, and set the buckets on the hearth.

Interested—God. "Burn, let her alone, you damn fool! She's damn near frozen!" <Burn licking cold nighthorse legs. Beautiful horse. Nice nighthorse legs.>

Damn fool, he thought, and poured the woman tea in one of the shelter's cups. "The water barrel's frozen solid," he said. "It'll warm up by tomorrow, maybe."

"Yeah," she said.

"I'll rub your horse down. She'll be all right. Gloves off. Boots off. There's aromatic rub and there's snow for water."

"Yeah," she said, and started pulling gloves off with her teeth. He took the salve, of which he didn't have but half left, and started in on the mare's legs, while Burn licked the ice off the mare's back. The mare nipped Burn. But not hard.

"God, save it," he muttered to Burn. "There's problems. God!"

Burn sent him <sex> and <warmth> and he got a feeling that he didn't know words for, but it involved pushing himself on a woman when she hurt. The rider was upset, the mare was upset—

"Let her the hell *alone*, Burn, you damn fool, give her a chance to catch her breath."

"Flicker," Chang said from the hearthside. "Name's Flicker."

He caught the image. A lot like Shadow, only light, not dark. She was picking up the other business, too, and while neither of them was acutely embarrassed—she was no junior—he felt himself pushed and set upon by his own horse. In most respects he and Burn were a match. Not in this.

"Sorry," he said, and squatted down, arms on knees, as far away from her as he could and still feel the fire. "My horse is a fool. You want to quiet it down?"

"They're all right."

"Are you? Hands and feet?"

"All right." Her feet were bare. She wiggled toes, and meanwhile downed a piece of biscuit—she'd found them; chased it with spirit-laced tea.

She seemed to be. So he got up and got several of the shelter's blankets down from the shelf, <intending wrapping up in them, intending sleep, him with his blankets, her with hers,> and he didn't invite approaches. She and her horse seemed all right, he was entirely sorry he'd given her a hard go-over and kept her out in the cold—but wherever she'd walked from, those feet hadn't been cold as long as his had, and Tarmin's troubles weren't just today's event. A day ago—at least. She'd been somewhere safer than he had.

She mumbled, "Two days. I think it's two days." <Fire. Rogue-feeling.> She gave a shiver, and poured more of the spirits into the tea. Offered the bottle to him.

He wanted more awareness than that while he slept, though he was very glad to see she would sleep soundly.

She gave him a narrow look, thinking, <rapist.> Or that was the uncharitable way his mind interpreted it.

"No," he said, taking offense. But her thoughts were skittering about so fast he couldn't catch them, a lot about people he didn't know, a lot about a camp he thought must be Tarmin, about a jail and an alarm in the night.

Not comfortable thoughts to sleep with. There was <anger,> when they got loose, and <desire to kill,> but he didn't think—he didn't *think* it was an unnatural anger, or an unnatural pain. It just resonated too well with his own, that left him touchy and on the edge.

She took a precautionary look toward the door, <checking the latch,> then wrapped her two blankets around herself, with a persistent thought about a man—a rider—<in this place. Anger. Two women, both riders. Both very young. Deep anger.>

<Fire. Shots going off.

<Wanting them. Here.>

He understood that, God, he wished he could put a damper on that feeling, smooth it down, ease the pain, distance the memories. It was her lost partners she'd looked to find when she'd smelled the smoke and come battering at the door.

<"Who *are* you?"> with so much anger—

<Rogue-feelings. Scattering. Wanting kill, shooting horse, horse with blonde child, wanting—this—wanting—this—>

Then it went away. Guil got a breath. The horses did, snappish and dangerous in a closed space.

While Tara Chang sat in her blankets, rested her head on her jacketed arm and stared bleakly into the fire.

Guil sat there a moment—asking himself what he'd let in and what was over there with Burn.

Grief, he decided. A day old, no more. A loss that racketed off his own, and left him raw-nerved. He probably made it worse for her—couldn't help but make it worse for her.

<Still water,> he sent, kept it up until the horses had calmed down, until he saw the woman sigh and settle, and felt the ambient quiet enough to dare let go and try to relax.

The mattresses on the bunks might have warmed if he'd dragged them over and left them an hour or so at the fireside; but right now he was exhausted and the hearthstones were warmer. He took his own couple of blankets, laid his pistol down, wrapped in them and lay down in the fire-warmth, head on his much-abused hat and scarf, that he stuffed under him from where he'd dropped them.

He was still cold—as if ice had gotten clear into the core of him, and another wave of it was coming out to chill his skin. He lay there by another heavy-coated, living body, as cold as she was, with no erotic notions whatsoever and wondering if he dared shut his eyes.

But in a few moments of quiet, Burn and the mare were back to their quiet muttering of grunts and sniffing and sneezing—

The mare was tired, snappish, and out of sorts. Burn, going too far, nearly got something important nipped. He heard the row. More, he felt it, and twitched into a spasm of cold chill, knees drawn up, and wishing intensely that Burn would quiet the hell down.

The woman in front of him was a solid sleeping lump now. Two drinks, as tired as she looked to be, and probably the roof could fall on her unnoticed.

Probably it was safe to shut his eyes and get some sleep. He didn't have any reason to doubt her. Burn didn't doubt the mare, and kept at his courtship, somewhat more gingerly—which didn't make Burn's rider more comfortable. Guil turned over, arranged his arm over the gun and belt beside him.

In very remote case, he was sure. But he didn't believe in deliberate chances.

Meanwhile the horses were bickering, Burn was exhausted, sore, and impatient, having made the one perilous try at a chilled, sore-footed, sore-backed mare, and settled to a sullen male posturing—imaging <handsome horse, male, male, *male horse,*> until Burn's male rider was <desperate, mad male human, trying to rest. Burn lying down.>

Burn wouldn't. The mare was on her feet. Burn was <handsome young male.> Burn wasn't going to lie down in the presence of any <female horse standing.> If Burn deigned <mating with cold, wet female.>

"God." Guil took several deep breaths, and imaged, <*Horses lying down,*> loud and mad. Which was fit to wake his own bedmate. So he sent, <Quiet horses. Beautiful mare. *Lying down mare.*>

The mare settled down fairly abruptly, imaging—he was sure it was the mare—<sore legs, sore back.>

Burn postured, Burn circled twice, lifted and flagged his tail, preened a foreleg, finally—

<Rump down,> Guil sent furiously.

Burn preened the other foreleg, and gracefully, gracefully, settled to a noble resting posture—not damned comfortable, but, hell, <handsome horse,> Guil agreed, asking himself if he'd ever in his human life possibly been such an ass.

<Aby laughing, and him chasing Burn across the hillside.

<Aby laughing and laughing.>

He grew warm, finally. He shut his eyes, drifted toward sleep, listening to another shifting-about with the horses. Horses didn't mind resting their legs, but give it about an hour and a healthy horse would be up to sleep a while standing; and down again, when he tired of that—they weren't quiet sleeping partners, unless the night was very cold indeed.

Which it wasn't, with the fire going.

And now—

Now Burn wanted <outside, call of nature.>

God.

But Burn had to. It wasn't Burn's fault. Sex failed and the other urge of nature took over. You couldn't ask Burn to wait. You could want to shoot him—but, hell, you woke up, took your gun to guard the door, you got up—

He let Burn out. He stood there against the wall, freezing in the brief blast of cold air, testing whether human beings could nap standing up—he could manage it.

But now that Burn was outside, the mare wanted <out.>

Fine. <Mare outside.> He couldn't keep his eyes open. He opened the door and Burn wanted in where it was warm. Immediately. Burn came in, radiating cold, covered with snow. Shook himself.

Guil shut his eyes, folded his arms tightly to keep himself from folding over in the middle, braced his heels, and waited for the mare. While the wind shrieked over the loose shingle.

In not so long the mare wanted back in and he wearily opened the door, accepted another horse shaking herself and spattering snow about, as he shut the door and double-checked the latch, arguing with himself that the mare was perfectly sane, that possibly now that the horses were settled, he might settle.

Chang was staring at him over the top of the blankets.

"God," she said, and collapsed. <Scared> for a moment. She'd wakened and been confused where she was.

"Sorry." He came back, gathered his blankets around him and sat down—lay down, shivering, and put the gun beside him.

"We're not the rogue," the woman said.

"We aren't either," he said, laid his head on his makeshift pillow and wrestled the blankets up to his neck.

"I knew that."

"How?"

"Because I know who is." <Blonde girl. Red coat. Tracks in the snow, going out a gate.>

"God." He wanted desperately to shut his eyes and sleep. And he didn't want to believe what he was hearing. It complicated everything.

But it felt true. Everything about the woman felt true—and disturbing.

"A kid."

"Village kid," she said. "Name's Brionne Goss." <Gate recently opened, traces in the snow, kid's footprints, a horse sick—>

"Kid's dead, if she's out in this."

The woman didn't answer. There was too much of <anger,> of <grief. Two men on horses, leaving a gate, into snowy woods.> "My partners went out after her. Didn't come back."

He remembered the rider shelter north of the village. Remembered <horse bones> and shied off from that image too late, sending <regret,> sending <sorrow,> all he understood to give.

For a long, long moment the air was thick with emotions. The mare came over and trod on the blankets, nosing her rider's leg. Burn came, disturbed, and Guil sat up to lay a restraining hand on the offered nose. Pushed at it. <Quiet horse,> he wished, and with the mare near the woman, there was no coherent thought in the ambient, just roiling, dark, disturbance.

Burn made a quiet, disturbed sound—next to a <fight> warning. <Quiet,> Guil sent, and got to one knee, and slowly to his feet, wanting to get provocation out of the mare's reach. It was hard even to breathe, let alone to think. He backed Burn up, wanting <quiet horses.>

Then <rogue-image> leapt into the ambient, <painted image, firelit> grotesque, horrid, in her sight, in her mind, and <anger> and <killing> flew around the room. Burn reared—Guil grabbed trailing mane and skidded and held on as Burn shied.

Held him. Burn stood trembling with anger. Chang had the mare, had hold of her, scared, and <wanting to kill.>

<Quiet,> Guil urged at her, at Burn, at everything in reach. <Quiet. Painted board. Room. Fireplace.> He reconstructed it out of the dark. He sent <horses standing. Horses quiet,> and felt, finally, Chang's help quieting the mare. Chang wanted <hitting him.> But she got it under control, got the horse quiet.

"Small room," he said. "Easy. Tight space here."

"That your idea of a joke?" Meaning the image.

"I didn't do it. Didn't *do* it. Haven't even made my mark up there. Swear to you. Didn't make me damn happy either. Throw a blanket over it."

She got a breath or two. Thought about <blanket> and didn't do it. She was calmer. She calmed the mare, who was still throwing off <warning.> Chang was doing the same, shaky and still <mad.>

It was cold on this side of the room. He wanted <her giving him blankets.> He wasn't going close to her horse. He had enough trouble keeping Burn still.

For a moment things stayed as they were, balanced on a knife's edge of Chang's temper and his nerves. Then he felt the anger unwind, slowly, slowly, into a quieter disturbance. A few more breaths.

She shook at the mare's neck, wanting <easy, relax,> and thought <him at fireside, wrapping in blankets.> She was shaken and upset. She wanted—<quiet.>

He understood—he didn't expect her to get that much steadiness back, not that fast. He wished he'd thought to cover that damned thing.

"It's stupid," she said, shaky-voiced. "Not that good a drawing. I ate your damn supper, I've no right to chase you off your own fireside."

He wasn't sure. Burn wasn't sure. Burn snorted and got between them, with him holding onto Burn's mane most of the way. But he ducked past Burn's neck, <not sure> about the offer. Flicker had her ears laid back. He wasn't confident the woman was all that steady.

"I knew," she said, "God, I knew, I just—"

—hadn't let it get loose, he thought, and stayed where he was as she made another effort and took a furtive wipe at her eyes. She turned deliberately and stared at the image on the wall. Stayed that way for a long moment, then patted the mare on the shoulder, jaw tight, eyes aswim with moisture, and went back to the fireside.

He stood there. He didn't know what else to do. She straightened hers, she straightened his. The horses were confused at this flapping of blankets and shadows, uneasy, not knowing clearly what the disturbance was. <Rogue horse> had been in her mind and his. It wasn't good.

She finished tidying up. Stood there in front of the fire and lost her battle. A man's face was in the ambient, and she couldn't breathe—*he* couldn't, and then the mare was coming at him, scored a nip on his sleeve as Burn snaked a neck past, defending him.

He cast about for a broom, a stick—and *she* dived in and grabbed the mare's mane—he flung himself in Burn's way, shoving at his chest, she was shoving at the mare—holding, pushing, <back, back, back, quiet> until they had a perilous quiet established. The bottle had gone spinning across the hearth, unbroken. The blankets were almost in the fire.

She was shaking. He was. They had it broken up, stood there reassuring horses until everything was quiet, inside—while the wind kept screaming its two notes into the spooked, treacherous dark. She wanted <him by fire,> wanted <humans sitting down, wrapped in blankets, wanted <horses quiet, beautiful horses> and he put his own agreement behind it. <Quiet Burn. Nighthorses together. Humans sitting. Warm us.>

Dangerous as hell. She was scared. He was scared. There were scars on the walls. There was blood drawn, minor nips, but it wasn't a time to push the horses. She put a cold hand in his, they made a tentative peace, pats on the shoulder, a demonstration of nonhostility while the horses were bickering and threatening each other. She'd pulled herself together. She'd used her head. He turned a pat into an arm around the shoulders, a quick, comradely squeeze with nothing behind it but thanks for her good sense, but she flinched away from it, and the ambient was still queasy.

In what seemed a second thought, then, she caught his arm and had him sit by the fire, shoved blankets at him and wrapped herself in her own. Her hands shook, holding the blanket under her chin. <Sun through evergreen,> she was sending, a calm-sending. <Sun through branches. Sun through branches, gentle wind.>

"I'm fine," she stuttered. "F-F-Fine."

A fool would breach that calm-sending. He said with feeling, "It's all right, woman. Just breathe."

"Didn't have a choice about being in here. They're dead. They're all dead. I th-thought I was handling it. Th-Thought Vadim at least—m-might have made it. He was the best. He was the best, but he—" <Kid in red coat.> "He'd g-go after that damn k-kid. Him and Chad. Both."

He didn't want to stir it up. But he asked himself <Woman and man leaving village,> and it couldn't help but be a question.

She shook her head. "No." <White. Moving white. Covering the whole world.> "Flicker. Flicker got me out. Wasn't thinking. Left my damn g-gun. I didn't do too well."

"Doing damn all right, woman. You're alive." He was <glad> of her calm. He was glad of her *life* after the thing he'd just felt. He felt the shakiness still in her, knew there wasn't a way in hell to reach into a woman's private thoughts and patch anything, no matter if he wanted to, no matter how good his intentions—couldn't prevent her doing what she'd do, wasn't right to want to. If he'd learned one thing from Aby, that was true.

He'd not held on to her. He'd not tried to change her.

And she'd died.

She reached out and laid her hand on his knee, shook at him to get his attention, her face glistening with tears, <throat tight> as his was. "Name's Tara," she said, pointed reminder.

"Yeah," he said.

"Aby?"

You couldn't hear words in the ambient. He didn't know how she came up with the name. But <Aby> was in her imaging, too. <Aby in the high country. Aby and somebody like Westman and herself riding together, in the winter snow.>

"You *knew* her," he said.

"A lot of years. Last winter. When she stayed over. You're *that* Stuart. *Her* Stuart."

He nodded. Wanted more of that image. Desperately wanted the missing pieces of Aby's life. The questions he couldn't answer.

"She's dead?" She hadn't known. "What in hell happened?"

He threw it into the ambient. It was easier than talking about what words didn't say anyway. <Rogue-feeling. Truck going off. Aby—>

"I saw the wreck." <Truck on the rocks. Tilted. Dead.> "I'd no idea—God."

"So I'm going after that thing. Get it stopped."

"By yourself?" Then <rogue-image.> "Like hell you are."

"I'd rather," he began on <you going to village.>

She shook her head, <seeing him,> now, <Guil in firelight.> "Two of us. That much more chance."

He wasn't happy about it. He wanted her safe. Didn't want any more dying.

"I need a gun," she said. "You can't use two at once."

"Woman, —"

"Name's Tara."

"Guil," he said. "*My* guns." That was damn selfish. He was being a jerk. But he wasn't getting killed, either. "I'll hand you one for backup. When it matters." He'd admitted she was going with him. He didn't see anything else to do but give her a gun and send her off alone. Which meant she'd still hunt it.

"All right," she agreed after a moment. "All right." She wasn't mad. She didn't blame him. Damn brave woman, he thought, going out there not knowing if she'd have a gun if he was incompetent.

She didn't feel like somebody who'd panic. She'd known Aby. That was something.

"We'll get it," he said. He didn't know, after that. Didn't have any plans, after that.

Except Cassivey's orders. Except next spring.

She sat there staring at the fire. He wrapped the blankets around his shoulders and looked at it too.

The horses wandered back to their courtship. She sat there remembering her village and her partners and trying for quiet.

Finally she lay down on her side and pulled the blanket up to her ears. He did the same, listening to the horses—<tired horses, both,> Burn having settled to better manners. The mare was still scatter-witted, concerned for her rider, a cold-water bath for Burn's attentions.

He wasn't sorry. He really, really wanted rest from emotional images and emotional situations. She didn't think about him. It was all, all <faces, moments, laughter around a rider quarters, man in bed, men on horses, women riding with her, sometimes Aby among them> as she sat there, still as the frozen dead.

Clenched fist. Steady stare. For a long, long time no thought but the patterns in the fire. She'd reached the angry stage.

Best help he could be, he decided, was do the same, image nothing but <fire patterns.>

She let go a sigh and lay down. Her concentration wobbled. He kept seeing <patterns in the coals,> and the horses settled, <tired horses, quiet horses, warm horses, side by side.>

One wasn't tempted to linger in the necessaries in the morning: the small add-on joined by a too-efficient door to the main cabin had no heat but the natural insulation, one suspected, of snow piled up over the roof—and one was very glad to be back inside and back in front of the fire.

Tara Chang took her turn while he put tea on and toasted biscuits over a renewed fire. Horses were hungry—horses had to be let out for their own necessities, and let back in out of the howling gale.

It was still whiteout outside. If Jonas had gotten back to shelter in Tarmin, depend on it that Jonas was going to stay put, postponing all questions until the storm had stopped, and hell if he wanted to see Jonas right now—he'd enough on his mind without dealing with Hawley.

"Autumn's definitely over," Tara said, shivering her way inside, and shutting the door fast.

"Looks like." He was uneasy. He wanted to keep the light mood she attempted, but he'd thought of Hawley and Jonas and his mind wanted to go ranging after questions he didn't want to ask himself. He was cooking a taste of bacon for the horses, to go with <grain> and he'd make hot mash, but <Guil and the woman eating biscuits.> He was being very firm about that. He had water heating for the mash. Which Burn liked adequately well. He wasn't in the least remorseful about the biscuits.

Tara made the mash, perfectly nice mash, mixed grains. A little bacon to flavor it.

Riders sat and toasted biscuits, and ate slowly, because it was certain they weren't going anywhere while the wind was howling like that.

He thought about Shamesey, in a long silence marked by horses bashing buckets against the baseboards. He thought about winter drifts, and evergreen, and high villages.

"Verden," she said. And he guessed it was Verden he was thinking about.

Where Aby'd spent no few days.

"Guys I've worked with, Aby's crew, they're back at Tarmin holed up. Guy who drew that thing—" He indicated the picture overhead. "You could go back there, if anything happened to me. They're all right, I mean, I think you'd be all right with them. They're probably after the thing too, but if something did happen—"

"I don't miss."

"I've been known to," he said. He hated infallibility. Considered it lethal. "I've decided you're right. One human hasn't a chance. So if anything happens, you go back, get Westman. Tell him—" He decided against what he'd like to say, which was Go to hell.

"I'm not going to tell him a damn thing. I know who you mean. I don't like those guys."

Didn't exactly surprise him. He didn't exactly like them, himself, but he couldn't find a cause against them.

It occurred to him that why was a reasonable question.

"What's the matter with them?"

"Just—stand-offish. Just not damn friendly."

"That's Jonas. And his horse."

She flung some small dark bit into the fire. Bark chip, maybe. There was a lot of it on the stones. She didn't talk for a moment. She wasn't happy with things. "Aby said—"

She couldn't leave that hanging.

"What?"

"Said she was worried. I don't know what about. I don't know what had happened. The last time, this last trip, before she went with them up to Verden with the trucks, she rode over to us, said—God, she said she wasn't staying around them longer than she had to, they were into her business . . . that was what she said."

He bit his lip. Found his pulse racing. <Wanted> to know. "Did she say what that business was?"

"I don't know. Only—you know, they don't run the Tarmin shipment uphill and then down again, they just set a date and our trucks meet them and join up at the downhill. So she gave us the date. And two of our guys, Barry and Llew, they took the trucks out with one of our road repair crews. And you know, usually when the convoys join the convoy boss sorts out who's going where in the line—"

"Yeah." That was normal.

"Some bosses, after they sort the trucks out, camp there that night. Aby did, usually. But they didn't ever stop. My partners were behind our trucks, and they just started rolling, and our guys, they stayed with the repair crew, ready to move them up when the trucks had cleared the road. But the whole convoy was just on down the mountain. Never did even *see* the riders. —It's not that unusual if there's weather threatening. There's a truck pullout a couple of hours on down. And some bosses just had rather make the time. Aby'd said she didn't want to spend time with them. I guess we all assumed she was anxious to get down—down the mountain. But she wasn't with them, was she?"

"No. She wasn't." He was very careful with his edges. <Still water.> "They were spooked. That's *their* story. The rogue showed up and spooked the convoy, sent Aby and Moon right off the mountain."

"I took supplies and more crew up to the road repair just a few days ago. They'd found the wreck <way down the mountain.> Our guys thought it could be a month old. They had no idea."

He was getting madder, and madder. Burn was disturbed. He tried to calm himself.

"Jonas knew," he said. And then broke a promise Aby'd died keeping: "There was gold on that truck. Whole year's shipment."

She wasn't knocked-down surprised. Mildly, maybe. "They said it went with the convoy before."

"They."

"Rumors. There are always rumors. But—"

She was confused. Thinking about <rogue.>

"Jonas imaged me about a rogue spooking the trucks," he said. "A rogue killing Aby. —Hell of a coincidence, isn't it? A rogue—and that one truck—the one with the gold?"

"The rogue's real," she said.

"Yeah," he said, and sat staring into the fire until he'd calmed himself from the attempt to add that up.

Sometimes things just happened. Sometimes the luck was just against you. But *bet* on it that Jonas Westman knew what was in that truck. Lead truck, it had been: he resurrected that from the image he'd gotten. Aby'd gone over the edge. It had.

<Wrecked truck. Logs scattered like straws down the rocks.> That was Tara Chang's memory. The way it had been when she'd visited the site. No bones. Nothing. What died in the Wild vanished before morning.

A lot of riders went that way. Just disappeared. Just gone.

* * *

The storm was still piling up snow in Tarmin streets—drifts were halfway up the windows, and they opened the door to shovel their way out—Danny worked up a sweat, and the village kids, shoveling with less fury but longer duration, made it to the porch.

Not senior riders. It was juniors' work. Senior riders sat warming their feet inside.

Juniors carried the wood. Filled the water barrel with clean snow that floated white in black water. Seniors complained about the length of time the door was opened, and burned more wood.

Something had turned last night. Danny tried not to think about it, but there was something unpleasant in the ambient, and Cloud was surly and snappish enough to match Shadow's disposition.

"What are they mad about?" Randy asked when they were out on the steps.

"Missing Stuart, probably." It wasn't the truth. He wasn't sure what was the truth; but something had gone skewed from the moment Jonas lectured them last night on false hopes, and that image had come to him which he didn't want to think about.

So he went back in. They had the storm shutters set back for the daylight hours, barred them only at night—and he'd found books, ten of them, the whole that the store offered for sale. He sat down by the window in the white light reflected from the snow, and read about <old kings and battles with swords.>

He found a strange lot of attention on him then. The boys were staring. Jonas and Luke and Hawley were. And the horses.

It was funny, he'd never read around the horses before. He'd just gotten into the habit of picturing things in his head since long, long ago, when mama would read to him and Sam and papa.

Sam never got good at it. Sam wanted to be down in the shop. Sam didn't want to study. Sam wanted to marry somebody who read.

Mama had read aloud.

"You can go on," Luke said, meaning he wanted more, but Luke wasn't going to admit it out loud. So he read to them.

It was an easy place to dive into, full of images. The horses were confused, but they liked some of it, he guessed—Cloud kept trying to fix the images so they looked more like Cloud understood, which wasn't a real help; and sometimes his audience did the same, until the images were something they more agreed on. Jonas cut in, on the king's side. You could guess. The boss-man couldn't be a fool. The story had to bend until the boss-man found some vindication.

He read until his eyes were tired, and until he was at a place and a turn of the story that he could shut the book and think about it and nothing else—like wanting the storm to end, so they could go out and go find Stuart before Harper did. And stopping the rogue so they could find someplace safe, and quiet, and he and the boys wouldn't have to take orders.

He sat by the fire and had himself a snack—he never in his life thought he could get tired of ham.

"Could go on another day," Carlo said. "Never knew it longer. But it could, I guess." Carlo ducked his head, <wanting to say something.>

"Quiet," Danny said, feeling the disturbance. "Calm down. Say words. Don't picture things."

"When they go out of here, after him, I mean, are you going with them?"

He'd shifted thinking about that. He'd begun thinking differently since last night. And he was scared.

"I don't know." He tried to think about the stove, whether it needed cleaning out: they'd been <burning a lot of wood.> About the story. <Kings and swords.> "I really don't know." He owed Stuart. He didn't trust what was going on. <Going with Jonas> put the boys in danger; going put the boys out there where their <sister> was.

"She's our sister," Carlo said urgently. "She might listen to us."

"She might not. You want your brother to be there?"

Carlo was scared, too. Cloud moved up and nosed in between them, jealous of anything that wasn't him. Danny shoved him with a hand on his chest, not even thinking about it. Carlo put his hand on Cloud from the other side. Cloud didn't offer to bite.

"I want her alive," Carlo said, and it was the truth. "I don't like her. But I want her out of this."

"What about Randy?"

"Is here safe?" Carlo asked. "Even if you stayed, is here really safe?"

It wasn't. Not with Harper loose. Not with a lot else that was going on. But he couldn't avoid Jonas.

There was leisure for shaving, for washing clothes to dry in front of the fire—not damn much else to do. They washed up the pans they'd used and then, with the wind still howling over the roof, Tara spent a long, long time working over Flicker's mane and tail.

That made Burn jealous. <Mare's rider combing mare's mane. Guil sleeping. Burn with twigs and leaves. Burn covered in mud.>

Mud, hardly. But he owed Burn on this trip. He got up and combed until Burn's tail and mane were drifting silk. Brushed a perfectly good nighthorse hide until Burn was starting to complain of pain.

"Pretty fellow," Tara said, and stroked <pretty nighthorse neck.> Burn did have male muscle and a healthy sheen that made ripples when he flexed it. As he did. Of course.

With Tara <scratching Burn under chin.>

Hell, Guil thought, seeing desertion and conspiracy. He wasn't feeling at all sociable this afternoon, if it was afternoon. He was stuck inside, under roofs, with the hearing company of a woman he liked, to whom he was bound to be polite, while irreconcilable facts were churning around in his head and he was wanting to shoot Jonas Westman for suspicions he couldn't fix in any world of fact.

So he skulked off with his surliness and his suspicions to clean his guns, which could take a considerable time if it needed to; and he took all the time and care he could justify at it.

But a man could only spend so long oiling guns and doing mending and washing dishes, while two fool horses were at a whole damned afternoon and evening of foreplay. It was going to be a lot worse come nightfall—he only hoped to God the storm kept going long enough to let two lovelorn horses get it worked out and at least quieter. He didn't want to imagine the rogue coming calling when the ambient was as erotically charged as it was—particularly since Tara was sure, at least in the ambient she'd relayed, that the rogue was female.

A scary situation if you were the one on the damn lunatic autumn-hazed male. He couldn't hold Burn. No way in hell he could hold Burn from going right off a cliff, the same way Aby couldn't have held Moon, on that road, with an edge too close.

A tightness hit his chest. He was a lot better. He really was. Temper wasn't helping it. Suspicion that Aby's death didn't need to have happened if people had been sane—wasn't helping it.

Aby'd been carrying secrets all right, secrets that the villagers had guessed and a horse would pick up on. Aby'd been carrying just too damn *much* without her partner. She'd picked up something from Jonas she didn't like. She *could* have thought it related to the gold. She was trying to protect Cassivey's contract—and if the word got gossiped about, Cassivey wouldn't be happy.

Jonas might not be after the gold as money. But the deal Aby had with Cassivey—Jonas could want that real bad. Aby and her regular partner hadn't been together much in the last two years. Maybe Jonas had just gotten ideas and *that* was why Jonas wouldn't face him at Shamesey. Aby's good living off Cassivey sure as hell explained Jonas coming back up here. She was making money. She was making a lot of money; by what Cassivey was paying him, she was stuffing it in that bank account hand over fist, —and for what? What did a rider need, beyond her supplies and her guns and her winter-over?

Time.

God. *Time.*

They *talked about* going into the hills and not working for a while. And they'd always made just about enough for winter-over. They spent too much. *He'd* spent too much. He hated towns. Hated the crowding, the noise—hung about them for her sake. She'd said—hadn't she?—that someday they'd make the money, buy the time, take the break to go back to the high country—and he'd known it would never happen.

Aby had *pleaded* with him to join her at Anveney. He'd refused. She'd gotten mad. And hurt. And they hadn't talked about it. But winter at Shamesey let her do those jobs at Anveney. And make money she wasn't spending.

That was what she'd been doing with her secrecy. That was why she'd been hurt. The big plan. The trip back to the south. The year off work. And Jonas moved in on her.

Tara sank slowly down on her haunches in front of him and rested her elbows on her knees, chilled hands in front of her mouth. The air was scarily tense. The wind screamed a steady song into the world.

Good man, Tara thought. Honest man.

And so damn much <anger,> so much <pain>—which he was so, so careful to contain in himself—all the signs of someone who'd been with the horses so early and so long that, hurt and hit, he had only the instinct to hold pain close and kill it, before it killed him, his horse, his partner.

She knew. She was smothering a lot of it herself. And she didn't know what to say that wouldn't intrude where only that partner ever had. Different from her—who'd had a set of lovers, interchangeable and easy. But with Aby Dale—and him—she got images of <children.> Of <yearling horses.> Of a whole life—

Fights. Reconciliations. Arguments.

Love had never changed, in all of it.

"Listen," she said, in the face of his skittish suspicions. "Don't—don't shoot Jonas Westman. All right? You don't know. If he shows up—and he could, when the storm quits, don't—"

"My business."

"Yeah," she said, and knew when to back off. She began to get up.

He caught her wrist. Not hard. Didn't have words framed—just—image. <Jonas Westman and the others. A gate. Village gate. Big town gate. Shots fired.>

"At you?"

"I don't know. I don't know. Now—I think so. But I've known them a lot of years. I don't know how to think. Maybe they just knew there was a secret. Maybe they were prying at it. Maybe they were just worried about her. —Maybe—I don't know how *she* thought, you know? —I don't know."

"I don't either," she said, and was going on to say—But Aby

would care what happens to you. I don't want you to do something you could be sorry for—

She was almost to saying—*I* could care. I don't want you hurt.

But another image overrode.

<Horse wanting out.>

"Hell," she said. It was Flicker. But it was Burn, too. One had the idea, and then the other did.

Guil shook his head, and then looked up.

In silence. Or near silence. The screech of the wind on the shingle had sunk away to an occasional flutter.

"Storm's letting up," she said. "Or we're covered up over the roof."

Burn was pawing at the floor. Nudging the latch with his nose.

"Damn, Burn. Hold it, can you?" Guil got up, snapped the loaded cylinder closed and gave it to her as she got up.

Meaning guard the door.

He went and shoved the latch up.

The door wouldn't budge. Burn shoved it, and it gave a little. Not much.

"Well," she said, meaning it had to be the snow-door, which meant moving a table, and unscrewing two heavy bolts that held a wooden bar as thick as her arm. Bear-bars, they called them. With reason.

She moved the table, he unscrewed the bolts, and pulled the door open on a shoulder-high wall of snow with dark above it and a wind still fit to blast cold air and snow into the room.

Burn pawed at it, got purchase and began digging furiously. "Burn!" Guil yelled in protest, nothing availing, and Tara got the snowshovel and began making a heap of it on the floor. Coats were definitely in order.

"Damn," Guil complained, pulling his on, and then took over the shoveling, piling the stuff in the middle of the board floor as first his horse, then Flicker behind him broke their way through a considerable drift. The wind was cold. A pile of snow in the room was quickly sending a trail of icemelt across the boards to a low corner under the bed. It was disgusting. And Tara inhaled a cold gust, shrugging into her coat, and felt like chasing out after the horses and breathing the free wind herself.

The horses had broken through into the night outside. They nipped each other and plowed through small snowbanks because they were there, they did their essential business when the urge took them, marking the area as theirs—and got to flirting with shadows, tails up, snow flying, while two humans froze, shoveling out the snow two horses had kicked into the room.

<Horses coming *in*,> Guil insisted, when they'd cleared everything but white traces of the shovel edge and a huge wet spot off the boards of the floor. <Snow on us. Cold, miserable humans.>

There was no sympathy. There was a rogue out there somewhere in the woods, and two fool horses wanted to play tag through brush that masked holes and drop-offs. <Flicker!> Tara sent furiously. <Flicker inside. Grain and water.>

Thirsty work, shoveling or digging. That drew the rascal, who came shaking her mane and shaking herself once she was inside, a spatter of quickly melting snow; Burn was right behind, hardly slower to spatter them and the room, with a whip of his tail to finish it—and no question in the world what was on both minds now. Flicker got her drink, from the bucket they kept full; and Burn moved in for a few gulps of water while two frosted humans were securing the snow-door to keep the heat in the room and the bears out.

But before they were done, the ambient was awash in <male horse> and <female> and there seemed to be a second source of heat in the room.

Two half-frozen humans went to the fire, nonetheless, to warm their chilled hands—impossible to ignore what was going on in the room, impossible not to feel the heart speeding and sensitivity increasing in areas one politely—desperately—tried not to think about.

And did, because it was impossible to believe a man and woman in the same room with those two were going to clench their teeth till daybreak.

She tried to concentrate on the fire. But she looked at him the same moment he looked at her, <seeing if she was looking> and it was like one thought, awareness of each other—impulses shooting through the parts in question. He was trying <not,> but she didn't think he was winning. She wasn't. Air seemed very scarce in the vicinity.

"Oh, hell," she said, or something like, and he was a degree closer and she was—they might both have leaned. A thickly padded hug gave way to a totally mindless intention, mouths meeting mouths and breathing finding some way to happen.

Burn and Flicker were down to basics; but humans had clothes to go, and bare skin in a chilled room, and blankets that somehow the other party was sitting on, that resisted being wrapped around fast enough to keep the chill away, so her rear was cold, but she didn't figure out where the end of the blanket was, and didn't care.

After that—after that were explosions, intermittent rest, and a quieter trial or two, with the horses quiet enough to let them feel their way around each other's sensations, new to each other, and old as their experiences, and full of ghosts.

He was thinking <Aby> through half of it. She was thinking, <Vadim> now and again—but not that she didn't care. They were both confused, and so much was still recent with them that neither of them could straighten out where they were.

But within the ambient, human heartbeats began to be in unison—which bothered the horses, whose hearts beat in a different time. A feeling ran through her like electricity, coming from his hands, coming from the air—the horses found their own preoccupations, but he was <holding on to her,> he was <body in body,> the sole shuddering link keeping them both from flying off into the dark. . . .

<Distracting her from the dark behind her brain—where <white-white-white> was safety.>

<That godawful dizzy turn out of a steep grade—> that was his personal terror.

Then <both falling.> Fright at first, then a long, pleasurable, leisurely descent until they were breathing together, settled together.

Hands held matching hands. Fingers clenched. The floor and the room still tried to come and go until the horses drifted to sleep, finally, themselves exhausted, and left them in a leaden, blind dullness of senses, just the physical touch, fingers on fingers, arm against arm.

They didn't talk. He just touched. That it kept on to its own unaided and less acute conclusion meant something, she wanted to think, if only that they each wanted the kind of human contact you got alone in barracks, in the few places riders found to do things the blind, strange way humans did alone—for different reasons. Like companionship. Like sensation in that blind, numb state, far from the horses, when the world seemed so scarily quiet.

It was an autumn craziness. It meant not a damned thing.

And did. He'd let her inside, all the while afraid he might have let Aby's killer inside with him.

He'd let her close to him—all the while skittish and wary of the betrayals he expected, and had gotten, from men who should have helped him.

Gold; and motives for accidents that weren't accidents—a boxful of gold hadn't mattered in his thoughts; it was his partner. It was only his partner.

Damned if she was going to ride off from him.

They were going out of here tomorrow. They were half dug out, only had to get the main door clear and bolt the snow-door tightly shut—in case Aby Dale's working partners wanted the shelter tonight.

They could go to hell. But you didn't leave a shelter so somebody else couldn't use it. Even the likes of them.

Fingers squeezed hers. With the horses asleep, higher things didn't come through. Worry could.

She turned her head. Stuart looked asleep. She kept watching. He gave no sign he wasn't. But he turned over and faced the fire then. So she suspected he hadn't been.

Truck. Rolling down the mountain. Faster and faster.

<Yelling—<warning—>>

Horses snorted. Danny waked with his heart thumping, the boys were awake—everybody in the room was awake, the ambient still awash with terror, and the remembrance of <falling. Brakes failed. Wrench—>

He suddenly felt <attack,> spun over on one arm with the realization it wasn't a dream—that somebody was coming at him, <mad—>

Cloud squealed a warning and dived for the man. Bit. Hard—and everybody was scrambling for their feet—horse hit the stove and recoiled with a squeal of pain and rage.

<"Calm down!"> cut through the anger: Jonas; and Shadow. It was Froth that had gotten singed, not bad, but it hurt, and Luke was trying to get Froth quieted, while Danny got his hands on Cloud and tried to keep Cloud from going for Ice.

"It's that damn kid," Hawley yelled. "It's that kid making the trouble, it's been him since Shamesey. We're leaving him. Him and the village kids. We don't need him."

Cloud wanted <bite Hawley.> Hawley's coat was all that had saved him as it was.

"I didn't do anything," Danny said. "I'm sorry if you think I did, but I didn't. I don't want any trouble."

<Machinery. Hydraulic line. Leaking.>

"Hawley," Jonas said. "Hawley, what's the picture? What's going on?"

It had become a quiet, all but breathless night—the wind, Danny suddenly realized, was quiet. He had his hands on Cloud, <quiet, quiet.>

"Fisher?" Jonas said coldly.

"I didn't say anything. I didn't *think* anything." The boys were <scared,> thinking of <gunfire in the streets. Fire. Murder.> Carlo was holding on to Randy, wanting <him in the shadows, behind him, safe.>

"Hawley," Luke said. "What did you do? What did you *do*, Hawley?"

"I didn't do a damn thing. I was watching them <fix the truck,> when we stopped, that was all, the line was <leaking,> that was all."

"Line was leaking," Jonas said. "What line was leaking?"

Hawley didn't say. But Danny didn't think Hawley needed to say.

"Hawley," Jonas said, and Shadow was a flickering, smothering

<presence,> loud, God, he was loud. "I want the truth, Hawley. Once this trip, I want the truth."

"They thought we were thieves! Piss on 'em, I said, you want I should stop us here, and no, they said—"

<Money. Bills. Paper money in men's hands.> "Hawley," Jonas said.

"Hell, it's *him* making it up! I didn't take any damn money!"

"Hawley. Aby's dead. Aby's <dead,> you son of a bitch. *What happened?*"

Ice was on the verge of attack. Shadow was. Froth was on edge with pain. Danny wanted <quiet. Quiet water. *Quiet*,> with all the strength Cloud had; joined Shadow's fight for the ambient, and Ice backed up, shook his head, snorted in confusion.

"They gave him money," Luke said, "they didn't want to stall up there, they'd been spooks all during the trip. They didn't want us to put a hold on that truck and leave it in the village, and they gave him money. Didn't they, Hawley?"

"I said I thought they ought to tarp that truck and leave it there, but they didn't like it, *we* knew what they had in that cab, they were being damn spooks about it. Aby was giving off like crazy she didn't trust anybody, all trip long—it wasn't my damn fault, Luke, the whole damn trip was screwed—I mean, Aby was boss, she was going to see that truck rolled right then, and they give me money, what was I going to do?"

"And they wanted to go on down. Right then."

"I was going to tell Aby. But they put the chocks off and they rolled, Jonas, I was going to tell her about the brakes."

"And not us. Why not tell *us*, Hawley?"

<Money.>

"You damned fool."

"Well, they give it to me. I didn't see any reason not to take it."

"Yeah," Jonas said. "Hawley, I want to talk to you. Outside."

"I don't want to talk."

"Then maybe you better come across with all of it. Here."

"None of their business."

Meaning him and the boys, Danny thought, and wasn't happy

about hearing whatever Hawley had done wrong, either. But Luke said,

"Pretty clear, isn't it? Hawley. We're not blaming you. You took the money. They gave it to you. So what did you do?"

Hawley took a while about it. "I was going to tell you. But I shouldn't've took the money. Aby'd be mad. I was going to give it back next stop."

Jonas was intensely frustrated. Angry. And trying to hold it. Danny stood patting Cloud's neck, wanting <quiet water.> Carlo moved up by him, full of questions Carlo didn't dare ask.

Jonas said, finally, "Storm's stopped. We'd better see if we can catch Stuart. Tell him what happened."

"Man's like to shoot us," Hawley protested. "We got the rogue out there—we got—"

"One hell of a mess," Jonas said. "One hell of a mess is what we've got. *Dammit*, Hawley."

"I didn't think it'd hurt. They said it'd hold. They was driving it, I mean they was willing to drive it. . . ."

"Yeah. They were stupid, Hawley, does 'stupid' make sense to you?"

Danny let go a breath. Luke said,

"Froth's got a burn. If we're going out there, I want to grease it down good—it's going to hurt like hell."

"Yeah," Jonas said. "Do that."

"So what happened?" Carlo whispered, at Danny's shoulder. "What did Hawley do?"

"I think the truckers bribed him, something about bad brakes."

But that wasn't the only question in his own mind. Bad brakes on a bad road. Truckers not wanting to stop, where they probably couldn't turn around.

Why?

Luke had found the salve. Jonas was putting his pack together. So was Hawley.

"Are we going?" Randy asked.

Danny said, "Not staying here. Pack up. Now."

Chapter — xxi —

THE RISING SUN CAST THE ROAD IN SHADOW, A BLANKET OF SNOW earlier trafficked by the ordinary dawn scurriers-about. Since they'd left Tarmin gate in the dark and in all the haste they could manage with two of their party afoot, the horses had been on edge, putting out hostile impulses, Shadow earliest and most assertive to warn a spook out of his path.

But they were clear of the attraction Tarmin posed to vermin. Cloud lazed along, thinking <cattle,> and not unhappy to have a separate place at the rear, the boys walking along on either side as Danny rode.

Everything was business, up front. Jonas wasn't pleased with Hawley, that was clear any time they came close; but Danny stayed out of it; and not wanting to push anybody including Hawley, with thoughts that Hawley could take for accusations, Danny thought <blue sky,> sometimes, and sometimes <evergreens and sunlight> and sometimes told for the Goss boys what creatures had made the various tracks, imagined them, little mental ghosts, that occupied the road-as-it-had-been in the boys' imaging.

So they could know what made them. So they'd learn what they watched for, and what was dangerous and what wasn't. Senior riders and a horse with a good nose had taught him. And he didn't know but what at some moment the seniors were going to take off at the speed they could use if they had to.

Hawley rode point. It hadn't been his habit earlier. Luke and Jonas rode to the center and back a little, but one in the track of the other, all in light snow that taxed the horses very little.

<Still water,> Danny thought, on the edge of notions he didn't want to think. He thought <ham sandwiches,> of which they had a great number—but he didn't want to fuss with getting food out of his pack, and he didn't want his hands encumbered. He preferred to wait for the sun and the greater surety they wouldn't have a sudden alarm.

So he began to talk idly to the boys about growing up in Shamesey town, about <his father and the shop,> about <working on the machines—>

<Mama and the furniture. Mama sanding and painting.>

But the boys were distracted, out of breath, thinking about what would happen if Jonas and the rest did decide to increase the pace as he began to feel they were doing.

"It's all right," Danny said. "They don't go long at a run. Horses won't take it. Sun's up, horses are wanting to move—they'll settle down."

"What if we meet something?" Randy asked.

"Hey, I'm not leaving you. I'm not moving with them, all right?"

So they slogged along at the best pace they could with their breath frosting in the morning light, Randy walking beside Cloud's shoulder, putting a hand on Cloud when the going got uneven. And the gap widened, as they followed the trail the three ahead broke through the snow.

Cloud wouldn't carry the kid. He'd remotely suggested it and Cloud was indignant. Cloud wouldn't carry Randy—Cloud wouldn't carry baggage.

But Cloud didn't mind being touched. He didn't mind <Randy walking> by him. He liked the boy's hands. Was easily seduced by brushing and combing.

Easier if Cloud would agree to <carry the kid,> Danny thought. Carlo had both guns—Randy was wearing out carrying what he'd brought, and they'd redistributed and divided the supplies, so that the kid had the lighter stuff.

Carlo was struggling. It was probably the farthest they'd walked in their lives; Carlo was strong, he'd grown up hauling iron about in the shop, Danny had gotten that from him and, warned what kind of walk they were facing, Carlo had picked a sturdier pair of boots out of the store supplies. So had Randy—but they were new boots, however designed for walking and padded with double socks, and Danny didn't want to think what was happening to unaccustomed feet.

"If I," Randy gasped, at one point, at knee level with him, and knocking into him on the tracked and thick-lying snow, "if I someday wanted a horse—do you suppose—one would want me?"

"Might," Danny said, figuring that brutal long walking had something to do with the thought. But he gave it an honest answer. "You can't say for sure. Even rider kids can wait for years. But, yeah, one might."

Randy wanted <horse,> at that thought—like letting something escape into the light; he wanted <horse> so much Cloud snorted and moved away.

"You'll spook him," Danny said, imaging <Danny on Cloud,> and assuring the silly fool under him that he wasn't going to let Randy bother him.

"Why's he scared?" Randy was upset. "I didn't do anything."

"They're like that. You want him. He doesn't like that."

"That's stupid," Randy said.

"No, it isn't," Carlo said, out of breath. "He's got his own ideas. You do what the man says, brat. You be polite."

"To the horse?"

"Damned right," Danny said.

Randy thought about it. He thought about <Cloud in the store,> and <Cloud leading them away from the jail.> And the ambient grew better and easier while he did it. So Randy found what worked with horses, and it wasn't what Randy'd thought it would be.

Randy did a lot of thinking after that. The air grew cluttered with it.

But up ahead Jonas' group had finally gone to walking, and they were catching up slowly. "We better close it up," Danny said, because he wasn't entirely easy with the gap they'd let develop. The boys were gasping with the effort they were already making; they looked at him as if he'd asked them to fly. But he got down and took Carlo's pack and Randy's, and that made a difference, the three of them slogging along in the track the horses had already broken through the knee-high snow.

Then to their vast relief Jonas pulled a full stop and waited—the only grace they'd gotten from Jonas since they'd started out.

And by the time they did catch up, Jonas and the rest had broken out food for them and for the horses—having breakfast standing, because there wasn't a warm place to sit except on horseback. Besides snow for water, they had a bottle of vodka to pass around, the only thing that wasn't frozen: the sandwiches were, and took effort.

But the borderers had known better than they had and kept one sandwich inside their coats—flattened, but not frozen; and they learned.

"You stay tighter," Jonas said to him, when he borrowed the bottle. "You're cat-bait back there."

"I'm trying," he said. "I know we're pushing hard, but those kids—"

<"Come here,"> Jonas said, led him up past the horses and pointed at their feet.

Horse track. He looked off down the clear-cut, and far as he could see, there was an unmistakable disturbance, a track clearly made since the snow had stopped last night, on ground not yet churned up by their own horses. They'd been riding down that trail and he, lagging back, hadn't even seen it.

It might be the rogue. It might be Harper. It might even be Stuart. The trail was clearly going Stuart's direction, and moving ahead of them.

<Harper,> Jonas said. Or didn't say. "Harper's on his trail. His smell's clear."

He'd been going along dealing with the boys. He could have ridden right into ambush. He looked in the direction the trail led, down the clear-cut of the road, mountain on one side and a forested drop on the other.

"There's a shelter halfway to the junction," Jonas said. "Stuart's got no reason not to stay there. He doesn't know Harper's after him. But Harper can figure where to find *him*. We're going to have to make time."

"Yeah," Danny said. "Quig with him?"

He didn't know about Quig. What he saw underfoot was one track. There was no second rider, no second horse. Maybe he *had* hit someone when he fired.

"If Quig's got sense," Jonas said, "he folded last night and got the hell to cover. Depends on how much he likes Harper. Or how much he hates Stuart. That's only Harper going this direction. Nobody else."

It was a clear, glaring bright morning. Burn and Flicker, let loose from the shelter, went immediately to roll in the snow, working the kinks out of building-cramped nighthorse backs and looking the total fools. Burn turned silly and luxurious, not a care in the world, wallowed upside down, feet tucked, belly to the morning sun, then righted himself and surged to his feet for a few running kicks.

They came back to the snow-door with snow caked to their hides and knotted in their manes—Burn had a great lump of ice started in his mane, where warm horse had met new snow. Flicker was starting a number of snowballs in her tail.

"God," Guil sighed, and went in and bolted the snow-door shut, the last thing of all before they went out the main door and left the latch-cord out.

They started out walking, he and Tara, the horses free to work their sore spots out—and break the way for them unencumbered, through an area drifted deep across the clear-cut of the road. The horses threw snow with abandon, kicked and plunged their way through the drift like yearlings.

They called the horses back after not too long, anxious for the hazards of the area. And Burn and Flicker came back to walk with them, sulking at first, but happier when they understood <Tara and Guil still walking.>

The skittishness of the season still had Burn and the mare flighty and spooked—Guil hoped that was all they were reacting to. And there seemed nothing more sinister than lust in the air when they finally coaxed the rascals to take them up to ride for the next while: a silly, giddy heat that made two humans feel awkward with each other in the memory of last night.

Guil at least felt awkward this morning—asking himself ever since they waked what he'd done and what he'd been thinking of, and where he'd lost his common sense in the blankets last night.

He hoped it had been Tara's idea. He hoped he hadn't dragged her into anything she didn't want; but he couldn't sort his thoughts from hers, the ambient was so confused and full of foolish horses this morning, who'd no damn thought of any serious business two minutes running. Autumn heat was no foundation to build on. You wished each other well, you vowed most times you'd not do that again—you rode off in the morning or stayed a few days as the mood took you or the weather required, and if need be that you stayed together a while longer than that, you didn't take it for anything permanent.

You didn't, after a night in the blankets, try to work together as if you'd known each other in any reasonable way or as if you'd any clear idea what your cabin-mate's abilities were, or her capabilities, or her strengths and weak spots.

And it wasn't—perhaps—that dizzy-brained a pair-up they'd almost formed. He began to believe that was a part of the disturbance he was feeling. They were out on the trail together, they were on business as serious to them separately as it was desperately vital to villages up on the High Loop. He felt the determination in the woman, a spooky, dead-earnest concentration interspersed with skittishness directed at him, and he didn't know why. They got up on horseback and rode for a time on a level part of the road, and he kept feeling it tugging at his attention—doubt of him, anxiety—he wasn't sure.

Both of them were facing as nasty a hunt as they'd made in their lives, they had two horses in desperate lust, and, worse, the rogue was a mare: Tara believed it and he had no reason to doubt. Much better a male that would provoke Burn to anger and defense. One more female—*that* was no natural enemy. God, lust was all over the ambient, and they were risking their necks, all of them were—only they hadn't their enamored horses' attention to get it through their skulls, and he couldn't tell whether the <female-female-female> nonsense running through Burn's brain and down Burn's spine at any given instant was Flicker . . . or a deadly dangerous scent coming at them on the wind.

He'd have been terrified if he hadn't, along with that feeling running down Burn's spine and up his own, been sensing the levelheadedness in the woman beside him, a common sense for which he was entirely grateful—and it was no autumn lust that conjured that feeling of companionship. This woman, however skittish toward him, wasn't going to fold on him in the hunt; she was no town rider and might be a damned good backup in a pinch—her attention patterns to the road and the brush and the hillside weren't the patterns of a townbred rider or a scatter-wit and he knew in what he'd learned the fast way, in the ambient, that she hadn't any intention of spooking out on him. She'd nearly lost herself to the rogue at Tarmin, but she'd had no damn help from her partners.

More to the point—she was alive after a night with no gun and no supplies in a winter storm—and in her mind was a grief and a certainty that her partners weren't.

And on the mundanely practical side—without a word of her intentions, or any need to do anything but laze in the blankets until he had the door clear, there being only one shovel in the shelter—he'd found when he'd finished his own job that the woman had their packs put together and a dozen flatcakes cooked, so when they'd set out onto the road, they had decent food in their packs that didn't use emergency supplies.

She'd also asked for a pocket-full of shells for the pistol—so, she-said, if he lent it to her in a hurry she had a reload without needing the belt.

This was no stupid woman. He decided he'd have liked her immensely if they'd met on a trail or a camp commons or, one had to think of it, in Aby's company: someone Aby had dealt with came with recommendations, so far as he was concerned.

More, the business about the shells had made him ashamed of his reserve of all the weapons, and he hadn't just given her the shells; he'd given her the pistol outright, belt and all, hers with no debt, in the hope she was going to be at his back—because with her to back him up, with her knowing the territory as she did, he wasn't obliged to stay and wait for Jonas' doubtful help.

Possibly his skittishness toward Jonas was autumn-thinking, too. Burn and Shadow were a bad pair. And with <male horse> occupying the ambient, the thought of dealing with Hawley had edges of very bad feeling, very violent feeling, that didn't make it a good idea for Hawley, for him, or for Jonas right now, to be sorting out what they thought about each other.

He and the woman, on the other hand, could be as noisy as they wanted to be, since they were looking for trouble. They didn't, either of them, they well agreed, want to spend another night waiting for the rogue on its terms, they were reasonably sure it wasn't behind them, and they meant to push on up the road, the only sane way up the mountain, until they attracted its attention.

They could agree on that. But it didn't mean he'd know the rest of her signals: working with a stranger, sensible as she was, meant they couldn't predict each other's moves if the ambient went as crazy on them as he was afraid it would.

Another reason she needed one of the guns.

It was likely she had her own doubts about him. She was mostly thinking about her partners, with that skittish, spooky skipping-about of thoughts she had—or Flicker had. Hard to pin down. Hard to understand, sometimes. Skittish as Shadow, and that was going some. But bright, not dark; she blinded you with sunglare when you came too close to her. She whited out your vision.

And he wanted—

Hell, he didn't know. Flicker's change-abouts were contagious. Confusing.

Just—Aby was dead. And he wasn't. He'd discovered that unsettling fact last night, felt guilty, and angry, and distracted, and glad—none of which he could afford right now.

Autumn promises. He *needed* his mind on present business. He needed his mind on the ambient, not pouring problems into it.

So he *wanted* the rogue to show, dammit—he saw no reason for them to freeze chasing it. He <wanted> it into the ambient, until Burn began to be disturbed with him and laid back his ears and nipped at his leg. Something ghosted at him in that second, drifted through the ambient—and stopped.

"Tell you something," Tara said to him then, in that moment that the air was still a little spooky and strange. "I was through this stretch of woods a few days ago with the rogue on my tail. I didn't know what it was at the time—but it's hard to be back here and not think about it. Sorry if I do it. Just so you know. It's a memory."

"Yeah," he said. He'd just had a momentary sending, just <white-white-white> for a moment as if the blizzard had come back. Scary. Something in the trees.

He'd provoked it, he thought.

Begging trouble. With a shell in the chamber. Driving his partner crazy. Making her doubt what she heard and saw. A help. A real help, he was being.

<Kid on that horse.> That was what scared hell out of him. Tara's image of that damnfool kid. It wasn't neat, it wasn't clean—they had a townbred junior to separate out of the problem.

A kid who, if she hadn't frozen to death, might not be sane.

Or might not want to be sane, if they did get her back.

"Kid opened a gate," Tara said sharply. "She went out where she knew she wasn't supposed to go."

"Not the only village kid who ever did it," Guil said. Her anger with the girl bothered him. There wasn't compassion. Maybe it was because it was a girl, and Tara made demands she'd have made of herself. He didn't know.

It was her village that was dead. It was her partners that were dead, the way Aby had been his. Her dead—her whole village, old people, kids and all—were because a kid who knew the rules had wanted what she wanted and to hell with the consequences. She was angry. And he couldn't argue with it.

It would have been a beautiful sight, all that untracked snow, blanketed thick around the trees, the rider shelter snowed-under up to its roof on the side; but the door was all shoveled out, there was no smoke from the chimney; and the single track of a horse went right up to that area, and lost itself in the general churning up of the snow, where at least one horse had broken through the drifts.

It wasn't what they hoped they'd find: they'd arrived too late to catch Stuart.

"*Third* set of tracks," Luke said in apparent surprise. "Somebody was with him."

Harper, Danny thought, was following. But when he caught the <tracks> Luke was looking down at, he saw the footprints of a third horse overlay *two* outbound horses—how old, that second horse-track, or whether the last was Stuart following the other two, wasn't clear in his inexperience. Cloud was imaging <female> and <Spook-horse.>

Harper was Spook's rider. But—Quig? he asked himself. Quig's horse wasn't a mare.

The rogue was.

"Suppose the first is the rogue?" Hawley asked. "Suppose Stuart went after it this morning? Or it's after *him*?"

"Check the board," Jonas said, basic common sense, and Luke went and pulled the latch-cord, carrying his gun, even though the horses imaged no other presence, and warily checked inside.

Luke shut the door again. "Stuart. And Tara Chang, of all people."

"*Tara's* alive!" Randy said, <delighted.> Carlo was excited, too, all but moved to tears—because, Danny suddenly thought, they weren't the only survivors any more. There was somebody else they knew in the world. They remembered <Tara in the camp,> remembered <looking for Brionne,> and there wasn't a doubt in their minds that that was why their rider had come here. <Tara looking

for Brionne. With Stuart.> On that, their hopes sprang up to a wild possibility—he felt it, even Jonas felt it, the whole ambient disturbed, but Hawley remarked, sourly,

"That son of a bitch was real comfortable last night, wasn't he? Didn't wait till Aby was a month gone."

That made Carlo <fighting mad.> It took Randy, on the far side and away from Hawley, a moment to catch what Hawley meant, and then Randy was <mad.> But Jonas told everybody to get back on their horses and get the hell back on the road.

Danny swung up, nudged Cloud with knee and heel until he caught up with Shadow, on the edge of the road, urgent with the only answer he saw. "Harper's out to kill Stuart," he said to Jonas, fast, because horses were moving. "That's all he wants. He knows who he's tracking now—he'll have seen that board, too. He's going to break his neck getting caught up and they're not hurrying—they're not going to know he's stalking them." <Jonas hurrying. Three of them. Up the road. Stuart and the Tarmin rider. Him going slower, with Carlo and Randy.> "Don't lag back for us. I'll take care of the boys. Just for God's sake get Harper before he gets Stuart."

Jonas didn't take to orders. Or suggestions. You never told him a thing and expected him to do it—for sheer stubbornness, if nothing else.

"Stuart's your *friend*, isn't he?" he flung at Jonas. "Isn't *he* why you came?"

<Truck,> hit the ambient. <Wrecked truck.> Something about a <box.> Jonas was as upset as he'd ever felt the man, spilling things that didn't make sense to him. And thinking <Stuart,> with an edge of anger. <Mad at Stuart.>

But Jonas gave a jerk of his head, said, <"Come on,"> to his partners, and hit a traveling pace, hard and fast, with <Stuart> the fading image in the thinning ambient.

<Cloud standing. Cloud stopped,> Danny wanted, and Cloud dropped out of a half-hearted run.

"Where are they going?" Carlo asked, panting, as he reached Cloud's side. "Danny?"

"Just stay with me." God, he wanted <running down that road.>

Cloud was exploding with the instinct to stay up with the rest, Cloud wanted <fight> and <follow.>

Cloud wanted—something that shivered in the air. There was everywhere the <smell of female about the trees, tracked in the snow—female and male horse. Sex. And winter.>

But catching Stuart and Chang wasn't the job they had. It was doing what riders generally did, getting villagers safely from one point to the other. Getting Carlo and Randy somewhere they wouldn't die.

Right now he wasn't sure where that was—whether to drop back altogether and lock themselves into the shelter, or to go on where he wasn't damned much use.

"They're going to shoot Brionne," Randy said, distressed, wanting to go faster. But a human body couldn't. They'd been going since before dawn and they couldn't go any faster, try as they would. "Tara wouldn't. —But they might."

"Stuart won't shoot any kid," he said. He believed that, the way he'd judged Stuart from the start. "He'll get the rogue. It's just—"

"Harper?" Carlo panted, struggling to stay with him, while he fought Cloud's tendency to pick the pace up. Because he was moving, Carlo and Randy with him; he *didn't* know about Harper. He didn't trust Jonas. He didn't like that <truck> business. Jonas had been mad about <Hawley taking money> and about the brakes. But Jonas hadn't come here purely for Stuart's sake. Something else was going on, to bring Jonas away from Shamesey and onto this trail. He remembered the camp meeting, remembered Jonas arguing for Stuart—remembered Jonas dissuading any hunt going out after Stuart himself; Jonas was that much of a friend to Stuart.

But not—he was convinced—not to the exclusion of other motives. There was something besides what Jonas had said was his reason.

He couldn't leave the boys. He couldn't go faster. But they were three guns if they weren't too late to matter; and they were witnesses if witnesses were any restraint to Jonas Westman, whatever the man was about.

* * *

They'd passed the small cut-off that Tara said led off toward the main road, on the downhill; and they were traveling an uphill now, a place where the wind had scoured the ground all but clear of snow despite the trees. Brush held drifts. But stone showed through on the roadway.

The horses had settled out of some of their foolishness—were breathing hard on the climb, at work again after the day cooped up close indoors, and beginning to think of thirst, snatching a lick at the snow as they moved.

And human minds had settled into businesslike purpose. Guil knew he'd bothered Tara—and he'd not pushed at her personal borders, not on a morning when reason wasn't working and the horses were doing their own pushing at each other. He felt under him the give and take of a body as entirely distracted as he was, as dangerously astray from their business as he was. He found himself gazing off up the mountain, where nothing was but snow and rock.

Not helpful, in a landscape where they weren't seeing the animal traces they were accustomed to see. Possibly something was laired up there. He didn't think it was a horse—not up in that tumbled rock.

Burn gave a surly kick in his stride, thinking about <horse. Guil walking. Tara walking. Burn walking with Flicker. Beautiful mare. Beautiful rump. Beautiful—>

He thumped Burn in the ribs, and Burn flattened his ears, threw off <warning> and slogged along with his mind on business, Flicker likewise, watching the mountain slopes and the trees with each swing of her head. Trees were still thick on the left hand and patchy clumps of forest were on the right, trees clinging among steep rock.

"No tracks," Tara said, watching the snow they alone were scarring.

"Noticed that." No animals. No life stirring across or down this road.

"We're not that far from the shelter," Tara said. "It's right around here."

"Last one, isn't it?"

"Only place left she could hole up, only chance that kid's alive."

"If that's a wild horse—indoors isn't real likely."

"Yeah," Tara said.

And was thinking thoughts of horse-shooting that sobered Flicker and Burn.

So was he thinking those thoughts, carrying the rifle balanced on his leg, hoping he'd see it or hear it at a distance and not—not close up in the trees; hoping he could get a clear shot at it in the woods; hoping he could get a bead on it and not hit the kid.

Tell that to the gate-guards at Shamesey, who'd missed a charging nighthorse much closer to them and hit him—Burn having that clever trick of imaging <horse> where Burn wasn't.

If it was a wild one gone bad, it might not know about guns.

But what had happened at Tarmin said the gate-guards hadn't had any luck aiming at it.

<Village,> was in Tara Chang's thoughts. <Kids in the streets. Kid on the horse. Gun firing.>

Maybe, he thought—one of those cold second thoughts that came only when they were past the point to do anything about it—maybe he *should* have waited for Jonas to show up.

Maybe he could have ridden side by side with Jonas and Hawley without wanting to beat hell out of them. Five were a lot stronger than two, if it came to an argument of sendings.

If their two sets of horses didn't go for each other instead of the rogue, and this morning it wasn't certain.

If he could only figure why that gunshot, or what Jonas was doing up here at such effort.

Jonas hadn't expected him to go to Anveney first. Hadn't expected him to talk to Cassivey. Yeah, Guil, go on up there, get that son of a bitch horse. Make the woods safe.

We'll just come up a few days late—

<*Coming apart.*>

<Trees, black against <white-white-white.>> Burn threw his head and skipped a step. Flicker threw a kick. It was that vivid.

"Sorry," Tara said. Her breath was shaky for a moment.

"Yeah, don't blame you. Easy. I'm not hearing anything but you."

"Vadim kept asking me—how close it got to me in the woods.

—And I don't know. He thought—not at all." Her teeth were all but chattering. "I couldn't judge."

"He was wrong."

"The thing was so damn loud—and it called that kid right out of the village without a one of us hearing. Granted Flicker was noisy—she was screening it out; I know now why she was as loud as she was all night. It was *out* there. But we didn't hear."

"When the kid went?"

"Her house was across the village. Closer to the other wall, that's all I can think." She built the village for him in the ambient; a row of houses, a single street, a rider camp protecting the one side, but only distance from the wall protecting the far side of that single street. And there were times, Guil thought, when distance wasn't enough.

"Damn kid claimed she heard the horses better than we did—but she couldn't hear Flicker about to back over her." <Kid in red coat. Snowy morning. Flicker sick, lying down in the den.> "But she damn sure heard the one horse she shouldn't have. She came to us the next morning. I told her get out, leave my horse alone. I thought she went back home. She didn't."

The whole business flowed past his vision, the frustration, the bitter anger.

<Footprints leading out the gate. The man, the boys, at sunset. The gunshot, and the mob and the riders—>

He couldn't follow all of it, it went by so fast. <Two male riders going out the gate. Tara at what looked like the village jail, the marshal's office—rogue at the gates, Tara running—running for her partners, empty camp, open gate—<white> rushing down on her, under her, carrying her away—>

Tara held it back then. The evergreens were around them again. The sun was shining. Tara said,

"It's my *fault*, you understand me? You can tell me all the reasons in the world. You can even tell me I was right, throwing the kid out of camp that morning." <Shaking kid. Hard. Anger, grief. A shiver through the ambient.> "But if I think I can get that kid free of that thing, I'm going for her—I'm going to save her, not shoot her. So you know."

"That's not what you're saying inside."

"No. It isn't. But I don't do everything I think of." <Walking down snowy road, Tara and Flicker and the blonde girl.> "Maybe I could teach her something. I don't know. What do you say? She's thirteen years old. —And she's killed my partners, dammit! Killed the whole damn village." <Kid reaching for Flicker. Flicker jerking away.> "She *wanted* things. She unsettled Flicker just being around her. Want, want, want. Push, push, push. Damn bottomless well of 'I want.' And temper when she didn't get her way. Real surly temper." Silence a moment, the ambient seething with anger that sank, sank, sank. Then: "You know what I ask myself? I ask myself—how much of the rogue is the horse, and how much is that kid? And that's a lousy thought for a rescue."

It wasn't at all a pleasant thought. But a kid wasn't innocent in the ambient. Just not as strong.

Usually.

<Rogue prowling the streets. Fire on window-glass. Rogue *hunting* for individuals. Woman. Girl. Boy. Minds going out. Guns going off. Predators and scavengers rolling through the village street like a flash flood. The girl riding through it blithe as a summer wind, searching out victims one by one—>

<Still water,> he sent. <Still water. Woods around us. Daylight.>

He wasn't getting her back. There was only <desire to kill.>

<Fireplace,> he remembered. That was *their* potent memory. <Skin on skin. Hands touching.>

<Partner-lover. Talking with him on the porch.>

For a moment the ambient stifled breath. Then Tara backed off the anger, drove it down to quiet, quiet, quiet.

"We do what we can," Guil said. He wasn't good with words. He sent <meadow with flowers.> He sent <new foals.>

She'd heard her village die. He'd not been on the mountain yet, the only way he could figure it. He didn't know how she'd stood it.

<White,> came back to him, just <white-white-white,> walling him out, all but blinding him. Burn threw his head and took small nips at Flicker's shoulder until <white> gave way to <branches> and <mountain road.>

"Her damn *choice*," Tara muttered finally, no weakening of her anger, just better control.

He rode thinking about that for a while, thinking he shouldn't have given her the gun.

"Don't do any heroics," he said. "My rifle may be able to take it—drop the horse and miss the kid. If the kid survives—best we can do."

Not damn easy, if it came at you—and it might, out of the trees at any moment. Aim low and hope you knew where the horse—

A chill went through the ambient, as if a cloud had gone over the sun. He looked left; and Burn pricked his ears up and laid them flat again.

The lump of snow among the trees—wasn't a lump of snow. It was a roof, blown partially clear.

<Rider-shelter,> Tara sent. She knew it inside and out. He heard the soft click as Tara drew the pistol. He became acutely aware of the rifle in his hand, where its balance was. They made a winding approach, through the outflung wall of a snowdrift, on the shelter's lower side.

Burn was smelling <female.> So was Flicker, he thought. But smelling something more, something confused, and upsetting.

Smelled it all the way to the shelter.

The door was clear. It had been opened. But there was nothing there. The place felt empty. There were tracks in the snow, both horse and rider—pointed-toed boots. Village boots. Drag of something in the snow, he wasn't sure what.

<Checking inside,> he thought and, rifle on his arm, slid down from Burn's back. He walked up to the door. The latch-cord was out. He pulled it, pulled the door open.

The place was a wreck. Pans on the floor, bed stripped, pottery broken. The place smelled of horse, smoke, burned food. Recent. The front of the mantel was smoked.

The kid hadn't known to open the flue. Or hadn't thought of it until she had a cabin full of smoke.

There were charred bones on the hearth. Small animal. He was almost certain—it was a small animal.

He shut the door fast, figuring Tara had seen what he'd seen, smell and filth and all.

Flicker shied from him. Burn was taking in scents, nostrils flared. The whole place reeked to their senses: <female horse, female human. Bad, unhealthy horse. Blood.>

He grabbed Burn's mane, got up, and Burn wanted to go back, turned his head downhill. Burn was agitated, thinking <Aby,> for whatever crazed reason. <Aby. Dead on the rocks.> Burn resisted the pressure of his knees, kept turning with him, a fit of refusal that wasn't like Burn, a fear and a confusion that afflicted Flicker, too, until Tara got her headed around, and moving.

Then Burn would go. <Flicker> was in Burn's mind. And <Aby riding away from us. Red hair in the sunlight. Aby on Moon.>

"Damn fool," Guil muttered. Burn had almost thrown him on that last fit. He'd slid far enough he'd thought he was going off into a thicket. He gave Burn a thump behind the ribs, wanted <going faster,> if Burn had so much energy to waste. They were on the road Tara imaged as <going up to the curves, past the junction, beyond the trees.>

Where he imagined the truck had gone off.

Tara straightened his road a small distance and thinned the trees and showed him the mountainside in her memory: a steep, badly slipped face of the mountain, a road crawling up a long, long curve that was a steep ascent and a hellish downhill, with all the mountain range spread out to see.

Burn calmed until that hillside conformed to vague memory, and it resonated with <truck falling> and that <Aby, Guil and Aby> nonsense. Burn was a smart horse—Burn *remembered* more than some horses; Burn put things together in spooky ways sometimes, thinking in nighthorse fashion through associations that had to do with smell and mating and group-making that didn't always find an echo in a human brain. Burn was right now on one of those autumn-hazed treks through the associations in his mind—probably, Guil thought, Burn was disturbed by the ambient smells. A smart horse *felt* the land-sense in ways that had nothing to do with the look of a place, and this place resonated in the memory he'd used all the way up here.

<Aby,> Burn was thinking, and <unhealth,> and <death,> with <female> somewhere in the mix. Burn was traveling with that ready-to-move feeling in his stride that made a rider aware how fast the fool could change direction.

"What's he smelling?" Tara asked.

"Horse," he said. He wasn't hearing Flicker that clearly—or hadn't been. Flicker was <uneasy.> Flicker wanted <quiet> and began to try to turn, except for Tara's pressure on one side and another. Burn was going willingly ahead. Flicker was confused and increasingly distressed as Burn picked up the pace. Trees were thinning out. They crossed a wide clearance, a place where three roads met, the one they were on, the one down the mountain, and the road Aby'd died on.

Burn went toward that place of open sky, wide vistas.

"Guil, that road's going to be hell up there, bad drifts. That kid's coming back here. This is where she's been coming to. Maybe we ought to fall back, just sit and wait. She's not going up that road much—"

<Aby,> he was getting from Burn, and then a feeling of <female> so intense he couldn't breathe for a moment, couldn't think, because it wasn't just <Burn.> And he kept going.

Up and up the road. Into the daylight.

"Guil!" he heard someone shouting at him.

<Aby,> Burn was thinking, and <death,> and back to <female,> all while traveling with that light-footed gait that made a rider know Burn could dive any direction.

A horse arrived beside him. It roused no alarm. But for a moment his vision was <white-white-white.>

Then he saw—

He saw <Aby on Moon, coming down the road toward him. He saw red hair. He saw her coming for him, after all, alive again, and beautiful.>

"No!" a woman yelled, and <white> and <anger> charged in front of him. A horse shouldered Burn and Burn reared.

He dismounted—no recourse but that as Burn recovered his balance. He landed on his feet and in that split second of landing the vision of <Aby on Moon> was <blonde kid in blankets, tangle-maned horse.>

Tara was on foot—Tara was beside him. A gun went off next his ear, rattled his brain, and then <fight> was coming at them, coming from a human, female mind, wanting <kill Tara. Wanting *him*. Claiming *him*.>

Moon. He had *no* doubt. Burn, beside him, knew. Burn sent out a troubled keep-away and Moon stopped. The blonde kid urged Moon forward with <kill> and <mine!> but Moon stopped again.

He only then remembered the rifle in his hand.

"Give me the pistol!" he snapped at Tara and held out his hand.

It was <Aby,> he heard her calling to him, <I want you,> he saw <Aby on Moon, coming down the road toward him, autumn-haired Aby, asking him where he'd been—>

<Wanting him—so much—>

He grabbed the pistol that arrived in his hand. He let go the rifle. He walked forward, <going to Aby. Moon and Aby. High-country meadows. Moon and Aby and Guil, and the sunlight on the mountains.

<Wind shaking the grass. Making waves like the sea. Moon and Guil—

<—making love.>

It was a hurt horse. A thirteen-year-old kid with a wish, on a horse in mortal pain. He saw it for a blink, but he said to Moon, <brave horse, beautiful horse.> He didn't see the cuts and the tangles and the blood.

He said, "Good girl, don't spook on me, you know me, it's <Guil,> it's just Guil. Let <Aby get down.> Let her get off. That's right—I'll help you. Come on."

He reached out his right hand, for the girl's hand that reached to him.

He fired with the left, the gun right under Moon's jaw.

He grabbed the icy fingers, snatched the girl against his chest and spun away as Moon went down—he held the kid crushed against him, blind to anything but the mountain—he couldn't see, either, for the blur of ice in his eyes, couldn't feel the ambient for the sudden silence he'd made, the murder of what he loved.

He knew Tara was back there, Burn was there. He began to hear. He couldn't see until he blinked and a shattered sky and a shattered mountainside whipped into order. The girl was in his arms, live weight, but there was utter silence in the ambient and his ears were still ringing. He only saw Tara with the rifle, Tara sighting toward him—

Second blink. He began to feel the ambient again.

<Burn and Flicker.>

<Tara. Anger.>

His foot skidded on ice. His balance was shaky. He saw the edge of the road under his right side and veered away from it. He set the girl on her feet, pulled the blanket about her, but she just stood staring into nothing, blue eyes in a tangled blonde mane. He shut her fist over the ends of the blanket, took her by the other hand and walked <going toward Tara and Burn and Flicker.

<Tara standing still. Burn standing still—still water.>

Something slammed into him, spun him half about in shock, about the time he heard the crack of the rifle echo off the mountain. He kept turning, trying to keep his balance, not knowing where he'd fall—

The rifle-crack rang off the mountain from behind them. Tara spun toward the sound and dropped to one knee, with the far figure of rifleman and horse the only anomaly in her sight of woods and snow. She fired on instinct at the distant figure, pumped another round, and looked for her target—

But there was only a horse. And the darkness of a body lying by it.

The man didn't get up. She stayed still, rifle trained on that target until her leg began to shake under her. <Angry horse> washed up at them; but Flicker imaged <threat> and <warning> at that distant horse—Flicker took out after it, ignoring her frightened <stop!>

Burn imaged <Guil hurt. Fight. Kill—> Burn was hesitating back and forth, sending snow flying—<staying with Guil.—Killing horse.>

She didn't want to shoot it. Didn't want to. She wanted <horse going.>

But it wouldn't. Damn it. It wouldn't. She put three shots near it. She didn't want another rogue on the mountain; but then Flicker charged into her line of fire, and she couldn't shoot. Burn followed, balance tipped, wanting <fight.>

She staggered to her feet, gasping for breath that wouldn't come, Flicker and Burn both going for the horse.

At the last moment it turned and ran back down the way it had come; Flicker and Burn stopped in their charge, circled back a little and maintained a threatening posture.

That horse's retreat told her the man she'd shot was dead. That Flicker and Burn both stopped told her the horse was reacting as it should, in ordinary fear and confusion. It hesitated in its retreat, probably querying its master. Burn called out a challenge that echoed in the distance.

Then it launched into a run, shaking its mane, going farther down the road. Nighthorses didn't altogether understand death. The total silence of a mind confused them dreadfully—in which thought—

She turned to see Guil getting up, leaning to one side, trying to stand. The girl just stood there, staring at nothing.

She started running. She saw from Guil's face he was in shock, even before the horses came running back to them, and she caught <pain> washing through the ambient.

"Stay down," she said to Guil, and made him sit. <Blood on snow, spatter all around them, around dead horse.> Burn sent out threat, <wanting Guil> and ready for <fight,> but she didn't admit guilt and she didn't retreat: she started unfastening Guil's coat, looking for damage, and Guil was coherent enough to wish <quiet horses, Burn standing, Burn quiet.>

She could feel the wound as if it was in her own side—felt entry and exit, as the numbness of impact gave way to <pain> that was going to be hell in another hour. Right now it was still a little numb.

"It could be worse," she said, and shoved his hands away. There was a fair amount of blood, but it didn't look to have hit the gut: it had gone through muscle and it was swelling fast. Guil kept trying to get his knee under him, <wanting bending over,> but she stuffed her scarf into his shirt around his middle and started wrapping it as tightly as she could.

It helped the pain. She could feel it. He was going to want to get to the shelter back there and lie still a while. She answered his confused memory of the gunshot with <man shooting. Tara shooting man.>

"Kid get hit?" he asked in a thready voice.

She cast a look at the girl who was still just standing there, holding the blanket. Staring at nothing. There was nothing in the ambient. Not from her.

"Didn't touch her. Hang on, all right. Don't faint. All right?"

"Yeah," he said, and pulled his coat to and started getting his knees under him—the fool was going to get up, and he couldn't stand; but he got the rifle and leaned on that before she could get her arm under his.

Burn was right there, nosing him in the face, in the shoulder, anxious and about to knock him over. He swatted Burn weakly with his hand and wanted <picking up kid. Getting kid safe.>

She had a wounded man on a mountain road bound and determined to pick up a girl who weighed most of what she did, and she didn't give a flying damn if the girl stood there and froze.

But *he* did. She left him to the wobbling assistance he could get from the rifle; she grabbed the kid herself and dragged her with them, with a wary eye toward the downhill road, in case she'd been mistaken about the man being dead, in the unlikelier case the horse had been mistaken.

In the far distance she saw a group of riders coming up.

<Jonas,> she thought. She didn't know who she'd shot down there. She hadn't stopped to ask. Jonas was her saner guess. But it didn't make sense.

Guil stood beside her, leaning on the rifle, trying to reason out who it was, too, and coming up with no better answer: <Man with rifle. Shot fired at him. Tarmin gate.>

"*Three* of them," she said. "Maybe it wasn't Jonas down there, Guil."

"I don't know," he said. The ambient was confused and muddled with his thoughts. Things from downland. Things from the village. From a long time ago, maybe. The shock was catching up to him, and he found a snow-covered lump of rock to rest on, rifle in one hand, his elbow tight against his side.

Burn came up close by him. Tara went and got the kid by the wrist, got the pistol from where it was lying in the snow, hauled the kid to the side of the road behind Guil and made her get down behind the rocks, out of the way of flying bullets.

She kept the pistol in her hand as the riders kept coming. She didn't need Guil's recognition to know them. She had a clear image of <Jonas Westman, of Luke, of Hawley Antrim—> and a notion of blowing them to hell if she didn't like the answer to her questions.

"Whoever shot you," she said to Guil without taking her eyes off the riders, "I got him. Whoever it was—I got him. Guil."

Flicker moved in. Made a solid wall behind them, with Burn. A wall giving off <warning> to the oncoming riders.

Guil put the rifle butt on his leg. Lowered it, slowly, and the three riders stopped a fair distance down the road.

"Guil?" the shout came up. "Guil Stuart?"

"Yeah," Guil shouted back, and hurt from the shouting. "So what's your story, Jonas? What's the story? Does it say why Aby's dead? Does it say why I shot Moon, Jonas? Does it say you're a lying son of a bitch *thief*, Jonas? I know why you're up here. I know what you're after, and you don't go up this road. You go to *hell*, Jonas!"

"Hawley wants to talk to you, Guil."

Burn wanted <bite. Kick.> Burn was <ready to go downhill, fight.>

But Guil sent, <Burn standing still.> Wanted <shooting,> and Tara held herself ready to grab Guil and haul him down behind the rock in the next instant, had her target picked, in Jonas Westman, but she kept the pistol at her side, while Flicker sent <fight,> ready as Burn was, if they got the encouragement.

"Who's that I shot?" she yelled down at them.

"Guy named Harper," Jonas called up. "Nothing to do with us."

It was somebody Guil knew. A lot of confused memories hit the ambient, an old fight. Another mountainside. Another edge of the road. She didn't believe it had nothing to do with present circumstances.

She waited.

She left Hawley to Guil. She still had her eye on the others.

Guil waited. Kept the rifle generally aimed at Hawley, as Hawley came up within easy range.

Then he brought it on target.

Hawley stopped. Hawley looked scared. With reason. Ice had followed him up the slope and arrived beside him, the way Burn stayed by him. Ice was loyal.

So had other things been.

"Moon's dead, Hawley. It was Moon gone rogue, you know that?"

"No. I didn't. I swear I didn't, Guil. It couldn't have. I *felt* it!"

That, in the ambient, was the undeniable truth.

But it was the truth as Hawley'd seen it. <From the back of the convoy. When a truck went plunging past the curve. Aby and Moon on that edge—in front of the truck that went over.>

"You left Aby's horse, Hawley, you left Moon hurt, you left her crazy. Moon maybe had a chance—she was a good horse, she never did a damn thing against the villages until she took up with that damned stupid *kid*, Hawley! You got yourself down that mountain and you left Moon on her own, the way you left Aby lying there for the spooks!"

"I saw that horse go over!"

That was the truth, too. He blinked, he at least considered a doubt of Hawley's guilt. It was what Hawley had seen.

But it wasn't what he'd just faced up the hill. It wasn't the truth lying there in the roadway, with a bullet in its brain.

"Guil, I'm sorry. I swear to God, I'm sorry. I wouldn't've left her. I saw 'em go, I swear. There was rogue-feeling all over—it *was* a rogue—"

"It wasn't any rogue driving that truck, Hawley. I can see that <truck.> I see it <rolling.> Right in your mind, I can see it. You can't see Aby from where you are. You can't see her, Hawley. You're at the back of the convoy. You're a damn liar!"

"I saw it, I did see it, Guil, I swear to you, I swear to God—"

The image rebuilt itself. <Truck moving, rolling out of control. Brake line—>

"You want to tell me, Hawley? I don't care about the money in the account. I don't give a damn. I want you to tell me what happened to Aby."

"I was going to tell her," Hawley said. There was <paper money> in Hawley's mind, there were <truckers,> there was <truck running away downhill—>

"Tell me. Use words. I want to hear it, Hawley."

"Jonas says—"

He brought the rifle up. "I don't give a damn what Jonas says. You tell me. About the gold, Hawley. What about the gold?"

"We didn't know about it. We didn't know! She just thought we did!"

He was <going to shoot. Dead center of Hawley's gut.>

"Guil, I swear—we just guessed it. I mean, anybody could guess, the truckers were guessing—"

"Keep talking."

"And Aby was mad about it. Aby didn't want anybody to know. And by the time we got up to Verden she wasn't speaking to us—she didn't want to be around us. I think she was rattled, she thought she'd spilled it, but, hell, we knew, Guil, once we was on to it, we could get it from folk all round us—"

You knew when Hawley was outright lying. And sometimes when Hawley was telling all the truth he knew. And this was, he thought, the truth as Hawley knew it.

"Guil, I swear to you—"

His arm was shaking. He let the rifle rest on his leg again. "I'm listening. Keep going, Hawley. You be thorough. I've got nothing but time."

"The truckers, they caught it, too. You could feel the upset all over, and this truck, its brakes weren't good. They was spooked, didn't want us to pitch that truck out of the line, and Aby, she told me she wanted them hurry up with that truck. I come along, you know, just walking the line—" <Trucks waiting in convoy, village center.> "And that truck, the one with the stuff, you know—they were at fixing the brakes when I come along, and they don't want me to see, but I know, and they don't want to have me pull that truck—they're logs they're hauling, but they got something in the cab they don't want across by daylight, everybody was watching, you know—and Aby was wanting us out of there—"

"The gold."

"Yeah. I mean, Guil, they didn't want to have to move that box. And we wasn't supposed to know about it. I don't think they trusted any of us. And Aby was madder 'n hell all morning. But they give me money, Guil, they give me money, they say shut up, don't talk about the brakes—and I had the money, and they'd fixed that brake line. I mean, they really fixed it. But then I'd got to worrying about it, I was going to give it back, I was going to tell Aby—I was going to tell her, Guil. I knew it was wrong to take the money. But she give the order, we started rolling then, and she was up front, and we was in the rear—Guil, I knew this one turn was bad, but I didn't think the drivers was going to risk their own necks. Aby was worried about the weather, worried about us getting down to the meeting-place, maybe after dark, but we'd get there—"

"So it was just the brakes. And there never *was* any rogue."

"There was a rogue, Guil, there was for sure a rogue—"

"*Before* that truck went off? Or later, Hawley? Was there a rogue when you got to that turn? Was there a rogue there then?"

"I don't know, Guil. It was there, was all."

"I *shot* Moon, Hawley. Moon was the rogue."

"Moon's dead. I saw her down there on the rocks, I saw <her with Aby.> I saw it, I saw it plain as plain—Ice saw it, Jonas and Luke saw it—we all saw it—Guil, for God's sake, we didn't lie to you!"

It hurt, that image. He thought about pulling the trigger and blowing Hawley off the mountain. He thought about not dealing with it at all, anymore. But Hawley—was so damned earnest, Hawley believed what he was saying.

"Hawley, go back and tell Jonas I want to talk to him. Tell Jonas get his ass up here. And get yours out of my sight. Right now."

"Guil, I'll give you the money—I swear, I'll give you the money—I was going to give it to you—"

His finger twitched. Twice. Stayed still, then, the gun unfired. Sight came and went. "Only thing that recommends you, Hawley. You got a single focus. Always know where you are. Always know what matters, don't you? Truckers put money in your hand and you don't know how to turn it loose. You get the hell down that road, Hawley, tell Jonas I said get up here. Now. Hear me? You tell Jonas get up here or I'll blow him to hell. Hear?"

"Yeah," Hawley said, anxious, confused as Hawley often was. "Yeah." He swung up on Ice, and rode fast down the hill.

Tara said, faintly, "I think it was the truth, Guil. But it doesn't make sense."

He was glad to know that. He didn't trust his own perceptions. He left the rifle over his knee. He watched as Hawley came down to Jonas; and Jonas looked uphill toward him, and then started up toward him.

"Give the son of a bitch credit," Guil muttered.

Tara said, his voice of sanity, "You asked him, Guil. Hear him out. You asked to hear him."

So he waited. He sat with the wound beginning to throb, and knowing if he shot now he was going to have to shoot from the hip.

Jonas rode up all the way, on Shadow. And sat there, to talk to him.

"So?" Guil asked. "Aby didn't trust you. Truckers bribed Hawley not to tell about the brakes. And the brakes failed. Not a lot of people trusted you, Jonas. What happened up there? You tell me. I want to hear this."

"We knew there was something on board. Aby didn't like us knowing. Truckers suspected. And they spooked. Didn't want to stop, didn't want to camp out on the road on that height and they didn't want to leave that damn truck on the High Loop. Guil, I swear to you—Aby didn't trust anybody. *She* didn't want to stop. She was spooked—she knew we knew something, we tried to talk to her, and she wouldn't have it. It spooked the drivers—"

"Her fault, is it?"

Jonas shook his head. "Brakes failed. Hawley told you—"

"Hawley told me about the brakes."

"They were taking it too damn fast. Riding the brakes too much. Aby wasn't with us, she wouldn't ride near us. The truck went runaway—she was down there. I swear to you, Guil, we did everything we could. It just happened—so fast—"

"She and Moon went over, did they?"

"Both of them." <Dead, on the rocks.>

"That's a lie, Jonas."

Shadow spooked. Made a move forward that Burn opposed with a snarl and a threatened lunge.

And Jonas didn't answer him. Jonas didn't know the truth.

"I saw her," Jonas said. And it was that image again, <Aby and Moon. Together. Dead.> "Guil, I didn't know about the brakes. Didn't know until Hawley told me, last night."

He stayed still, his finger on the trigger. But the pieces fell together, finally.

<Lying on the rocks. Dead horse.> That was where Moon had imaged being. With Aby.

He said quietly, "She fooled you, Jonas. Moon fooled you. You understand. Moon *wanted* to be down there. In her mind—she *was* down there. And wasn't. She was up on that hillside looking down the same as you were, and you saw what *she* imaged. I tell you, Jonas, I believe you. I believe you about Aby. I believe you about the gold. Which I think is what you came up here to find. Is that true, Jonas?"

"Yeah," Jonas said after a moment. "Yeah. —But I didn't know Hawley'd robbed you, Guil. I'd no idea."

"Just going to turn that box in yourself, weren't you? Nobody the wiser. You, with big credit with Cassivey."

"I'd have dealt you in."

"Yeah, me, who never took the Anveney jobs. I tell you, Jonas, you go on down to the junction. You take that downhill road. And I want you to take Hawley somewhere we won't meet for maybe, two, three years. Then maybe we'll talk. You understand me?"

"Guil, we'd take you down country."

"I'll handle it. You get to *hell* off this mountain."

Jonas stayed still a moment, turned Shadow half-away, then looked back. "There's some kids, Guil. Rider named Danny Fisher, couple of village kids, on this road. Looking for you. They didn't have anything to do with this. You want to sweep them up, see they get somewhere safe? Road down's hell when the snow builds up."

"Fisher."

"You know him? He knows you. Horse named Cloud."

He couldn't place the name.

But he knew, in one of Jonas' rare slips, that Jonas had gotten three kids out of Tarmin. Got them on the road. Wanted them safe. Personally—and earnestly—wanted them safe.

A lot like the man he'd known a long time back. He almost relented.

Almost.

Said, "See you another year, Jonas."

So Shadow went, and Jonas with him. And the ambient was only themselves, and the horses, and the wind.

Chapter — xxii —

YOU TAKE CARE!" TARA CHANG SAID, WHEN THEY WERE GATHERED in the yard of the rider-shelter, and take care was what Danny meant to do, personally. He'd said his good-byes to Guil Stuart inside: Guil wasn't on his feet, but would be, they had confidence of that. Meanwhile Burn was taking advantage of an open door and a sunny day. So was Flicker, and Burn was sending Cloud a serious warn-off, <Burn and female, strong male horse,> that had everyone's nerves on edge.

That was one reason for leaving. The kid bundled in the travois was another: Brionne Goss and her brothers weren't comfortable companions for nighthorses in a winter shelter, and the first crystal-clear day, with the sun burning bright in the high-altitude sky was a chance Danny knew they couldn't turn down.

Guil didn't mind much, Danny figured that for himself. Guil got a winter-over with a damn pretty woman, all to himself, and had a village down the way with a store full of supplies. They'd shared <ham> with Burn and Flicker and, nighthorses being what they were, Burn and Flicker didn't mind saying they'd take the ham, thanks, but Cloud could take his rider, the <rogue-girl> and the three <males-not-welcome> and hit the road.

Down the mountain or up the mountain wasn't Burn's urgent concern. But Guil said, "If you go up, don't linger in the shelters."

And Tara: "The mountain doesn't give you many days after the snows start. Either one's dangerous. You make time. Make time, all you can do."

So in this bright, clear morning, they went, and he thought up, all considered, was the best choice. Cloud wasn't against it. Avalanche on those lower slopes scared him personally worse than the high, hard climb did. Jonas had taken the chance. He thought maybe Jonas had won the bet with the mountain; but they'd been holed up and couldn't prove it.

The days that that downward road would be passable were getting fewer, if they weren't gone already.

And Guil said he hoped Jonas made it. About Hawley, Guil still wasn't sure, but he said Hawley was a thorough-going jerk, that was what he was guilty of, and he'd forbear to shoot Hawley, in colder blood, when next they met.

Assumptions. Assumptions was the thing that had been so fatal. Lives that touched one another and never knowing they'd touched at all.

Aby Dale had never figured, when she'd died, that she'd have cost so many lives.

Jonas Westman and his friends had never figured, when they came clear down to Shamesey, that they'd bring rogue-taint with them. Likely, was Danny's private opinion, that the disturbance in his own family owed something to the contagion the Westmans had brought; likely that Harper's private vendetta owed something to it, too. Harper had been a haunted man. And rogue-craziness had been very close to what drove him. The man had carried a grudge for years and, crazy-mean that he was, had had it set off by something, maybe rogue-sending, maybe just the scent of blood in the ambient when they'd shot at Guil down by Shamesey, and a hunter-sense when Guil had taken to running.

Maybe then in Harper's head the balance of fear had shifted and he'd seen his chance to settle old scores.

But it hadn't been a good place, the mountain hadn't, for a man with a guilty past. A rider could lie to other riders, sure, but he had to lie to himself first, had to lie to himself. And Guil Stuart hadn't had a thing to do with Gerry Harper's death. Stuart hadn't known that Harper was on his tail, hadn't even known how Harper's brother had died.

A kid who'd come up from town had had the pieces of it shoved at him, that fell into place once Guil told what he knew: a whack in the head from a winch cable, a partner dead, Gerry Harper going off from Ancel in a fit of rage, the Harper brothers not dealing with each other any more for years.

"Gerry was all right," Guil had said. "A lot more reasonable than his brother. I got along with him. —So Ancel shot him." Guil was surprised and sad. That came through the ambient. Harper believed his brother had gone rogue.

"Maybe he did," was Guil's opinion. "God knows. I don't. So Ancel shot him. Shot his horse."

At a campfire. Late one night.

Harper had told himself it was all Guil's fault. Told it well enough at least other men had followed him up a mountain looking for blood.

Harper had found blood, all right. They heard his horse at night. Spook came in looking for him—but it wasn't a rogue, itself, just lonesome. And they hadn't the heart to shoot it or the guilt to let it haunt them. Harper'd taken a shot at Guil at Tarmin gates; he'd taken his second at the start of the Tarmin Climb.

But Harper wasn't the marksman Tara Chang was. She'd snapped off that one shot and nailed him dead through the chest. So all Harper's hate, all Harper's craziness had ended right there, in the snow. The horse mourned him. Nobody else did.

Guil hadn't known the Westmans were on his track, either: when he'd found out, he'd blamed them for the shot at Tarmin village and wouldn't trust them. He damn sure hadn't known Harper and his lot were on his heels, hadn't remotely expected the shot out of nowhere that had gone through his side. He hadn't, he swore, cared a damn about Harper, hadn't spoken to him for years.

But Harper'd paid his life for a grudge Guil didn't know Harper was carrying.

And come to find out—Guil had had no idea in the world there was a kid named Danny Fisher. Riders weren't prone to polite lies: the horses didn't let them do what townfolk did, and Guil didn't deny there'd been a rainy afternoon on a porch, and a kid asking him questions, Guil just didn't remember him. All the way he'd tracked Guil up on this mountain to pay a debt Guil didn't remember.

In his way he supposed that he was as crazy as Harper was. But it was a debt he still held valid. He'd heard. He'd listened. He'd learned.

He'd remember some time when some kid came to him: he'd know what he said could save some kid's life and he'd take the time.

He might not remember doing it, either. He supposed the moments that came on you to do something good or something evil weren't necessarily lit up in flaming letters. The things you assumed all needed looking at, and the way you answered a kid's asking help needed looking at; if you mistook as few as possible of the former and did as much of the latter as you could, the best you could while doing your honest work, he figured that answered all morality a rider was responsible for.

That and his ties to his partner. He wouldn't ever forget the way Guil had come after Aby Dale. He hoped some day to have a partner like that, man or woman. It wouldn't be Guil.

And it shouldn't be. He couldn't give anything in that relationship. He could only get. And maybe Tara Chang was it for Guil. Or maybe she wasn't.

A winter in a one-room cabin might be a start on finding it out.

Meanwhile he had two boys in his charge. Carlo and Randy; and a kid who might never get any better: Brionne Goss. He knew things he didn't need to tell.

He was, right now, their best hope of living.

So it was a down-payment on the debt he had.

"Come on," he said to the boys, and sent Cloud on ahead to break the trail, Cloud's three-toed feet being quite adept at doing that. It was what Cloud was born to, the High Wild, and the mountain.

There were villages on the High Loop that would take strays in. There were villages where the boys could find a place and a rider could earn a living if he wanted to stay.

But down by spring, he thought. He wasn't ready to settle yet. Neither was Cloud.

<Winter and females,> was in Cloud's thought.

And an upward road.